"I'd like a cosmopolitan," A woman at the bar behind him ordered. "with olives."

Who ordered olives with their cosmopolitans?

The server said something he couldn't understand. And the woman laughed.

Noah froze. Then in slow motion lifted his head and turned enough to see the woman in the red suit.

She had not been a vision. She was Savannah Skye Richards. His college sweetheart all grown up.

He'd recognized her, but his mind had refused to accept the reality that after twenty years, she'd be standing in front of him.

Closing his iPad, he laid it on the table and silently turned his chair around so he could watch her. He leaned back, his six-foot frame appearing relaxed – disguising the cat-like tension coursing through him.

She hadn't spotted him yet. Her gaze was glued to her phone – her fingers typing rapidly. The years had been good to her. She'd always been pretty, but now... she was drop-dead gorgeous. There was an air about her that hadn't been there when she was struggling in college. She carried an air of assurance and confidence now that hadn't been there before.

Twenty years. Then twice random crossings in less than an hour. It was more than he could ignore.

She must have felt him watching her. She glanced up, typed a couple of key-strokes. Then looked up again. He could tell by the way the corners of her mouth twitched the moment his presence registered with her. With her new self-assurance, he was certain that only he could tell. He'd spent, after all, countless hours studying her. For nearly a whole year.

Their gazes locked. He smiled. God, but it was good to see her.

Unbreak My Heart

BEGIN AGAIN - LOVE AGAIN - FALLING AGAIN

THE WORTHINGTONS

KATHRYN KALEIGH

THE GRAVITY OF US
(Suggested Reading Order)

Just Breathe
Just Surface
Just Melt

All of the books in the Gravity of Us Series are standalone and can be read out of order. However, the books are best read in order.

VOWS OF INHERITANCE SERIES
(**Reading Order**)
Vow to Protect
Vow to Redeem

All of the books in the Vows of Inheritance Series are standalone and can be read out of order. However, some books have characters from the previous stories in them.

ALPINE FALLS ROMANCES
(Suggested Reading Order)

Secrets and Second Chances
Honeymoon with a Stranger
Not Our Wedding
Stranded in Alpine Falls
Belonging in Alpine Falls
The Spirit of Christmas in Alpine Falls
Christmas Wishes in Alpine Falls
Finding True North in Alpine Falls
A Ghost of Christmas Magic in Alpine Falls

All of the books in the Alpine Falls Series standalone and can be read out of order. However, some books have characters from the previous stories in them.

Contemporary

(ALPINE FALLS)

Secrets and Second Chances

Honeymoon with a Stranger

Not Our Wedding

Stranded in Alpine Falls

Belonging in Alpine Falls

The Spirit of Christmas in Alpine Falls

Christmas Wishes in Alpine Falls

Finding True North in Alpine Falls

A Ghost of Christmas Magic in Alpine Falls

(SILVER PINES)

The Way Back to You

Back to Where We Began

When We Were Us

(ONCE UPON FOREVER)

My Forever Guy

Our Forever Love

Forever Vows

Finding Forever

Accidentally Forever

(TRUE NORTH)

Borrowed Until Monday

Still Mine

The Moon and the Stars at Christmas

Perfectly Mismatched

On the Way to Forever

A Merry Little Christmas

On the Way Home to Christmas

It was Always You

(UNBREAK MY HEART)

Begin Again

Love Again

Falling Again

(FOR THE LOVE OF THE FLIGHT)

Just Stay

Just Chance

Just Believe

Just Us

Just Once

Just Happened

Just Maybe

Just Pretend

Just Because

(MAGNETIC NORTH)

Second Chance Kisses

Second Chance Secrets

First Time Charm

Three Broken Rules

Second Chance Destiny

Unexpected Vows

(FALLING FOR CHRISTMAS)

The Heart of Christmas

The Magic of Christmas

In a One Horse Open Sleigh

A Secret Royal Christmas

An Old Fashioned Christmas

(CITY SKYLINE BILLIONAIRES)

Billionaire's Unexpected Landing

Billionaire's Accidental Girlfriend

Billionaire's Fallen Angel

Billionaire's Secret Crush

Billionaire's Barefoot Bride

(TRULY, MADLY, DEEPLY)

The Lady in the Red Dress

On the Edge of Chance

Sealed with a Kiss

Kiss Me at Midnight

The Heart Knows

(STOLEN ECHOES)

When Cupid's Arrow Strikes

Chasing Fireflies

A Chance Encounter

(EDGE OF THE HORIZON)

The Forever Equation

Pretend Boyfriend

All our Tomorrows

Kissing for Keeps

Out of the Blue

The Princess and the Playboy

(RED LIPSTICK KISSES)

Red Lipstick Kisses and Small Town Wishes

Stolen Dances and Big City Chances

Chance Connections and Upside Down Plans

A Christmas Kiss on the Twenty-Fifth

Believe in the Magic of Christmas

All of the books in each Series are standalone and can be read out of order. However, some books have characters from the previous stories in them.

ROMANTASY

(IN THE SPIRIT OF LOVE)

Spirits of the Heart

Out of Dreams and Ashes

Etched Upon the Heart

WESTERN ROMANCE

(LONE STAR HEARTS)

Wanted by a Texas Ranger

Saved by a Texas Ranger

(WHISKEY SPRINGS)

Finding Natalie

Promising Samantha

Falling for Allyson

Saving Savannah

Claiming Charlie

Rescuing Keira

Protecting Gabriella

Courting Isabella

TIME TRAVEL

(INTO THE MIST)

Written in the Wind

Scripted in the Stars

Destined in the Twilight

Promised in the Mist

Trapped in the Melody

(DRAGON'S BLOOD)

Dragon's Blood

Lavender Blue

Champagne Silver

Twilight Frost

Mountbatten Pink

(WHEN HEARTSTRINGS BECKON)

Rescued in Time

Meet me in 1879

(WHEN HEARTSTRINGS ECHO)

Messages Across Time

Falling Through to Forever

Once Upon a Winter's Spell

(BECKONED)

Before the Storm

Twist of Fate

When the Stars Align

Once Upon a Christmas

Once in a Blue Moon

A Wish Upon a Star

(BEGUILED)

When Lightning Strikes

Storm of Time

Midnight Storm

When the Moon Falls

Stormborn Angel

(SPELLED)

Time Tempest

The Heart Remembers

A Moment in Time

Moonlight Shadows

HISTORICAL

(TAPESTRY OF BLUE AND GRAY)

Shadows Beneath Magnolia Blooms

Secrets Among Southern Roses

(IT HAPPENED BY ACCIDENT)

Accidentally Alluring

Accidentally Married

(SOUTHERN BELLE CIVIL WAR)

Beyond Enemy Lines

Love Always

Hearts Under Siege

Hearts Under Fire

Away Down South in Dixie

The Reluctant Bride

Stay with Me

Jasmine Kisses

Magnolia Kisses

Gardenia Kisses

(THE QUINNS)

Wait for Me

Take Me Home

Keep Me Safe

FATED MATES

Riley's Mate

Aiden's Mate

Brayden's Mate

STANDALONE SUSPENSE

Lost and Found

All I Want for Christmas

Serenity

Courting Alley Cat

Sign up for my NEWSLETTER to get all my romance releases, sales, Kickstarter announcements, and a **FREE** romance, SEALED WITH A KISS

UNBREAK MY HEART:
BEGIN AGAIN
LOVE AGAIN
FALLING AGAIN
PREVIEW: JUST STAY

Written by Kathryn Kaleigh.
Published by KST Publishing
Cover by Skyhouse24Media
www.kathrynkaleigh.com

Unbreak My Heart

KATHRYN KALEIGH

Begin AGAIN

THE WORTHINGTONS
UNBREAK MY HEART SERIES

Begin Again

THE WORTHINGTONS

CHAPTER

One

Savannah Richards didn't believe in chance.

But there he stood, head bent, focused on his iPad. Handsome in his black uniform - black tie, white shirt, silver stripes at his wrists. A captain's cap sitting atop his head His hair graying around the edges.

Noah wouldn't recognize her now – even if he remembered her.

He would be forty-two now. A far cry from the college senior who had been attached to her hip for a year. He'd been a boy then, but his features were the same. A few pounds heavier, but that was to be expected. The five o'clock shadow that never failed to appear by early afternoon. The same brow that she had seen furrowed over a calculous problem seemed to have made a permanent home between his eyes. No wonder, as he had worn it often. Sometimes even as he'd studied her, though he thought she hadn't known.

As a college senior, the only time he'd left her side was when he was flying or training to fly. Sometimes she'd gone with him to practice on the simulator. She usually ended up using the time to study her own biology textbooks or read an English lit novel. Side by side, each lost in their own world.

The time, she thought wryly, had been well spent. After her freshman year, Savannah had immersed herself in her studies and graduated top of her class with a bachelor's degree in science.

Noah also had displayed a singular passion – aviation. And everything that went with it. Flying. Airplanes. Weather reports. When he hadn't been engrossed in aviation, however, he'd turned that singular focus on her. The memory brought a flush to her cheeks.

And a familiar stab to her heart.

As the terminal train arrived at the station and the door opened to allow people to exit, it occurred to her that she could take six steps to the left, get in his train car, and speak to him. It was a much more logical thing to do than just watching him – letting him breeze by her.

Two ships passing in the night.

No. He was a ship from the past. She would let him go.

She was still mad at him.

Noah Worthington glared at the flight schedule displayed on his iPad and wondered if his lunch had not agreed with him. The terminal train at Atlanta airport was interminably slow. He wasn't sure if he wanted it to hurry up or to never arrive. He struggled to find a middle ground.

He was seeing an apparition. He knew it had to be a vision because the girl he recognized wore a snug red pencil skirt with matching suit jacket. Her black pumps, though, had a matching red bottom. She carried a black leather Louis Vuitton handbag in a cross-body style, freeing up her hands. He recognized the LV twist-lock on the front – its only readily identifiable feature. The silver on the handbag matched the buttons on her suit. And the gray of her camisole. Her long brunette hair fell in loose waves around her face. Her make-up was flawless down to the shiny, but muted glossy red lipstick.

The college freshman from his indelible memory wore jeans ripped at the knees, white canvas sneakers, and either a sweat-shirt or t-shirt depending on the weather. She'd kept her hair pulled back in a loose ponytail. The only time he'd seen her dressed up was when she wore a dark gray cardigan and matching shell with black slacks to a dinner with his family. She'd worn low heeled dark gray moto boots. He'd been impressed, at the time, at how put together and cute she looked. Her hair had fallen straight to her shoulder and though he hadn't commented, he'd known she had taken the time to straighten it with a flat iron. Her hair was naturally wavy and thick and she hated it. Hence, the ponytail.

All in all, perhaps that was a precursor to the woman who watched him now. Or perhaps she was his mind's rendition of the girlfriend he'd so inconsiderately left behind twenty years ago. Besides, what college freshman gained no more than a couple of pounds and in all the right places after twenty years?

The vision watched him, though she didn't know he knew. He recognized the expression she wore.

She was still mad at him.

The train rolled in, the door opened, and throngs of people rushed out of the cars. She got into the car behind his, moving with that same lilt in her step that even he hadn't managed to dull.

She's only a vision. Probably some random girl from California who just happened to have similar – very similar facial features.

However, he knew the saying that one never forgot his first love to be true.

He glanced at the time on his tablet. He had time for dinner before his flight, now delayed, took off for Dallas. He didn't feel like going to the officer's club. Didn't feel like talking aviation. Or hearing about someone's new aircraft acquisition. He just wanted to enjoy some peaceful time to read his novel, order a martini he wouldn't drink, and have a meal.

He scanned his ID and slipped into the Diner's Club – away from the other pilots. He wasn't exactly nondescript in his pilot's uniform, but he'd learned over the years that the typical flyer tended to not bother the pilots. He'd never quite discerned if it was out of respect, awe, or fear. Perhaps just disinterest. Whatever it was, he'd grown to count on it when he wanted to be left alone.

He took a small table for two near the bar, his back to the room. He found it less distracting to read when he couldn't see people hurrying to and fro.

He ordered a sandwich and water. And resumed his attention on the novel he read on his iPad. It was about a man who never slept. In theory, he liked the concept, but in reality, sleep was one of his favorite pastimes.

And allowed the world to fade into the background. Which was exactly where he preferred it these days.

"I'd like a cosmopolitan," A woman at the bar behind him ordered. "with olives."

Who ordered olives with their cosmopolitans?

The server said something he couldn't understand. And the woman laughed.

Noah froze. Then in slow motion lifted his head and turned enough to see the woman in the red suit.

She had not been a vision. She was Savannah Skye Richards. His college sweetheart all grown up.

He'd recognized her, but his mind had refused to accept the reality that after twenty years, she'd be standing in front of him.

Closing his iPad, he laid it on the table and silently turned his chair around so he could watch her. He leaned back, his six-foot frame appearing relaxed – disguising the cat-like tension coursing through him.

She hadn't spotted him yet. Her gaze was glued to her phone – her fingers typing rapidly. The years had been good to her. She'd always been pretty, but now… she was drop-dead gorgeous. There was an air about her that hadn't been there when she was struggling in college. She carried an air of assurance and confidence now that hadn't been there before.

Twenty years. Then twice random crossings in less than an hour. It was more than he could ignore.

She must have felt him watching her. She glanced up, typed a couple of key-strokes. Then looked up again. He could tell by the way the corners of her mouth twitched the moment his presence registered with her. With her new self-assurance, he was certain that only he could tell. He'd spent, after all, countless hours studying her. For nearly a whole year.

Their gazes locked. He smiled. God, but it was good to see her.

Déjà vu was an understatement.

He'd been working registration his senior year. She was a freshman. Her first day on campus at Auburn University in Auburn, Alabama. He'd taken one look at her and fallen head over heels.

This time, however, instead of smiling, she was looking… displeased to see him.

He stood up, closed the distance between them, and sat at the bar next to her. "What brings you to this gin joint?" he said.

"Work," she said, clicking off her iPhone.

"It's been awhile," he said.

"Twenty years," she said, as the server set her cosmopolitan in front of her. She picked it up. Sipped.

"What are the odds?" he asked.

"I don't believe in chance." She kept her eyes focused on her drink.

"I guess a date at the casino is out."

She scoffed. "A date is out."

"Savannah Skye," he said.

"Savannah," she corrected.

He rubbed his chin. "Savannah. Look at me," She lifted her eyes and he saw a glimpse of the pain before she checked it.

"It's been twenty years since we saw each other. Let's at least say hello."

"Hello," she said.

"That's better."

She scowled again. "You started it."

He shook his head. "You're right. I did. I'm sorry. I was caught off guard."

She smiled, albeit a little wobbly. "I'm sorry, too. I've seen you twice in one day. That can't be coincidence."

"I agree," he said. "You look good. You look like I imagined."

She raised an eyebrow. "You imagined me."

He chuckled. "On occasion, yes."

"You're married," she pointed out, nodding toward his ring finger.

He glanced down. Saw the line on his ring finger, no more than a shadow to most. She always had been observant. "Divorced. Separated actually."

"Right," she said, looking at him askance. "Aren't you all?"

"What?"

She shrugged.

"It seems you've been hanging around the wrong crowd."

"Is that so? When's your divorce hearing date?"

"I don't know."

She rolled her eyes. Sipped her drink.

"Seriously. It's uncontested. I'm not even sure we have to go."

She glanced at him. Unlocked her phone.

"Ok. Here," he said, taking his own phone out of his pocket. "Let's call Matthew. Let's call my attorney."

"Let's don't."

"Why are you so interested in my marital state?"

"Ok, let's say for now I believe you."

"No, really, why are you?"

Her gaze met his now. She chuckled. "You've already asked me out."

"I most certainly did not."

"The casino," she said, locking her phone again.

He shook his head, "It's a figure of speech. When did you become so literal?"

She leaned back. Sighed. "After being hit on about five hundred times."

"Admirable," he said, "I can see the attraction."

She laughed. "Not like that. As part of my job."

He considered her in a different light now. Her clothes were much too fine for a stripper. Definitely not a prostitute.

"You're an escort?"

She sighed. "I see you never developed a filter."

He shrugged. "Some things never change."

"I'm not a call girl." She glared at him. "Or a prostitute. So don't get any ideas."

"I think you're about twenty-one years late on that request."

"Yeah, well, you're married now."

"Separated."

"Same thing."

"You're difficult. I'm impressed. What about you?"

He'd yet to get a glimpse of her ring finger. Truthfully, he'd been too enthralled to even think to look.

She held up her unadorned hand.

"Divorced?"

"Never married."

"Are you telling me that you never..." He trailed off. This conversation was completely unfair. He had no way to know what damage he'd done to her all those years ago.

"I work a lot."

He nodded. Self-sufficient. Successful. Hence the air of confidence. "What kind of work?"

"I'm a drug rep."

"Really?" Not at all what he expected.

"You may recall I was a science major."

"I do recall. And I'm sure you excelled."

"You could say that."

He smiled to himself. She had that slightly pouty expression that had always worked on him.

"I'm a pilot," he said, before he could stop himself.

She laughed. A genuine laugh now. Her green eyes twinkled with sincerity.

And it was in that moment. Just like that, that the years fell away and he was that college senior all over again. In love with the freshman coed.

"I never would have guessed."

"Did the uniform give me away?"

"That and the unerring devotion you put toward achieving that goal."

He sat a little taller in his chair. "You're successful at this drug rep thing you do," he said.

She tilted her head with a little smile. "I suppose. Why would you say that?"

"Because you're good at everything you do and…" he lifted one eyebrow suggestively. "You have a way of making a man do whatever it is you want."

She shook her head. The smile disappeared back into the little pout. "That seems a little odd coming from you." A silent message appeared on her phone. She checked it and pushed her unfinished drink aside.

"I'm sorry," she said.

She had managed to do it again. She had mesmerized him and he had no idea what she was talking about. "Sorry about what?"

"I have to go."

"Go?" He checked his watch. Such a short time had passed since he'd come into the club… yet his life, it seemed, had been altered forever.

The girl he had spent twenty years wondering about. Twenty years with a love in his heart that hadn't died.

And here she was. In the flesh.

"Yes," she said, with the flash of a smile at the corner of her lips. "I have a flight to catch." She stood up.

"Of course you do." *Why else would she be here?* For a mere moment in time, he'd allowed himself to think that she was there in his world just for him. Just for him and no one else.

She stood up. Pushed her chair to the bar. "It was good to see you again, Noah," she said, her lips curved in a polite smile no doubt used successfully when working with doctors.

"It was good to see you, too," he said, automatically.

She held out her hand.

He took her hand, but didn't shake it as she had obviously intended, but held it. Stared into those mesmerizing green eyes. She pulled back almost imperceptibly. He held tighter. Felt a gut-wrenching juxtaposition of familiar and new as she gave in and squeezed back. Just for a moment.

A moment in time. When his heart was light and the world narrowed down to them. Just the two of them.

"I'm gonna miss my flight," she said, pulling back in earnest now.

He released her. "Go," he said.

She picked up her bag and turned. Took a step.

His heart sank. Heavy again.

"Wait," he said, out of his chair in a flash and closing the distance between them. Stepping in front of her.

She raised an eyebrow.

"How will I find you?"

Her lips curved into a smug little smile. The smile he'd seen her wear after she aced a chemistry exam. "Perhaps we'll bump into each other again," she said.

"No," he insisted. "It's been twenty years. We both travel all the time. Right? You travel?"

"A fair amount."

"Well, you don't believe in chance. Yet in one day, we've bumped into each other twice... in one hour."

She shrugged. "What are the odds?"

He scoffed. "Out of the mouth of the one who doesn't believe in chance."

"I believe in science."

"Well, scientifically, we could never see each other again."

"You could always look for me this time."

He absorbed the jab. Owned it. "I could. I will. But the world is a big place."

She seemed to consider. Squinted into his eyes. Searching for something only she knew to look for.

"New York."

"New York what?"

"I'll be in New York for the next five days."

"Ha. New York doesn't narrow the world by very much."

She nodded. "It is a big city. But you know enough about me to find me."

"Wait," he said. "Until Monday?"

"Tuesday."

"Come on," he said. She turned. Smiled over her shoulder. That smile that had once been reserved only for him.

"See you around," she said, and walked away from him. He watched her walk through the door.

And took a deep steadying breath. Glanced at his watch. Now was not the time for a panic attack. He had a plane to fly in less than an hour.

Savannah rushed down the corridor. She could not afford to miss this flight, but she wasn't late.

She wasn't thinking straight. Her blood pounded in her ears. She'd only known that she had to get away. Before her composure shattered.

Noah Worthington had been the last person she had expected to see today. When he'd disappeared out of her life twenty years ago, she'd waited for him. She'd waited longer than she cared to admit, even to herself. She hadn't dated any one else in college. She'd gone into a dating moratorium after he left. Then, after graduation, she'd gone through a phase of serial relationships until ending up in a five-year engagement that had ended four years ago. She'd gone back into her no dating phase with the exception of a couple of dinners here and there. She'd never even signed up for a dating website service.

It was like Noah had taken it all out of her.

She took a seat in the waiting area and found herself studying the pilots as they, too, waited for the plane to arrive.

She wondered again, as she often had while raking in frequent flyer miles, what kind of life they had. Even though they were a little like taxi drivers, as Noah had so oddly pointed out to her so many years ago, they had professionalism and respect and an aloofness from the rest of the world.

Very few were invited into their worlds. Flight attendants seemed to have the most direct route. From her view in first class flight, she'd watched a romance or two unfold between pilots and flight attendants. She had yet to see anything more than cordial interaction between pilots and passengers. And to think that she'd been a part of that world once. At least to some extent. She'd been on the ground floor of a pilot in training.

Did their wives feel part of their world? Or did they feel like they perched on the fringe of an elite group? Only the elite group got to travel around the world with the lives of innocents in their hands.

As she allowed her musings to keep her from thinking directly about Noah, a pair of tall, blonde flight attendants went up to the pilots and after quick hugs all around, and sitting next to the pilots, moved into their private world.

Drug reps were more private. More competitive. She knew a few of them, but they were reluctant to trade secrets. Too much at stake. There were exceptions, of course, mostly among the more seasoned ones like herself. It seemed that the more knowledge they had, the firmer their hold on the industry, hence, they were less afraid of losing it.

Savannah knew that she was moving into that point in her career where she would have to start looking for different options. It was a daily struggle to keep up with, not only the constantly changing drug market, but also the technology alone required to make the presentations.

The young ones, coming out of college, came readily equipped with what she thought of as updated software. Just like her iPhone, Savannah had to constantly make updates to her brain. And it wasn't just technology and drugs. In order to establish rapport with the doctors younger than she was, she had to stay up with current culture. She had to know which movies were popular... which restaurants were popular in an area. Even what music people were listening to. And that didn't even begin to touch on what she had to keep up with in the political world. Who was supporting what movement. Such as the medical psychologists. Louisiana and New Mexico were allowing psychologists to write prescriptions. Several other states were right behind them. She had to be able to either support the idea or not depending on who she was interacting with.

All these things took their toll.

How dare Noah Worthington to waltz back nonchalantly into her life!

Hearing them call for first-class boarding, she gathered up her bag and was ushered through the gate. Following a couple down the corridor, she watched their heads tucked together, laughing at things unique to them, the rest of the world nonexistent.

A pang shot through her heart as they invoked unbidden, but now newly invoked memories of her year with Noah. They, too, had often walked hand in hand, oblivious to the rest of the world.

She followed them into the plane where they sat together and she sat across the aisle in her own private first-class seat. She always booked a single seat when possible. She enjoyed the privacy to read, work, or just rest her mind. Resting her mind often meant preparing herself for upcoming meetings.

She heard glimpses of the couple's conversation.

"Did you see the look on your father's face when his ex-wife asked him to dance?"

"I can't believe Meredith caught the bouquet. She's already thirty. Everyone knows she'll never get married."

Savannah smiled to herself. A happy couple on their honeymoon. This should be an interesting flight.

She accepted a bottle of water from the flight attendant and settled into her space. Flying at least once every couple of months, she was comfortable here. She had all the rules down. Drink lots of water. Stand up every hour. Avoid alcohol. Well, at least on the flight itself.

She took out a highlighter and a stack of notes. It was about time to unplug from the world for a few hours. But first, she sent a quick text to her mother. Another to her sister. Confirmed two appointments for next week. Set up a meeting with a new doctor she'd been assigned.

As the plane taxied down the runway, she turned off her phone and iPad. Sipped her water and relaxed a few minutes before getting to work.

She used the sway of the plane to prepare her mind to focus on reading.

The muted laughter of the couple next to her, snuggled in together now beneath a blanket provided by the flight attendant, faded into the background.

And Noah Worthington's face invaded her thoughts.

He looked better, she mused. He was nearing what Savannah considered a man's prime.

Handsome. Mature. Successful.

The very same profile of many of the men she dealt with on a daily basis. She had refined her interactions to an art. She knew how to get a man's attention and to keep it. She knew what to say to keep his focus in the midst of a busy day long enough to have him agree to use her medications.

She also knew when to let him down easily enough. Leaving him looking forward to their next meeting without feeling rejected.

In fact, she'd never dated a doctor. Or nurse. Or anyone in the health sciences.

Her five-year engagement had been to the construction manager who'd built her house on Lake Martin. She kept business and pleasure in two completely separate compartments.

Savannah Richards was good at her job. She knew her science. She knew her marketing techniques. She preferred solitude but was good at social interaction.

She hadn't however, been good enough at social interaction to keep the interest of Noah Worthington.

Noah gathered up his iPad, tossed a tip on the table he had barely touched, and rushed out of the club. He had a flight to Dallas, then back in the morning.

Then his schedule was about to change. He had somewhere unexpected he needed to be.

He made his way down the concourse, into the terminal, and

onto the plane. His copilot, a woman named Michelle, was running late from a delayed connection, so he had a few minutes to himself. To reflect on the conversation he'd had with his ghost from the past. He knew exactly when his divorce hearing was – December, but he hadn't wanted to talk about it with her.

Whether intentional or not, she'd presented him with a puzzle and Noah Worthington could not resist a challenge. Especially not one wrapped in such an appealing package.

She'd said she was going to be in New York for five days. That either meant she traveled so much that she would only be home for five days or she was travelling to New York. The thought of finding someone who lived in New York was daunting to say the least. But finding someone in a hotel narrowed it down slightly.

He began checking the weather. Skies were clear, so the routine check allowed him to think about Savannah Skye. He smiled at the name she obviously no longer used. He'd always thought how ironic and convenient, that both the girl he loved and the place he loved to be had the same name. Skye.

So she was a sales rep. What would a sales rep be doing in New York? Assuming she didn't live there, it was unlikely she would have clients there. "Ah ha," he said, picking up his iPad.

"Ah ha what?" Michelle asked, taking her seat next to him.

"You decided to show up for work?" he asked, pulling up google.

"You know how I am. Always trying to avoid a flight."

"Yep," Noah said. So, far, he'd found no gatherings of drug reps in New York. Did drug reps even gather? Perhaps drug companies sponsor events. He googled drug companies and immediately found a list of twenty-five companies. This was going to take a while.

"So what's her name?"

"What?" Noah asked, after a few more clicks.

"Who is she?"

He stopped. Looked up blankly at his friend. Shook his head. "Who?"

"I haven't seen you this distracted since you had that crush on the brunette from Idaho."

Noah laughed and put his iPad aside to continue going through the pre-flight checklist with this copilot who had, over the years, become a friend of sorts. She was physically attractive, he supposed, but he'd never thought of her that way. She was tall, thin, and blonde; hence, she had a never-ending run of men. But it wasn't her looks so much that kept Noah at bay. It was the personality that doubtless came from the daily battle of trying to fit into a man's world.

"Back on match.com?" she asked.

"Nope."

"If you need a date, I can hook you up with a flight attendant."

"I'm good on my own. Thank you." He had made the mistake of allowing Michelle to *hook him up* once. One time too many. The match.com thing hadn't been for him either. He told himself that after seventeen years of marriage things had changed far too much in the dating world. It was a little more difficult to admit that he couldn't find anyone he could have a conversation with that he also wanted to kiss.

"Just say the word," Michelle said.

Noah preferred a woman who spoke like a lady. More times

than not, Michelle's words could just as easily have come from a man.

"No crush," he said, needing to keep his thoughts about Savannah as far away from Michelle as possible. "Just information seeking."

"Ok," she said. "Looks like we should have an uneventful flight."

"The only way to fly," he said, automatically, truly not in the mood for pilot banter at the moment.

CHAPTER

Two

Noah sat in the cockpit of his plane, a Cessna Mustang with gray interior, running down the pre-flight checklist. He would be in New York by evening. It was already Thursday. That left only 4 days to not only track Savannah down, but also to convince her to spend time with him. He frankly didn't care if it was no more than a cup of coffee.

The plane was new – he'd only had it a few months, and only flown it three times, but he was already in love with it. He liked the idea of having his own space. No pilot banter. No crude jokes.

No forward flight attendants.

Noah supposed he was not the typical pilot. He loved flying. Passionately. He just didn't care for much of the culture that went along with it.

He taxied out to the runway and waited his turn. It would be a little while, but he didn't mind. He still had internet.

He'd run into a dead end with the twenty-five drug companies. Nothing seemed to be going on in New York that would attract a drug rep. Her words kept replaying in his head. *You know enough to find me.*

Had she been to New York before? That was a place she had always wanted to go. He recalled a cool fall Saturday they'd spent on Lake Martin on his boat. He winced at the memory that he'd told her it was a friend's.

There were so many things he hadn't told her.

The weather had been perfect. A soft breeze. The sun warm, but not hot. The leaves on shore starting to turn. The water calm. They were anchored in a quiet cove. Difficult to find this time of year. But Noah knew the lake inside and out. When he wasn't in the air, he had been in the water. His mother used to joke that he'd had something against land.

That's how it had been, anyway, before he met Savannah. After that, all bets were off. Even when he'd been in the air, he felt her pulling him back to her. Actually, now that he thought about it, he hadn't gone out in his boat again that year without taking her with him.

He'd brought a blanket and she had lain with her back against him, snuggled against his chest.

They had nothing to do that day. Mid-terms were over and they were taking a break. It was Saturday, so she wasn't at her student worker job.

"I can't think of anywhere I'd rather be," he'd said.

"Really? I can."

He hadn't answered right away.

"I'd want you with me," she added quickly.

He laughed. "I wasn't fishing. I was just trying to think of someplace better."

"Not necessarily better. Just different."

"I'm listening," he kissed the top of her head. He loved the way her hair smelled. He didn't tell her that, of course.

"San Francisco seems nice."

"California? That's like a whole different country out there. People are different."

She shifted, to glance at him. "How do you know?"

"I'm a pilot."

"Have you been there?"

"No. But I hear things."

"Ok. New York then."

He stroked her arm, instinctively holding onto her as a wave from a jet ski hit them. "Too big."

"That's what makes it so cool," she said. "So much history and so much energy. Right there in such a small space."

"Hmm."

"It's so big that most of it is in the sky."

He chuckled. "You like the idea of people living in the sky?"

"Yeah," she said. "Don't you? I mean of all people you should like it. You love riding in the sky, why not live in the sky?"

"That's an interesting concept, my love." He took her hand, held it in his. Marveled at how much smaller it was than his. How soft. "And very perceptive of you. I do love everything related to the sky." He waited a beat. "Savannah Skye."

"I have my moments."

"What would you do in New York in the sky?"

"I'd spend the day at the Empire State Building."

"It's not the tallest."

"Doesn't have to be. It's one of the oldest and has a wrap-around view."

"They have a restaurant that turns while you eat."

"No way? How do you know that?" She shifted to glance at him before settling back against him.

"You have so little faith in how much I know."

He felt her laugh against him. "I don't think you know as much as you think you do."

"What would you do on the Empire State Building?"

"I'd look around at everything. I'd even look through those telescopes they have. And..." she squeezed his hand. "I'd let you kiss me."

"Well," he said, pulling her around to face him, "Since you're taking me with you to your land in the sky, I suppose we'd better make sure we're in good practice."

She always smiled when he went to kiss her. It had bothered him at first, so much so that he'd once asked her about it.

"Why do you smile when I kiss you?"

She'd looked a little perplexed. "Because I like kissing you."

The voice on the radio indicated it was time for take-off. Pulling himself out his memories, he went to work. As he left the safety of land, his thoughts left the safety of the past.

Had she been to New York before? Had she been to the Empire State Building? Had she kissed someone there?

He should have been the one kissing her on the Empire State Building.

Landing in New York, he had to wait again. A line of planes all waiting their turn to get to a parking space. Opening his iPad, he went for a broad google search this time - *medication conferences.*

It took no more than a few keystrokes for him to feel the jolt of success.

There was a psychopharmacology conference going on right now.

In New York.

The American Society of Clinical Psychopharmacology.

She hadn't said she had a specialty.

It made sense though. He was only certified to fly certain types of airplanes.

It was being held at the Grand Hyatt Hotel.

He scrolled through the program.

And grinned like a cat who just stuck the claws of his paw into the tail of a mouse.

Savannah sent out for room service – a big salad with turkey and a bottle of water. She had read all the articles she had down-loaded to read. And she already had a working draft that she'd started six months ago. She still had revisions to do on the PowerPoint before her presentation tomorrow morning. Her presentation was scheduled for 11:00 am. *The Drug Rep: An Inside View of the Unconscious.*

She'd done a similar presentation a couple of years ago, but this was a bigger – much bigger, conference and she wanted to make sure all her references were updated. And she had to make sure she had appropriate psychological jokes. Psychiatrists and psychologists wanted entertainment with their information.

Her plan was to give them just enough of a peek beneath the

curtain, or as Sigmund Freud would say, a peek at the ankle – enough to keep them interested, but not enough to give anything away.

She looked at the notes scattered across the hotel desk and wondered how that had become the whole purpose of her life. Give them just enough – then get out.

It would be nice to just, once in a while, be able to let her guard down and say what she really wanted to say instead of what was expected. Or what would be most effective.

While she munched on a bite of egg, turkey, and spinach, someone knocked on the door. "Room service."

They must have made a mistake, she thought, walking across the room.

"I already have what I need," she said, through the door.

"We have a delivery for you," the man insisted.

Savannah didn't open the door. She trusted most of the strangers she came in contact with in her travels. However, the story of the drug rep brutally murdered in her hotel room in Minneapolis had imprinted itself in her mind and she'd often considered how that could have happened. There were so many possibilities but Savannah always went for the most parsimonious.

"Just leave it," she said, "Thank you."

The man put something next to her door and walked off.

Savannah waited. She really couldn't be sure he'd left.

But if they'd brought her salad twice, she needed to call and straighten it out.

She walked back to her desk, drank some water, and walked back to the door. Waited. When she heard voices coming down the hall, she opened the door. If she was going to be nabbed, at least she'd have witnesses.

Instead of the food service tray she'd expected, there was a vase of red roses next to her door.

Two women walked down the hall, passed her, and no one else was visible.

She picked up the vase and took it into her room, locking the door behind her.

Keeping the flowers at arm's length, she took them to the bathroom and set them on the counter. Kept her eyes on them as though they would bite if she looked away. No one had sent her flowers since the construction worker and that had been at the beginning of their relationship.

Why would someone possibly send her flowers?

After several minutes had passed, with her mind frozen, she thought to look for a card and found one. The note was printed, so no handwriting to decipher.

Good luck with your presentation tomorrow.

She turned it over. There were no other identifying notes. Not even a florist name. That was odd.

Perhaps the conference coordinator had sent flowers out to all the presenters. That was the most logical explanation she could fathom.

If she, however, had been the conference coordinator, she would most definitely not send out the flowers of love to wish someone luck. White roses perhaps. Even better, would have been a bouquet of flowers with lilies, white roses, and white mini carnations in a blue vase. Maybe some white daisies. Definitely white flowers.

Instead, a vase of long-stem red roses with assorted fresh

greenery and baby's breath in a silver vase sat on her bathroom counter.

Deciding they weren't going to do any damage, she took each bloom, one at a time, and examined it. They were perfectly formed rose buds. She sniffed. Definitely high quality. She counted them.

Frowned.

Counted three times more.

There were only eleven roses in the arrangement.

She shook her head, pushed them to the back of the counter against the mirror.

Unable to sort the whole thing out and make further sense of it, she double-checked the hotel room door lock, put it out of her mind, and went back to work on her presentation.

Around nine o'clock she realized her presentation was done. Sure, she could change up the font. Again. Or google some more images.

But as of right now, it was professional and comprehensive, but still entertaining.

She saved it on her computer. On the cloud. And emailed a copy to herself.

The next morning, she got up early, ran five miles on the treadmill in her room, and took a long hot shower after having eggs and fruit sent up for breakfast.

She put on a black pencil skirt with matching short jacket and an emerald camisole – to match her eyes.

She was focused and had her mind trained on her presentation as she went down to the conference area at the hotel. In order to get into the social mode, she went into the vending area where the other sales reps would be.

"There you are," Adam, one of the reps from the Denver area pounced on her when she'd barely gotten in the door.

"Hey Adam. I see you made it." Adam was always at the conferences and he'd stayed in touch with Savannah throughout the years. They had drinks occasionally while at the conferences. They had, in fact, originally met in Chicago at a smaller conference.

"Wouldn't miss it," he said. "I've got to get back to my booth, but make sure you check out the STIM display back there."

"I thought you were anti-STIM."

"I am. They're gonna steal our business. Mark my words. But in the meantime, they have a cool display."

Savannah laughed. "I'll check it out."

Adam started to walk away, "Oh hey, drinks tonight?"

"Not tonight," she said. "We have that black-tie dinner thing."

"Right." He made a face. "Love those things."

"Just part of the job, Adam."

"Yep. Tomorrow night, then?" he asked, walking backwards.

"Sure," Savannah said absently. She never made casual commitments ahead of time at these things. Just in case she needed to be available for a business meeting. But she didn't really consider Adam a commitment. She was sure he felt the same way.

A little later, she stepped into a crowded meeting room. Everyone, it seemed wanted to know about the unconscious thoughts of a sales rep. *That's what I get for having a catchy title.*

Putting a smile on her face, she stepped into her extraverted role and began her presentation.

Everything went smoothly until a little over halfway through. "So as you can see," she said. "from the next slide, the mechanism of action isn't all we worry about."

The next slide elicited a laugh. She had a cartoon up on the screen that had nothing to do with a drug's mechanism of action. It was Sigmund Freud himself, cigar in hand.

"However, back to busi." She froze in mid-sentence.

Her eyes fell on a man sitting in the second row on the left that she hadn't noticed before. He had been hidden behind a couple of what looked to be young physician assistants.

But this man was no doctor. She didn't need her knack for classifying people to figure this one out.

This man wore a smug grin that said *I found you sooner than you thought. And I just caught you terribly off guard.*

"Back to business," she continued, deftly putting Noah Worthington out her mind.

For a full two seconds.

After her presentation ended – exactly on time, several psychiatrists, two psychologists, and three other mental health workers came up, introduced themselves, and wanted to further the conversation.

She found the enthusiasm of the medical psychologists to be the most refreshing of all the medical professions she worked with. The medical psychologists used medications judiciously and effectively. They were apt to try other things in addition to medication. Savannah liked that about them and they responded well to her nonjudgmental response to their methods.

Psychiatrists, on the other hand, tended to see non-medication interventions as a waste of time. Depending on who they were speaking to, they may not come right out and say it, but medication was their only thing.

When the two psychologists asked to take her to lunch, she agreed, enjoying the twist of events. Usually, she was the one trying to take doctors to lunch to woo them into using her medications over another company's. But the psychologists seemed genuinely interested in establishing a relationship with her and learning more about the drug business.

She soon learned that they were from Louisiana. The woman, middle-aged, but looked Savannah's age, was a newly licensed medical psychologist. The man, in his early sixties, was her business partner. Though he was not a medical psychologist, he actually had more experience in the medical field than the newly licensed medical psychologist did. They seemed to work well together and enjoyed each other's company.

As they left the presentation room, Savannah scanned the room for Noah, but he had disappeared. She had the fleeting thought that she had imagined him. She had only glimpsed him the one time and then her view had been obstructed. The psychologists took her to the hotel café and they had a pleasant lunch. Savannah was honest with them. She didn't get to Louisiana often, but she could send an associate in the interim. She warned them that the associate would do her best to sway them to use their medications over those from other companies. They, however, seemed to expect this and weren't alarmed.

They ordered cocktails, so Savannah ordered a mimosa, her standby lunch drink. She found it difficult to keep her attention on them, even though she considered herself working. The thought that Noah was out there was disconcerting to say the least.

That despite insurmountable odds, he had managed to locate her in New York. She hadn't thought to ever see him again.

But there he had been, sitting in the audience of her presentation. The knowledge that he had found her sent little shivers through her. Little shivers that she thought had been eradicated from her system.

There was also the anticipation that she was destined to see him again. Although she could have doubtless found him after the presentation, she had needed to work. And... she had needed time to process the fact that he was, indeed here, in her hotel.

She finished her lunch and excused herself from the couple of psychologists. They had one more presentation they wanted to catch, then they were headed out to see the Statue of Liberty. She didn't blame them. If she didn't have obligations to be there, she would cut out, too. That was half the fun of going to conferences.

Not wanting to go back to her room just yet, she went to the courtyard and found a quiet place to respond to texts and emails. Her mother and sister had checked in. They had a bit of anxiety about her traveling alone though she'd been doing it her whole career. Her sister was a stay-at-home mom who devoted far too much time to worrying. And her mother was a retired school teacher, which pretty much summed things up in Savannah's mind. Her mother had pushed her relentlessly until she'd left home. Then Savannah had continued to push herself. Now her mother insisted that Savannah worked too hard.

MOTHER: *It's your, what, fourth or fifth time to New York? And you've never seen anything other than the inside of a hotel.*

SAVANNAH: *I happen to be sitting outside right now, Mom.*

MOTHER: *That doesn't count and you know it. Go see the Statue of Liberty, go to the Empire State Building, go shopping, for goodness sakes. You love shopping. And you're in the shopping mecca.*

Savannah sighed.

SAVANNAH: *I will, Mom. I go shopping every time I'm here. In fact, I might even go today.*

MOTHER: *Good. Just be careful out there.*

SAVANNAH: *Love you, Mom.*

There was a black-tie event tonight at the Art Institute. Although she had brought something to wear, it wouldn't hurt to take a walk down 5th Avenue.

She gathered up her bags and went back inside the crowded hotel, making her way toward the elevators. She had the smile back on her face and greeted several acquaintances along the way.

She was looking forward to getting out of her heels and putting on some flats, at least until tonight.

As she reached the elevators and pressed the button, her smile faltered.

"Well, hello, Savannah Richards," Noah said, pushing himself off the wall to step toward her. "Are you staying here, too?"

Her heartbeat ratcheted up a notch. "You're stalking me now," she said.

He looked hurt. "I like to think of it more as… hunting."

She laughed. "Is that what they're calling it now?" She pressed the elevator button again.

"I'm always up for a challenge," he said.

"I wasn't challenging you, Noah. I was merely trying to… get away."

"It sounded like a challenge to me," he said, unable to hide the hurt on his face.

She sighed. "I'm actually rather impressed that you found me."

"It wasn't easy," he admitted. "Looks like you're having a busy day."

"Very."

"So, since I'm here. And you're here." He put his hands in his pockets and joined her in staring at the elevator. "Do you want to go have coffee?"

Coffee. With the man who broke her heart twenty years ago. That was exactly what she wanted to do. "I'm actually on my way out."

"Oh. I see," Again, that crestfallen look.

"But," she said, narrowing her eyes. "I have a black-tie affair tonight at the museum – a work thing. I was planning to go by myself, but I wouldn't mind having an escort." The offer of a black-tie affair usually sent most men running in the other direction.

"Black tie, huh? That happens to be my specialty."

She narrowed her eyes, looking for the joke. Didn't find it. "Great. I'll meet you in the lobby at 7:00."

Noah watched the doors of the elevator close and turned away. He'd been loitering around the elevators so long that the security guard had questioned him. Apparently waiting for someone at the elevator was a questionable excuse for standing around at this hotel.

He had a ridiculous grin on his face. She had been on target.

He had felt like a stalker standing at the elevators for nearly two hours. His perseverance had paid off, though. In a hotel this large with this many people wandering around, it would have easy to lose track of her. It had been an anomaly that he'd seen her name in the presentation program. After her presentation, she'd been swamped with what he thought of as fans, then swept off to lunch with some people.

Although he wanted to talk to her, he wanted to do it in private. The last thing he wanted was to be an embarrassment to her.

But now… she had invited him to be with her in public. That meant he didn't embarrass her. She would have to introduce him. Spend hours with him.

There was just one problem.

He had to find a tux.

Savannah sat in the back of a taxi, locked in traffic. Tapping her foot. Tapping her fingers against her phone. She had taken far too long at the shops, but she had found the perfect dress for tonight. She didn't need shoes – wasn't into shoe fads. She liked basic pumps for all work and social occasions and wore flats on days like today. Of course, she also liked boots. Boots were sort of her weakness, but too big to travel with.

And added to that, she'd stopped in at one of the Blow Dry Bars to have her hair washed, blown and styled, then she had her make-up done and, finally, her nails. She'd chosen the mysterious look from a menu of make-up choices – smoky eyes, glossy lips. Her hair felt light, bouncy.

She checked the time on her phone. Again.

Took a deep breath.

She had plenty of time to get back to the hotel, change, and get back downstairs.

She should have just gotten dressed at the salon, she berated herself for the hundredth time. But her shoes were in her hotel room as well as her perfume.

I'll be fashionable late.

Nonetheless, with the magic of the New York minute, she arrived at the door to her hotel with forty-five minutes to get to her room, change, and make it back to the lobby.

Rushing into her room, she threw everything on the bed, plugged in her phone for a quick charge, and checked on the roses. They were still there and there were still only eleven of them.

With a little trill of girlish excitement, she unwrapped the black taffeta beaded gown with an off-the-shoulder bodice. The flower clustered sequins crowded the bodice and dispersed along the waist becoming scattered on the skirt. There was a royal blue sash at the waist, adding an elegant touch. The slit at the side was high – mid-thigh giving the formal column dress an unexpected edge.

She spritzed perfume high into the air, and walked through it. She adjusted the little diamond necklace she had bought herself last Christmas at Tiffany's and stepped into her shoes.

Checked the time. She had fifteen minutes to get downstairs. She grabbed her phone, tucked it into her handbag, and twirled in front of the mirror.

Black tie events are important to my career. Not everyone gets to go.

She ignored the other voice that reminded her that this one was different. She'd never taken a date.

It's not a date.

She'd never taken an escort.

It's Noah Worthington.

She laughed. Told herself to just enjoy the moment.

When she stepped into the lobby, she immediately realized she should have been more specific when she said to meet in the lobby.

Air and Water.

She found him near the waterfall, leaning against a column.

Her heart fluttered. She was again astounded that he was even more handsome than he was twenty years ago. Their clothing couldn't have matched more perfectly if they had tried. He wore a black tux with white shirt and royal blue tie. Six feet tall, broad shoulders, trim. A smile that would melt any female heart. He was clearly the most handsome man in the crowded lobby. A lobby the size of a basketball court.

She could tell he had watched her look for him. Felt the pink flush on her cheeks at his unwavering perusal.

He took a step forward, kept one hand in his pocket and one behind his back.

She returned his smile. Their gazes locked.

"You're beautiful," he said.

"You're not so bad yourself."

He took another step forward, brought a single long-stem red rose from behind his back. "To complete your set," he said.

She looked at the rose. Looked back at him. Back at the rose. Oh. My.

It all clicked together for her. The eleven roses in her bathroom. The rose in his hand.

He held the rose out to her. She took it, her fingers trembling as she took it in her hands, avoiding the thorns. A white ribbon wound up the stem, and was tied into a bow.

She sniffed it, her eyes misting. Squeezing her eyes closed, she steadied herself.

Opened her eyes, her lips curving into a smile.

"Shall we make our way to the museum?" he asked, crooking his arm and holding it out to her.

She put her hand on his arm and followed him toward the front doors of the hotel. As they walked through the crowded lobby, people moved aside for them, but Savannah barely noticed them. She was ensconced in her own world.

With a handsome pilot. Off to a black-tie gala at the New York Metropolitan Museum of Art. Not bad for a girl from Birmingham, Alabama and a guy from Ft. Worth.

Outside the hotel, the doorman hustled to hail a cab.

"Wait here for a second," he whispered in Savannah's ear.

He stepped up to the valet stand, spoke to the valet, and came back to her side. "Our car will be here in five minutes," he said, waving off the taxi.

"We're not taking a taxi?"

"Not tonight," he said.

It was more than five minutes, but less than ten, when a sleek, black limo pulled up to the curb. The valet appeared at the car, opened it, and ushered them forward.

Settled into the back of the limo, he smiled.

"Nice touch," she said.

"Can't be riding around in a taxi dressed like this," he said.

"I'm a little impressed," she said.

"Then it was worth it."

"I'm not easily impressed," she said.

"I didn't think you were. So, who are we meeting with tonight?"

"It's hosted by one of the top five drug companies."

"Big pharma."

"None other."

"Is this the one you work for then?"

"It's crazy, but no. You might say I'm one of the competitor representatives."

"That sounds like quite an honor."

"It's actually more like an obligation."

Noah pulled a bottle of champagne from the ice bucket in front of them and filled two flutes. Handed one to her. "Here's to obligations," he said, touching his glass to hers.

"To obligations," she said and sipping. This was a Noah that she didn't know; nor had she expected.

The Noah that she had known was a devil-may-care daredevil. He drove a black Mustang and wore white t-shirts. Though she knew him to be disciplined and hard-working, her memory had created an image of him as something of a bad boy.

Noah had never given her flowers, nor had he ever taken her to a gala in a limo. While wearing a tuxedo. And he had certainly never given her champagne.

They had drunk beer on his boat on Lake Martin, wearing swimsuits, and shorts.

"Penny for your thoughts," he said.

"I was remembering beer on Lake Martin. Wondering how

we'd ended up drinking champagne in New York in what feels like the blink of an eye."

"Life is full of surprises, isn't it?" he asked.

"How did you find me?"

"You told me you'd be in New York."

"How did you know I didn't live here?

"I was betting on the come."

"There you go with gambling references again."

"It means I'm betting on the future."

"I know what it means," she said, sipping bubbles from her glass. "I'm not sure what it means in this case."

"It means if you lived here, I never would have found you. But if you were visiting, you had to be staying at one of the hotels. And you were obviously here for some kind of business thing. From there, I looked for drug conferences."

"It's not really a drug conference."

"Not exactly, no, which made it a bit more difficult."

Before they could finish their conversation, they pulled up in front of the Met and the driver opened their door.

Replacing the typical tourist crowd from daytime, the Met was overflowing with ladies dressed in formal evening gowns and men in tuxes. These were the business moguls of the drug companies, physicians, and representatives like Savannah.

And their dates.

Or escorts.

It was all semantics, Savannah mused as she walked up the steps with her hand on Noah's arm. They could be perfect strangers, having met in the cab, but once they appeared together at the gala, they were automatically thought to be a couple.

Adam was the first person she recognized. He must have been watching for her. She ignored the little pang of guilt at not warning him that this time, unlike years before, she wouldn't be sitting with him.

"Adam," she said, "this is Noah."

Noah and Adam shook hands, seemed to size each other up.

"Savannah didn't mention she was bringing a date," Adam said.

"I don't think she knew until today," Noah said.

"I see," Adam said.

"Noah and I were friends in college," Savannah stated.

"I see," Adam said, seeming to bristle a bit. "Are you a doctor?"

"No, I'm a pilot."

"Oh," Adam said, then was silent.

"Well," Savannah said. "We should go inside. It's about time for them to get started."

"Of course," Adam said, stepping aside.

Savannah and Noah went through the museum to the room set aside for tonight's occasion. There were several small groups clustered around the room.

"We should really spend some time in here," Noah said, as they passed several paintings.

Savannah glanced at him askance. "Really? You like art?"

"Yeah," he said. "Who doesn't?"

She shrugged and took a glass of champagne from a passing server. "Not a lot of free time," she murmured.

He shifted. Faced her. "Are you telling me your life is all work and no play?"

She studied the bubbles in her glass. "I work a lot."

"How long has it been?"

As her thoughts went places she typically didn't think so much about, she felt her face flush. "How long?" she echoed thickly.

He beamed. "Since you had a date."

She laughed.

"But we can talk about… the other if you want to."

"Four years," she said. "Four years since I had a boyfriend. And I haven't dated really since then."

"Haven't dated much or at all?"

"You're awfully inquisitive," she turned her gaze to an abstract painting – splashes of black and white that resembled the work of a three-year-old.

"I want to know everything," he said.

This time, she flushed in earnest. "My life is rather boring."

He scoffed. "Your life has never come close to being boring."

She bit her lip. A flurry of possible responses ran through her head. Before she could land on one of them, they were interrupted by Mr. Pence, CEO of one of the big drug companies hosting tonight's gala.

"Miss Savannah Richards," he greeted her with obvious enthusiasm, taking her hand. "I'm so glad you could make it tonight."

"I wouldn't miss it for the world. Mr. Pence, I'd like you to meet my friend, Noah Worthington," she said as she pulled her hand from his.

"It's a pleasure to meet you. Are you a physician?"

"No, I'm not a doctor, I'm a pilot."

"Oh," Mr. Pence said, a similar expression to the one Adam had worn upon hearing the news that Savannah had brought an outsider into their folds. "Well, then, this should be interesting to you."

"It is interesting to see the inside of Savannah's world."

"She's had a successful career," Mr. Pence said.

"Hopefully you're not putting me out to pasture yet," Savannah said, with a laugh.

"Absolutely not," the older man said. "In fact, I should warn you Mr. Worthington that if you have designs on Savannah, we won't let her go without a fight."

"I wouldn't think of taking her away from the thing she loves."

"Good. Good," Mr. Pence said. "Well, enjoy yourselves. There's food in the next room."

After he walked out of earshot, Savannah rolled her eyes. "Designs on me?"

"I think it shows great affection on his part to be worried about you."

"Designs?"

"It's cute," he said. "Remember, he's from a different generation."

"Oh, I get that. But he made an awful lot of assumptions by you standing next to me."

"You did introduce me as your friend," he reminded her, "Come on, I'm starved."

When they stood in front of the food display, he pinned his gaze to hers. "Just say the word. I'll have you out of here and in a fancy restaurant."

She shook her head and led him toward the other room. "As tempting as that sounds, I don't think it's a good idea. They would put me out to pasture for sure."

He handed her a plate, stepped aside for her to go first. She put some cheese, a raspberry crepe, and some crab salad on her plate. He followed suit.

"I can get us in to a nice restaurant," he said as they sat at an empty table, covered with a white tablecloth.

"This is just the appetizer," she said.

He chuckled. "If you insist."

Another of Savannah's colleagues came up and hugged Savannah. She looked at Noah with a big smile.

"I'm a pilot," he said, before she could ask.

"Oh. Wow," the young woman said, glancing at Savannah.

"We're friends," Savannah said.

"Oh. Ok. I thought…"

Noah laughed.

"We'll talk later, Savannah," the woman said and moved away.

"She thought I brought my pilot to dinner," Savannah said, under her breath.

"Actually," Noah said, biting into a crepe. "It's customary."

"Customary?"

"It's not unusual for people to bring their private pilots with them to things like this."

Savannah tucked her hair behind her ears. "You work for the airline."

"I do," he said. "But they don't know that."

Savannah looked around the room. Many of the guests were wealthy, powerful people. She was a drug representative. Not really part of this world. Not on a day to day basis. Only during special events like this.

"They think I hired a private pilot."

"That would be my guess," Noah said, keeping his focus on her. "So, you can expect that they'll look at you a little differently from now on. Unless, of course, you set them straight."

Her lips curved into a mysterious smile. "I don't know why I would do that. I rather like the idea of having my own private pilot."

"That opens all sorts of doors in my head."

She rolled her eyes at him, but secretly enjoyed that he still had those doors he was willing to open for her.

"Have you thought about doing that?" she asked.

His eyes widened and she had to quickly swallow her water to avoid spewing. "Let me rephrase that. Have you thought about hiring out as a private pilot?"

"I have thought about that," he said.

"Well, have you ever done it?"

"Yes," he said, but she could see the shutters close in his face. And she was not surprised when he changed the subject. "What do you want to do after this?" he asked.

"After the conference?"

"After the gala."

"It'll be late," she said.

"You have an early morning?"

"Only if I want to. With my presentation over, I don't really have any obligations."

"Yet you're staying until Tuesday."

"Yeah, I'll probably catch some workshops."

"Savannah," he said. "You do know the real reason people go to conferences."

"To learn," she insisted.

He rolled his eyes.

"And to network."

"Those are good reasons. They also go to get away. To have fun."

"I am having fun," she said.

He smiled. "That's good to know. Then perhaps you'd like to have some non-conference fun. Unless of course, you can't handle it."

"Of course, I can handle it."

"Name one thing in New York that you've always wanted to do, but haven't done."

"Easy. I'd like to go up the Empire State Building."

"And… you've never done that."

She shook her head.

"You do realize that's the first thing people do when they come to New York."

She shrugged. "I've never done it."

"You've never been to the Statue of Liberty."

She shook her head. "But…" she held up her hand. "I've been shopping on Fifth Avenue. In fact, I was there today."

"That's a relief. I was beginning to worry about you."

"Now you're making fun."

"Nope. Now I know what I can do for you."

"Ha."

He grinned. "One of many things."

The speaker, Mr. Pence, came on the microphone, and Savannah realized the room had filled and people were seated all around them.

Mr. Pence began talking as dinner was served. Savannah quickly regretted her decision to not duck out and go to that fancy restaurant Noah had offered. The food was bland and the speech predictable.

She leaned over, put her lips next to Noah's ear. "Do you still want to get out of here?"

"Just say the word," he said, turning, his face near hers. His lips a hair's breadth from hers.

Her heart stuttered as her gaze landed on his lips. Although she had kissed those lips hundreds of times before, it was as though she never had.

He was a different man now with twenty years between. Twenty unknown years. The disconnect was intriguing.

What would it feel like to kiss him? Would it be familiar or would it be brand new? She swallowed thickly. She lifted her gaze back to his and she was lost in those pools of blue.

Noah Worthington was an intriguing man. There was so much she knew. So much she didn't know.

And, oh so very much that she wanted to know.

Getting her out was proving to be more difficult than he had expected. Savannah, unfortunately, was obligated to be here for work. If she boldly got up and walked out, she would be noticed. And judged. Noah could do black tie events in his sleep. Especially one where no one knew him and he was free to sit in the background and observe.

That didn't mean that he wanted to be here.

He wanted to be with Savannah, but preferably alone with her.

As Pence was wrapping up his speech, Noah took the opportunity to set their exit in motion. "When I say go, meet me out in front of the restrooms," he said.

She nodded. Waited until the applause started.

"Now," he said. And was pleasantly surprised when she got up and made her way out of the room.

He waited a couple of minutes. Then followed her out.

She smiled sheepishly as they dashed out the front door of the museum. She waited while he had the limo brought around. Her cheeks were flushed a bit with excitement. He couldn't help staring at her. She was glowing.

And he was spellbound.

And honored that he had been the one to talk her into doing the thing that put that flush on her face.

He didn't want to let her down.

Ever.

Again.

"Where are we going?" she asked, as the car pulled out into the traffic.

"It's a surprise," he said.

"I don't like surprises."

"I know. But you'll like this one."

She grinned at him, shook her head. "You haven't changed one single bit."

"And you've developed a mean streak," he said with a feigned look of hurt.

She chuckled. "You have no idea."

"You have my attention now," he said.

"I'll keep that in mind."

They rode in silence for a few minutes. He soaked in every angle of her face, every movement of her lips. Even in twenty years, she was perfect – better even than before and he couldn't take his eyes off her.

"You're staring," she said.

"You're pretty," he said.

She chuckled again, her face flushing. "You're being silly."

"It's like that first day all over again."

She stared back him then, her lips curving into that sexy little confident smile that he loved. "It is, isn't it?"

The car stopped and he helped her out, taking her hand. He didn't let go as they went into the doors of the Empire State Building.

"Aren't they closed?" She asked.

He led her to the ticket counter, bought two tickets and went to the elevators where there was a line. "They're open," he said. "And the best time to visit is at night."

"Hmm," she said.

They got into the elevator and started up. He watched the play of emotions on her face. The emotions she hid well. There was a bit of trepidation as the elevator creaked and started up, mixed with a bit of excitement.

When they got out at the top, they went to the outside door and, stepping outside into the wind and darkness, high above the streets of New York, she gasped. "Wow."

"Yeah," he said, keeping a firm hold on her hand as they stepped out to the railing.

"This is so beautiful." She whispered.

"Come around here. Look at Central Park."

They walked around, gazing at the busy life of New York far below them. The cool breeze picked up on the other side. She shivered.

He took off his jacket and placed it around her shoulders. With a look of gratitude, she slipped her arms in the sleeves and disappeared into his jacket that was much too big for her.

"Wouldn't it be awesome to live here? So much energy," she said.

"A far cry from the small town of Birmingham or Auburn."

"There isn't even a comparison."

"Where do you live now?" he asked.

"Lake Martin," she said.

She answered easily, not realizing the effect her words would have on him. They had spent countless hours there on the lake. The fact that she had chosen to make her home there, almost caused him to come undone.

"You remember it, right?" she asked, focused on the city.

"Yes," he said, his voice hoarse. He cleared his throat.

She turned, looked at him. Studied his face. "You're surprised," she said.

Noah felt a lump in his throat that threatened to send tears to his eyes. After all he put her through, she was able to stay there, where they had been connected, and make her life.

"Noah," she whispered, placing a hand on his cheek.

He sucked in his breath, determined not to allow his thoughts – his regrets to overcome him now.

He put his hand over hers, smiled, wobbly as it felt, and squeezed as he enveloped both her hands in his. They were mere inches apart. He moved forward, kissed her on the forehead.

Her eyes fluttered closed. He gently turned her, pulled her against him, and rested her back against his chest. His chin fit perfectly on the top of her head.

Just as he remembered.

Together, they watched the traffic below, the lights of the city all around them. Others, mostly couples, walked around them, leaving them alone in their own little world.

He could feel her heartbeat against his chest. Or maybe he imagined it. Maybe it was his own heart beating. He could feel her warm breath against his hand as his arms were wrapped around her. She hesitated, but rested her arms against his.

Noah could not have been more content in that moment.

He was in a beautiful place with the most beautiful girl in the world. There was no one else he could possibly want to be with.

He didn't know how long they stood there, neither one wanting to move.

He heard a clock strike midnight and she tensed against him.

"We should go," she said.

He wasn't sure if it was a question or a statement. "Are you going to turn into a pumpkin?"

"Cinderella didn't turn into a pumpkin, the carriage did."

"But something about the stroke of midnight..."

"Makes it feel like it's all going to end."

"It doesn't have to end. She could have stayed with the prince instead of running off." Noah had never understood that.

"She couldn't let him find out who she really was."

"It wouldn't have mattered. He was already in love with her."

"He only met her hours before."

"It happens."

"But she couldn't have known that."

"She needed to have faith."

"Then there wouldn't have been a story."

"There was a story alright."

She sighed. "A big part of the story was that he had to search for her."

"It didn't have to be that way, but you're probably right," he admitted. "Men often don't

realize what they have until it's gone."

"You know this from experience?"

"No," he said. "You're right. We should probably go."

He led her back to the elevators, and silent now, they traveled down. She kept her hands hidden in his jacket. He stared at the numbers as the dial ticked downward.

He wanted to tell her everything. He wanted to explain. He wanted her to understand.

But not now.

He wasn't ready to break the spell.

He wasn't ready to risk her rejecting him for what he had done.

He told himself that the damage had been done twenty years ago. If he told her the truth, would it only make things worse? He just wanted it all to be behind them.

He wanted to begin again.

Savannah knew the moment Noah retreated into himself. She kicked herself all the way down the elevator.

It was too soon to bring up the past.

They were just at the beginning of starting over. It would do no good to bring it all up again anyway.

They had to let it go if they were going to start over.

She just had so many questions. So many unanswered questions.

They couldn't deny the unfinished business. It was part of who they were.

But she would give it time.

She would give it time because she liked who he was. Liked who they were together.

They got back to the hotel and went through the lobby, nearly deserted now.

At the elevators, she took his hand. Smiled at him. "Thank you for coming with me tonight."

He brought her hand to his lips, kissed her palm. "Have breakfast with me," he said.

She knew better than to try and understand his changing moods. "I plan to sleep through breakfast," she said. "Remember, I turn into a pumpkin at Midnight."

He chuckled and pulled her against him in a hug. "Lunch then?" he asked, holding her elbows.

"Alright. I'll have lunch with you."

The elevator door opened and they went inside. "Keep the rest of the day open, too. I have a surprise for you."

"I don't like surprises."

"I know, but you'll love this one."

They got off at her floor. She handed him the rose she had remembered to pick up from the seat in the limo and pulled her phone out of her handbag. "I'm here," she said, when they got to her door. She held her phone to her door and it unlocked. He reached behind her, opened the door and stepped aside for her.

"Good night," he said, handing the rose back to her.

"Good night," she said, walking through the door, letting him close it behind her.

She stood staring at the closed door. Let the range of emotions wash over her.

This was a day she had never, ever expected. After twenty years.

In the span of mere days, she had accidentally run into her college sweetheart, set an impossible path for him to find her a second time in New York, and spent a fairytale evening with him.

She stepped out of her shoes and walked into the bathroom with her rose. She pulled the vase forward and slid the rose into the vase. Twelve roses now.

She smiled to herself at the romantic gesture.

She took the roses into the bedroom and placed them on the dresser. She sat on the edge of the bed and realized she still wore his jacket.

Taking it off, she pressed her face against it. And inhaled deeply.

She missed him.

How could she miss him already?

This was not a good sign.

He had told her two days ago that he wasn't even divorced yet.

She groaned.

She wasn't sure what it said about her, but she didn't care. She wanted to spend time with him. She wanted to know the answers.

Twenty years ago he had gone back to visit his parents. He had called it a summons. He had evaded telling her much other than it was a business meeting with someone his father had known since childhood.

Three weeks later, he had graduated, packed up and gone back to Ft. Worth.

They hadn't broken up. He'd said he'd call. That was before they had cell phones.

He hadn't called.

She'd never even known if he made it home. She'd gone to the Internet to try and find news of an accident.

All she knew was that he lived with his parents in Ft. Worth. She knew their names were Martin and Mary Worthington. She had looked, but she hadn't been able to locate them online.

She'd gone about her summer – school and student worker job.

But she had grieved.

And buried herself in her studies.

She'd looked for him a few times over the years, but unsuccessfully. As far as she had been concerned, he had fallen off the face of the earth.

She wanted to know the answers.

Because she had never stopped loving him.

Savannah was up at seven the next morning. She jumped on the treadmill, and ordered room service – yogurt and granola today. She flipped through the conference program and found a couple of presentations that she had highlighted to possibly attend.

Instead, she indulged herself and ran a hot bubble bath. She replayed last night over and over in her head.

Found herself looking forward to the day. With Noah. Whatever it may hold.

She put on some jeans and a casual shirt, pulled her hair back, put on a pair of dark sunshades, and slipped out to the elevators.

After stopping by Starbucks for a grande vanilla latte with caramel drizzle, she went to the blow out bar around the corner. She had her hair washed and dried and her make-up done in what they called natural.

With it being Saturday morning, the blow out bar was packed. Whoever came up with the idea was an absolute genius and her credit card was fortunate that this New York indulgence hadn't caught on in Birmingham. Sure, she could go to a salon, but that was typically for a haircut, too, and they didn't do make-up.

After her morning of being pampered, she went back to the hotel and changed clothes three times. She decided against blue jeans and quickly ruled out a skirt and jacket.

She put on the red dress she'd originally brought for last night's gala, added a little cardigan, put on the chunky red lace-up heels she had bought to match, and studied herself in the mirror.

The dress was red jacquard flower print, with a high low hem – just above her knees in the front and halfway down her calves in the back. The sales lady had said it could be dressed up or down. Since she had no idea what Noah had planned for the day, she thought she could pass for whatever he came up with. She could always remove the cardigan for a dressier look for dinner.

She checked the clock and paced a bit. He hadn't said what

time he would be there to pick her up or even where they would meet.

It was ten to noon. She sniffed the roses, and fought back the panic that he wouldn't show up.

What if he just didn't? She had no way to contact him.

He won't disappear again.

He had acted a little distant after she'd brought up the past, but then he'd asked her to spend the day with him.

If he stands me up, I won't see him again.

Going to the window, she took deep, steading breaths.

I shouldn't have gone to so much trouble getting ready.

Feeling a little foolish, she located the remote and checked the weather. It was going to be a beautiful day.

If he's not here by one o'clock, I'm going to walk around the city myself. She'd seen an interesting little restaurant around the corner that looked like a good lunch spot.

When he knocked on the door, she jumped and fumbled the remote.

She went to the door, confirmed that it was him, and opened the door.

"Hi," he said, "you look a little startled."

"Do I?" She turned her anxiety into a bright smile.

"Yes, you do, but nonetheless stunning."

"You look good," she said. He was wearing khaki pants with loafers and a pale pink shirt, open at the collar. He wore a leather case hanging from a strap across his shoulders.

"I'm overdressed," she said, biting her lip.

"You're perfect," he said. "Ready for lunch?"

"Starved."

They fell into any easy rhythm going downstairs, out onto the street.

He glanced at her shoes, "I'll get a taxi."

Once inside the back seat, he gave the driver an address.

"What's for lunch?"

He winked at her.

"I know," she said. "It's a surprise."

He laughed. "You always were a quick study."

"Yeah," *And I've always been a sucker for you.*

They only went three blocks before the driver pulled up to the curb and they got out. Taking her hand, Noah led her to the door of a quintessential pizza parlor.

"Pizza," she said, letting her guard down.

"This may be your third time to New York, but this time you get to really experience it."

He was staring at her again, but she didn't care. There was a line out the door, but she didn't care.

He was right. She'd never had New York pizza.

As they stood in line, he asked. "Exactly what have you done during your time in New York?"

"Let see… I've ridden the subway. I've been to the Met obviously. And I've been shopping on Fifth Avenue. Oh. And I discovered blow out bars."

He gave her an odd look. "Blow out bar?"

She laughed. Swirled her hair.

"Ah. Haircut."

"Not a cut. Just a blow dry."

He ran a hand through her hair. "Nice," he said. "Ok, so shopping, art museum, and hair."

"And subway."

"Right. And art isn't really your thing."

"I don't dislike it."

"There's a big difference between liking something and disliking it." He unzipped his case and pulled out his iPad.

"Ah," she said.

"Ah what?"

"Ah, I wondered what you had in there."

"A pilot is never without his iPad."

"Really? We use iPads, too, for medications."

"Then you understand."

"Yeah, but I'm not working right now."

"A pilot is always on call."

"Always?"

"Pretty much. Yeah."

He made a few clicks on his iPad. "Done," he said.

"Work?"

"Not this time," he said with a wink.

"Personal?"

"Part of your surprise."

Noah had to make some last-minute adjustments in his plan. The weather had been perfect for the Staten Island Ferry and the Statue of Liberty. But Savannah had come out wearing something looking more like an evening dress and heels than for walking around as a tourist. He would ask her to wear jeans and flats tomorrow. But not yet. She had obviously put a lot of detail into today's attire.

And he was enjoying it far too much to ruin it for her.

After cheese pizza, they hopped back in a taxi and went to

Broadway.

She didn't even ask where they were going.

Instead, she wore a look of eager anticipation. He considered that a huge step for someone who didn't like surprises.

The taxi dropped them at the door to the Phantom of the Opera house. Her eyes widened. "Really?"

"We have tickets for the two o'clock showing."

She beamed.

"Since you don't like surprises," he said. "I'll go ahead and tell you the plan so you know what to expect. After this, we'll have drinks at the Rainbow Room followed by dinner."

That part of his plan, at least, they could keep.

She put her arm on his, leaned in, and kissed him on the cheek. "Thank you."

Once they had made their way to their seats, he took her hand. "I'm sorry," he said. "about last night."

"What do you have to be sorry about?"

"You asked me a question I wasn't ready to answer. I didn't want to ruin the mood. But I owe it to you to answer questions you might have. And I will. I'll tell you what happened tonight."

"I should be the one apologizing. You obviously weren't ready to talk about it. Whatever it was that happened, I'm sure you had a good reason. Anyway, I don't want to ruin the mood either."

"Sounds like we're on the same page. When you're ready to know, I'm ready to tell you."

"That means a lot."

Noah preferred a good movie with a storyline he could understand to singing he couldn't. But halfway through,

Savannah was moved to tears. He had to admit that the special effects were quite impressive.

"What do you think?" she asked at intermission.

"I don't dislike it," he said.

She laughed.

"If you want to stretch your legs, I'll buy us a drink,"

A few minutes later, they returned to their seats with glasses of red wine.

"This should make it much better," he said.

She shook her head. "Only spoken by the guy from Ft. Worth."

"What can I say? We had rodeos, not operas."

After the play, they went to the Rainbow Room for drinks as he had promised. Savannah ordered a cosmopolitan – with olives and he ordered a crown on the rocks.

"You look beautiful tonight," he said.

"I never once imagined us here."

"I knew our paths would cross again."

That elicited that look again. The one that said perhaps he should be on an antipsychotic medication.

"Why would you think that?"

"Because I would have looked you up. And you have to admit I'm a pretty good detective."

"You did find me in New York. And I am impressed by that. But I gave you enough clues. Do you know how hard it is to find someone without clues?"

"You could have found me."

"Really? Tell me how."

"You knew I was from Ft. Worth. You knew my parents'

names – unless you forgot, which is quite natural. And you knew I was a pilot."

"Actually, that wasn't enough."

"No?"

"No. I looked for you."

"It's ok," he said. "It wasn't your job to find me. It was my job to find you."

"Anyway," she said, tipping the lime into her glass and sliding an olive off the toothpick into her mouth. "I've always had a gut feeling that it had something to do with the summons from your father that weekend."

"The summons."

"Am I right?"

"You are exactly right."

"What was it about?"

He stirred his drink.

"You said you'd answer. But if you don't it's ok."

Three

NOAH — BEFORE

Noah didn't want to be here. A summons from his father, Martin Worthington, was never a good sign. And this was two in less than thirty days.

He tied his shoes and smoothed out his tux. *Just get it over with.*

He walked down to the drawing room where his father was already entertaining. His father had promised that there would be only a few guests.

A few guests to his father could be five or a hundred.

Noah saw his mother, fussing with a flower arrangement, her blonde hair in a simple updo. She was elegant in a dark blue sheath dress.

"Noah," she said, hugging him. His mother hadn't come from money. She'd been a self-employed florist until his father had swept into her life and given her a fairytale romance – at least for a while.

Noah knew he wasn't supposed to be an only child. But he

had been. His mother wouldn't talk about it. Whenever the topic came up, his mother had a haunted look in her eyes and his father turned away, with silence.

Always silence when he was displeased.

Growing up, Noah had loved it when his father was away on business. Without his father there, he and his mother would veg out on pizza and watch movies. Sometimes she would even play video games with him. Of course, when he'd hit teenage years, he chosen to do things with his friends.

Nonetheless, his mother was the one he could talk to.

"What's Dad up to?" he asked.

His mother kept her eyes on the flowers. "Just his usual," she said. "Everything is a business deal."

"I can't imagine why that would require a summons for me."

He expected his mother's usual *It's not a summons, Dear, he just wants to see you.* Instead, she said, "He's getting older. I think he's trying to get everything in order."

Noah glanced at his father, his head bent in deep conversation with another man, a little older than he. "Dad? Older? He'd never admit to that."

"Whether he admits to it or not, it's inevitable for all of us."

Before he could question his mother further, his father had spotted him and called him over. "Noah, get over here. This is Mr. Henry Beauchamp. We've been friends since we were in high school."

"Really?" Noah shook the older man's hand. "I'm surprised we haven't met."

"Mr. Beauchamp moved to California shortly after high school and we lost touch for a few years."

"Have you moved back, then?" Noah asked.

"Oh no. Just expanding a business venture back this way."

"Oh, well, Dad is the one to meet with on that."

His father had laughed, but even to Noah, it had sounded a little nervous.

"My wife will be here shortly," Henry said. "It was good of you to have us for dinner."

"You're welcome here anytime," his father said.

"Your father tells me you're a pilot," Henry said.

"I am," Noah said. "I'll have my degree by the end of the month and I have several job options available."

The two older men exchanged looks.

Noah no longer questioned his father. The two of them weren't close. Martin made sure Noah remembered that he was the son and Martin was the father.

"That should make you invaluable to the family business," Henry commented.

"Why don't you make yourself a drink, Noah?" his father suggested.

"I apologize," Henry said, "I would never keep a man from his evening cocktail."

Noah obediently left the men and went to the well-stocked bar across the room. He dismissed the men's conversation. His father's business, really, was no concern of his. He was a pilot and would soon be flying for the one of the larger airlines.

This party, it seemed, was going to be smaller than his father's usual. Noah was still perplexed about why his father had asked him to come tonight. He hadn't overly questioned it, however, because it had given him an opportunity to fly. And any opportunity to fly was always welcome in his book.

Noah poured scotch into a glass. Added ice. Wondered what

Savannah was doing. Checked his watch and thought about calling her. He looked around for his mother, but she had disappeared.

Noah took his glass and went out on the veranda. There was a cool breeze at the moment. Summer had yet to take full root. But it wouldn't be long before the summer heat was unbearable.

He had wanted to bring Savannah. He wanted to bring her everywhere. In fact, he would have brought her, but something in his father's voice had alarmed him. That alarm coupled with Savannah's pending final exams had kept him from pushing at her to come along.

It was just as well, he thought. Savannah knew him as the laid-back college student majoring in aviation who had an occasional beer.

She would not know him as this man who wore a tux to an everyday business dinner meeting with his family and drank scotch from what she would call fancy crystal glasses. And had dinner in a dining room twice the size of her whole dorm common room.

Female voices caught his attention and he turned his thoughts back to the present. Whatever it was his father wanted, he was waiting until morning to discuss it with Noah. *I could have flown in tomorrow morning and missed all this.* For some reason, his father seemed to enjoy torturing him whenever he had the opportunity.

Hearing his father call his name, he went back inside and stood watching for a moment.

Two women had entered the room. One appeared to be Henry's wife – a brunette with shoulder-length hair, but it was the other that sent the hairs standing up along his nape.

She was a tall blonde, with long, straight hair, a pretty smile. She was young – about Noah's age and wore a seductive red dress with matching red heels. Even her lips, curved into a bow, were red.

Noah's first impression was *trouble.*

"Noah," his father insisted. "Come meet Claire."

Noah stepped forward. Claire held out her hand, but with her palm down. It was the way women of wealth shook hands with men. Noah imagined that older men actually would kiss the lady's hand.

Savannah would have laughed. And said that Claire would never make it in the business world. What she wouldn't have understood was that Claire would never have to make it in the traditional business world. This was her world. And this was how she would make it.

"I've heard so much about you" Claire said.

"And I've heard absolutely nothing about you," Noah admitted, after a brief touch of the girl's hand.

"It seems our fathers have known each other our whole lives."

Noah began to get a sick feeling in the pit of his stomach.

"There's plenty of time to get acquainted," Noah's mother, who had reappeared stated. "Dinner is ready. Shall we?"

They went into the dining room. Noah was surprised that the dinner party only included six people. The alarm bells in his head were at full decibel as he was seated next to Claire at the table.

Nonetheless, the dinner conversation was pleasant enough. Claire and her mother talked about their flight from California and their day of shopping in Ft. Worth.

Apparently, they found great humor in Texas styles. None-theless, they had each bought themselves a Texas cowboy hat as a souvenir.

"Where in California do you live?" Noah asked.

"Los Angeles," Claire answered. "I can't imagine living anywhere else. The climate is great and the food is good especially for me, being a vegan. I had trouble finding anything I could eat today."

"Everything has beef in it," Claire's mother added.

"Image that," Noah said. Checking his watch under the table. He needed to call Savannah, but didn't want to call too late. She liked to go to sleep early, but had promised to wait up until after he called. "I guess that explains the salad and vegetables."

"I guess it does," Claire answered, her smile curved into a knowing bow.

After a few more minutes of inane conversation, Noah excused himself. "I have to make a call to someone back east," he said, pushing his chair away from the table. "Please excuse me."

He truly couldn't get away fast enough. His father was obviously trying to push through a new deal, but he would have to do it on his own. He'd done it enough times before.

"Hi love," he said when Savannah answered.

"Hey," she answered sleepily.

"I'm sorry it's so late."

"It's not late. Studying makes me sleepy."

"I know."

"Did you find out what your father wanted?"

"No," Noah said, "He had some guy over for a business

meeting. I'm sure he'll let me know tomorrow what he needed me for."

"Maybe he just wanted to show off his son."

"Not likely. That isn't his style."

"How's your mother?" she asked.

"A little reserved," he said.

"Hmm."

"It seems a little odd, doesn't it?"

"I don't really know them all that well, but, well… yes."

Noah smiled. That was one thing he loved about Savannah. She didn't mind saying what she thought. Coupled with her high level of perceptiveness, he found she was one of the few people he actually enjoyed talking with.

They hung up with Noah promising to call her in the morning.

Turns out his father wanted him up for breakfast. Whereas most of his friend's fathers took them out duck or deer hunting or even fishing before daylight, Noah's father took him to the country club for breakfast.

Noah had an ominous feeling that day.

"Son," his father said, with next to no preamble after they ordered. "I want you to marry Claire."

Noah felt the bottom fell out from under him.

The problem with his father was that Martin Worthington got what he wanted. And Noah knew that when his father wanted something, no matter how much he protested, it still happened.

"I don't want to marry Claire. I'm going to marry Savannah."

His father waved him off. "You can use the company plane

to go see Savannah whenever you want, but I need you to marry Claire."

"I don't understand," Noah protested. "Why would I possibly want to marry… her?"

"You don't have to want to marry her," his father insisted. "Do you think I married your mother for love?"

"I kind of thought so,"

"Of course not. Men in our position make the most of every opportunity."

Noah shook his head. "Not marriage."

His father sighed. "Let me lay it out for you. With you marrying Claire, her father and I will merge our companies."

"Just merge them without me."

"It doesn't work like that, son. You're the incentive. Our family name is what he's after."

Noah gaped at his father. This was a new level.

"There's plenty in it for you," his father continued, digging into his omelet. "You'll have your own company plane and be over the other pilots. You'll be able to choose which trips you take."

"I have other job offers," Noah insisted. "that don't require me to marry someone I don't love."

"You can take the plane to see Savannah whenever you want. Until you get tired of her."

Noah glared at his father. "No," he said.

"The alternative," his father continued, "is that your mother and I disinherit you. You get nothing from this day forward."

Noah dismissed it. "Mother wouldn't do that."

His father put down his fork, reached into his coat pocket

and pulled out a folded, notarized document. Taking his time, keeping his eyes on his son's, he unfolded the papers and laid them on the table in front of Noah.

Noah broke his father's gaze and looked down at the signed document. His mother's signature – disinheriting her only child. The money going to charity upon his father's death with a small stipend going to take care of his mother unless she remarried.

Noah glared at his father in disbelief. His father merely smirked.

Noah pushed back his chair and stood up. His fists clenched reflexively. He would never hit his father. But this was one time in his life when he was tempted.

Grabbing the document, he turned and stalked away. He couldn't look at his father. The man disgusted him.

Going outside, he started walking. He just needed to get away.

Ridiculous. His father's demand was insane. Why would he possibly agree to do it?

He didn't need his father's money. He could get his own job. He didn't have to be rich. He just wanted to be happy. And he was happy. He loved Savannah. There would never be anyone else for him.

His flash of anger settling, he stopped and sat on a park bench. Stared at the golfers hitting their little balls. Plotting their businesses. Ruining people's lives.

No. He did not want to be – would not be – part of this world.

Able to focus a little better now, he began reading the four-page document.

When he was finished reading, he knew he didn't have a choice.

He had to marry Claire Beauchamp.

CHAPTER
Four

Savannah excused herself from the dinner table and went to the ladies' room. She paced a bit in the parlor area, then perched on one of the oversized chairs. Got up and paced some more.

What she took from Noah's story was that he had fought for her. But his father had been too much. Too powerful.

The bottom line was that Noah had been forced to choose between her and his inheritance.

He had chosen his inheritance.

She had to respect him for that.

Didn't she?

He could have talked to her about it. Explained that he needed to marry someone else or his father would disinherit him.

Savannah scoffed and put her head in her hands.

A woman, old enough to be her mother, placed a hand lightly on Savannah's shoulder. "Are you alright, Dear?"

Savannah looked at the older woman. Forced herself to smile. "Yes. Thank you. I'm just trying to sort something out."

The woman apologized for bothering her and left.

Savannah knew that Noah knew that she never would have understood. The result had been the same. Perhaps it was best that he never contacted her again.

She had looked for him.

Watched for him even. Stayed home on the weekends, studying. Secretly waiting for the phone to ring.

He should have at least told me.

But he hadn't.

And life had gone on.

She wanted to hear the rest of how he got to where he was now.

Checking her appearance in the mirror, deeming herself presentable, she went back out to the table where Noah waited for her. His expression anxious.

"Are you alright?" he asked.

"I'm good. I just needed to take a moment." She gulped the rest of her wine. "So, did you do it? Did you marry Claire?"

"I did. It was fast. Two weeks after I got back, I was married," he lowered his gaze. "I couldn't tell you. As long as I didn't tell you, it wasn't real. Any day, I thought, I would wake up and it would have all been a nightmare. And I was so ashamed. Ashamed that I had let my father decide who I was to marry."

"I can see where you would be."

"Yeah," he ran a hand through his hair. Savannah could see the pain his eyes. After all this time it was still there. "I married her, but it was in name only."

She watched him carefully.

"Anyway, we had separate bedrooms. The day we got back from the honeymoon I told her I was going to work for the airline. She got mad and it made avoiding her easier from there on out."

"But you stayed married."

"We did. We'll be divorced soon though."

"Why now?"

"My father died eighteen months ago. My mother and I own everything now."

"Rather ironic, isn't it?"

"Hmm. I refused to spend any of his money while he lived."

"You were really angry."

"I never forgave him. He destroyed my relationship with you."

"I am so sorry."

"Don't be sorry. I made my choice."

"You didn't really have a choice."

"Looking back, I think he was bluffing. I don't think he would have done that. But, I was young and couldn't imagine living without the money I'd grown up with."

"You made what seemed to be the best decision at the time."

"You always were understanding. I knew that. But I didn't think even you could handle what I was doing."

"I don't think I could have. The end result would have been the same. Except that I would have known what happened. I actually thought I did something wrong – something to make you stop loving me."

"You were perfect. I would never do that to you now. I hope you can find your way around to forgiving me."

She nodded. Did she forgive him? Even if she did, she couldn't bring herself to say the words right now.

The server brought their meals which lightened the mood somewhat. Savannah had liked it better before they'd dug into their pasts. Noah had been right to avoid the topic.

"You were right," she told him.

"That's always good to hear. What was I right about?"

"It was too soon to talk about all that."

"It's out there now," he said. "Can I change the subject?"

"Please."

"How do you like your tour of New York so far?"

That brought a smile to her face. "I like it very much."

"Good. Does that mean you're available for tomorrow?"

She nodded, taking a bite of fish.

"There is one requirement. You have to wear jeans and flat shoes that you can walk in."

"I can do that," she said.

They finished eating in silence. Now that Savannah had a little information regarding his past, her brain began to focus on the future. Was he going to just show her around New York, then disappear again? Was this his way of atoning for his past?

She still felt that pull toward him. That dangerous pull. Dangerous because the pull was at her heart.

It had always been there.

She allowed her mind to wander. He had filled out in the last twenty years. She'd always felt safe around him. That hadn't changed. Last night when he'd held her against him, it had felt right.

He was keeping her at arm's length, nonetheless. It would be so easy to slip back into that close physical relationship. What was holding him back? Was he no longer interested in her that way?

She watched him under her lashes. Longed to feel his lips against hers again.

In the year they had been together, they'd spent countless hours with their lips locked together. They had never gone all the way though. They had agreed that they should wait. She had only been a college freshman. If they had, would it have changed anything?

They hadn't talked about marriage. They had just… been in the relationship. Savannah hadn't questioned the future.

But now…

Now she wanted to know. She wanted to know how much to invest in him. It had been two days now and he hadn't even tried to kiss her.

"Do you still like mint chocolate chip ice cream?"

Her jaw dropped. "You remember that?"

"I remember a lot of things," he said, placing a hand over hers, his eyes twinkling with mischief.

"I haven't had it in so long, I really don't know," she said, her thoughts scattered with the feel of his hand over hers.

"There's an ice-cream parlor around the corner if you'd like to find out."

"Ok," she said simply.

He paid the check and they got on the elevator to go downstairs."

Since it wasn't far to the ice cream shop, they walked along the sidewalk. Steam from the subways drifted up creating a unique urban fog.

It reminded Savannah of their long walks along Lake Martin after the rains.

"Do you remember," she asked, "when you had me out on the lake hunting for frogs?"

He stopped. Looked at her and broke out into a deep male laugh. "What on earth made you remember that? While walking downtown New York?"

"The fog," she said, and he laughed harder. "What?"

"Fog," he said, bent over now.

"Steam. Whatever," she said, biting her lip to try to keep from laughing with him. It wasn't long before they were both walking hand in hand down the sidewalk laughing at a joke only the two of them could fathom.

"It wasn't my idea," he said. "Johnny Ray told me that girls were impressed by guys who could catch frogs."

"What? Please tell me you're kidding."

"Scout's honor," he held up his hand.

"I'm not concerned about what he told you. I'm concerned about the fact that you believed him."

"I didn't know. He said it was an Alabama thing. I was from Ft. Worth. It seemed possible at the time."

"Do I look like the kind of girl who would be impressed by her boyfriend catching frogs?"

"Well, no, not now."

"I think you should have just said no and let it go at that."

"I didn't know you all that well at the time."

"Oh, my. I can't believe you were trying to impress me. I thought you were just some country guy dragging me out to look for frogs."

"I guess it's a good thing we didn't find one."

"Probably. Especially if you thought I'd know what to do with it."

"He said you'd know."

"Johnny Ray was an idiot."

"He's an attorney now."

"No way! You stayed in touch with him?"

"Sort of. He calls about once a year."

"Well, you can tell him, attorney or no, he's an idiot."

"Turns out he's not a bad attorney."

"I never would have guessed that."

They arrived at the ice cream parlor and stood in line. They were the oldest ones there. The clientele consisted mostly of young couples.

"We used to be like that," she said, without thinking.

He put his arm around her, pulled her close. "We still are. Actually, we're better. We can take any one of these couples."

"Take them how?"

He squeezed her close. "I don't know. It just sounds good."

"One scoop or two?" he asked when they got to the counter.

"One," she said.

He ordered her a scoop of mint chocolate chip and he ordered a two scoops of fudge swirl vanilla.

They found a bench and sat side by side.

"Is it as good as you remember?" he asked.

"It's even better," she said, licking her spoon.

"Mine too," he said, "Here, try a bite."

Without even thinking, she allowed him to feed her a bite of his ice cream. "That's good, too," she said, holding her spoon out to him to try hers.

"Not bad."

She was reminded that they had shared pretty much every-thing. She couldn't imagine that there were two other people more attached at the hip than they had been back in college.

She gazed at him. He smiled.

It was though a piece of her had been missing all those twenty years.

And here was the missing piece.

She'd been hurt. There was no denying that. But in that moment, sitting outside a New York ice cream parlor surrounded by young people, many of whom were the same age they had been, she realized that she forgave him.

They were different people now. Yet they were the same. It was odd how after twenty years, they still fit together so well. Despite the changes each had undergone.

She smiled back at him. "Thank you," she said. "Thank you for showing me the fun side of New York."

"It is my honor," he said.

His lips cold from the ice cream, he bent over and kissed her cheek, only a fraction from the corner of her mouth.

Her nerve endings went on edge. And craved more. She wanted more. She wanted to feel his lips against hers. Instead, she settled for another bite of ice cream.

And wondered.

After all this time, when would the time be right to begin again?

Sunday in the park.

Although Savannah knew the lyrics to the Chicago song were actually Saturday in the park, she changed the words around to fit Sunday in her head as she sang silently to herself.

They'd started off with a hot dog from the hot dog stand. Then boarded the Staten Island ferry.

The sky was clear. The breeze was perfect.

The day was perfect.

They had to wait in line after a long walk to the Statue. Thank goodness for flat ballerina shoes.

"She's so… big," she said, looking up at Lady Liberty.

"The tall buildings of New York make her look small, but in her day, she was huge."

"From where I'm standing, she still is."

There was a middle-aged couple in line in front of them. The woman turned around, smiled at them. "Make sure you go up to the crown," the woman said. "We come here every year and until last year, we never remembered to get advance tickets. You can't go without advance tickets. And there's always a long line. But last year, we remembered and decided to wait it out. It was so worth it."

"How long is the wait?"

"It was what, honey, about two hours?"

"I don't know," the man said. "I just remember we missed lunch. So we made sure we ate before we came out today. And it's really strenuous."

"Oh, yes, "Sue added. "You only want to wear comfortable shoes."

"You come every year?" Savannah asked. "Where are you from?"

"We live in Pittsburgh."

"I've been there. It's a really pretty city."

The woman nodded. "You know, Honey," she said to her husband. "Would you go get me bottle of water?" She turned to Savannah. "I'm diabetic, so I have to keep hydrated."

The man looked at Noah. "Want to come with me to get water?"

Noah looked questioningly at Savannah. "Do you want some water?"

"Actually, yes, I really do."

"You'll be ok here?"

"Sure," she said, waving her hand.

While Noah was gone to get water, Savannah learned that Sue and Mike were not originally from Pittsburgh. Sue was from Iowa and Mike was from Arizona. They'd met while in school at the University of Pittsburgh. Then had decided to stay.

"But enough about us," Sue said as the line inched painfully forward. Savannah could see Noah in line at the concession stand.

"Where are you two from?"

"Birmingham," Savannah said, keeping things simple.

"You're such a cute couple. How long have you been married?"

"Oh, we're not," Savannah said, relieved to see that Noah and Mike were on their way back

"Really?"

"No. But we've known each other forever, Since college actually."

"That's the best way to start a relationship – as friends."

Savannah wanted to say that she and Noah had never been friends. Instead, she smiled and nodded.

But the thought startled her a little.

Noah had been it for her since the day they met.

Being with him like this, now.

This uncertainty.

Was dangerous territory for her.

A few minutes later, when she and Noah had a moment of privacy, Noah took the tickets out of his pocket and handed them to her.

They had advance tickets to go up the Statue of Liberty's crown.

Dangerous territory indeed.

CHAPTER
Five

She was here.

She was actually doing this.

She was a freshman at college.

She waited in the registration line with Betty, her friend from high school.

Betty was what Savannah's mom called boy crazy. Even now, Betty had already pointed out three different guys that she'd like to go out with. And they'd only been here for thirty minutes.

Savannah wasn't looking at boys. Savannah was worried about whether her classes would be filled by the time they finally got up to the registration desk. Being first-time freshmen, they didn't exactly get first pick of class times.

By the time they got to the front of the line, Betty had struck up a conversation with a guy standing next to her.

"Next."

Betty waved Savannah off. "You go ahead," she said. "I'll take the next one."

Eager to get enrolled, so they could hit the bookstore, Savannah didn't hesitate to go ahead.

Registration was completed in booths manned by older students. She went up to the upperclassman and, her hands shaking, handed him the form that had been signed by her advisor.

"You can sit down," the student worker told her.

She sat on the edge of the seat and watched as he typed in her information.

"Savannah Skye Richards," he said.

She nodded, glanced at him and returned her eyes to the screen.

"From Birmingham."

"Yes."

"That's only, what, a couple hours away? So you'll be commuting?"

"No," she said, "I'll be living on campus."

"That's good." He clicked the keys. "Your English is closed."

"Oh no," she groaned.

"And your math."

She felt the tears welling in her eyes. Here she was, ready to start classes and couldn't even get in.

"Hey," he said, "your biology is good. And I got you in the psychology class. Let me check the history."

She held her breath.

"Closed."

"What do I do?" she asked. "I only have two classes?"

"Oh no. We're not finished," he said, watching her carefully.

I won't cry, she repeated over and over to herself.

"I can move your history to 9:00, so that's done." He clicked deftly on the computer keyboard. "Then I can put you in the 2:00 English. So I just switched those two out. You'll like this English professor better. Trust me."

She turned her eyes to his. And was mesmerized by the deep blue. His smile was kind.

"What about my math?" she asked, a glimmer of hope shooting through her.

"Math always fills up quick," he said, "Even though no one wants to take it. I've yet to meet anyone who actually likes math."

"I like math," she said, her voice no more than a whisper.

"No kidding?"

"Yeah. I went to state."

"No way," he said. "How did you do?"

"First place," She began to relax a bit.

He looked back at the computer. "There is seriously nothing open."

She really needed the math. She had her whole schedule worked out and math was a prerequisite that would put her whole schedule behind.

"Hold on a minute." He picked up the phone. Spoke briefly to someone on the other end. More tapping on the keyboard. "Alright," he said. "You are in."

"But how?"

"I got you an override."

"You can do that?"

"I've found that if I ask only about once every now and then, they realize how important it must be and give it to me."

He gestured over to the booth next to him where Betty now sat. "She calls ALL the time and only rarely gets an override."

Poor Betty.

He hit print and said, "I'll be right back,"

Savannah waited, much calmer now. She was ready to hit the bookstore.

He came back, handed her a printout of her schedule. "Just what you wanted. I only had to switch out two classes, but your times are the same."

Savannah studied her schedule. Looked up and smiled. "Thank you so much."

"I'm happy I could help." He seemed to consider.

"Is this it? What do I do now?"

"The next stop is fee payment." He leaned back, his expression quizzical. "There is one other thing."

She looked at him questioningly.

"I'm supposed to go to the orientation dance on Friday."

She knew there were lots of activities this week, but hadn't paid much attention. "Ok."

He laughed. "Will you go with me?"

"I don't usually go to dances."

"I don't either," he said. "But I kind of have to go to this one. And it's a good excuse to get to know you better."

"I'm just a regular freshman."

"I have a feeling you're anything but regular. So what do you say? Can I be your escort to the dance?"

"I don't know," she said. "Maybe I'll meet you there if I go."

He swirled around, picked up a flyer from his desk. Handed it to her. "If you change your mind, this is where I'll be."

She took the flyer. Glanced at it. "I don't even know your name," she said.

He pointed to his Auburn University name tag. "Noah," he said. "I'm fully vetted." Then, as though on impulse, he took the flyer back from her, scribbled his name and a phone number. Handed it back to her. "I'll walk you to your next station," he said, standing up.

She stood up. "I have to wait for Betty," she said, glancing at the line of students waiting for their turn at registration. "Besides," she said. "I think you have a line."

"All right," he said, "you win. See you Friday Savannah Skye."

Betty walked up at that moment. "What happens Friday?" she asked.

"Nothing," Savannah said, turning and steering her friend away.

"What? Do you have a date with Mr. Hunk?"

"Mr. who? No. I don't date."

"Then what?" Betty saw the flyer clutched in her friend's hand, lifted it enough to see the header. "He invited you to the dance?"

"Yeah," she said. "I can't go."

Betty grinned from ear to ear. "What do you mean you can't go? We're freshmen. We have to go."

"We don't have to go anywhere but class."

Betty glued her feet to the ground. "Savannah, president of the high school student class, is not going to go to college and be a hermit."

"I'm not a hermit."

"Sounds like it. If Mr. Hunky guy asked me to go to my own dance with him, I would most certainly go."

"You would go if anyone asked."

Betty's eyes widened.

"I'll think about it," Savannah acquiesced.

Betty frowned, but started walking again. "I guess that's something at least."

Later that evening, Savannah sat in her new dorm room and arranged her desk. Betty, also her roommate, was out, somewhere, with a group of girls who had come by recruiting freshmen. Savannah had waved them off, not paying much attention to where they were going.

She turned on her little lamp and opened each one of her textbooks, thumbing through them in anticipation of the worlds of knowledge they held.

She settled on her biology text and started reading.

After a few minutes, she laughed at herself. Studying the week before classes even began. She got up, stretched, and went to the refrigerator for a soda.

Betty had tacked the dance flyer to the front of the fridge. Savannah took it down, read it for at least the tenth time, and stared at Noah's name and phone number. A number she had memorized.

She hadn't gone on a date since her high school prom. Her date, Timothy had gotten drunk, and decided he really wanted to be dancing with Mark. Granted, Mark was a good-looking guy.

But something about having one's high school prom date coming out on the night of the prom had left her with a slight aversion to dating.

Savannah had never been "boy crazy" anyway. Not that she didn't like boys. She just preferred to be a little more selective. In fact, she never would have gone to the prom with Timothy if Betty hadn't insisted that they should double date.

Noah had seemed nice, but she really didn't have the time to even be thinking about a boy, much less spending time with one.

No, she decided, putting the flyer back on the refrigerator, she definitely would not be going to the orientation dance.

Two nights later, Savannah followed Betty into the student union.

Against her better judgment.

"I really don't do dances," she said to Betty for what must have been the fifteenth time, that night alone.

"I know. I was there when the whole senior prom thing fell apart. If anyone is qualified to keep you away from dances, it's me. But this is college," Betty insisted. "You have to move on. Get back on the horse."

Savannah kept her comments to herself. Betty had been dogging her for two days now. She ran her hands along her jeans. Straightened the sleeves of her pink polo. She was actually a little nervous.

She'd agreed to come along to keep Betty company. She didn't like the idea of her friend walking around campus at night by herself. *I've really got to get past this. I can't follow Betty around for four years.*

She justified her decision to come along with the newness of college for both of them. As they entered the room, she found herself searching for a glimpse of Noah. Would he really be there? He was an upperclassman. Why would he be at a freshman dance?

Betty went to the check-in desk and presented her ID.

"Savannah," Betty said, tugging at Savannah's sleeve. "Show the guy your ID."

Savannah pulled her ID out of her back pocket and, after glancing at her friend who was grinning like a Cheshire cat, presented her ID.

To Noah.

"Hello Savannah Skye Richards," he said, without looking at her ID card.

She felt the flush in her cheeks. The very person she'd been searching for was sitting right in front of her.

He leaned over, whispered something to the girl sitting to him, and pushed back his chair. He was tall – at least six feet. He came around the table, nodded to Betty. "I'll show you around," he said, turning his attention back to Savannah.

"I'll get something to drink," Betty said, bouncing off toward the concession area.

Frowning, Savannah watched her friend desert her.

"I wasn't sure I'd ever see you again," he said.

She met his gaze. "You had my address, not to mention my class schedule."

"True," he said, "But that would be stalking. I'm not saying I never would have used it, but I was hoping not to have to."

"Why?" she asked simply.

"You're the only girl I ever met who likes math."

She scoffed, turned away. "That's not a good reason."

"Ok," he said, putting his hands up. "You got me. I don't have a reason."

She turned back to him. "You're a strange man, Noah Worthington."

He broke into a wide smile.

She couldn't help it. She smiled back.

"Savannah," he said, taking her hand. "Just give me a chance."

With Chicago blasting in the background, they made their way around the crowded floor to an empty table.

"Aren't you supposed to be working?" she asked, leaning close so he could hear.

"I was just here to help out if they need anything. It was just an excuse so I wouldn't look like a weirdo stalking freshman girls. So I was hanging out. Waiting for someone to show up."

"Just anyone."

"No, I had the possibility of a date."

"What were you going to do if I didn't show up?"

"I was planning to stay about thirty more minutes, then head home. I didn't think you were coming."

"I wasn't."

"But you're here."

"I just came to keep Betty from being out after dark by herself."

"You really know how to boost a guy's ego."

She laughed. "Sorry."

"It's ok."

"You don't have a girlfriend?"

"No."

"Are you a senior?"

He nodded "It's my last year."

"In…"

"Aviation."

Noah had been cool before, but now he was… out of her league.

"You should definitely have a girlfriend."

"I agree."

"But not a freshman just out of high school."

"I don't see anything but college girls here."

Her lips curved into a smile. "I suppose you're right," she said. "However, I maintain my stance."

"Tell me your major again."

"I'm undeclared."

"That's what I thought," he said. "And as a very wise senior, I think you should declare a very lofty major."

"Something akin to aviation?"

"Nah. You're not the mechanic type. You need something more abstract. Like law."

"My uncle's a lawyer. It's overrated."

"How about psychology?"

"Maybe," she said. "I looked at it. But there's only one math."

"Yeah, the math thing. They have statistics."

"I'll keep it in mind."

"You'll figure it out."

"Yes, I will."

"I don't want to spend our whole first date talking shop."

"When did this become a date?" She looked around at the awkward freshmen, just getting their footing in the college world.

When he didn't answer, she turned back. His face was ever

so close. He placed his fingers on her cheek and his thumb next to her mouth. Then his lips were pressed softly against hers.

Time froze as she absorbed the sensation of having his lips against hers and his fingertips on her skin.

As the Chicago song ended and faded into the next, he pulled back. "Now," he said. "Now it's a date."

Six

Savannah's phone vibrated. She glanced at it. Groaned. "It's my mom," she said.

"Answer it," Noah said, slathering marmalade on a slice of toast.

"I'll call her back," Savannah said. "How can you eat all that sugar?" she asked, picking up a cluster of grapes, pulling one off and popping it into her mouth.

"You should really try it," he said, breaking off a piece of toast and handing it to her.

She took and tasted. "Too sweet," she said.

"I don't see how you do it. I could never live without sugar."

"If," she began, but picked up her phone. It was her mother again. Twice in a row. "Hello."

"Savannah," her mother said, her voice shaky.

"What is it?" Savannah said, turning, walking toward the balcony, her heart racing.

"The house was robbed."

"What? What do you mean? Are you hurt?"

"No, I wasn't home. I came home and the front door was open."

"Thank God you weren't hurt."

"Savannah," her mother sniffed. "Whiskers is gone."

Savannah had watched her mother bury her father. Her eyes red from crying. Other than that one time, never, not once had she heard her mother upset like this.

"What do you mean he's gone?"

"The front door was open and I can't find him anywhere."

Whiskers was her mother's fifteen-year-old cat. Whiskers had never put his feet on the ground outside.

"Did you look everywhere? Maybe he's hiding."

"He's not here. I looked everywhere."

"You'll find him, Mom."

"I called and called. The police looked for him, too. When are you coming home?"

"My flight doesn't leave until 9:00 in the morning. Where's Charlotte?"

"Your sister went somewhere with the school on a bus. She can't come."

"Mom, I'm in New York."

"I know. I just don't know what else to do."

Savannah had to do something. She couldn't bear to see her mother like this. "Did you check with the neighbors?"

"I checked with everyone. I'm only calling you because I don't know what else to do."

Savannah put the phone away from her ear, looked back at Noah. He'd stood up and was watching her.

"Can I help?" he asked.

"My mom's house was robbed and the cat got out. She can't find him."

She put the phone back to her ear. Her mother was sobbing. "I can't lose Whiskers. Your father and I raised him from a little kitten."

"I know, Mom. Let me call the airline. I'll see if I can get back sooner. I'll call you back. Just hold on ok. We'll find him."

She hung up and paced for a moment before turning around. "It's funny, huh? I can handle almost any crisis except when it comes to my family."

"Seems normal to me," he said, going to her. He pulled her against him, hugged her, and released her.

"You need to get home," he said.

She nodded. "I have to call the airline."

"Wait," he said. "I can… um. I have some pull. I can get you home."

"Alright."

"How soon can you be packed and ready?"

She had showered and dressed before he came to her room for breakfast. She was used to packing, so it never took her long to get out of a hotel. "I need thirty minutes," she said.

"Good," he said. "I'll make a call, grab my things, and be back here in thirty."

As he headed out the door, Savannah called her mother back. Assured her that she was on her way. Her mother sounded a little calmer now. Having heard her mother in a hysterical state only one other time, it was almost Savannah's undoing. "I don't know how I can help," she said, putting her mother on speaker while she tossed her clothes into her suitcase and gathered her things from the bathroom.

"Just get here and help me look for him."

"I'll call you when I know my ETA."

After hanging up, she scanned the room, stood her luggage next to the door, and went to stand in front of the dresser where the roses sat. She pulled out the single rose with the white ribbon tied around it. Dried it with a towel, and took it with her.

They hadn't time to wait for a bellhop, so when Noah returned, he had a luggage cart with him. She had no idea how he had gotten to his room and back, packed, arranged a flight, and located a cart, all in thirty minutes. It didn't matter. He was here and she was grateful.

He stacked their luggage on the cart and they made their way out to a taxi.

"How is she?" he asked once they were loaded into the vehicle and on their way to the airport.

"Hysterical."

"I don't remember your mother being the hysterical type."

"Exactly. That's what's so disconcerting about the whole thing."

"What did they take?"

"The robbers? She didn't even say. I don't think she cares. All they had to do was close the door behind them. And not let the cat out."

"She's had this cat a long time."

"Fifteen years. He's part of the family. He's a cool cat though. He talks."

"Is that so? That is special."

She laughed. Felt her eyes tearing up. "Poor little guy."

Noah took her hand. She held it a moment, but had too much nervous energy. "When does my flight leave?"

"Our flight leaves when we get to the airport."

"Our?"

"I'm going with you."

"No," she said, but felt her phone vibrating. "I'm on my way to the airport, Mom."

"Thank God. I'm going to go sit out back and wait. In case he comes home."

"What did they take?"

"I don't know. Nothing important."

"I'm glad you weren't home."

"If I'd been home, Whiskers wouldn't be out there."

"Mom?"

"What?"

"Never mind. I have to hang up now, but I'll call you when I land." She hung up the phone. "I hope they didn't take Whiskers."

"I take it your mom hasn't thought of that."

"Apparently not. God help them if she finds out who did this. Especially if they hurt her cat."

"No kidding."

"You don't have to go with me," she said.

His lips curved into an odd smile. "I kind of do have to."

She kind of didn't understand why he thought so, but her mind was preoccupied, so she let it go.

The taxi driver didn't stop at any of the gates. "Which airline are we flying?" she asked.

He shook his head.

Savannah began ticking off in her head what she could do when she got to her mother's house. They could make signs with Whisker's picture on them and plaster them around the neighborhood. She scrolled through her photos looking for a picture of Whiskers. They needed to call the local vets. Alert them. She was fairly certain Whiskers had a locater chip. Especially if he was stolen, they needed to be on the lookout.

Noah spoke briefly on the phone, but she tuned him out as he spoke flight jargon.

Her mind preoccupied, focused on her phone, she followed him out of the taxi, waited while their luggage was unloaded. Her suitcase rolling alongside her, she finally looked up. Squinted in the sunlight.

"We have to walk a little," Noah said.

Savannah looked around. And followed him toward a small jet sitting alone on the runway.

"You hired a private jet?" she asked, stopping to stare at him.

"No," he said. "I'm a pilot, remember?"

"They let you use planes whenever you want?" Truly, there was so much about the aviation industry that she was clueless about.

"Something like that," he said. "Come on, we're cleared to get on the runway."

The flight assistant took their luggage, tucked it away. Noah helped her up the stairs into the plane.

The plane smelled new. Like a new car.

She turned right to go into the cabin. There was no else on board.

"You can sit back there," he said. She stopped and looked at him. He nodded toward the back of the plane. "Or you can sit up here," he said, turning his head toward the cockpit.

She frowned. Why would she want to do that?

"With me," he said.

Her feet were glued to the floor. She wasn't sure which way to go.

Her gaze locked onto his. On the pleased smile on his face.

And everything she knew about Noah clicked into place.

His passion for flying.

The story he'd told her about his father.

Her face broke into a wide smile. "This is your plane."

His expression was not what she expected. It was more like a deer in headlights. "But you didn't want me to know that."

He squared his shoulders, shook his head, and returned her smile. "Nothing gets past you, Savannah Richards. Come on," he held out his hand.

If not for her mother's plight, Savannah's excitement would have been uncontrollable. She sat down in the co-pilot's seat, took the headset from him, and nearly bounced in her seat. "It looks a lot different than it used to look," she said. The cockpit was all glass, providing a clean view of everything. Gone were the old round dials and gauges. Everything was displayed on what looked like three large computer screens.

"That was a long time ago," he said after she pointed that out to him, "and this is a much better plane." The pride in his voice was evident.

"It is yours then?"

He winked at her as he put his own headset on. "All mine."

CHAPTER
Seven

Savannah had flown with Noah before, but always in little prop planes. This was different. Faster. Higher. Not so loud.

They could actually talk without wearing headsets.

He put the plane on autopilot and leaned back to get them bottles of water. Savannah stared nervously out the window.

His attention was only off a few seconds, but her imagination was nearly her undoing.

One look at her face as he turned back, handing her the bottle of water, was all it took. "I can see that I'm going to have to teach you to fly so you won't panic."

"I think it's best if you just keep our hands on the wheel."

He laughed. "All right, but..." he gestured toward the empty sky. "There's not exactly a lot to run into up here."

"Easy for you to say," she said. "You never know when some crazy driver will come out of nowhere."

"If another plane comes within a hundred miles, all sorts of alarms start to go off."

"Really?"

"Well, no, but it sounds good. We have our own flight path and no one else should be near us."

"What if someone deviates?"

He shook his head. "It rarely happens."

"Rarely."

"When did you become such a nervous flyer?"

"I watch too much TV."

He looked at her, disbelief evident.

"I do fly a lot, but it's different up here. Up front."

"You get used to it."

"I don't think that's a good idea. I could never afford private charter fees."

"You'll never pay a fee with me," he said matter-of-factly, his attention focused on the computers.

His words brought a little flush to her cheeks, and some unexpected emotion. Fortunately, he was busy checking the displays and didn't notice.

Despite her occasional anxieties, the flight was uneventful. Noah assured her that an uneventful flight was the ultimate goal.

After they landed at the Birmingham airport, Noah secured a car. "They keep cars on hand for us to use while we're here," he explained.

"Yeah, that part I remembered," she said, but he was busy signing some paperwork and didn't seem to hear. How many times had they dashed to a town, took a car to get a burger and dashed back to the plane to fly home? That wasn't exactly something a girl could easily forget.

He retrieved their luggage and together they rolled their bags to the borrowed car.

Savannah checked her phone. No calls from her mother. No calls from anyone.

"No news is good news," he said. "right?"

"Not with my mother. She may be in full blown crisis mode by now."

"That thought terrifies me."

"Ha. You and me both."

When they pulled up to her mother's house, there was still a cop car in the driveway. Her mother lived a suburban cul-de-sac in a white Victorian style home with four dormer windows across the third story. The house had been built when Savannah was an infant. She'd lived there until she went away for college at eighteen.

A little sliver of panic shot through her as the memory of driving up to her parents' house two years after Noah left came back in a flash. There had been an ambulance and three cop cars in the drive way, their lights shattering the peaceful night air.

Her mother had called her cell phone, while she sat in a night class, focused on neurotransmitters and the myelin sheath – something she had never forgotten. She'd been hysterical – waiting on the ambulance to come and save her father from a heart attack. Unfortunately, they had gotten there too late and by the time Savannah pulled up to the house, they had her father in the ambulance. They had not been able to save him. Her mother sat on the front steps, her head in her hands.

"Savannah?" Noah asked.

"I'm sorry," she said, trying to smile. Pulling herself back to the present. Her mother's house had been broken into and Whiskers was missing. No one was dying.

"Tell me," he said.

"My father died two years after you left from a heart attack. I was just… I was just…"

"I didn't know. I'm so sorry."

"It was a long time ago."

"It may have been, but you don't just get over something like that."

"Let's check on Mom and see if we can find Whiskers." She jumped out of the car and rushed inside, her heart racing in spite of telling herself she was overreacting.

Normally, she would have knocked, but the door was unlocked. Her mother was sitting on the sofa talking to the policeman when Savannah walked in. As usual, her mother, who did cardio daily, and could easily wear Savannah's clothes, was impeccably dressed in black slacks with low pumps and a deep emerald tunic. She had recently cut her hair to her chin, and it bounced healthily against her cheek as she shook her head.

She got up when she saw Savannah and drew her into a hug, holding her as though she wouldn't let her go. "I'm so glad you're here," she said.

"Whiskers?" Savannah asked, pulling back to meet her mother's gaze.

Her mother's eyes glistened with unshed tears. "I've looked everywhere."

"I'll look for him," Savannah said, desperate to remove the agony from her mother's face. "Mom," she turned to Noah. "this is…"

"Hello Noah," her mother said. "Please sit wherever you like. The officer is just leaving."

Noah obediently sat on the edge of the loveseat and waited.

Savannah began looking for the cat, first checking under the sofa. It was as though her mother just saw Noah last week, not twenty years ago. How could she not show at least a little surprise? Savannah would have to think about that later. It was too overwhelming to think about at the moment.

After her mother saw the officer out and returned to the living room, she went up to Noah and hugged him, too.

"You don't seem surprised to see me, Mrs. Richards," he said.

She shrugged. "I knew you'd be back. It was just a matter of time. Please, call me Emily."

Savannah moved her search upstairs and Emily followed behind her. After Savannah had searched every inch of the house for a place a cat could hide, they went back to the living room where Noah waited.

"Which door was left open?" she asked.

"The back door. Did they take anything?" *Other than Whiskers.*

"I don't think so. I don't have any valuables just lying around. Anything valuable is in your father's gun safe."

"Did they take his guns?"

"No, it looks like they tried to pry it open though."

Savannah held out her hand to Noah. "We're gonna go out back and look around for few minutes."

"Go ahead. I've looked everywhere. I'm gonna call your sister again."

Savannah led Noah out the back door. And they sat on the

big porch swing, not touching, but only inches apart. Savannah was flooded with memories of them doing more than sitting out here.

"Whiskers must be pretty scared," Noah commented, seemingly unaffected by such memories.

"I'm sure." She scanned the yard, looking for any sign whatsoever of the white Persian cat.

"Has he ever been outside before?"

"I don't think his feet have ever touched the ground."

"Did you tell her I was coming?"

Savannah turned and focused her attention on Noah. "I hadn't even told her that we ran into each other, much less that you were coming with me."

"That's odd."

"It's very odd."

"Did you ever talk about me?"

Savannah frowned.

"I mean, it's just weird that she reacted like that."

"She's stressed out. Anyway, you never know what she's going to say. I wouldn't worry too much about it."

"It's almost like it was yesterday and not twenty years ago."

She laughed. "I'm telling you, you'll drive yourself in circles if you keep trying to figure it out."

"I'll ask her about it."

"She always liked you."

"Really?" His face lit up.

"Of course. My dad liked you too."

"That's good to know. You two were close."

"Our family was close-knit. My sister, though, is more like

my mom. A little 'odd' as you would say. I'm more like my dad. More scientific."

"Wasn't he a professor?"

"Good memory."

"I remember him being kind of quiet, but always very polite"

"That's my dad. Quiet and polite."

"You're kind of a cross between your two parents."

"Thank you," wondering if that had been a compliment. Her mother could be a little difficult at times.

She got up, went to stand at the edge of the porch and looked toward what had been her father's tool shed.

She squinted. Something moved.

Could it be?

She dashed down the stairs, across the lawn, toward the tool shed. Huddled there, next to the edge of the tool shed, was a bright-eyed white cat. "Whiskers!" she said, walking slowly, so as not to spook him.

He stood up, swished his tail in the air, and walked toward her. Reaching down, she picked him up and held him close as he clung to her shoulder. Noah watched her from the top step.

"Where have you been, little guy?" she asked. "Your mommy is going to be so happy."

"I take it this is Whiskers," Noah said, opening the back door for them.

"This is Whiskers. The one we flew all the way from New York to find."

Once Emily and Whiskers were reunited, Savannah and Noah sat side by side, again, not touching, but only inches apart, on the sofa.

"What do we do now?" he asked.

She shrugged. Hugged a blue throw pillow to her.

"Do you want to go back to New York?"

"Not right now. I'm a little tired."

"Come here," he said, shifting to rub her shoulders. As he massaged the tension from her neck, she moaned softly.

"Good?"

"You have no idea."

"Ok," Emily said, coming into the room. "I have the guest room ready. You two can sleep there tonight."

"Oh, um." Savannah was torn between coherent thought and the feel of Noah's hands on her neck and shoulders. "We don't sleep in the same room."

Her mother narrowed her eyes in that way only mothers could do. "Well, I suppose you'll work it out."

Noah stopped and sat back. Savannah's head began to clear. "What about one of the other rooms?"

"Your sister's room is the process of being painted and there's no bed in there anyway. I made the other guest room into my hobby room."

"Maybe I could sleep with you."

"Not a chance."

"It's ok," Noah said, glancing around. "I can sleep on the couch." His words carried very little conviction.

"Figure it out," Emily said, "and don't even think about getting a hotel. I'm making dinner. And I have wine. Noah if you'll come open it."

They got up and followed Emily to the kitchen where she had salad greens and pasta spread out on the large kitchen island.

She handed Noah the opener and the bottle of Pinot Noir.

Noah poured wine into three glasses. Savannah picked her glass up and gulped down several sips.

It was disconcerting being in her childhood home with her mother pushing her to spend the night with a man from her past whom she was barely reacquainted with.

For some odd reason, her mother seemed completely unsurprised to see them together. And determined to get them in bed together.

Perhaps she had fallen down a rabbit hole.

The irony of it all was, twenty years ago, there was no way in hell they would be allowed to sleep in the same room together in this house. Had that been her father's rule? Or had time merely mellowed her mother?

As her mother stirred her famous Italian sauce, Savannah washed and broke up lettuce and spinach and added it to a large salad bowl.

"What can I do to help?" Noah asked.

"You get a free pass this time," Emily said. "Next time you come over, you can help."

"Fair enough," he said, perching on a bar stool to watch them.

"Where do you live Noah?" her mother asked

Savannah cringed inwardly. She hadn't even bothered to ask Noah such a basic, albeit important question. Part of her hadn't wanted to know. As long as she didn't know such basic information, they still lived in a fairy tale world.

"I'm living in Ft Worth," he said.

"Near your family," she said.

"Actually, my father passed away a few years ago and my mother lives in an assisted living facility."

"I am so sorry to hear that," Emily said.

"Why didn't you tell me?" Savannah asked.

"It didn't come up yet. Actually I live there because I'm close to my daughter."

Savannah froze. Her hands chopping carrots. She looked up and met his gaze. "It didn't

come up yet?" she asked.

"I didn't want to freak you out."

"I'm not freaked out," she said. "You're a grown man. You should have children," she insisted, knowing her voice conveyed her surprise, nonetheless.

"Just one," he clarified.

She wiped her hair from her forehead with her wrist, continued to chop carrots, with a vengeance now.

Her college sweetheart had a daughter. The man she had thought, in her delusional world, was exactly the same man she had loved so many years ago, was now a man with a child.

Her brain attempted to integrate this new information. That Noah Worthington was a father. But her mind only wrapped around itself and ended up back where it started.

In a shock of disbelief. There was a time when she had thought they would have children together. And a picket fence. He had shattered that dream when he had disappeared.

Even now with their reconnection, that fantasy had been fanned back to life where it simmered in embers at the back of her mind.

But now…

"How old is she?" Emily asked, no doubt recognizing the look on her daughter's face.

"She'll be eighteen in a couple of months. She's a senior in high school."

Well, at least he had waited a little before getting someone else pregnant. Savannah kept her eyes down, picking up a stalk of celery and chopping it into a pulp.

The anger that welled into her was unexpected.

Anger wasn't one of the emotions she had ever connected with Noah.

But now… now that he was back in her life, her emotions had become more… well-rounded.

"I'm sorry," he said, softly.

I have no reason to be angry. It's not rational.

"Sorry for what?" She forced herself to look up, meet his gaze, forcing her lips to curve up at the corners in a semblance of a smile.

Emily had slipped out of the room, leaving them alone.

"I don't know," he said.

She forced herself to smile. "I'm just surprised, that's all. You must be very proud."

"I am," he beamed. "Would you like to see a picture?"

"Of course," she said.

"Here's her senior photo," he said, showing her a picture on his phone.

Noah's daughter was blonde. And beautiful. She had her daddy's eyes and someone else's bow shaped mouth.

"She's gorgeous," she said, and meant it. Of course, Noah would have a beautiful child.

"Guess the marriage was a little more than name only." She hated herself for saying it out loud. She just couldn't help herself.

"It was on our wedding night. It's the only time I ever touched her. Every time I even looked at her, I felt like I was cheating on you."

Savannah digested that information. Allowed it to sink in. She hadn't been the only one in pain.

She inhaled deeply, steadied herself before looking into his eyes. Twenty years had passed between them. But there one thing she had to remember.

He was here now.

"I'll sleep on the couch," she said, dumping the celery and carrots into the salad bowl.

"Not a chance," he said.

"Ok, you can take the couch."

"Do you remember the last night we slept here?" he asked. "It was after midnight before I could sneak into your room."

"I was already asleep."

"Not for long," he reminded her.

She felt the heat creep up her cheeks. Being here reminded her just how much this man knew about her.

"I never told you," he said, picking up a carrot stick and munching on it. "I ran into your dad in the hallway."

Her eyes widened. "My dad saw you coming to my room?"

Noah nodded. "My hand was on the door knob."

Her dad had never said anything to her about seeing Noah that night. "What did he say?"

"He said 'good night Noah.'"

"Wow," she said. A whole host of emotions rushed through her.

She quickly tamped them back down and laughed. "I guess

it wouldn't be all that strange, after all, for us to sleep in the same bed.

"Not for me," he said.

Before Savannah could process that comment, Emily came back into the kitchen and took plates from the cabinet. "Who's hungry?" she asked.

After dinner, the three of them went around and checked the door locks. After this morning's break in, Emily seemed to still be a little shaky.

Noah mostly followed along just in case he was needed.

"I'm gonna stay down here and read for a little while," he said, after Emily had gone up to bed.

"Sure," Savannah said. "There are blankets in the closet in case you get cold."

"I'm good," he said, opening his iPad.

Savannah went upstairs to her room, washed her face, and took a pair of sleep shorts and a t-shirt from the dresser. They had left their luggage in the car. Noah must have gone out to get a few things, but Savannah had basic clothes and toiletries here, at her mother's house.

She climbed into bed and listened to the familiar quietness of the house. The sounds were different from her house on Lake Martin. Here, the central air conditioning unit was just beneath her window. Subsequently, she didn't need the little white noise machine she used to lull herself to sleep at home. She blamed this air conditioner on her inability to sleep without a constant roar in the background.

The presence of other people in the house was different, she mused, from living alone. There was comfort in it.

She estimated that she spent about one fifth of her life in

hotels. There was comfort in knowing that there were strangers sleeping next door, but it was a different kind of comfort.

It was unsettling that her mother's home had been broken into just earlier that day. She felt an uncertainty that resulted in knowing that they were vulnerable. Yet, with Noah downstairs, she felt safe.

Noah, the father.

Though she thought he should have told her about his daughter, she could understand why he didn't. He was divorced – almost, and they were getting reacquainted. There were several things they hadn't discussed. Several things left over from years gone by. His daughter was just one of them.

Why he had left without a word was another. A big one. One she was beginning to understand.

But they seemed to have a tacit agreement that those things would be sorted out in good time. In the meantime, they were getting to know each other again. Getting to know the people they were now.

The same. Different.

She liked who Noah was now. He'd been cute when they were young, but now he was handsome. Successful. A pilot for a major airline.

She smiled as she considered that he had dropped everything to not only track her down, but also to stay with her. To show her the sights of New York. To get her home to resolve a family crisis.

He hadn't belittled the nature of the crisis as many others surely would have.

There was still a spark between them. Was that something that never completely died?

She was confused by the range of new emotions that he invoked in her.

She'd felt sad when he hadn't returned to Auburn all those years ago. But she'd quickly kicked that sadness into her studies.

Perhaps she hadn't dealt with his leaving. Perhaps she had unresolved issues.

Focusing on the moonlight shining through the bedroom widow, she attempted to quiet the thoughts rambling through her head.

Using the relaxation techniques she'd learned over the years, she drifted into sleep.

And in the darkness of night, with moonbeams shining through her window, she dreamed that Noah snuggled next to her as she slept, holding her cradled with her back against his chest, his arms around her. His chin on the top of her head. The way they had slept so many nights so many years ago.

But when she woke, with the moonbeams replaced by the glow of the morning sun, she was alone in the bed. Only the faintest hint of masculinity lingered in the air and she dismissed it as her imagination.

It was most likely just the coffee and bacon she smelled drifting up from the kitchen.

Noah loved to cook breakfast. There was something about starting the day with a home-cooked meal that always put him in a good mood. He enjoyed the routine of it. The smell of it.

Emily had already been up when Noah went into the kitchen

for morning coffee. There was a fresh pot next to the latte machine – no doubt there for Savannah's use.

He found a mug, left his coffee black. Searched out the Verismo pods needed to make Savannah's latte when she woke up. Considered taking coffee to her in bed, but decided that with her mother here, it was one gesture that should probably wait.

Instead he joined Emily in the sunroom. "Good morning," he said. "Am I interrupting?"

"Not at all," she said. "Please come on in. I spend more time alone than I care to admit."

"It's nice out here."

"I've got my plants and my birds out there. They'll be back." She nodded toward the bird feeders set up outside the window.

"Do you mind if I make breakfast?" he asked.

"Are you kidding? A man who can cook? And enjoys it. Does Savannah know how rare that is?"

"Savannah and I are slowly making our way back to being reacquainted."

"It shouldn't be all that hard."

"It takes a minute."

"Not much, I would think, after the way you two were attached at the hip."

"I apologize for the way that ended."

"I'm not the one you need to apologize to."

"You're absolutely right. I'm getting around to straightening all that out."

"It wasn't your choice, was it?"

"You're a wise woman, Mrs. Richards. You're right. There was a… problem with my father."

"I told her you had a good reason for what you did."

"Turns out the reason wasn't so good."

"I also told her you'd be back. I'm not sure that was the best thing to tell her. I think she waited for years for you."

"You can't know how much I regret that."

"Well… it seems I was right after all."

Noah laughed. "You were right after all."

They sat in silence for a few minutes. A couple of sparrows flitted around the bird feeder, but seemed more interested in each other than the bird seeds.

"How did you know?" he asked.

"I could say a mother knows these things, but honestly, it was just a lucky guess. And like I said, I had it off by too many years for it to count and for her own good."

"I hope to make that up to her."

"I would expect no less. I just have one thing to say."

"Sure," he said, steeling himself.

"Don't disappear on her again."

"Only if she runs me off."

"Ha. I hope you're not counting on that happening."

Noah drained his cup. "I think I'll get a refill and get started on breakfast. That is if you don't mind me in your kitchen."

"Absolutely I do not mind."

Emily's kitchen was organized to the hilt. It took him no time to find what he needed for a hearty breakfast.

He cracked eggs, flipped bacon, and grated some potatoes. It occurred to him that Savannah didn't eat this kind of breakfast. At least based on her menu choice of breakfast items yesterday.

Nonetheless, he made the things he liked to eat.

He did a double-take when he saw her standing in the door. She had on a white mid-calf length cotton robe that flowed around her, tied at the waist, fuzzy slippers on her feet, and her hair was tousled with sleep. He'd never seen her look so sexy.

"Good morning," he said, taking a step toward her to pull her into a hug. Her softness against him sent shock waves through his body. He had to remind himself that he had taken a personal vow to take it slow with her. To allow the trust to rebuild between them, at least on her part.

"Hi," she said, bending down to pick up Whiskers and held him close, petting his head. Whiskers meowed. "Meow. Meow. Me. Meow."

"The talking cat."

"See, I told you."

"I know you're not all that big on breakfast, but if you want to join me, I have enough."

Enough was an understatement. He'd counted on her eating with him. Somehow it had become very important that she be the one he could share his love of cooking breakfast with.

His ex had managed to always sleep through breakfast. The few times he had attempted to share, she had been on her way out. *Breakfast with the girls.* He always wondered why breakfast with her husband was never an answer.

But, then, neither one of them had ever been overly enthusiastic about their arranged marriage. The fact that they had a daughter was a miracle in itself. If his child's eyes hadn't looked so much like his own, he would have wondered…

It had happened on the Celebrity cruise during the honeymoon. There was a martini bar right outside the main dining room. The bar was refrigerated and had a layer of ice on top. Kept the martinis deliciously cold. Martinis that were the best he had ever had before or since. Even extra olives, chilled to perfection, soaked in vermouth.

What happened after the martinis from heaven was a little hazy. He remembered rambling about how there should be benefits of holding the husband title. More benefits than what his father and his blackmail could provide.

He had no doubt she'd been willing. No haziness on that part. He wasn't the only one drinking martinis, after all. And it was their honeymoon. They'd spent the last two days pretending to like each other. *Fake it 'til you make it,* his mother had always said.

After the confined cruise, his society wife had managed to quickly find her way into Ft. Worth high society with frequent weekend trips home to California.

The trips had come to an abrupt halt, however, after the pregnancy. The math had been the easy part. Her obvious distaste for being confined to Ft. Worth was not.

He often wondered what her own father had threatened her with in order to make sure she married Noah. She never said and he had only asked once. Noah was a quick learner.

"You cook," Savannah said, gazing at him as though he was a unique specimen. Which, apparently he was. A man who could fly a plane, cook a meal, and look at her in a way that made her feel like she was the only woman on earth.

She sat at the little breakfast table and he set a plate of scrambled eggs, bacon, hash browns, and toast in front of her. No jelly. Not her usual breakfast of granola and yogurt, nonetheless, one bite and she was hooked.

"You're a man of many talents," she said, between bites.

"I might be," he said, teasingly.

"You know," she said, holding her breath just a little, then plunging in. "I've kind of gotten used to you planning our days." She kept her eyes on her plate, nibbled a corner off the toast. She could so get used to this homemade breakfast thing, too.

He didn't respond. She actually wondered if he had left the room. When she looked up, he was grinning from ear to ear.

"I'm glad you said that," he said.

She smiled back. It was an involuntary reaction around him. "Why is that?" she asked.

"Because since I knew that you're still on vacation, I was toying around with a few ideas."

"Is that so?" She found that little smidge of cockiness irresistible. Always had.

"Yes," he said, sitting down to join her. "But first, I have to run a quick errand. Are you ok with staying here for a couple of hours?'

"Sure," she said. Cockiness and mysteriousness all swirled into one.

After breakfast, he rinsed and she placed the dishes in the dishwasher. "Have you seen my mom this morning?"

"She's in the sunroom."

"Still?"

He shrugged. "Maybe she was giving us a few minutes alone."

"Maybe," she said, though that truly did not sound like her mother. Her mother's philosophy was if someone came to visit, especially her daughter, they should have stayed home if they wanted alone time. But then, technically, with Noah here, it wasn't exactly alone time.

"I think I'll check on her, then get my shower."

"Sounds good. That'll give me more than enough time to get back."

He took her hand, kissed her knuckles, then pulled her into a tight bear hug. And held on like he never wanted to let go.

He pulled back enough to press a kiss against the corner of her mouth.

Then he was gone and she was left feeling a little bereft. A feeling she hadn't experienced since Noah had shown up at her hotel. Noah was going to be trouble, indeed.

On the way to check with her mother, she smiled to herself. In just a few short days, it seemed, she and Noah had once again become attached at the hip.

Eight

"Don't you have to be at work?" Savannah asked, cradling her Starbuck's coffee cup.

"I'm on vacation," Noah stretched out his long legs, watched her like a cat. "Don't you have meetings?"

"Not until Monday. I gave myself plenty of time to recover from the conference."

"Good idea."

"How much longer do you have off?"

"I haven't really decided yet," he said.

Savannah frowned. "That must be nice."

"Yeah," he said. "I kinda like it. It's giving me some ideas."

She looked askance at him. "What kind of ideas?"

"I'm thinking maybe I should quit and venture out on my own."

"That's kind of a giant leap, isn't it?"

"Now that I have my own plane, it isn't so much."

"Why now?"

"After my dad died, I decided to spend some of his money after all."

"Ironic."

He smiled. "It is ironic, I know."

"Has anyone ever told you that you have a… determined streak?"

"It may have come up." He sipped his coffee. Stared into space a moment. "So, if you could pick one place that you wanted to go, where would it be?"

"That's easy. I want to go to Venice."

"Ok," he laughed. "Let me rephrase the question. One place in the states."

"I don't know."

"Really? I could name five places right off."

"But you only said one. That's harder."

"Ok. Name five then."

"Denver. San Francisco. Salt Lake City, Las Vegas. Seattle."

He coughed, nearly spit out his coffee.

"That's interesting. You kind of like the west, I see."

"I've been to all these places for conferences. They were nice. Places I'd like to visit again."

"Oh. I see," his eyes took on a curious expression. "Name one place you'd like to go that you haven't been."

"That's harder. How would I know if I've never been there?"

That elicited an odd expression.

"Ok," she said. "I'll play along. I've always wanted to visit Mackinac Island."

"Where in the world is that?"

"Michigan."

He pulled out his iPad. Began typing. "It's a small airport," he said. "But the Mustang can handle it."

She chuckled. "The Mustang?"

He glanced at her, then back at his iPad. "The airplane."

She giggled a little, sipped her coffee. "You named your airplane."

"No, Silly," he said, turning his attention to her. "It's a Cessna Mustang. Cessna is the brand like Toyota. Mustang is the model name like a Camry."

"Oh," she said, trying to keep a straight face.

"It's like a Ford Mustang."

"Ok," she said, keeping an almost straight face. "I get it."

"Anyway," he said, shifting back to his iPad. "The weather looks good, but if it turns, we can land at Cheboygan and take a ferry."

She nodded, serious now. "No cars allowed on Mackinac."

"How do you even know about this island?"

"Seriously?"

"Yeah. An Alabama girl knowing about an island in north Michigan is a little… unusual."

"It's where Somewhere in Time was filmed."

He waited a beat. "I saw that movie. It was set there?"

"Yeah."

"I didn't know it was a real place. And if I remember correctly, he drove."

"He did drive, but that was just for the movie."

"Hmm. It says here there's a golf course just north of the airport. We can get a horse drawn carriage and stay at the Grand Hotel."

"Sounds nice."

"And you've never been there?"

"Never."

Five minutes later, he turned the screen so she could see.

He had pulled up a map from Birmingham to Mackinac Island with a line connecting them highlighted in magenta. There was a splash of green here and there and one splash of yellow, but nothing over their direct route.

"Good weather," he commented. "The green means light rain and the yellow means a little heavier rain."

"I'm well acquainted with the Weather Channel," she said, the amusement still playing about her lips.

According to the map, they could be there in two hours and ten minutes.

"Cool," she said. "It's a lot closer than I expected. Wouldn't you have to get approval to fly?"

"I would," he said, turning the iPad back so they could both see it. "We have to tell them when we're leaving." He looked at her questioningly.

"Let's say we wanted to leave now."

"Alright," he said. "We tell them there will be two souls on board." He clicked two.

"Souls! That sounds morbid. Almost like they're counting on a crash."

He grimaced. "Yeah. It's an archaic term, but it's still the way the FAA counts the number on board."

"Ok. Now what?"

"We're not far from the airport, but I'll give us an hour. So..." he checked his watch. "We should eat lunch first."

She nodded.

He typed in one o'clock. "That should give us plenty of time to eat lunch and get to the airport and get boarded." He hit enter.

"We're all set," he said.

"What else would you have to do?"

"We need to go eat and get to the airport."

"Now?"

"Sure. The flight plan is filed… and, your suitcase is packed from New York."

A little bubble of panic blocked her throat. She coughed.

"Our luggage is in the trunk of the car we borrowed from the airport," he reminded her.

"Well, yeah, but…" She did have her luggage packed. Hell, she practically lived out of suitcase. "I have a suitcase full of heels, cocktail dresses, and business suits."

"The dress and heels will come in handy when we have dinner at the Grand Hotel."

"What about clothes? This is my only clean pair of jeans."

He clicked on his iPad again. "The hotel has a laundry and…" more clicking. "They have shops in town."

She took a deep, steading breath. Closed her eyes.

Noah put his hand on hers. "Savannah," he said. "No strings attached."

Savannah felt tears welling in her eyes. *No strings.*

She couldn't do no strings. Especially not with him. She shook her head, felt a tear slip down her cheek. She couldn't go down that route again.

"Hey," he said, "No, no."

He slid her against him, kissed the tear from her cheek, kissed her eyes, kissed her forehead. Tears started spilling from her eyes. Cradling the back of her head in his hands, he wiped them away, kissed the dampness of her cheeks. "I think I said the wrong thing," he said into her ear. "If you come with me, I insist on strings. Lots and lots of strings."

She laughed a watery laugh.

"I didn't mean to do that," she said. "I must look like a raccoon." She wiped at her eyes and came away with mascara on her fingertips.

"I like raccoons."

She laughed and looked into his eyes – his beautiful blue eyes. Eyes she knew so well. Eyes that now had little lines at the corners. Oh, so very sexy little lines. Her heart skittered the way it always did when she was this close to him.

"Give me a chance," he whispered.

With his words, she felt twenty years of heartbreak begin to melt away. Heartbreak she thought had been healed long ago.

Noah couldn't remember the last time he'd had so much fun. Flying was the one thing that had always brought him true happiness. Sitting here in his very own Mustang, the plane he'd been dreaming about owning for years was enough to make him ecstatic. But having Savannah sitting next to him, in the four-point safety harness, was enough to just about send him over the edge.

Did she have any idea the effect she had on him?

She wore jeans under what looked like a burgundy sweater dress with cute little motorcycle boots. Her eyes were bright as she watched everything he did. She had picked up the headset on her own so she could listen in to the traffic control chatter, even though she didn't need to. She could just as easily have stuck her head in a book and waited for him to get them to their destination.

But Savannah Richards was no spectator.

She was full of life and wanted to be a part of whatever she was doing.

While they had waited on their lunch at a local sandwich shop, they made a reservation online for the Grand Hotel. She hadn't objected when he'd reserved a two-bedroom suite for two nights. The anticipation of exploring the area with her was enough to have him pinching himself to make sure this wasn't another of his fantasies.

"That's us," she said, with her hand over the microphone, when their plane was cleared to taxi to the runway.

"I'm impressed," he said, after responding to the control tower. "By the way, you can talk," he told her. "I have you muted."

"Gee thanks."

He grinned. "I thought you might enjoy the freedom."

"I do." Nonetheless, she sat in silence as they taxied out to the runway. With Birmingham being a small airport, there was no wait.

He watched her clutch the edges of her seat as the plane went airborne. His favorite part of flying. Feeling nothing but air beneath him. For a moment in time, he was a bird.

As he checked controls, his mind went into autopilot.

How was this supposed to work? How long before he could begin thinking of her as his girlfriend again?

Ok. How long before he could begin calling her his girlfriend again? For twenty-one years, Savannah Richards had been his girlfriend.

She always was.

She always will be.

The thought came out of nowhere. Perhaps from the free air around them.

Oh, there was so much he had to make up for. The very fact that she had agreed to come with him meant that the stars had aligned, for once, in his favor.

He had been given a gift – a second chance and he would do everything in his power not to screw it up this time.

There was nothing anyone could say that could keep him from Savannah now.

With one exception.

Savannah.

He wouldn't have blamed her if she had never spoken to him again. But it was almost like they had picked up where they had left off.

He wondered how long he was supposed to wait before he kissed her again.

And again, the wind brought a swift answer to him.

She had settled into her seat now. It was hard to be excited for very long - when there was nothing to see but clouds and sky. And acres and acres of land beneath them. Besides, Savannah was a frequent flier, so that part wasn't new.

Once he had the plane leveled off, he set the autopilot control and, reaching out, took her hand. Their seats were close enough that if he leaned toward her and pulled her toward him just a little, he could put his arm around her.

She came willingly, tilting her head as though she thought he was going to tell her something.

He placed his hand under her chin and placed his lips lightly against hers.

They hit a pocket of air that had them reflexively clinging to each other.

All he could think was divine intervention.

His tongue lightly swept along her lower lip. He felt her shudder, whether from turbulence or his kiss, didn't really matter.

Everything he had pushed out of his memory. Everything that had faded from his mind about her, flooded back in a wave of sensations. Her feel. Her taste.

She dug her nails into his upper arms to bring him closer. There was no closer. Not with their harnesses in place and he wasn't about to release them with precious cargo in flight.

He deepened the kiss. His tongue swirled against hers. He wanted to taste everything. Feel everything all at once.

Don't rush. Take your time.

Forcing his sanity to return, he kissed her in a series of little short kisses. Little promises of more.

He pulled back, her eyes were closed, her lips parted.

He groaned. Kissed her again, lightly.

Willed her to open her eyes before he tossed caution to the wind and took her to the more comfortable back of the plane.

She blinked, opened her eyes. Smiled.

He scooted back in his seat. Checked his controls.

"We'll pick up there again soon," he said, his voice sounded gruff, even to his own ears.

Noah had a lot to do before landing. He checked the weather again. Spoke to the traffic controller in Minneapolis. Nothing coming in on Unicom. They were clear to land.

Curious about the island, he made a little loop around before lining up to the runway. The Grand Hotel, at least from the air, lived up to its name.

The landing took all his concentration. The short runway gave him no leeway for error.

After a smooth landing, he parked the plane and they climbed out. There was no car waiting for them here.

However…

Noah had called ahead, while Savannah had been in the restroom at the sandwich shop, and a horse and carriage waited for them, a driver dressed all in black standing at their beck and call.

"It's like a fairy tale," she said, turning to him, her face glowing.

Noah beamed. Pulled her against him and kissed her on the lips.

A fairy tale indeed.

Savannah huddled in her sweater, next to Noah. Her first purchase was definitely going to be a jacket.

The driver of the little carriage didn't seem to notice the cold.

"You two barely made it before the Grand Hotel closes next month," he said. "There are a few places open in winter, but it gets a little more difficult to get here. Especially after winter really gets going.

"Do people live here in the winter?" Noah asked.

"A few hearty souls. You won't catch me here though."

The ride to the hotel was elegant. The driver took them around so that they traveled along the tree lined road up to the hotel. When the Grand Hotel came into view, it nearly took her breath away. It was truly an American castle.

She smiled at Noah. It was hard to believe that just less than three hours ago, they had been sitting in Birmingham, Alabama. Not much longer than it would take her to drive from her home on Lake Martin to Atlanta for a day of shopping. Now here they were on the other side of the country in another world.

The driver stopped at the front of the hotel, and like royalty, they were greeted by the valet. The valet took their luggage and helped her from the carriage.

Noah took her hand as they went up the stairs, across the front porch, and through the lobby to the check in desk.

"Good afternoon," the clerk greeted them.

"We have a reservation for Worthington," Noah said.

"Ah. Welcome Mr. and Mrs. Worthington," the clerk said. "We have you in a lovely two-bedroom suite."

Savannah opened her mouth, but Noah just shrugged.

She didn't say anything. Didn't correct the clerk to tell her she wasn't Mrs. Worthington.

The clerk handed them keys – real keys, not key cards, and they followed the valet to the elevator and up to the fourth floor.

He opened the door, "Welcome to the newly renovated Cupola suite," he said.

"I tried to get the Somewhere in Time room," Noah said, "but it was already booked."

"No," Savannah said. "This is perfect." Everything was elegantly decorated. The walls were papered in a cheerful blue color, the drapes, the flowers. "It looks like a room for a princess."

After the valet left, Noah pulled her into a hug.

The clock on the wall chimed five times. "Hey," he said. "It's five o'clock."

"Time for a martini?" she asked.

He grinned. "You read my mind."

She laughed. Give me a minute to freshen up.

"Take your time."

Suitcase in hand, she paused, turned back to him. "Which one is mine?"

"You can have whichever one you want."

Savannah dragged her suitcase into the room to the right, which had two queen beds, dug her toiletry bag out of her suitcase, and went into the bathroom. She brushed her teeth, brushed her hair. It had been a long day, so there wasn't a lot she could do. She freshened her make-up, added some lip gloss.

Took a deep breath and stretched. Looked around. What were they going to do with all these beds?

At thirty-nine, she was not easily impressed.

And she knew better than to be swept off her feet.

This was a no strings trip.

It was important to keep her head out of the clouds. Noah may have been the one she'd always loved, but...

She ticked off the things to be wary of.

He was still married.

He had a daughter.

He had walked away from her once.

He had shattered her heart.

She shook her head. But she was here. Mentally rewrote her list.

He was almost divorced.

His daughter was an adult, so not a big issue.

He was here now.

There was still a place for him in her heart.

Much better. Putting a smile on her face, she went back to join him.

He was standing at the window so she could see his profile.

What she saw surprised her.

Instead of the carefree man he attempted to portray, in this unguarded moment, she saw pain.

What had caused him so much hurt?

She realized that whatever it was, she wanted to make it go away. Even if that meant setting aside the pain that he had caused her.

They sat next to each other at a little table in the huge lobby of the Grand Hotel, generously decorated with burgundy mums.

Noah drank a crown on the rocks and she sipped a pretty pink cosmopolitan. With olives.

"Tell me about your job," he said.

She shrugged. "It's really not all that interesting."

"Is that so. Well, let's see. You get to travel a lot."

"Travel is overrated."

"She said to the pilot."

Savannah laughed. "Right. No offense intended."

"None taken. You know a lot about prescription medications."

"I know a lot about psychotropic medications."

"Really? You specialize?"

"There are so many meds out there, you almost have to."

"So you only visit psychiatrists?"

"I prefer psychiatrists and medical psychologists, but

Alabama doesn't recognize medical psychologists yet. I've visited a few in Louisiana and one in New Mexico. I'm a very strong advocate. They have their act together. I believe in medication. I have to. But I believe it works best with psychotherapy."

"I take it that doesn't go over all that well with general practitioners."

"I rarely even bother to mention psychotherapy to primary care providers. They don't have the time or energy to do more than prescribe a pill and send the patient on their way."

"That's unfortunate. I had a friend who tried the full range of SSRIs and finally landed on Lexapro. He pretty much had to figure out his own dosing regimen."

"Higher functioning patients can do that. But those are few and far between. Believe it or not, my most recommended SSRI is Prozac."

"Why Prozac? Isn't that the oldest one?"

"It has a built-in titration schedule. If the patient stops taking it all of a sudden, it stays in their system long enough to not cause any side effects from withdrawal."

"What about something like Xanax?"

"Ah. The benzos are wonder drugs. But docs don't like to prescribe them."

"I heard they're hard to get. What's the problem with them?"

"Unlike the SSRIs, they have to be titrated off. If not discontinued properly, seizures can occur. Also, in the elderly, they can cause dizziness and falling."

"They're ok in low doses, though, right?"

"I take Klonopin to help me sleep sometimes. Xanax works well, too, but it doesn't stay in the system long."

"You have to know all these drugs."

"I also know their systems like GABA. It's not required, really, that we know all that, but it seems to impress some of the docs and it's a good way to establish rapport. Besides, if I'm gonna be selling something, I want to know how it works."

"I can see why you're good at what you do."

"What makes you think I'm good at it?"

"You may recall that I heard you speak at a national conference."

She winced. "Right. You did, didn't you?"

"It's ok to be good at your job."

She swirled her drink, enjoyed the relaxed pace.

"Is it true?" he asked. What they say about drug reps?"

"What is it that they say?"

"That they'll do just about anything to get a doctor to agree to use their medications."

She scoffed. Refused to answer. "What about you? How good are you at your job?"

"I'm ok."

"Ok, my foot. You're with a major airline. Which I understand is hard to break into. And," she held up a finger. "You're good enough that you're thinking you can give that up and go out on your own doing contract work."

"Yeah," he said, rubbing his chin. "It's a hard decision with a daughter in college."

"It's weird to picture you as a dad."

"Hard to imagine, huh?"

"Not hard, just weird. In my head, you're still the college senior who wanted to grow up and be a pilot." She picked up a napkin. Held up the two sides. "Here's the Noah I knew," she

said, "on this side and on this side is the Noah you are now."
She put the two corners of the napkin together. "It's like all
this," she swept a hand around the bottom of the napkin. "never
happened. This is where all the mystery is."

"I'm still me," he said.

"Maybe. To some extent. But life has molded, changing you
in perhaps small ways. It's like... Maybe you should get another
drink."

He nodded. "Are you good?"

She placed her hand over the top of her glass. "Good."

He took his empty glass with him to the bar.

Savannah was enjoying her pretty pink cosmopolitan, but it
was making her a little light headed. A little bold perhaps.

Or perhaps it was just sitting here in the Grand Hotel. From
the movie she'd watched over and over as a teenager. And
developed a huge crush on Christopher Reeve. She was actually
here where the movie was filmed. It was almost like the movie
had come to life.

She smiled, feeling like part of a private joke when Noah
came back to the table.

"Are you having a good time."

"Absolutely."

"Good. Me too," he put his hand over hers. "What were you
saying?"

For a moment, gazing into his clear blue eyes, she forgot
what she was thinking, her thoughts scattered.

"It's like the neurons," she said, finding a thread of her
previous thoughts.

"The neurons?"

He glanced at her drink. Frowned.

"When we have new experiences, we form new neuronal connections. Different experiences lead to different kinds of connections. These connections basically make us who we are. You've been married, you've had a baby, all sorts of things in the last twenty years. All those things have given you new emotions, new experiences. They've made you who you are."

She swirled her drink, took a swallow. He was watching her closely.

"Are you nervous?" he asked.

"Me? No. Why would I be nervous?"

"I don't know. But you've only had about a fourth of that drink and I've seen you be unaffected after drinking a whole lot more." He slid the drink over, sniffed it, slid it back.

"Is my drink ok?" she asked, with a mischievous smile.

"There's nothing wrong with your drink."

"Good. Because I'm enjoying it."

"I haven't seen you like this since…"

"Since when?"

"Never mind," he said, "There are probably some things we need to talk about."

"Oh no," she said, leaning forward. "Listen. I understand the whole concept of being in the moment. I'm into the moment. Let's not look into the past and let's not look forward tonight."

"Ok," he said. "I thought you wanted to look into the napkin."

"I changed my mind."

He ran his hand through his hair. "Sure."

"Look where we are," she said, sweeping her hand upwards. "Did you have any idea that we'd be thousands of miles away from home tonight on this beautiful, historic island?"

"No, but technically we were thousands of miles away from home two nights ago, too, when we were in New York."

"And that was lovely. But it was planned."

"Planned for you, perhaps."

"Ah ha."

"Ah ha what?

"No, we're not talking about that tonight."

His eyes narrowed and she smiled.

"Tonight we're on the same page. We're doing something together that neither one of us planned."

"You're right," he conceded. "So what do you want to do tomorrow?"

"I just want to be with you," she said. Then smiled broadly. "We can do whatever we want because neither one of us has any expectations from the other."

Noah downed the rest of his drink.

Savannah knew exactly what she was doing.

She was getting him off-guard. He wasn't sure yet, but he knew she wasn't intoxicated and she wasn't blonde. However, at the moment, she could easily have passed for either.

He figured she wanted to talk about their past. Wanted to so bad she could taste it. She was toying with him. Making him think she didn't. Making him think she was not concerned with their future. He was pretty sure she was very concerned with their future.

Her being here was quite a leap of faith. Savannah Richards didn't do anything lightly. And she was not spontaneous. She was a planner. He knew that if he checked the electronic calendar on her phone, she would have meetings scheduled and trips laid out for the next few weeks, conferences planned for the next year, and who knew what else.

This lack of structure, this ambiguity was enough to drive her over the edge. She did nothing without purpose, but she would deny it. She believed she was spontaneous.

At least, he reminded himself, that was the Savannah he had known before. Perhaps it would be interesting to test his theory. To see if that had changed.

"When's the last time you had free time like this to do whatever you wanted?"

She pursed her lips. "It's been a little while. Why?'

"Just curious. I feel lucky that you were able to get away with me."

"I didn't plan on it," she said.

"I know. That's why I feel lucky. When is your next conference?"

"There's a three day at New Year's."

"You have a conference on New Year's?" He ignored the flash of disappointment.

"Technically, it doesn't start until the day after New Year's, but I usually go early. They always have some sort of New Year's Eve party."

It was worse than he thought. Even her New Year's Eves were planned months in advance.

"How often do you see your daughter?"

"At least once a week."

He also knew that she did not want to talk about his daughter. But she wouldn't be able to resist it. His daughter represented everything she missed out on with him.

But she didn't realize yet that it didn't have to be that way.

"What about you?" he asked. "No children?"

She shook her head. Gave him the canned response. "My lifestyle didn't really allow for it. I always thought there would be time someday."

"So you never got around to it," he said.

"Exactly."

"Savannah." He held her gaze. "You always told me you wanted two kids and a cat. You said you wanted everything normal in life."

"I do want everything normal in life."

"You say that, but you don't have those two kids. You don't even have the cat."

"I could have a cat."

"Your mother has a cat. You don't. You're gone too much and you wouldn't do that to a pet."

"You're analyzing me now."

He laughed. "I'm a pilot. I don't analyze people. You do."

"I push medications. I don't analyze."

"How many conferences have you attended on psychology? To learn how to analyze people and push their buttons to make them want to choose your drugs over someone else's? Why do you think you're so good at your job?"

"I'm good at my job because I work hard."

"Yes, you do. And you make time for things that are important to you."

He'd pushed her too far. He could see it in her face. Oh no! *Please don't cry again.*

She recovered quickly, though. "When I meet the right person, I'll think about having a baby."

"Aren't you worried about the ticking biological clock?"

"I'm only thirty-nine. I've got another good five to ten years before I have to worry about that."

"It takes a minute to meet the right person and get all that in place."

There was that look again. That deer in the headlights look.

"I'd like another drink," she said. "Would you get me a martini with extra olives?" She held out her glass with the unfinished cosmopolitan.

Noah took the glass and went back to the bar. He should feel pleased that he'd turned the tables on her and now she was the one unsettled instead of him.

But he didn't. He, too, wanted to talk about their past. He wanted to explain everything. Tell her everything about his life for the last twenty years. But he knew it would be painful for her to hear. He would have to continue to tell her little pieces at the time.

He also wanted to talk about the future. He wanted to be on her daily day planner. But before he could get to the future, he had to right the past.

He took the martini from the bartender, tasted it. It wasn't bad. Not too strong. He wanted Savannah clear-headed. He wanted her to make good decisions where he was concerned. He didn't want her judgment clouded with alcohol.

Well, maybe just a little.

The lobby was filling up now. They weren't the only people staying here after all. Dinner would be served soon. Tomorrow they would go downtown and look around at the shops. They might even walk around the beach.

A few feet from their table, he froze.

She wasn't there.

In fact, there was no sign of her. Her handbag was gone, too. He looked around frantically. He'd brought her all the way to Michigan only to have her snatched?

His heart pounded in his chest. Had she left him? Had he pushed her too far after all?

Setting the drink on the table, he had the most bizarre sensation that she had been no more than a fantasy. He traveled alone so much, that perhaps it had gotten to him. Now he was imagining conversations with people.

He stood at the table, frozen. Not sure whether to get himself home and admitted to a psych ward or to turn this island upside down in a frantic search for Savannah.

He turned, then, and saw her walking toward him. Relief flooded through him. When she reached him, he hugged her tightly.

"You missed me?" she asked.

"I was trying to figure out what I was going to tell your mother about your kidnapping."She laughed. "You make it sound like having your dates kidnapped is a common occurrence."

"I don't date," he said.

"What do you mean?"

"You're the only girl I've ever dated."

An elderly man in a dark gray suit came around to each table, one by one to let them know that dinner was being served in the main dining room. "The meal is included with your stay, but you have to put on a tie, sir and, miss, I'm sorry, but no denim allowed."

"That's not a problem," she said. She had a suitcase full of formal attire. And knew that Noah had a tux with him. After all, they hadn't changed out their clothing after returning from New York.

"Very good," the man said, "we look forward to seeing you there."

"What do you think?" he asked. "Should we go or look for someplace less formal?"

"I think I'd rather put on a dress than venture out tonight. How about you?"

"Sounds good. Want to finish your drink first?"

"Nope. I'm good."

It was a bit of a walk back up to the room. Once inside, they went into their respective rooms and dressed for dinner.

Savannah put on her red high low dress and black heels. Her floor length gown seemed a bit formal for the occasion. She felt a bit rushed as she ran a brush through her hair and reapplied lip gloss.

They met back in the parlor and didn't waste any time for the hike back down to the dining room.

The dining room was surprisingly crowded. The required formal attire gave it a different atmosphere than it had earlier. It looked less touristy now and more formal and historic. They were seated at a table with an excellent view of the water – just as the sun was setting.

Noah ordered a smoked salmon roulade for an appetizer and a bottle of pinot noir.

Savannah wanted to get back to their earlier conversation. At the moment, however, he seemed to be intent on distracting her with small talk.

"Did you know that the hotel has three hundred ninety rooms and no two are exactly the same?"

"I did not. That's pretty amazing."

"And," he continued. "The front porch is the longest in the world."

"Did you know that there's a Somewhere in Time fan club that meets next week?"

"That's unfortunate. We just missed it."

"It's ok. I think it would be distracting."

"I thought that's something you would enjoy."

"Maybe," she said, "I'm in more of a low-key mood right now."

The server appeared to take their order. She ordered the roasted eggplant casserole and he ordered the whitefish.

"We have to order one those Grand Pecan Balls for dessert. It's their most famous dessert."

"I don't suppose they have a treadmill."

"With all the bicycling, walking, and such on the island, I doubt you'll need it."

"I guess I can count that as cardio."

"I admire your health consciousness," he said.

"With everything I know about biology, it's hard not to take exercise seriously."

"I need to follow your example."

"I don't mind the company."

The server brought their bottle of wine, uncorked it, and poured a taste in Savannah's glass. She sipped. "Wow. This is really good wine."

"Only the best, Miss. Is this your first time to the Grand?"

"It is," she said, glancing at Noah. "We're quite impressed."

"Thank you miss," he said. "I hope you enjoy your stay."

He filled their glasses, wiped the bottle with a white cloth, and went to check on their appetizer.

"We are impressed, aren't we?" she asked, turning back to Noah.

"We are ecstatic."

She smiled, glanced around before turning her gaze back to Noah. "I know we haven't had a chance to explore the island yet, but based on your first impression, which do you prefer, New York or Mackinac?"

"That's like asking me if I like apples or oranges. They're both great, and I couldn't possibly choose one over the other."

"Aw. That's a cop out and you know it."

"I know one thing."

"What's that?"

"I like you."

She paused, her glass halfway to her lips.

"I certainly hope so since you brought me up here to the top of the world."

He laughed. "It seems more like you brought me."

She smiled. Either way. "I hadn't planned on taking a vacation right now."

"Unplanned vacations are the very best kind."

"I had no idea."

The server brought their appetizer and Noah tasted it first. "Oh wow. You've got to try this."

She took a bite of the salmon with dill cream and caviar.

"This is...hmm. Unlike anything I've had before." She took another bite.

"You like it?"

"It's like heaven."

Noah beamed as though he had made it himself.

"You've had this before," she said.

"I've actually made this before."

"You? No way."

"I did. I took a cooking class last year and this is one of the things we made. You take some cream cheese and some dill and roll it up like a jelly roll."

This was a Noah she did not know. And hadn't expected. "Why did you do that?" Was all she could think to ask.

"I knew I was getting divorced and it just seemed like something interesting to do"

She couldn't help the accusing tone that came next. "You wanted to attract women."

"You're attracted to men who can make salmon roulade?"

"That would be strange," she said.

"Perhaps, but you avoided the question."

"I do like a man who can cook and will cook," she took another bite of salmon. "There is huge difference in the two."

"Sounds like you're speaking from experience."

"I might be."

"Well, in my house, if there was cooking to be done." He stopped himself in mid-sentence. Appeared to regroup. "Let's just say that in my previous relationship, I'm the one who of us who cooked."

"You just kept something from me," she said.

He sat back, sipped his drink. "Very perceptive, my dear."

"I think that's the problem," she said. "You've been holding out on me for a while… about twenty-one years."

"Why would you think that?"

"At the time I didn't notice, but in retrospect, you knew everything about me and my family, but I knew nothing about where you came from. I met your parents once. And they were not ordinary parents."

"I'm not sure that's a compliment."

"Noah," she said, setting down her fork. Leaning forward. "I know now why you kept me from your family."

He shook his head, imperceptibly.

The sounds of live musicians drifted from the other end of the dining hall.

"Looks like they have live music," Savannah pointed out.

"No. No. Don't change the subject. Why did I keep you from my unordinary family?"

"I was an ordinary girl and your father was a tycoon."

"What makes you say something like that?"

Savannah knew she was on the right track by the way his eyes widened. "He had the tycoon look."

"I didn't realize tycoons had a look," he glanced around the dining area. "Are any of these men tycoons?"

"No," she said. "Besides the tycoon look, you obviously inherited enough money to use *some* of it to buy yourself an airplane. I can add, Noah."

The server, dressed in black tie, brought a tray to their table, two plates, covered with silver domes. He uncovered each one to serve their food. Heat from the white plates, elegantly presented, wafted between them.

Noah appeared relieved to have a moment to collect his thoughts.

"I apologize, Noah. I shouldn't have said anything."

"It's ok," he said, tasting his fish. "This is awesome fish!"

Savannah tasted her own food. It was, indeed, tasty.

"You're right," Noah said. "My father was wealthy."

"Noah…"

"No. I always tried to keep that from you. I wanted to be normal. Regular. In college. Even the boat. It was my boat. But I didn't want you to see me that way."

"Noah," she breathed. "You should have known. It wouldn't have changed anything. I loved you from the very beginning."

"I didn't know that then. I needed to know that it wasn't my money you were after."

Savannah lowered her lashes and set her fork down. Everything she knew about Noah shifted into place. Everything she had suspected after he went away. Now that she knew, she expected it to matter. But it didn't.

He was still Noah.

They finished their food in silence. Savannah ate a few more bites, but she had lost her appetite.

By the time the server removed their plates, one of the couples was dancing a few yards away. They watched as another couple joined them.

Suddenly, Noah stood, went around the table and stood in front of her and held out his hand. "Dance with me, Savannah," he said.

She shook her head.

"Come on. Don't make me look foolish."

She put her hand in his and allowed him to lead her to the

dance floor. He put one hand on her waist and, holding her other hand, led her into a waltz.

Another one of Noah's secret talents.

"I went to a boarding school," he said, when she looked at him questioningly.

"I have no idea how to do this," she said.

"Just follow my lead," he said, sending her into a twirl.

Noah was indeed a good dancer. So much so, that they drew a bit of an audience. After the first dance, other couples joined them until the area around them was crowded.

Then the music slowed and he pulled her to him. Put his arms around her waist. Her hands wrapped around his neck and she laid her cheek against his chest.

Safe.

Cherished.

Those were the two emotions that flooded her senses.

Noah.

She sighed.

Nothing in her life had made as much sense before or after him.

The years faded. Folded in until, although it may still exist, the time that had elapsed no longer mattered.

She was in Noah's arms. The one place she had always belonged.

Noah swayed with Savannah in his arms. How had he let her go so long ago?

There must be a God, indeed, for him to have not only found her, but to have the honor of her allowing him back into his life.

A second chance.

He'd been granted a second chance. And he would not. Could not. Mess it up this time.

He slipped a hand up to her chin, gently tilted her face up. Her eyes were closed. He stroked her cheek, the edge of her lips. Her lips quivered ever so slightly.

He groaned.

Pressed his lips against hers.

She melted against him.

A room.

He needed to get her to their room.

He reached down. Picked her up.

Her eyes flew open.

He carried her back to their table. Slid her down against him.

His body still pressed against hers, he swept her hair back and tucked it behind her ears. "What am I going to do with you, Savannah Skye?" he asked, his voice next to her ear.

"Is it so difficult to figure out?" she asked, her voice quivering.

"Turns out I'm a little slow sometimes."

He felt her laugh against him.

"You're the smartest man I know."

"Spoken by the girl who cavorts with doctors."

"I wasn't thinking of them."

"You really know how to stroke a man's ego," he said.

"I think I had too much to drink," she said.

He glanced toward the table at the glass of wine she'd barely touched.

"You didn't even have half a glass."

"Must be the elevation," she said.

"Must be," he agreed, releasing her enough to pick up her handbag, but still steadying her with his other arm. "How about we get out of here?"

"I thought you'd never ask."

He took her hand and after a chaste kiss on the forehead, led her toward the elevators.

They walked in comfortable silence, only the sound her heels echoing softly down the long hallway.

Noah wanted more than the chaste kisses on the cheek. He wanted more than kisses while locked in a four-point shoulder harness.

But he also wanted more than passion in the sheets.

He wanted everything. And the heat was still there between them. Perhaps even more so. They were stoking a fire than had been smoldering for twenty years.

But most of all, he wanted her heart back. Once and for all.

They had waited this long. There was no reason not to wait a little longer before rushing into consummating their relationship.

"I need a minute," Savannah said, once they were in the room.

She went into her part of the suite and Noah, knowing it would be more than a minute, went to his room and changed into a pair of warm sweatpants and a t-shirt. Washed his face and brushed his teeth.

He went back to the common area and stretched out on the sofa to wait.

A few minutes later, Savannah joined him, her face scrubbed free of make-up, she also wore a t-shirt and long pajama pants.

"It's cold," she said, as he gathered her into his arms on the sofa.

"I'll keep you warm," he said.

"Ok," she said, snuggling against him. He gently rubbed her back, making little circles at the back of neck.

She grew still against him. He shifted slightly. Her eyes were closed and her lips slightly parted.

She'd fallen asleep.

He gathered her into his arms and carried her to her bed, tucked her beneath the comforter.

He watched her sleep for a few minutes.

Then went to the sofa, stretched out his long legs, and pulled a fleece throw up to his chin. Tucking his arms behind his head, he watched Savannah's door.

Guarding her perhaps.

Definitely struggling with the magnetic pull to go to her.

CHAPTER
Ten

Savannah woke early the next morning. Disoriented. Despite her frequent hotel stays.

She checked her phone. It was only five thirty.

Then she realized why she was disoriented. It was pitch black in the room. Typically, she liked to keep the curtains open whether in a hotel or in her second story bedroom at home.

She climbed out of bed and opened the curtains. No street lights.

She wandered into the living room.

Noah was curled up on the sofa beneath a blanket.

He had his own room.

She walked over, peeked inside. His bed was still made. His suitcase stood next to it. Unpacked.

Perplexed, she went back to the living area and sat in the chair next to the sofa.

Wondered if the hotel did room service.

After about three minutes, she went to her room and dug

into her own suitcase for her workout clothes. She had a pair of tights which, according to her phone, should be weather appropriate. She tied her sneakers, tucked her phone and room key into a pocket on her tights and headed outside.

It was early and she appeared to be about the only one up and about.

Stepping outside into the chilly air, she skipped her warm up and started jogging down the main road. It felt good to stretch her legs. To have a few minutes to herself when she didn't have to think.

Her mind could just wander down its own path with no direction.

Naturally, it wandered to Noah.

Why on earth had he slept on the sofa when he had a perfectly good bed?

She didn't remember how she had ended up in her bed last night. But she did remember being so incredibly sleepy.

Her path took her downtown next to the waterfront. There were a few people about, mostly headed to work, it seemed.

She spotted a Starbuck's and was instantly ecstatic. Going inside, she was the only customer.

She ordered a vanilla latte, paid with her phone app and strolled back outside. Walking now, she studied the quaint little town. Mostly tourist shops and restaurants.

It was perfect.

She found a bench on a path next to the beach and sat watching the sun come up.

A young couple, walked past, hand in hand, and Savannah decided she should get back to Noah before he got up and discovered her missing.

She finished her coffee as she walked back through town. At the edge of town, she began jogging again. The warmth of the sun, the jog, and the hot coffee had her perspiring a bit.

She went back through the lobby, up the elevator, and down the long hall to their room.

Used her key and stepped into the room.

Noah was there, holding his phone with one hand, the other hand pressed against the side of his head. He turned, saw her. "She's here. Thank God. I'm sorry I bothered you. Yes. Thank you."

Noah stared blankly at her.

"What's going on?" She asked, taking her phone out of her pocket.

"Savannah." He looked a little pale.

"What?"

"Where have you been?"

"I went for a jog," she picked up a bottle of water, opened it, and drank about half of it.

"A jog."

"The town is really pretty," she said. "And they have a Starbucks."

"I was in the process of reporting you missing."

"Missing?"

"You weren't here."

Oh crap. "I'm sorry."

"Hand me your phone," he said.

She handed him her phone.

He clicked, handed it back. "You have to unlock it."

She used her fingerprint to unlock it, handed it back. She drank more water. Watched him warily. "What are you doing?"

He was typing into her phone. "Here," he said, when his own phone started to ring, handing her back her phone.

He clicked the keys on his own phone. "Now I can call you when you're lost."

"I wasn't lost," she said, but knew exactly what he meant. "I'm sorry," she said again.

"You really are used to being alone."

She shrugged. He appeared to be calming.

"So, where's my coffee?"

Her eyes widened. She should have brought him coffee. "It would have been cold by the time I got back."

"I'm only kidding. It would be hard to jog with coffee in your hand."

"Why did you sleep on the sofa?"

He picked up the blanket. Folded it. "I fell asleep," he said.

She waited for him to expound on his answer, but instead, he went toward his bedroom. "I'm going to take a shower," he said.

"Good idea," she said. "Me, too." But she didn't think he heard her.

Letting the hot water run over her head, Savannah tried to sort out what had just happened.

She'd been awake and restless. So she'd gone jogging. It wasn't like there was a treadmill in the room.

And, she admitted, she had taken time at the Starbucks and watching the sun come up. She'd been gone, what? A little over an hour. She hadn't kept track.

She really hadn't expected him to even know that she was out. Had he gone into her room?

If they had true separate rooms, instead of a suite, he certainly wouldn't have known.

They had, it seemed, progressed a bit in their relationship.

She got out of the shower and put the same jeans back on that she had worn yesterday. She could not however, bring herself to wear the same sweater. Consequently, she wore a silk blouse. She never wore the same clothes two days in a row. But she didn't want to wear a dress or slacks.

Noah had promised that there would be shops.

Unfortunately, she wasn't sure he was talking to her now.

She put on her make-up and dried her hair.

Noah was waiting for her when she went back into the living area.

"Ready for breakfast?" he asked.

"Sure."

He took her hand and together they went into the hallway toward the elevator.

"I'm sorry I overreacted," he said.

"I'm sorry I left without telling you. You're right. I have spent too much time alone."

"I guess we both have some adjustments to make," he said, with a smile.

"Yes, I suppose we do," she returned his smile. His comment gave her hope that he was thinking forward to the future.

They rode in a horse drawn carriage downtown, then Savannah had her second, albeit smaller cup of coffee. She didn't have the heart to tell him she'd already been to Starbucks.

She bought a gray sweatshirt, one that zipped and wore it out of the store.

They had an early lunch and watched the ferry bring in the tourists for the day. Some of them had luggage with them.

"Flying is definitely the way to get here," Savannah commented.

"I'm glad you're finally on board with the whole flying thing."

"I've always been on board. But after this past week, I'm not sure I'll ever be the same."

Her comment elicited a smug look which Savannah found amusing. Noah was so easily complimented. As long as it was about flying.

After lunch, they rented bicycles for the rest of the day and started their trek around the island. It wasn't crowded. They only saw a few others out walking and one other man riding.

About halfway around, they stopped to take a break and admire the view.

"I'm glad you picked this place," Noah said. "There are so many beautiful places to see in this country. I'd like to see them all."

"It would take a lifetime," Savannah said. "How would you even find all the places to see?"

"We could go state by state. Research it."

"You sound almost serious. What would you do? One state every year?"

"We'd have to do more than that. I guess it would depend on the state. And how much time we had to devote to it."

Savannah leaned back and savored the sun shining on her face. They had settled into their old companionship. Savannah was reminded that she'd had no other relationship like the one she'd had with Noah. Had he? Had he had other relationships like this?

He had definitely set the bar for her early.

"There's something you should know about me," she said.

He turned his attention to her. "I'm listening."

"Just before you start planning these trips, you should know that I'm not really an outdoor kind of girl."

"Is that so? You seem to be riding that bicycle ok."

"Yeah. But I'm not into the whole camping thing. I prefer to sleep in a warm bed. With room service."

"No need to worry, ma chérie, we are of like mind when it comes to that."

She smiled at the endearment. And turned her gaze to meet his. "There's a chill in the air," she said.

He pulled out his phone. "I should check the weather."

"Now?"

"Unfortunately, our return flight home depends on the weather."

"Let's just stay here."

"Don't tempt me," he said.

After an afternoon of bicycling, Savannah was exhausted. She'd used muscles she didn't know she had. She made a mental note to add cycling into her workout routine.

Noah determined that they should leave early the next morning due to an impending cold front. Savannah was disappointed. There was so much more on the island that she wanted to see. Noah was opening up worlds she didn't even know existed.

They had a quiet dinner at the hotel, then rented a movie in their room. Noah didn't drink, but Savannah had a glass of wine. "Twelve hours bottle to throttle," he'd said. Apparently, that rule also applied to sleep. At nine o'clock he announced that he was going to sleep – in his bed.

"I'm glad you're going to get some use out of your bed," Savannah commented.

"Ha. So, you'll be ready by seven?"

"I'd prefer to stay here for a week," she said.

"As would I," Noah agreed, "instead, we'll put this on our list of places to visit again."

"Deal," she said, as he kissed her good night.

And, with his kisses, he was bringing to life fantasies that she had given up on years ago.

It seemed he would only be getting eleven hours of sleep, she mused, as they settled into the kiss.

Eleven

Noah landed the plane and taxied down the runway. Glancing at his watch, he knew he would be early for his three o'clock meeting.

He took a deep breath and forced himself to relax. There was a lot riding on the meeting, yet, no matter how it went, he knew he had more options.

Two hours later, Noah stepped out of the bank building and went straight to his BMW SUV. The meeting had gone well.

In less than a month, he would begin his transition process toward retiring from the airline and doing his own contract work. The older pilot, Sam Allen was ready to give up his business. He was ready to spend his days on the beach with the love of his life.

Noah loved Sam's story. It reminded him a lot of himself and Savannah.

Sam had only been married for ten years, but those ten years had been a long time coming. He and his wife had gone to high school together, but they hadn't gotten to know each other until twenty –five years later after they had run into each other in their hometown. Neither one of them had lived there since high school, so it was rather happenstance that they had even recognized each other. They had both been married at the time, but had stayed in touch as friends. Then, ten years later, they had met again, this time he was divorced, but she was still married. They had begun talking on the phone anyway. As friends. After her husband died from heart disease, they had gone on their first date. They were married a week later.

Sam knew that had created quite the gossip flurry, but neither he nor his wife cared. Now that they were in their sixties, they found the whole thing amusing. They just wanted to live out their days on the beach, holding hands, and drinking Piña coladas.

Sam had built up quite the business. So much so that he had three younger pilots flying for him.

Unfortunately, Sam had no children, so there was no one to pass the business along to. Sam and Noah had met years ago at a week-long training for certification for flying the Learjet, and had become friends immediately.

They'd stayed in touch and Sam had been telling Noah for years that he should come work for him.

Noah had picked up the phone the day after he returned from Mackinac and set up the meeting with Sam to work out the details.

Now that Sam was retiring, Noah was getting more than he had bargained for. He was getting Sam's business. That meant he could take the jobs he wanted and let the younger guys have the other ones. Noah liked the idea of having that kind of freedom mixed with security.

And the great thing about being a pilot was he could work from anywhere.

He was meeting Sam and his wife, Beth, at a restaurant in Dallas. Noah didn't mind. It was on his way home. Sam had to run home and pick up his wife, so Noah would have a few minutes to have a drink at the restaurant bar and unwind.

He chose a seat toward the back, at the bar, away from the noise, ordered a crown on the rocks, and opened his iPad.

He had an email from Claire, his soon to be ex-wife.

Hi Noah,

I hope you're doing well. It seems like we haven't spoken in forever. I met with the attorney today and we have court day for December 16. The week before Christmas! I got a sick feeling just thinking about it. I don't know why. Lol. It's not like we had the best relationship. And I know I was one to initiate the divorce. At least I think I was. I think you smiled quite a bit during the whole packing process.

Anyway, I thought that if you were having second thoughts, this might be a good time to talk about it.

Love ya,

Claire

Noah stared at the email. Where was the Claire he had been married to?

Had she ever told him she loved him?

For his daughter's sake, sure, but truly of her own volition? He was certain she hadn't. They had only been intimate that one time on their honeymoon on the cruise.

He had been fairly certain she was only biding her time, based on the prenuptial agreement.

The server brought his drink. He sipped. Considered. What was her angle? She was after something, he had no doubt. Perhaps their daughter had been looking over her shoulder. Whatever it was, he couldn't possibly imagine it being anything sincere. Or good.

It didn't matter anyway. There was no way this side of hell that he was going to rethink this divorce. In fact, December 16 was much farther off than he would prefer.

"Mind if I sit here?" The decidedly female voice interrupted his contemplation.

"Sure," he said, absently, barely glancing toward the blonde in the sleek red dress. He returned to his iPad. No other emails. He reminded himself that Savannah didn't have his email address.

She did have his phone number though. He checked his phone. No text messages.

It had been five days since he'd dropped her off at her home. He hadn't gone inside. He'd wanted to give her some space. He didn't want to make too many assumptions. He knew he couldn't expect to just waltz back into her life and upend everything. She was obviously busy and successful.

She wasn't however, seeing anyone, which he found comforting. He liked knowing she was out there. Busy. Perhaps thinking of him.

Just a little.

"Busy day?" the woman asked.

Jarred out his thoughts again, Noah looked up to the woman

sitting on the bar stool next to him. The bar wasn't crowded. There were about a dozen other places she could have sat.

"I'm Abigail," she said, holding out her hand.

"Noah," he said, automatically shaking her hand.

He refocused on his iPad. Not seeing it now.

"Can I buy you a refill?" she asked, indicating his drink.

When it rained, it poured.

"No, I'm good."

"No, really… Bartender," She gestured for the bartender. "I'll buy him another of what he's having."

Noah shook his head, but the bartender was already off to fetch his drink. Noah knew how this game played out. He'd end up buying the drinks. If she had her way, they'd end up in a room together.

But that wasn't going to happen. Noah was no saint. He'd done two one-night stands years ago. Each time, he woke up feeling unfulfilled.

Besides, all he could think about was Savannah. Then and now.

Perhaps he should call her tonight. But he was more of a show up out of the blue kind of guy. Maybe he liked the effect it had or maybe he just wasn't sure what he should say to her.

Perhaps he should at least send her a text.

He typed *Hi. It's Noah. How's your week?*

Abigail's drink arrived.

"No thanks," Noah said. "I'm meeting someone." He hit delete.

"Alright," she said, "But I don't think she's coming."

Noah stared at his phone. Still no text from Savannah. He'd

had to text her a couple of times while they were at Mackinac and she had responded immediately. He knew she had his number because he had put it there himself.

"No," Noah said, not even looking at her as he stood up and started toward the door. He'd wait for Sam outside if he had to.

Sam and his wife arrived at the restaurant a few minutes later. Beth was an elegant woman, charming, always wearing a smile on her face. She hugged Noah in greeting.

After they were seated, Sam ordered a bottle of champagne. Noah was reminded of Savannah and her love of mimosas. He suddenly wanted her there with him. Badly. She should be here.

She would enjoy Beth and Sam and they would enjoy her company. His idea to surprise her with the news of the deal he was making suddenly felt like not such a good idea. It would have been better to involve her in the process.

He took out his phone, stared at the offending blank screen.

It was Friday night. What was she doing?

Was she out?

Savannah had told him she didn't do the whole going out with girlfriends thing. She could be with her mother or her sister.

Or she could be on a date.

"Is something wrong, Dear?" Beth asked.

"No, not at all," Noah said, and put his phone away. He would deal with this later.

Over appetizers, Noah asked Beth to tell him how she and Sam got together. He had heard Sam's version. He wanted to hear hers.

"Oh, in high school, he didn't even know I existed. Then we kept running into each other over the years."

"I knew you existed," Sam protested.

"It's alright," she said. "I had a huge crush on the football captain."

"You never told me that."

"A girl has to have a little mystery," she said, with a bright smile at Noah. "Right, Noah?"

"Most women do," he said.

"We have to keep you interested somehow," she told her husband.

Sam took her hand, kissed her knuckles.

Noah looked away and his gaze landed on Abigail. She had taken a table just out of earshot. She smiled broadly at Noah.

He scowled.

And had a flash of boiling bunnies.

"Noah, do you know that woman?" Beth asked.

"I met her at the bar before you came in," he said.

"Do you want to invite her over?" Beth asked.

Noah shook his head before the words were out of her mouth. "I tried to discourage her, but she's persistent."

"Well, you're a good-looking single man."

"I'm taken," he said.

Sam and Beth both leaned forward.

"Your divorce?" Sam asked.

"No," he scoffed. "I just found out we have a court date a week before Christmas."

"I think being separated allows you to see others," Beth said, with a knowing look at Sam.

"I'm seeing someone," Noah said, "someone else."

"Oh? It must be serious."

"I've reconnected with my girlfriend from college."

Sam sat back. Ran a hand through his hair. Sam had been the one person he had confided in over the years.

"This was a long time coming," Sam said.

"We ran into each other about a week ago at the airport in Atlanta."

"This sounds like a romantic story," Beth said.

"You can tell her," Noah said, turning his back squarely away from Abigail who was still watching him.

"Worthington made a business arrangement that required Noah to marry Claire. What he didn't know was that Noah was planning to marry..." he turned to Noah. "I'm sorry. I can't remember her name."

"It's ok. It's been twenty years. Her name is Savannah." Just saying her name out loud sent a warmth through his body.

"Noah was planning to marry Savannah."

"I handled it very badly." Noah said.

"You were young," Beth pointed out.

"No. Really badly. I just walked away from Savannah. No explanation. No good-bye. Nothing."

Beth watched him closely. "You loved her very much."

"Yeah," Noah said. "I loved her too much to watch her heart break."

"But now you're back together."

Noah nodded. "That's part of why I've made this decision. I want to be able to set my own schedule. To be able to spend as much time with Savannah as possible. I have some serious making up to do."

Sam took Beth's hand. "Sounds like they're going to have the same happy ending we have."

Over the course of the next couple of hours, Noah and Sam

worked out a few details, but the deal had been sealed with that initial phone call Noah had made to Sam.

Halfway through dinner, Abigail had disappeared obviously abandoning her efforts to pursue Noah.

Noah left the restaurant in high spirits.

Tomorrow he would give his final notice to the airline.

CHAPTER

Twelve

"How are the children, Mary and Todd?" Savannah asked.

Dr. Smith beamed. "They're good. Todd is still at Yale and Mary is getting ready to graduate."

"Time really flies, doesn't it? Is Mary following his footsteps into architecture?"

"Oh, no. Mary is thinking about going into fashion design."

"Oh, how fun! She and her mom must have really enjoyed that trip to New York. She must have caught the fashion bug."

"I think maybe she already had a touch of it. Do you have a medication to treat the fashion bug?"

Savannah laughed. "If I had a drug for that, I'd take it myself."

"What about you? How have you been?"

"I've been good," she said.

"Still single?"

"Yeah."

"My wife's cousin is coming into town next week."

"Oh," she said, "that will be nice."

"You know she's been talking about this for a while."

Savannah knew exactly what he was talking about. She'd had dinner with Dr. Smith and his wife and they had offered to set Savannah up with Mrs. Smith's cousin.

Savannah had never given a direct answer. She didn't want to offend either the doctor or his wife. Besides, she'd seen a picture of the cousin and he wasn't bad to look at.

"Do you want me to have my wife call you to arrange a dinner meeting?"

"You know what, I'm actually seeing someone."

"Oh, good for you. Is it serious?"

"Well, it's actually kind of new. But, yes, I think it might be."

"My wife will be disappointed, but I'm happy for you. It's been a long time for you."

Savannah had a propensity to keep her social life separate from her work life. However, in an attempt to establish rapport, especially with good clients, she disclosed certain personal information. Especially clients like Dr. Smith and his wife that she occasionally met outside the office in a social setting.

She considered it to be part of the job. Considered them to be work friends.

However, it was times like this, that she regretted the need to blur those boundaries.

After the meeting, she sat in her car, jotted down a few notes regarding the meeting.

It was helpful to keep notes to remind her of details.

She firmly believed that her attention to detail was one of the things that made her successful at her job.

She checked her phone.

No message from Noah.

Reminded herself that he was working. He'd dropped her off at her house, then dashed off to catch a flight home to Ft. Worth so he could work the next day.

"Twelve hours bottle to throttle." He'd told her that was his personal rule. It meant no alcohol twelve hours before flying, but it also meant he needed to be asleep twelve hours before takeoff.

But it had been four days and she hadn't heard from him.

He had sent her a couple of quick text messages while they'd been on Mackinac, so she knew he had put her phone number in his phone correctly.

Her thoughts wandered back to those days they'd spent together and a smile played about her lips. It had been like old times, only better.

Then his words came back to her. The words he'd spoken before they left. "No strings attached."

He recanted after she'd inadvertently starting crying, but the words were there. It seemed he'd meant it.

She admonished herself for thinking that things would be different this time. That they would have something serious.

It would be a long time before she would be ready to spend time with another guy.

Being with Noah had reawakened feelings in her that had lain dormant for twenty years, but there they were, back again.

An old wound, it seemed, was the hardest to heal.

She checked the calendar on her phone. This was her last meeting for the day. Friday afternoons had gotten progressively more and more empty over the past few years as offices started closing early for the weekend. She really didn't mind.

Putting her phone away, she started the two-hour drive home.

As she pulled into her driveway, it became evident how she would spend her afternoon.

She dragged her suitcase and computer bag out of the trunk of her BMW. The house was quiet and seemed a little empty.

She tossed a load of clothes into the washer, then changed into a pair of old jeans and a t-shirt.

There were occasions when she paid the neighbor's son to clean the yard, but there were also days when she needed to do the work herself. This was one of those days.

She took a rake from the tool shed in her back yard and, after picking up stray limbs from a recent storm, began raking leaves from the pine trees that shaded her house.

Two hours later, she had several large piles of pine straw around the yard. With November around the corner, this was just the first round of required raking.

Exhausted now, she decided that she could bag the straw tomorrow. Going inside and upstairs, she ran a bubble bath in her garden tub that overlooked the backyard below. Used the jasmine gardenia scent that she always found soothing.

She checked her phone for messages, turned the volume on, and set it on the stool next to the tub.

As an afterthought, she turned on the volume and the sounds of Taylor Swift drifted through the air. After twisting her hair up and securing it to the top of her head, she stepped into the hot water and relaxed against the back of the tub.

Her thoughts were instantly filled with Noah. Seeing him across the hotel lobby in New York, handsome in his tuxedo. Sitting in his plane with his headset, deftly maneuvering them through the air. Holding her hand as they rode side by side in the carriage on Mackinac Island.

His kisses. Ah, his kisses. She closed her eyes and allowed the memory of the sensations to envelope her.

His words whispered in her ear as they snuggled on a bench looking out over the water, watching the sunset. *I missed you,* he had said.

I miss you now. Where are you Noah? Was that just a fling for old times' sake?

She'd never gotten over him. It was a hard thing to admit.

I need to let him go.

How many times had she wished for just one more night with him?

She had gotten a whole week. *I should be happy.*

Shoring up her resolve to be happy, she got out of the tub and got into her cozy fleece robe.

Went to the refrigerator, opened the door, and sighed. She should have gone to the market instead of heading home to rake the yard. Nothing in the freezer either.

She picked up her phone and located the number to the pizza parlor and called in a Hawaiian pizza.

She poured a glass of cabernet and sat on the sofa while she waited. Checked her phone. Clicked on the weather channel. There was a band of storms across the Ft. Worth area. Was Noah home? Or was he flying across the country right now?

It would have been decent for him to call.

She opened the photo album on her phone and found the selfie they had taken on the porch of the Grand Hotel.

One hand holding the camera, the other arm pulling her against him, their cheeks pressed together, both of them grinning from ear to ear. She pressed the picture, bringing it to animation. He'd captured a perfect photo. In the three seconds captured in the live photo, he turned, kissed her on the cheek, and grinned back at the camera.

She'd watched it a thousand times. Every time, it brought a smile to her face.

But tonight it brought tears to her eyes. A tear landed on her hand just as the doorbell rang. Her pizza was here and she'd lost her appetite.

The pizza turned out to be better than she had expected. With a full stomach and a glass of wine, she decided to turn in early. By the time her head hit the pillow around nine o'clock, she was sound asleep.

Her phone alarm went off at five.

Savannah checked her phone. How had her alarm been set to five o'clock?

After making sure it was off, she rolled over and closed her eyes to go back to sleep.

Five minutes later, her eyes were wide open. She sighed.

And reluctantly rolled out of bed.

This getting up early was getting to be a bad habit.

She put on her fleece robe and made a latte with vanilla syrup and creamer, her only indulgence of sweetness. Out of habit, she sat at her little writing desk and turned on her Mac computer.

But instead of pulling up her email, she paced a bit, her coffee mug in her hands.

She felt restless.

She sat back down, checked her email - mostly deleted

emails, and scanned the headlines. Nothing seemed out of the ordinary.

After putting on her running skort, running top, and sneakers, she got on the treadmill and took a five-mile run in her living room via Norway - according to her iFit program.

She chugged a bottle of water and felt some better.

She had no yogurt and no fruit. A trip to the market was definitely on the list today. So, she scrambled an egg, added some cheese, and toasted two slices of bread she found in the freezer. She ate her egg and cheese sandwich while watching Fox news.

The sun was up now and she needed to bag the pine straw she had piled around the yard.

It was a bit chilly outside, so she pulled on a pair of old sweatpants and a sweatshirt. Grabbed some big garbage bags from the pantry and went outside to start cleaning the yard.

By the time she had two bags stuffed and dragged to the curb, she was sweating.

She had about three bags to go. One more and she had to trade in her sweatshirt for a t-shirt. After the fourth, she was ready for a break. She dragged it to the curb and left it along with the others.

A dark blue sedan pulled up to her driveway. She watched as it turned in and pulled up to her garage door and stopped. Since she was on the other side, she couldn't see the driver. A little spurt of anxiety shot through her. The car was between her and the door of her house. She considered her options. She could run to the neighbor's house and call the police. The nearest neighbor was behind a grove of trees and it would take her about three minutes to jog to their front door.

She held her breath as the driver turned off the motor and the driver door opened.

And Noah stepped out.

A rush of emotions shot through her. Relief that it was someone she knew, but more importantly her heart did a little summersault at seeing him and the blood rushed to her cheeks.

That was followed by a dash of panic. She'd run five miles then gotten even more hot and sweaty bagging leaves. She badly needed a shower.

He stood on the other side of the car, watching her over it. Even from where she stood, she could see his smile.

Her feet were glued to the ground. He started toward her. She clutched the rake as he slowly approached.

He stopped three feet in front of her, still smiling.

She smiled back, her heart tripping dangerously in her chest. Did she have that effect on him?

"Hi," he said.

"Hi."

"You've been busy," he said.

He looked good. He had tucked his sunshades in his collar as he walked toward her. He had on faded jeans and a light blue oxford shirt with loafers.

Her eyes widened. This was not how she wanted him to see her. "I'm a mess," she said.

His smile widened. "Then this is a good thing."

"How could this possibly be a good thing?"

"I've seen you at your worst and I still think you're gorgeous."

She licked her lips, unsure how to respond. Did she look that bad?

"But since I know you, I'll make you a deal. You go shower and I'll bag up that last one over there."

"I look that bad?"

"Not in the least."

"You don't want to get dirty."

"He nodded toward the car. "I brought extra clothes. That is if you'll let me use your shower."

"You brought old clothes?"

He glanced down. "These are old clothes."

She frowned. "Seriously?"

"Yep."

She really wanted to shower. He did, indeed, know her well. "Ok," she relented.

He held out his hand. She put her hand in his. "I was reaching for the rake, but this is better." He pulled her into a hug.

"Alright, shower for you," he said, taking the rake.

She laughed. "I warned you."

Giving up the rake, she took off toward the house, smiling now that he wasn't looking at her.

Inside the house, she sprinted upstairs and turned on the shower. What to wear?

She stood for a moment, contemplating. Deciding the first order of business was to get clean, she stripped and hopped into the shower.

Noah was here! At her house. And he had brought extra clothes. Did that mean he was staying overnight?

Her mind raced. Was the guest room clean enough? Her sister had stayed there last. She had no food in the kitchen.

Thank goodness she'd washed her dishes from breakfast. Why hadn't he called first? Why hadn't he called at all?

How had he even found her without her address?

Noah always had been a show up kind of guy. He liked the element of surprise. He had a cell phone. A text only took a second.

She rinsed the conditioner out of her hair and gave up.

He was here.

She was happy.

No strings.

As the words came back, her good mood dissipated somewhat, but so did some of her anxiety.

No strings meant she really had nothing to lose.

She stepped out of the shower and wrapped herself in her big, cozy towel. Then went to the bedroom window and peaked outside to the side yard where she'd left the other stack of pine straw.

Noah was there, his sleeves rolled up, raking an area she hadn't gotten to. He was giving her plenty of time to make herself presentable.

She felt a little twinge of guilt having him outside working in her yard. She bit her lip. Told herself he could have called first and she would have been up and presentable for him.

Something nagged at the back of her mind, but she couldn't quite put her finger on what it was.

Going back to her bathroom, she washed her face and combed out her hair.

Took out her hair dryer and began to blow dry her hair.

Lost in her thoughts, she jumped and turned off the

hairdryer when she spotted Noah standing behind with a goofy grin on his face.

"Sorry," he said.

"It's ok. I'm not use to anyone else being in my house," she admitted.

"That's good to know."

"Yeah," she said. "You took a leap of faith."

"You did say you weren't in a relationship."

She smiled, picked up her hairbrush. "I suppose I did."

He stepped forward, put both hands on her face, and kissed her. Really kissed her. And all logical thought evaporated from her mind.

"I'm just gonna be out back," he said. "finishing up the raking. Then I'll take you up on that shower."

"Ok," she said. And watched as he turned. "Did you need something?"

"Yeah," he said. "Thank you."

A slow smile spread across her face as she listened to his footsteps going down her stairs.

Noah had just enough cockiness to make him charming.

She finished drying her hair, confident now, that they would figure out what to do next. What to do if her house wasn't exactly guest ready. What to do about her having nothing to eat. What to do about their no strings relationship.

She put on some basic makeup and went back into her bedroom to unpack – something she had neglected to do last night.

CHAPTER
Thirteen

Noah stepped out of Savannah's shower and dried off with the towel she'd left on the counter. Her bathroom smelled like her – jasmine and gardenia.

And, he supposed, he smelled like her, too, now, since he'd just used her soap.

He smiled at the thought of smelling like a girl.

His daughter would give him a really hard time if she knew.

He went to the sink, dug around in his man bag and pulled out his toothbrush and toothpaste. While brushing his teeth, he noticed that the sink had a drip.

He would have to fix that.

He pulled on a fresh pair of jeans and a sweatshirt before wiping up after himself and, walking through her bedroom, went to find Savannah.

Walking around in her house was a little presumptuous, he would be the first to admit.

However, they had spent a great deal of time together lately and it felt, well, normal.

At least to him.

Perhaps he should ask her if she was ok with him being there.

Was it a bit too late?

He found her in her laundry room, sorting clothes and putting a load in the washer.

"Did you know you have a leak in your bathroom?"

She looked over her shoulder. "Oh yeah. I've kind of gotten used to it. I'll try to remember to call a plumber Monday. I don't really want to pay the weekend rate."

"You shouldn't have to pay a plumber for that at all."

She turned and looked at him.

"Where are your tools?" he asked.

"What kind of tools?"

"An adjustable wrench," he said, a sinking feeling in the pit of his stomach.

"I don't think I have one of those. I only have a few tools."

She pulled a basket from a shelf next to her dryer.

She had a couple of screwdrivers, a hammer, and tape measure. No wrench.

"Is this it?" he asked.

"I have some scissors and some glue in the kitchen."

"All right," he said. "I think I saw a hardware store on the way in. I'll run get what I need."

"There's no need to do that," she insisted. "I have a plumbing company that will come out and take care of it."

"You're cute," he said. "But don't you dare pay a plumber to come out and fix that faucet."

"All right," she said, pressing buttons on the washer.

He liked her calmness. Her ability to not worry about things.

He also found it charming that there were basic things she didn't know how to fix and really didn't want to know how to fix.

He always figured that if a woman could fix everything, she would have no use for a man around the house.

"I'll be back in a few minutes."

"Okay," she agreed, shooting him a quick smile before going back to sorting clothes.

He locked the front door behind him. She'd just have to let him back in. And drove the couple of miles to the local hardware store.

He purchased a wrench, some replacement washers, just in case, and some O-rings.

Back in the car, his phone beeped indicating a text message. Thinking it was Savannah adding something to his list, he picked up his phone with a smile on his face.

His smile quickly faded into a frown. It was a text from his daughter.

Daddy, can we talk?

Noah groaned and ran a hand through his hair. Conversations with his daughter were never short and simple. She took after her mother in that way

"Is it urgent?" he dictated to Siri.

Not an emergency.

He'd taught both his wife and daughter a long time ago not to contact him while he was at work unless it was an emergency.

Ever since that time he'd been taxing out on a runway at DIA and got a message from his daughter urging him to come home. She needed help.

It had taken some work, but he'd managed to turn the plane around, get off the plane, and make it home.

The emergency was a lost teddy bear.

The passengers had been told there was a problem with the engine.

Danielle had been five, but that hadn't happened again. Her mother had taken the blame for that one.

But he wasn't working today. This was a Savannah day. As he waged an emotional war with himself, he dictated to Siri.

"Can it wait until Monday?"

No response.

Noah closed his eyes and knocked his head against the back of his seat.

"I'll be home Monday. Let's talk then."

Silence on the other end.

Ok. The text came in finally.

Noah groaned and dialed his daughter's number.

"Hey Baby," he said when she answered.

"Hi Daddy."

"What's wrong honey?"

"Nothing. I just wanted to hear your voice."

"Are you ok? Any trouble with boys?"

Was that a laugh or a snort? "I'm taking a break from boys."

"Seriously? Hold on. I think I dialed the wrong number."

It was a laugh this time. "Maybe not completely, but I'm trying to get ready for graduation."

"I know, Baby, you have lots to do."

"It's a lot."

"Do you need me to help you with anything?"

"Not really."

"Ok, honey, I'll see you next week, ok?"

"Ok, Daddy."

"Think about where you want to go eat."

"I will."

"I love you sweetheart."

"I love you, too, Daddy."

Noah breathed a sigh of relief. He put the car in gear and started back toward Savannah's house.

He did not need to be worried about his family when he was with Savannah. She deserved more than that.

His mood a little heavier, he drove back to Savannah's and stood on the front porch ringing the doorbell like any Joe Blow.

That, too, added to his foul mood.

She opened the door.

"I'll just be a minute," he said.

He went up to the bathroom and after turning off the water supply, tightened the screws and, true to his word, no more leaky faucet.

Savannah came into the bathroom, admired his work, and putting a hand on his shoulder, pressed her lips against his.

Almost like a magic spell, his black mood dissipated and he even forgot why he'd been in a bad mood to start with.

"I suppose I should have asked," he said, "if you minded if I came to visit.

"It might be a little late for that, don't you think? I mean, you've done it now. You've cleaned the yard and fixed a leaky faucet and you've been here, what, less than two hours. I think I might have to keep you."

"Is that so?" he said, nuzzling her neck.

"It is so," she said, her eyes drifting closed.

"We may have to see about that."

"Right," she said, as his lips claimed hers again.

Without taking his lips off hers, he put one arm beneath her shoulders and one beneath her knees and lifted her into his arms.

He took her to the little settee he'd scoped out earlier, purposely avoiding her bed, and sat down with her in his lap

Their lips merged, hungrily. She laced her fingers through his hair and he put one hand behind her neck, his fingers splayed on her cheek, holding her close.

She moaned softly, fueling his desire.

And reminded him of his promise to himself. Not to push her.

Not to rush things.

He pulled his lips away and held her tight against him, feeling her heartbeat pounding against his chest.

"You probably had lots to do today," he murmured against her ear.

"I did have lots to do today," she said.

His fingertips made gentle circles on her back.

"You have something planned, don't you?" she asked, her voice muffled against his chest.

He nudged her back, smiled into her eyes. Tucked her still damp hair behind her ear. "Nothing gets by you, does it?"

"What is it?" she asked.

His expression turned sheepish. "I thought we could go to the game tonight."

Her eyes widened. "Football?"

"Auburn," he said. "We always went to the Auburn games."

"We were college students." She looked askance at him. "You still go to college football games?"

"No," he said. "I haven't been to a college football game since I left here. I usually go to see the Cowboys."

"Oh wow," he felt her pull back imperceptibly.

"It's ok," he said, "I won't make you go."

She laughed and relief shot through him. "It's ok. It might be fun. I haven't been in… a really long time."

He smiled broadly. "The game starts at 3:00."

She sat up. "I really needed to do some things today."

"Ok. I'll help you. What do we have to do?"

"I have to buy groceries. And pick up my meds from the pharmacy. And dry cleaning. Saturdays and Sundays are catch up days."

"We already cleaned the yard and fixed the faucet leak. I think we're on a roll."

"Ok, then," she said. "Let me get myself ready and we'll get started. I think we can make the game."

She disappeared into the bathroom and he breathed a sigh of relief.

She hadn't rejected him.

He knew he had a bad habit of just imposing himself. Somehow it seemed so much easier to get forgiveness than permission. He'd started to call a hundred times. *Hey, how's it going? Want to spend the weekend together?*

Besides, he hadn't been a hundred percent sure he could get away until yesterday.

•　•　•

Savannah straightened her hair and pulled it back into a ponytail, tying a navy-blue bow to hold it in place. The bow was something she'd picked up to give her niece for her birthday, but she could easily pick up another one later. She put on an oversized gray sweater with her jeans and mid-thigh boots.

Studied her appearance in the mirror. The glow on her face could not be manufactured. Her heart was beating a little faster than normal.

She realized she was the most genuinely happy that she had been in a very long time. But she quickly decided that it was unwise to contemplate just how very long that had been.

She went downstairs to find Noah stretched out on her couch, his feet on the coffee table – no shoes. His attention focused on his iPad.

He still set her heart aflutter.

She was still amazed that he was there. In her home.

It was almost like they'd never been apart.

Almost.

"Ready?" she asked.

He put his iPad aside and, standing up, held out his arms.

She went into them.

"Thanks for letting me just barge in like this."

"Did I have a choice?" she asked teasingly.

"Always," he said, seriously.

She pulled back. "I'm happy you're here."

"Are you sure?" he asked.

"Absolutely," she said, smiling.

"Ok, then."

"Let's take my car."

She drove to the pharmacy drive-in first, pointing out things along the way that had changed since he'd been there. Things like the shopping center and the new stadium seating movie theatre.

"Are you hungry?" he asked. "We should eat lunch."

They went to a sandwich shop next. The crowd was boisterous, filled with college students and alumni getting ready for the game.

"They look so young," he commented.

"You really haven't been back since graduation."

"Not once."

The server brought their burgers and fries.

"And you never left," he said.

"I lived in Birmingham for a few years – first with my mom, then in an apartment."

"What brought you back to Auburn?"

"I always thought the lake was where I wanted to live," she said, setting down the ketchup bottle after an unsuccessful battle.

He took the ketchup bottle, got it started, handed it back.

"When I was ready to build, I just knew."

"I love your house."

"Thank you," she said. "I designed it myself."

"No. Now you're kidding me."

She laughed. "I'm not kidding. I took a basic blueprint and changed some things around."

"Now I'm seriously impressed."

"Really?"

"Absolutely. It's one more thing about you that impresses me. You're very impressive."

"I'm just ordinary."

Noah laughed. "I don't think you have an ordinary bone in your body."

She smiled. Took a bite of her burger.

What was he up to? There were so many things she wanted to ask him. So many things he would tell her when he was ready. However… if he didn't start talking soon, she would have to start asking. Perhaps there was no time like the present to start the conversation.

"Tell me about your daughter."

His eyes widened with that deer in the headlights expression that came with unexpected questions. It only fueled her determination to start asking for the information she wanted to know. Nonetheless, she took pity on him. "Does she have a boyfriend?"

"Danielle has had a string of boyfriends since she was fifteen."

Savannah laughed.

"You just think it's funny."

"Well, she is pretty."

"Having a pretty daughter is sometimes actually a curse."

"What about you? Does she have you wrapped around her little finger?"

"Of course," he said. "Though the divorce has put some strain on our relationship."

Now we're getting somewhere.

"Where did you say she was planning to go to college?"

"There are a couple of universities in Dallas that she's looking at."

"Not following daddy's footsteps?"

He scoffed. "Not at all. She's planning to major in nursing."

"That is a bit different from aviation. Does she take after her mother?"

"No," he said, keeping his eyes focused on his plate.

Ok, so obviously this was not a conversation he was ready for.

"Do you know who Auburn is playing?" she asked. Switching a conversation that wasn't going well was one of the things she was good at.

"Ole Miss," he said.

"Uh oh," she said.

"Yeah, we lost last year, but we won the previous two years."

"You have kept up."

He shrugged. Smiled. "I googled it."

She shook her head. "And here I thought you were one of those men who keeps up with his alma mater."

"A lot of people do."

"I know. Especially in a college town."

At least he was distracted now from the mention of his soon to be ex-wife.

A few minutes later, the server brought the ticket. "Who gets the honor?"

Noah took the ticket. "It seems dating has changed over the years."

"Maybe she didn't think we were dating."

"Really?" He leaned across table, put his hand over hers. "Then we need to do more things to let people know that we're a couple."

"You want people to think we're a couple?"

He smiled wickedly. "I think we make a cute couple."

Unsure what to say, she allowed him to lace their fingers together.

She most definitely had questions to be answered.

Their next stop was the grocery store. Savannah had a habit of bringing a list with her, but she'd forgot and left it on the counter. So, as Noah pushed the cart, she picked up the necessary things she could remember that she needed. She didn't have to travel next week, so she bought vegetables for salads, yogurt, and multi-grains.

"Do you need anything?" she asked as they approached the checkout counter.

"Do you have eggs?"

"I think so."

"I'll grab a carton, just in case," Noah said, and headed back to the dairy section.

"I'll wait here," Savannah said as Noah headed back to get the eggs.

The line was unusually long, but then it was game day.

As she waited, a man in his mid-forties wearing navy scrubs walked up to her.

"Savannah?" he asked.

She turned. It took a moment, but she recognized him from one of her early clinic assignments. What was his name? He was a nurse practitioner. "Yes," she said, putting on her professional smile. "Hi, how are you?"

"I'm good."

"It's been awhile. Are you still at the family clinic?"

"Unfortunately, yes," he said with a laugh. "So... you stopped coming around."

"Yeah," Savannah said. "I got reassigned."

"Oh. That's too bad. I was hoping we could do lunch or even coffee."

Savannah saw Noah coming toward her out of the corner of her eye. "Oh, well, that would have been nice. But I've got to run for now. It was good to see you."

Noah came up next to her. "I got some cheese, too," he said.

The line moved and Savannah began putting things on the counter.

"I'll see you around, Savannah," the nurse practitioner said.

"Sure," she said, turning with a quick smile in his direction. "Later."

He went to the next checkout line and out of earshot.

Noah helped her put the groceries on the counter and waited while she checked out.

Together they carried the bags to the car. Savannah didn't see the nurse practitioner again. Relieved to have gotten out of that situation, she took her place behind the wheel.

Noah had been quiet since they'd checked out.

"Who was that guy?"

Savannah didn't even try to play dumb. She knew exactly who he was talking about. "I don't even remember his name. I think he's a nurse practitioner at one of the clinics I used to go to in Birmingham."

"And he recognized you."

She backed out and pulled out of the parking lot. "I guess it's a hazard of the job."

"I have that, too, sometimes."

"Job hazards?"

"Yeah. Flight attendants. Sometimes they take advantage of access to pilots. I guess doctors do that with drug reps, too."

"Way more often than I would like."

"Do you enjoy your job?"

"I do," she said. "In spite of the job hazards."

"That's important."

He was being far too quiet. "Should we go ahead to the stadium?" she asked, checking the time.

"Sure.

"Do you?" She turned on her blinker and got on the highway. "Do you enjoy your job?"

"I like flying."

"I don't think that's exactly the question."

"No, you're right. It's not. I was waiting for the right time to tell you."

"What is it, Noah?"

"I turned in my resignation this week."

"What? Why?"

"I got a better offer," he said, with a tentative smile on his face.

"This is kind of a big deal."

"I suppose it is."

"Are you going to tell me about this better offer?"

"I'm going to be doing contract work."

She wracked her memory. "I don't remember you wanting to do contract work. I mean, you mentioned it last week, but I didn't think you were serious. All I remember is you wanting to fly for the airlines."

"It seems like it's time for a change."

"Do you have clients set up? Or connections?"

He went over the highlights of his deal with Sam.

"Noah, that sounds awesome. It'll give you more flexibility, right?"

"That's the plan."

"Are you excited about it?"

"I'm a little apprehensive about leaving behind the security, but yeah, I'm looking forward to it."

It seemed like there was something he wasn't telling her, but she would have to ask him later. They pulled up to the stadium and she focused on finding a place to park.

Tailgaters were everywhere. The smell of different foods reminded Savannah of a county fair. The smells combined with the noise. People yelling. Cheering. The band was warming up somewhere in the distance.

As they made their way through the crowd to the gate, Savannah heard the cheerleaders already getting into high gear.

As they waited in line, a man about Noah's age called out to him.

Noah looked at Savannah. Shrugged.

The man, nonetheless, made his way through the crowds and stood in front of them. "Noah Worthington, right?"

"Yeah, I'm Noah. Do I know you?"

"It's me. Mike."

"Mike?"

"Yeah, Mike from flight class. We flew together."

Savannah actually recognized Mike. Sort of. He was balding now. And much heavier. But she recognized his voice and the way he stood.

She saw the moment Noah's memory clicked and he remembered him. "Mike. Yeah. It's been so long. Hey, this is."

"Savannah," Mike said, pulling her into a hug. "It's good to see both of you guys. How have you been?"

"Good," Noah said. Savannah nodded. "Good. And you?"

"I'm good. I gave up flying."

"Why?" Savannah asked. If her memory served, Mike was one of the better students in Noah's class.

"I went into the Air Force. Did two tours in Iraq and three in Afghanistan."

"Oh wow. That's a lot."

"Yeah, I just retired."

"The crowds don't bother you?" Savannah asked, remembering that most guys coming back from active service avoided crowds at all costs.

"Don't make me go to Wal-Mart," he said with a chuckle. "But I cut my teeth at this stadium. This is comforting to me."

Savannah found that fascinating. She would mention this to one of the psychiatrists she was seeing next week who specialized in PTSD. Of course, Mike may not have PTSD, but with five tours, how could he not have at least residual symptoms? Enough anyway, it seemed, to make him stop flying.

They were inside the gate now. Mike gave Noah a quick hug. A pat on the back. "I got to run now, but I hope I see you around," he said.

"You too, buddy," Noah said. "Hey, thank you for your service."

Mike saluted him. "The pleasure was all mine." He took a step, stopped, and turned back around. "You know. I always knew you two were going to make it as a couple."

Then Mike disappeared in the crowd.

Savannah looked at Noah, but his face was expressionless.

This must be their day to be recognized by people from their past.

Savannah was beginning to see the benefits of her typical quiet evenings at home. "That was kind of odd, seeing him here," she said as they walked toward their seats.

"Yeah," Noah said, still distracted. "I had no idea he'd joined the Air Force."

"He looked like he was handling it well though."

"Mike was always a good guy."

They took their seats. It was nearly time for the game to start.

"I guess you got your wish," she said.

"What wish is that?" Noah asked, looking at her now.

"You wanted people to think we're a couple."

Fourteen

Noah wasn't a big fan of college football. He had gone to a few Dallas Cowboy games over the years, but it was more of a networking thing than a love of football. It had just occurred to him that now that he was going to be relying on referrals for business, he was probably going to have to start doing a lot more of this. The idea did not exactly thrill him.

He'd brought Savannah to the game, hoping to awaken more memories of their time together for her.

Noah didn't need any awakenings. He had very vivid memories of their time together and wanted to pick up where they left off

Savannah, however, was going to take a bit more convincing.

He had to tell her what had happened with Claire. Talk more about why he had left her so abruptly.

She was being so forgiving. He hated to bring up something that might awaken old wounds. How had it been for her? Her mother had said Savannah had waited for him. Noah felt like such a cad for the way he had treated her. She'd done absolutely nothing wrong

She'd been perfect.

If she'd left him that way, he wasn't so sure he would have been all that forgiving. Would he have welcomed her back so easily? Somehow he didn't really know.

It must have been hard for her to bring up the topic of his ex-wife. Soon to be ex-wife.

He suddenly regretted bringing her here. They should be sitting somewhere with him explaining everything to her.

But she seemed to be having such a good time. Perhaps the memories of their time as college students – back when Noah had insisted they go to all the football games, were good for her. Heck, she'd built a house on the lake where they had spent so much time.

Perhaps the memories weren't painful for her like they were for him. He should really try and find out how she did it.

He returned her smile. Squeezed her hand.

He'd brought her here. He needed to get himself together. Later, after the game, at dinner, they could talk.

Then she could decide if she wanted to continue to see him. It was only fair that he give her the straight story before he spent the night at her house.

Before they got in too deep again.

Something told him, however, that it was a little late to be worried about being fair to Savannah. He'd crossed that bridge long ago.

He watched Savannah more than he watched the game. He was fascinated by her approachability. His soon to be ex-wife had also been beautiful, but in more of an ice princess kind of way.

Over the course of the game, Savannah had conversations with the woman in front of them, the guy sitting to her left, and the elderly gentleman sitting behind them. She had a way with people that he found spellbinding.

Noah was ready for the game to end. He wanted to talk to her. To clarify some things. And, he had to admit, he wanted her alone.

By the time they finally got to the restaurant, Noah was beginning to think he'd missed his opportunity to talk to her.

There was a line, of course, at the restaurant, so they waited for their table in the crowded bar. They managed to snag two bar stools and Noah ordered her a cosmopolitan and a crown on the rocks for him.

They could barely hear each other with all the noise from people around them.

"Are you ok?" she asked, leaning close to his ear.

"I'm ok," he said.

"You seem a little edgy today."

"I wanted to talk to you about some things, but there hasn't been a chance."

She lowered her eyelashes and sipped her drink. She remained quiet while they waited for their table.

Thirty minutes later, they followed the hostess to a much quieter table in the back of the restaurant.

"Will you drink some champagne with me?" he asked.

"Sure," she said. "We're celebrating your new job."

He nodded. Savannah should have become a psychologist.

He told her so.

She laughed. "No thank you. I think I've had enough school."

"You're not too old," he said.

"I couldn't afford to be a student. I have a house note, a car lease. You know, all the usual things."

The idea had wound itself into his head, though, and he couldn't shake it. "But if you didn't have all those things, you think it would be something you would consider?"

"I don't know. Maybe." She broke a piece of bread, dabbed some butter on it, and chewed slowly.

He decided to let it go for now. But he would come back to it later. "What are you in the mood for?" he asked.

"The blackened salmon with hollandaise."

"That sounds good. I was looking at that too."

The server came back and he ordered a shrimp cocktail along with their entrees.

Alone at last.

He took her hand, laced his finger through hers.

"Something's been bothering you today," she said.

"See," he pointed out. "psychologist."

She shook her head. Looked the other way. "No. I just know you."

"That's sort of what I wanted to talk to you about."

"Ok," she said, turning back, her green eyes meeting his.

Noah swallowed the lump in his throat. He didn't want to mess up what they had now while dealing with the past. But he didn't want the past to tarnish what they had now.

"I'm sorry," he said.

"For what?"

"I'm sorry for leaving you without an explanation."

"Noah," she said, her voice full of compassion.

"No. Let me say it. I was a jerk. We had it all and I just walked away."

"You had a good reason."

"No. I didn't have a good reason. I had my father. But in the end, I'm the one who did it."

"Your father pressured you."

"He threatened to cut me off from my inheritance."

Her fingers grew still. Pressed against his. "How significant was that?"

"Not worth leaving you."

"Noah," she said, searching his eyes. "What was the significance of you losing your inheritance?"

"It was a lot," he said. She narrowed her eyes. "But I didn't take any of it. At least not until after he died."

"Why? Why didn't you take it Noah? After giving up your life, why didn't you take it?"

He lowered his gaze. Felt her nail pressing into his hand now. "I didn't do it for me."

She released his hand. Sat back. Even out of the corner of his eyes, he could see the hurt.

"I did it for my mother." There. He'd never told anyone that before. He couldn't face the thought that his father might actually have left his mother destitute.

"I don't understand," she said, leaning forward again.

Noah took a deep breath and looked up. "My father threatened my inheritance, but I told him I didn't care. I told him I was going to marry you and take a job with the airlines."

Her eyes were moist now. "You did take a job with the airlines."

"I did. But I married that girl – the daughter of a business associate that allowed their companies to merge and somehow make my father richer. As a result, my father dropped the threat to leave my mother destitute."

"Would that even be legal?"

"I don't know. I didn't check it out. You met my father, but you didn't see that side of him. That side that got whatever he wanted."

He swallowed the rest of his drink. "After I got back from the honeymoon, I told my father to go to hell. I wanted nothing to do with his company or his money. And I didn't. I went to work for the airlines and lived off my own money." He scoffed. "That wasn't good enough for Claire. She took money from her father and made sure we lived up to par. She was never happy."

Savannah sat back. Her drink forgotten, melting. "You think your father would have done that to your mother?"

"No, I don't think so now. But at the time, I didn't know. At the time, I believed him when he threatened to. I don't know. I guess I thought he would leave her."

"That's awful."

"It was pretty bad. I wasn't going to do it until he pulled her into it. Then I was too ashamed to tell you. I couldn't look at you and break your heart."

Tears slipped down her cheeks. She wiped them away. "I guess if you don't see it, it isn't real," she said, with a watery laugh.

"I guess so. I was young. And dumb."

"It was a long time ago, Noah," she said.

"It feels like yesterday. And yet forever ago."

She nodded. "I know what you mean."

Their entrees arrived and both of them picked at their food.

"Did you love her?" she asked.

Noah scoffed. "How could I?"

"You stayed with her for almost twenty years. You must have felt something for her."

"The agreement was that we stay married for eight years. But ultimately it was for the child. Danielle. I stayed for my daughter. I knew that if I left, they would find a way to keep her from me."

"I'm so sorry, Noah."

"I was ashamed to tell you. Even now. I'm not proud of how it all went down."

"It wasn't your fault."

"I never should have left you."

"You didn't have a choice."

Noah pushed his plate aside. This had been a bad idea. He never should have told her about his family. He should have let the past die with the passage of time.

All he'd wanted to do was to start over with Savannah.

To begin again.

But here she was, trying to comfort him for doing the thing that had caused her so much pain.

He froze at the thought that occurred to him.

Perhaps he had been the one in pain. Much more than she was. Savannah was a resilient person. Maybe she had just moved on.

"What about you?" he asked. "What must you have thought of me?"

"I didn't know what to think."

"But you had to wonder. I mean, at what point did you figure out I wasn't coming back?"

Did he have the right to ask these questions? He didn't know.

He probably didn't even deserve to have her sitting here with him now.

But she was.

"I don't know," she said. "I looked for you, but I didn't know how to find you. That was before everything and everybody was on the Internet. You might be fortunate in that."

He barely breathed as she talked.

"I didn't date anyone. Not until I'd graduated and gone to work. I put everything into my studies. I don't think I ever really gave up on you."

"There was no one serious for you?"

"Oh sure. I was with one guy for five years. I guess he was the most serious relationship I had."

"You never got married."

"It never worked out for me."

"That's my fault," he said.

"Don't be crazy. I just spent all my time working. I didn't have time for anyone hanging around all the time."

He suspected there was more, but he didn't push her on it. Not now. Maybe not ever.

He'd done enough damage.

Was it possible for them to start over and build on the embers of what had been before?

When Savannah spoke, it was as though she'd gotten into his thoughts. "Noah, we're the same people we were twenty years ago, but time has passed. Experience has changed us, molded us into two different people. I think we have a good foundation that we can build on if we want to. But for all intents and purposes, we have to let the past go. If we're going to move forward, we both have to let it go. Thank you for sharing yours with me. It helps me to understand what happened. I needed to know. I needed to know that it wasn't just some careless thing that you did. But now is now."

"You're a wise woman, Savannah Richards."

"I'm not wise. I've just had a lot of time to think about this."

"I guess that's what I wanted you to know. I wanted to let you know that I didn't want to leave you. I needed to know if you could forgive me."

"I forgave you a long time ago."

He smiled. "Thank you."

He took her hand, kissed her palm. "Here's to tomorrow," he said.

As she brewed decaf coffee, Savannah poured a touch of amaretto into two mugs. Her hand shook a little as she poured. She and Noah had been close in college. Both emotionally and physically.

She had been young and he hadn't pressured her beyond the normal fooling around, usually with her roommate on the other side of the room. Fortunately for them, the roommate snored loudly enough that they knew when she was asleep and when she was awake.

Now that they were adults, at what point would Noah expect more? Their relationship – their current relationship, was evolving. She felt it in the way he kissed her.

She didn't know why she was nervous.

Perhaps she felt there was more at stake now.

They were no longer just a couple of college kids fooling around.

No, she mused, they were undefined.

And undefined meant no strings.

Savannah had tried the whole no strings thing. It hadn't worked for her.

She didn't know why she was so nervous. *It's just Noah.*

Noah, whom she trusted.

Noah, whom she loved.

Noah, who had a propensity to walk out of her life with no explanation.

Going back into the living area, she handed one mug to Noah and kept one for herself.

"Spicy," he said, with a wink after tasting her concoction.

"Amaretto is good for digestion, right?" she said.

"That's what my grandfather always said."

She sat next to him, their thighs touching. Was everything he ever told her engraved upon her memories from so long ago?

She shook her head.

She had been young and impressionable.

"What's going on in that beautiful head of yours?" he asked.

She chuckled.

"A whole lot of nothing important."

"Huh. A whole of something. Always."

"Maybe. Just enjoying the moment."

He glanced at her quizzically.

"That's not your enjoying the moment expression."

She laughed. Set her mug down. "Maybe I just need a little distraction," she said, as she wrapped her arms around him.

He set his mug down next to hers. "I'm nothing, if not good at distraction."

He kissed the corner of her mouth first, sending her nerve endings into electric shock. The pressed his lips against hers. Held them there until she couldn't stand it any longer. She moved her lips against his. And he responded.

He shifted her into his lap. Tilted her back until he was on top of her. He nudged her lips apart with his tongue and while caressing her cheek, tasted the roof of her mouth with his tongue.

She threaded her fingers through his hair, pulling him closer.

With one hand caressing her cheek, his other hand roamed down her arm, settling on her waist. His lips left hers long enough to linger over her cheeks, her eyelids, then back to her lips.

She couldn't get enough of him.

He shifted. Nearly fell off the sofa.

Savannah chuckled. "I think we're too old to make out on the sofa."

"Never," he said. "But I wouldn't mind if we got a little sleep… in the bed."

"All right," she said, allowing him to pull her up.

They went upstairs and Savannah paused at her bedroom door. "Do you want the guest room?"

He raised an eyebrow. "Even if I promised to be good?"

"Ok," she said, "but only for sleeping. Otherwise, we're back to the sofa."

"That's a funny rule," he said.

"I thought it was pretty good."

Nonetheless, after he wrapped his arms around her and nestled against her, Savannah was soon sound asleep.

At four a.m. Noah's cell phone rang. It was a ringtone on his phone she hadn't heard before. Pleasant, almost like Christmas music or church bells.

Noah stirred, but didn't wake up. Savannah waited, but no message came through. After a few minutes, she went back to sleep.

At six thirty-five, his cell phone rang again. This was a different ring tone. Not urgent, but not as pleasant either.

This time Noah woke and looked at his phone. He didn't answer it.

When a text message followed, he jumped out of bed and paced to the window and back while he returned the call.

Savannah kept her eyes closed, pretending to be asleep.

"Claire" he said. "What is it?"

"Where?"

"Is that all you know?"

"I'll be right there."

He went into the other bedroom and Savannah could hear him getting dressed.

She got up, put on her robe. Went into the bathroom and brushed her teeth.

When she came out, she heard Noah downstairs. The front door opened and she heard his car unlock.

A couple of minutes later, he sprinted back upstairs, stopped when he saw her standing there. "I have to go," he said. "I'll call you."

Savannah watched as he raced back downstairs and slammed the door. Within seconds, she heard his car backing out of the driveway.

Stunned, she went downstairs and checked the lock. He'd locked the door behind him, at least. Realizing she hadn't set the alarm last night, she keyed in the code.

She stared down the driveway, but it was though he had never even been there.

She clenched her fists, then rubbed her forehead.

The grandfather clock tolled seven o'clock.

Awake, she went into her kitchen and made a cup of coffee. Then sat down at the little breakfast table in her little breakfast nook. She rarely took the time to watch the magic of daybreak. But today she watched the lake as it ever so slowly became illuminated by the rising sun.

Alone.

And unlike the sunrise she'd watched at Mackinac Island, even in her own home, the house she loved, she did not want to be alone.

Sometime. Somehow. Her heart had shifted back to once again accommodate Noah. It had been seamless. So seamless that she hadn't even noticed when it happened.

Whatever may come from here, didn't matter.

She was in love with Noah Worthington.

Always had been.

Always would be.

Fifteen

Noah sat on the leather sofa and stared at the monitors. His beautiful daughter Danielle had tubes and wires all over her body.

He watched the beeping of the monitor that told him her heart rate was ok. With each blip of the monitor, his anxiety relaxed only to increase in the next moment.

He could see Danielle's mother through the glass. Talking to the nurses. That was her way of coping. Gathering information.

Noah just wanted to hover over his daughter, and wait. Wait until she was better.

Until her eyes opened.

And she could tell him herself what had happened.

They said she attempted suicide.

Noah didn't believe it.

Couldn't believe it.

He'd just spoken to her yesterday. While he was at Savannah's. He'd said he would call her back and they could talk next week.

How was he to know that there might not be a next week?

Why hadn't he heard the pain in her voice?

Why hadn't he listened?

He reminded himself again that it wasn't true. His daughter wouldn't do that. It had to have been an accident. They had gotten it wrong. Or someone had done this to her. Heaven help the person who did this to her.

As soon as she opened her eyes and told him who did it.

There would be hell to pay.

He felt the tears running down his cheeks. He didn't bother to wipe them away.

He had a missed call from his daughter this morning. But that was something he would have to think about later.

His soon to be ex-wife came back into the hospital room. Took one look at him and handed him a tissue.

"They said she should pull through," she said.

"Should." He focused on the monitors. Everything was stable. He pulled his gaze from the monitors long enough to focus on Claire's face. "She will."

"Yes," Claire said. "She will."

"Did you know about this? That she was in emotional pain?"

"I guess I had an idea."

"Why didn't you tell me?"

"You weren't there, Noah."

"It doesn't matter. You have a phone."

"You might recall that you don't answer your phone when I call."

Noah shifted back to watching the steady beep of the monitor. This wasn't about Claire. He wouldn't allow her to make it about herself.

This was about Danielle.

Claire had found her in Danielle's bedroom. Thought she was asleep. An hour later, when she didn't respond, she'd called the ambulance.

They said they found an empty bottle of Xanax and a half empty bottle of crown… and a two liter of cola.

Noah knew the crown belonged to him or had belonged to him before he left. The Xanax belonged to Claire. Someone had exposed Danielle to crown and coke.

So, together, he and Claire had done this to her.

In more ways than one.

He scooted his chair closer and took her small hand in his. The one thing he and Claire had done right. The one thing that prevented him from regretting his marriage to Claire. The only thing.

They had a meeting scheduled with a psychologist sometime that afternoon. Whenever she made her rounds.

Just yesterday, he'd urged Savannah to become a psychologist. Was it some connection with his daughter that had him needing that from the one person he would have trusted to take care of his daughter?

Whatever it took, he would get Danielle through this. He vowed to himself in that moment, he would make it right. No matter what.

With her hand gripped in his, he lay his head on the side of the bed and for the first time in over thirty-six hours, his body overruled his mind and he slept.

Noah woke in a panic. But Danielle was still lying in the bed, the monitors beeping, her hand in his. He gently unleashed her hand and rubbed his face. Looked around.

He was alone with her. No nurse. No Claire.

He leaned over and pressed his lips against her forehead. "Wake up," he whispered. "Please wake up."

He almost promised her he'd never leave again. But Savannah…

Please, not that. Don't make me stay.

"You can come live with me," he said, his eyes tearing up. His beautiful little girl was almost grown. By her standards, she was grown. She would be on her own soon.

Just don't die.

He took his bottle of water to the sink and filled it with water. Not up to his usual standards, but this was not his usual scene.

He drank water. Paced.

Stared at the monitors.

A young woman, mid-thirties, knocked on the door. Smiled.

"Mr. Worthington?"

"Yes," he said, taking a deep breath.

"I'm Tara. I'm a psychologist." She held out her hand. He shook her hand.

"Come in," he said, "Please take the chair."

"Let me grab another one," she said, turned back to the door and a moment later, returned with another chair.

Noah took the chair, sat it next to the one he'd been camped out in.

"How are you holding up?" she asked.

Noah shook his head. Felt the lump in his throat. "Not very well."

"That's understandable. Is there anything I can get you?"

He shook his head. Stared at Danielle.

"The doctor said it might be a few days before she wakes up."

"They told me she might not," he said, his voice barely audible.

"No one has said anything like that to me."

Her voice was soothing. Calm.

Like Savannah.

"What can I do?" he asked.

"You can first of all, take care of yourself. When she wakes up, she's gonna need you. A lot."

He turned, met her gaze.

"Are you able to sleep on that couch?" She nodded toward the couch strewn with his bag, a pillow, and a blanket.

"I don't know. I guess."

"Then I suggest you get as much sleep as you can."

"She might need something."

"If she needs something, the nurses will know."

He turned back stare at Danielle. At the monitors.

"This is not your fault."

Noah's mind couldn't let go of the crown he'd left in the house.

"You didn't know. Now that you know, you can do something."

"What?"

"She's going to need counseling. Counseling by herself, but also with you and your wife."

"We're divorcing."

"I know. But you're still her parents."

"Poor kid."

"No. She's very fortunate. I spoke to Claire a few minutes ago. She's willing to do what needs to be done. In spite of the divorce."

"I'll do anything."

"You'll need to be here for a while."

"I can do that."

Oh God. He had a new job. He had a new girlfriend. His life was crashing down around him.

Without Danielle, nothing else mattered. Not the job. Not even… Savannah. He turned his head so she couldn't see the moisture in his eyes.

"You're in a lot of pain right now."

"I just need her to wake up."

"She will Noah. Just don't give up. I'll be back tomorrow." She handed him a business card. My cell number is on the back of this card. "Call me if you need anything at all."

He needed to call Savannah. He needed to talk to Savannah.

He couldn't talk to Savannah.

It was starting all over again.

Noah took the psychologist's advice. Tara. Interesting name. One that people would remember. A nurse had brought him a warm blanket and he had slept through most of the night, waking only a couple of times to check on Danielle.

The sun slanted across his face, bringing him to a startled awakening.

Something was different.

He sat up. On alert now.

There were no nurses in the room. Danielle lay in her bed, the monitors beeping.

He stood up, went to stand next to her at the bed. Picked up her hand.

And she opened her eyes and looked at him.

"Danielle," he said, putting his arms around her. "Baby, are you ok?"

"You're here," she said.

"Of course I'm here, Baby."

Tears leaked from her eyes.

"How do you feel?"

"Not so good. Can I get some water?"

"I don't know," he said. "I have to call a nurse. Don't go anywhere."

He rushed out the door, called, "She's awake," to no one in particular and bounced back into the room.

"There's a button here somewhere," he said, searching her wires. The nurse had shown it to him yesterday.

He mashed the button. "Somebody will come," he said. "Are you ok?"

"I'm ok, Daddy." She smiled and his heart melted.

A nurse stuck her head in the door, then returned shortly with two other nurses. They were joined by the doctor ten minutes later.

Noah watched as she was examined. He should probably call Claire.

Claire could wait. This was his moment with Danielle.

Hopefully, since he supposedly was the one who caused this whole thing, he could have a moment alone with his daughter to make things right.

After they all left, Noah went back to sit next to Danielle. "What happened, Baby?" he asked.

She turned her face away. Her chin trembled. "It was an accident."

"It's ok, Baby. We'll figure it out." He smoothed her hair back from her forehead.

She turned back. Took a deep breath. She looked so much better without the oxygen in her nose. "I feel good though," she said. "Where's mom?"

Noah took Danielle's phone from her handbag in the nightstand and handed it to her. "You call her."

It was an hour before Claire made it to the hospital room. Tara was there thirty minutes sooner.

She asked to meet with Noah and Claire alone.

Noah was reluctant to leave Danielle, but the nurse assured him that she would be ok. Besides they were just going to a room down the hall.

Tara sat facing the two of them. "How are you doing?"

"Good," Claire said.

"Relieved," Noah said.

"You're very fortunate," she said.

They agreed.

"Danielle is a very emotionally troubled young woman."

"But..." Noah said. "She's ok now."

"She tried to take her own life."

Noah sat up straight, ready to defend his daughter. "But she's ok now."

"She's very emotionally distressed," Tara repeated.

Noah felt ill. Looked toward the door. He should get back to her.

"Not at this very moment," Tara told him. "But she needs to be in an inpatient clinic."

Noah couldn't think. Tara kept talking.

"There's a good inpatient hospital in Dallas. I'll make a phone call and have her transferred there as soon as she's released from the hospital here."

"No," Claire said. "I don't want my daughter to be put in a nut house."

"It's not a nut house," Tara said. "It's a reputable psychiatric facility. They'll do a full evaluation, start her on antidepressant medication, and she'll go through both individual and group therapy sessions."

"I won't do it," Claire said.

Tara focused on Noah. "Tara will be eighteen shortly, so we'll put her in the adult unit."

"Why?" Noah asked.

"It's common for people who attempt suicide to feel euphoric after the attempt. Danielle just woke up, but I fully expect this to happen. She's already saying that she feels better."

Noah nodded. "She told me she feels better."

"After the euphoria wears off, she'll try again."

"Try again? You mean attempt suicide again?"

"Yes. And many people are successful on their second attempt."

"Oh my God," Claire said.

"I'm not saying this to alarm you. I'm saying this to let you know how crucial it is that she receive the best care possible. You want your daughter to have the best care, don't you?" Her gaze was locked on Noah.

Noah glanced at Claire. He knew Claire would fight this to the bitter end. She'd rather have a dead daughter than a daughter who was in the "nut house." This didn't surprise him. He knew the importance of social appearances to her.

"We don't have to tell anyone where she is," Noah said. "No one has to know."

"How are they not going to know?" Her voice was verging on hysterical. "They already know she's in the hospital."

"You say she's at a retreat," Tara suggested. "Or on a trip to Europe to rest and recover."

Claire appeared to consider this option.

"I know you both love your daughter dearly."

Noah nodded. "I'll do anything for her."

"Good," Tara said. "Because I'm gonna need you both to be available every day to meet with her and her therapist for the next few weeks."

Noah knew this was what had to be done. He didn't even mention his new job. He would call Sam and explain the situation. Unlike Claire, Noah did not have qualms about anyone knowing that his daughter needed help.

Tara went back to Danielle's room with them and explained her plan to Danielle.

Noah sat on the couch and watched his daughter cry and resist. "I'm not crazy," she said. "I promise I won't do it again."

So much for his hope that someone had tried to kill her. That would have so much easier to solve. Now he had no one to beat up on except himself.

After a while, Danielle realized she had no choice in the matter.

And cried herself to sleep.

Claire went to the window and stared outside.

"Can you stay?" she asked. "I'm supposed to meet the girls for lunch."

Noah stared blankly at her. He had actually married this woman. Had given her so many good years of his life.

"Before you go," he said, "we need to talk." He patted the couch next to him.

Surprise on her face, she sat. Waited.

"Let's talk about your email," he said.

"Oh that. I had forgotten all about it."

"What was that about?"

"I just thought we should stay together for Danielle's sake."

"When you wrote that, you knew she was struggling."

"I did."

"Then it really had nothing to do with you having feelings for me."

Her lips twitched in that way that meant she had so much to say, but would say nothing.

"We're not getting back together," he said.

"What about Danielle?"

"Danielle will get through this. She'll have divorced parents like all her friends. She'll get past it."

"What about…"

Noah ran his hands over his face. "What about what, Claire? What about what you'll tell your friends? Tell them you're divorced. You'll be the topic of conversation for a minute, then no one will care anymore. They'll forget all about you. Maybe you'll even find someone who meets your standard and get married again. I hope you do." He stood up. Walked around to the other side of the bed.

"Go," he said. "I'll stay here with Danielle. We'll work out a schedule when you get back so we're not here at the same time. I wish you well."

Finished with his tirade, he watched his soon to be ex-wife quietly gather up her Gucci bag and, with a flip of her blonde hair, kissed her sleeping daughter on the cheek, and walked through the door. She told the nurse good-bye as they passed in the hallway.

But no word to her husband. No thank you for sitting with our daughter while I go have a nice lunch. No wish you well, too.

Nothing.

Noah went back to his chair and sat down.

Such was the way of his life for the last twenty years.

The nurse walked in, took one look at him. "Are you ok, hon?" she asked.

Noah looked up at her. Smiled. "Yeah," he said. "Actually I am."

Sixteen

It was December 17. Saturday.

Savannah rolled over and turned the alarm on her phone off. It had gone off every Saturday morning at 5:00 a.m. since they got back from Mackinac. Savannah was very careful with her alarms on her phone.

She was one hundred percent certain she hadn't set it.

And since she hadn't set it, she didn't turn it off. Before she turned it off, she wanted to figure out how it got set to start with.

She lay on her back and stared into the darkness. Listened to the rain slamming against the window panes.

One week to get ready for Christmas. She hadn't decorated. Not that she ever decorated all that much. She spent Christmas at her mother's house or her sister's, so there wasn't really any need.

However, she hadn't bought a single gift either. That was out of character. She usually did her shopping online the day after

Thanksgiving. This year, she'd sat at the computer doing some research instead of shopping.

Doctor's offices pretty much closed for the season, so she had no meetings scheduled until after the new year.

She had two weeks to do whatever she wanted.

The problem was she really had nothing she wanted to do.

She hadn't heard from Noah since the night he'd gotten the call from his wife in the middle of the night. Something about his daughter, she was certain.

Her fingers had hovered over his phone number a thousand times. She had written him little text messages a hundred times and deleted them.

The bottom line was Noah was still married. His wife beckoned and he left her in the middle of the night.

Then he didn't contact her.

For Savannah, that spoke volumes.

After a couple of weeks, she decided she wouldn't hear from him again.

She told herself she was ok with it.

That's how Noah operated.

He breezed in, upset a girl's life, then like the wind, he was gone.

Chasing Noah was like chasing the wind.

Perhaps in another twenty years, they would meet up again. Perhaps their timing would be better and they would have another go at it.

In the meantime, there was no point in worrying about it.

Unfortunately, her brain worried over it constantly. Trying to make sense of something that made absolutely no sense.

Doubtless he had family things to do.

Maybe he wasn't even really getting divorced. Maybe he just told her that to make her feel better about spending time with him.

Out of all her theories, out of all her crazy explanations, that was the one that made the most sense to her.

She'd been played.

He lived in a world of his own. A world that she wasn't part of. It was, after all, why he'd left her before.

It really was less painful this way. It just would have been nice if he would tell her ahead of time how many days she should wait before declaring him MIA.

After Mackinac, he'd shown up after a week. So, apparently a week was within range. But how long?

One week to get ready for Christmas.

Today was as good a day as any to get it knocked out. The rain was forecast to be out before noon.

She would get dressed and head out to the mall with everyone else.

If all else failed, she could get everyone gift cards.

She dragged herself out of bed, threw on a robe, and went downstairs to make a latte.

With latte in hand, she started back upstairs. She would drink her coffee and do some preliminary scouting on the internet for gifts. She had to have some kind of a plan after all.

The doorbell rang when she had her foot on the first step.

She nearly dropped her coffee and fell off the stairs.

Who could possibly be at her door at 5:30? A spurt of fear shot through her. Something could be wrong with her mother or her sister.

Somebody must have died.

Or else somebody wanted to kill her.

She inched to the door, peeked out. Noah?

She stepped back. Hallucinating.

The doorbell rang again.

"Ok," she muttered. Maybe it's not a hallucination. "Noah?" she called.

"Yeah, it's me. Can I come in? It's raining out here."

She peeked out again. Squinted. "Savannah," he said.

She keyed in the alarm code and opened the door. Noah stood there, dripped from the rain that had drenched him. How long had he been standing there?

"What is it with you and phones?" she asked.

"I'm old fashioned," he said.

"You're an idiot." She opened the door wider, and stepped back. "Come in out of the rain."

He stepped inside. Pulled a single red rosebud from under his trench coat. Held it out to her.

She took it from him, feeling a little clutch in her heart.

Noah was her weak spot. Her drug of choice.

One look from him and she was off the wagon.

She wasn't, however, about to let him know it. "I'll get you a towel," she said, going to the guest bathroom downstairs and returning with a dry towel.

He had already shed his raincoat and shoes. "I knew it was going to rain today. Of all days."

She looked askance at him. What did he even mean? "How did you even know I'd be up this early?"

He smiled that mysteriously cocky smile that sent her heart rate into high gear. "Don't you always get up at 5:00 on Saturdays?"

Her alarm clock. Mackinac.

Seriously?

She folded her arms. "If you tell me you had this planned for all these, what, nearly two months, I'm going to...."

He grinned. "You're going to what?" He took a step forward.

She stepped backwards, but bumped up against the stair post. Then he was standing next to her, blocking her from moving.

"I hope you were going to say you're going to kiss me. After all, I had a long trip."

"You live for travel, Any excuse."

"Can't deny it," he said. "Nonetheless..."

He bent his head, pressed his lips against hers.

She moaned, leaned into the kiss. *And this is what I live for.*

He deepened the kiss and their arms wrapped around each other. She couldn't get close enough.

His cell phone rang and he jumped. It was odd. Noah was usually exceptionally calm. And rarely worried about his phone.

"I have to take this," he said, walking back to the kitchen and answering the phone.

Savannah stood where he left her. Her lips tingling from his kiss. Her emotions running rampant.

No. I won't do this. I won't allow him to keep doing this to me.

The words hurt her. Even in her head. And tears gathered in her eyes.

She dropped to the step, gathering her robe around herself. Shivering.

Felt the tears dropping onto her hands. She swiped at them. Not caring.

A few minutes later, he came back, saw her sitting there, saw the tears on her face. He rushed to her side. Pulled her to him. She didn't resist. Allowed him to cradle her against his chest as the dam broke free and she sobbed against him.

"Hey," he said, rocking her. "What is this? Sh. What is it, my love?"

Her chin trembled. She sobbed harder.

"I can't," she said, but couldn't catch her breath.

He held her, made soothing noises, and rode out the storm with her.

Savannah's pain must have been a culmination of past hurt, because the intensity was unlike any she could ever remember experiencing. She felt like she was going to explode from the inside.

She grasped at him, holding onto him for dear life.

Then, just like that, it was over.

She had no more tears.

He continued to gently rub her back.

They were both soaked now. She was soaked not only from her tears, but from his wet clothes.

She disentangled herself from him and was surprised that she still held the rose in her hand. A drop of blood landed on her robe and she saw that her hand was bleeding from a thorn.

A perfect illustration of what Noah was doing to her.

"Are you going to tell me what just happened?" he asked.

"I can't," her chin trembled. *I won't cry again.* "I don't cry around anyone else. Ever."

"I'm not sure what that says for my character," he said wryly.

"You must think I'm pathetic."

"The thought never crossed my mind."

She steadied herself. Plunged forward before she lost her nerve again. "I can't do this," she said. "I can't be your... girlfriend."

She couldn't look at him. She expected him to walk out right then.

But he didn't move.

"Ok," he said.

She looked up. The calm Noah she knew so well was back. So, he didn't care. The thought turned her tears to anger.

"You can't just come around here when you feel like it. What am I supposed to do? Just wait around until you show up again?"

"I had something to do," he said.

"We all have things to do." She wiped the blood on her robe. Handed the rose back to him.

"Look at me," he put a hand under her chin. Kissed her lightly on the lips.

She kept her face blank. At least she hoped it was blank.

"That was my daughter on the phone."

"You don't have to explain anything to me."

"My daughter just got out of the hospital last night – the psychiatric hospital."

"Oh Noah," she was flooded by remorse. "Is she ok?"

"She is now. When I was here and got that call, she was unconscious. She attempted suicide."

"Oh no. Noah." She took his hands.

"I felt responsible. She called me the day before, but I barely had time to talk to her. I told her I'd talk to her later."

"Oh, God. It's my fault."

"Not in a million years. It's no one's fault."

"You went to counseling, too."

He nodded. "She's ok now. I had to stay close for the last few weeks to go to counseling with her every day."

"Wow."

"I wanted. I needed to get through that."

"It's ok. I understand."

"I should have called you. I'm sorry."

"You had something you had to take care of."

He laughed. "Obviously another of my bad choices. But there was something else that had to be resolved before I came back."

"Something else?"

"Yes. It seems we reconnected at a bad time in my life. I needed to get it straightened out."

"And have you?"

He retrieved the bag he'd dropped at the door and sat back down next to her. Pulled out a document, about a quarter of an inch thick, bound with a binder clip at the top.

"Read this," he said.

She wiped her hands on her robe. Took the document from him.

"I'm going to make us some coffee while you read that."

"It might take me awhile," she said.

"You can skim it," he suggested. "Want to sit on the couch?"

She followed him to the couch, took the throw he offered and settled in.

She opened the document and began reading. She could see immediately that it was a divorce settlement.

"Are you sure you want me to read this?" she asked, looking up at him. This is private."

"I need you to read it. I'll be right back."

As she read, he handed her a hot cup of coffee and holding his own cup, sat across from her, watching as she read.

She skimmed a few pages, but read almost all of it word for word.

Thirty minutes later, she clipped the document back together and handed it back to him.

He looked at her expectantly. Savannah wasn't sure what she was supposed to do with this information. Did it change anything?

"You got divorced yesterday," she said.

"That was the other thing I had to take care of. Now you don't have to worry about me lying to you about being married."

"I wasn't worried about that."

"And you're not a good liar."

"Of course I am. Just not with you."

"I think that's a good thing."

"You're a wealthy man, Noah."

"I have enough to get by."

She scoffed. "You have enough to buy, what, twenty more planes?"

"Probably more like ten, but I can only fly one at the time, right?"

"Why are you showing me this?"

He moved to sit next to her. "I want you to know. I don't want any more secrets between us."

"I have some news, too," she said.

"What?"

She went to her little desk where she kept her computer and paid her bills. Picked up an envelope. Handed it to him.

He opened the letter and his face broke into a wide grin. "You're going to be a psychologist."

"Maybe," she said. "I haven't accepted yet. The clinical psychology program is full time. I'd have to quit my job and use my savings to live. It takes about six years since I don't have a master's degree yet. I have to decide if I can do that. If I want to do that."

"I think you should do it."

"Thanks for the vote of confidence, but I don't have your bank account."

He kissed her on the cheek. "It's an honor to be accepted," he said.

"You're right," she agreed. "it is."

She put the letter aside. "So what happens now, with your daughter?"

"She goes back to school. Graduates in May and goes to college."

"Just like nothing happened."

"Better than before."

"And your new business?"

"A slight delay, but it's going. I have my first flight next week."

"It sounds like you're all set."

He grinned. "As I said, I had some things to take care of."

She didn't bother to tell him that a simple text message would have made all the difference. "I didn't think I'd see you again."

He nodded. Held up his hand. "I promise to never, ever

disappear on you again. If I do, you have my permission to send the authorities to look for me because it means foul play."

She laughed.

"I know you don't believe me. And I don't blame you."

"You don't have the best track record."

"I'll make it up to you."

"Ok," she said, but she knew that even though her heart was willing, her head was not so quick to jump on board the Noah wagon.

"So," he said. "In celebration of my newly divorced status, I'd like to take you to dinner tonight."

She hesitated. Hadn't she just told him she couldn't do this anymore?

"Please," he said, holding his hands under his chin. "I promise I'll have you home by midnight."

She laughed. "Ok."

"I'll be back to pick you up at 3:00. Wear something formal."

"Three o'clock?"

"Yep," he glanced at his watch. "You've got plenty of time."

She scowled at him, but he laughed and kissed her on the mouth. "Lock the door," he said, as he went outside, closing the door behind him.

She followed him to the door, which he had already locked, clicked the deadbolt, and set the alarm.

Glanced at the grandfather clock in her foyer.

She had enough time.

Energized in spite of herself, she sprinted upstairs, and ran bath water.

Comforted by the hot water, she digested all that she had learned about Noah that morning.

She didn't know if it changed anything. It hurt her head too much to even try to sort it all out.

He wanted to take her to dinner. To celebrate and she would go with him. There would be plenty of time for Christmas shopping tomorrow. Or the next day. A light week. A vacation really.

Wishing for a New York blow dry bar, she dried her own hair and put in some hot rollers for a more formal look.

He wanted formal. She could do formal.

She ate a quick lunch of grapes and cheese, then studied her closet.

There was really no choice. She had recently purchased a dress for no particular reason other than the fact that she'd fallen in love with it on sight. The sales lady had called it a mermaid dress. It was white silk, strapless, with a daring neckline. The sequined asymmetrical sash at the hip emphasized her slim figure.

Since it as too early to get dressed, she checked her email and skyped her sister.

"You look good," her sister complimented.

"Thanks." Savannah studied her sister. Charlotte rarely wore make-up and kept her hair pulled back in a pony tail. Her sister was wearing full make-up including eye liner and lipstick. And her long hair fell softly around her face. "So do you," she said, her thoughts churning. Why would her sister be dressed in the middle of the day? "What are you wearing?" she asked, straining to see what her sister wore.

"Just a t-shirt," her sister leaned back, tugged on the collar of her blue shirt. "A date with Noah?"

"What?" How could her sister even remotely know that?

"You look kind of excited and your hair is in those soft curls you only wear when you're dressing up for a date."

"Might not be Noah."

Charlotte shrugged. "Ok, then," her sister played along. "What's his name?"

"Never mind about me," Savannah changed the subject. "Where are you anyway? Why is it so quiet? Did you give the children away?"

"They're off doing their thing. Let's just enjoy the quiet moment, shall we?"

"Of course," Savannah said automatically, but couldn't let go trying to discern what was different about her sister. "Are you at home?"

"Where else would I be? I'm always at home."

Savannah checked her watch. Her sister obviously wasn't in the mood to give up any personal information. "Ok, well, I have to run. We'll talk tomorrow."

Her sister grinned. "Sounds good. Hey."

Savannah waited before she clicked off. "What's up?"

"Have fun and enjoy the moment."

Savannah clicked off and put her sister out of her thoughts. Charlotte always had marched to the beat of her own drum.

Savannah shut down her computer and went to get dressed.

Studying the finished product in the mirror, she decided she was probably over-dressed, but he'd said to go formal, so formal he was getting.

She packed her evening handbag, pulled her phone off the charger, and went downstairs to wait for Noah.

While she waited, she straightened. Shredded her mail.

Checked the window twenty times.

Wondered why they were leaving for dinner so early. Probably driving into Atlanta. Perhaps he had tickets to a play or some such.

It was easy to be full of surprises, she mused when you didn't see someone very often. She wondered what he would be like on a day-to-day basis.

You know what he's like. He's kind and funny. And considerate. And thoughtful. And ever so sexy.

Savannah sighed. The past was in the past. Right now, in this moment, her head was swirling with Noah. The Noah she knew before. The Noah who was in her life now.

He pulled into her driveway at ten minutes to three. Sat in his car for nearly ten minutes before coming to the door. She knew this because she watched him from the window.

Her breath caught as he came up her walkway.

He was incredibly handsome in his black tuxedo. She no longer felt overdressed.

She opened the door and his jaw dropped.

"Wow," he said.

"You're kind of wow yourself. I think divorce agrees with you."

"Nah," he said. "It's the company."

They went to his car, a rented BMW sedan and he helped her get inside.

"Where are we going?" she asked.

He grinned.

"You know I-"

"Don't like surprises," he finished her sentence for her. "I know you don't, but I think you'll like this one."

When they turned down the road toward the airport, it all fit together for her. "I should have known."

"You should have," he agreed. "Like you said, any excuse."

"You're incorrigible."

"That might be why you like me."

She looked at his plane as they drove up. And in that moment, decided to just embrace the fact that she liked everything about him.

She couldn't even be mad at him for more than a few minutes.

"I'm not sure I can get in the plane in this dress."

"Yeah," he said, "I should have had you get dressed when we got there. But I'll help you."

Seated in the plane, Noah did indeed look happy. And it was contagious. She could think of nowhere else she wanted to be and no one else she wanted to be with.

She was amazed, again, at the clear view from the cockpit. Surrounded by glass, it really was like being a bird.

Once they were in the air, he took her hand. "I missed you," he said.

"I missed you," she immediately responded and smiled. "I don't suppose I get any clues as to where we're going?"

"And ruin all the fun?"

It turned out to be a long flight. But the sunset was absolutely gorgeous. It gave a clue, however, to their direction. They were traveling west.

The flight was uneventful. Savannah closed her eyes and relaxed, enjoyed the sway of the plane.

Her eyes opened when they began their descent. She straightened in her seat, searching the land below. Gasped.

Las Vegas.

She turned to Noah, her eyes wide.

"It was on your list, right?"

Savannah's thoughts flew back to their conversation in Starbucks when he'd asked her to name places she wanted to visit. He'd asked for one and she'd given him five. Impressed that he had remembered, she smiled broadly into his eyes, but turned her attention to the view.

Savannah had never flown into Las Vegas at night. The view was outstanding. The lights. She could almost feel the energy from way up here.

"So is this my date to the casino?" she asked as their wheels hit the ground.

"Something like that. Since it's early," he said, "do you mind if we have drinks before we have dinner? Our reservation isn't until 6:00 local time."

She shrugged. Smiled. "I'm with you."

A limo waited for them. Savannah didn't comment, but this was certainly different from the dash and dine cars they used at the airports in their youth.

In the backseat of the limo, Noah pulled her into his arms, his fingers entwined with hers, resting their hands against her shoulder. The silence was companionable. Serene, even, after the four-hour flight.

The driver took them to the Stratosphere Hotel, then hand in hand, Noah led her up the elevator to the 107th floor to the rotating Sky Lounge. The view was breathtaking. And they were there just in time for sunset.

Once they were seated with drinks, Noah took her hand, looked into her eyes. "Are you happy?" he asked.

"Yes," she said.

"I feel so fortunate that we ran into each other again. I hope we have a new beginning."

"I thought we already had a new beginning."

He nodded. "We did." He seemed to study the view – watching the lights. Stirred his crown on the rocks.

"You're not going to drink that," she observed.

"You know I can't. But the olives are great."

She knew that Noah was firm on his twelve-hour bottle to throttle rule. And she respected that. And she knew that flying for Noah was rewarding in itself. Nonetheless, the prospect of flying all the way back to Alabama tonight seemed a bit daunting to say the least. "It would have been fun to spend the night," she said, hoping her voice sounded light.

He shrugged, kept his eyes on the view. "We can check into it if you like," he said.

What was wrong with Noah all of a sudden? "Maybe next time," she murmured and stared at her drink. He, of all people, should know that she wouldn't travel without luggage. Besides clothes, there was make-up, hair products, medication. A girl didn't just hop in a plane without a go-bag. It took all her reserve to tamp down the annoyance she was feeling at the moment. Taking a deep breath, she forced herself to look at him.

"What's on your mind, Noah?"

He turned back to her. "I'm sorry for the way I treated you."

"Like you put it," she said. "A new beginning."

They were alone in their private world, the sunset creating a glow of warmth.

"I'm sorry you've had to go through so much lately. With your daughter and your divorce."

"Speaking of my divorce," he said.

"What about your divorce?"

"I've come to the conclusion that divorce doesn't suit me very well."

A little pang of panic shot through her. "Are you thinking about getting back together with Claire?"

"Hell no."

That was a relief. "What then?"

"I'm thinking of getting married again."

"Well, you made it, what, a whole day?"

"About a day and a half, more like."

She laughed. "You men just can't stand to be alone."

"That's it," he said. "We need someone to take care of us."

"Do you have someone lined up for this marriage thing?"

"Nope," he said.

She frowned at him. "I think maybe you need time to reset after your divorce."

"You know how us men are."

"True. I have to go to the restroom, Noah."

He stood up, and she found her way to the restroom. There was a little sitting area there in the restroom. She sat on a chair in front of mirror and reapplied her lip gloss. Noah was acting strange.

Almost like he was going to break up with her. If he hadn't brought her all the way to Las Vegas…

Any excuse to fly.

She went back to the table, and Noah stood up to help her in her chair, but instead of sitting, he knelt.

"What are you doing?" she asked, her heart tripping up a notch.

"Your napkin fell," he said, picking up a white napkin from the floor and setting it aside. "I'll get you another one."

"Thank you," she murmured, taking the napkin from his hands. She kept her gaze down. Berated her treacherous heart. She closed her eyes and took a long, slow, calming breath. It's just drinks and dinner. In Vegas. The ink was not even dry on Noah's divorce papers.

Perhaps the gentle rotation of the lounge mixed with the alcohol was causing her head to spin a bit.

"Hey," he said, a mysterious smile playing about his lips.

She looked up. Answered his smile with her own.

"Why don't I call the car around to take us to dinner? But we can walk a bit when we get to the strip."

"Sure," she said. A walk sounded better than good. Some fresh air to clear her head.

Hand in hand, they went down the elevator and out to where the car waited for them.

They drove about ten minutes, then the driver stopped and let them out of the car to walk

along the crowded Vegas Strip. Hand in hand, they were engulfed by the sights and sounds of the city that never sleeps.

His hand tightly gripping hers, he suddenly stopped. People funneled around them, mostly ignoring them.

Her eyes widened and her heart tripped as he put his hands on her waist and lifted her off the ground and twirled her around. Her thoughts collided. He'd gone mad. He was ill. He was doing this right here on the strip of Las Vegas like it was nothing.

He stared at her with an intensity that blocked out the rest of the world. "Savannah," he said, not caring who heard him. "I love you."

She felt her heart open and a smile exploded on her face.

She lifted her gaze to the people walking around them.

No one had any idea how long she had waited for this moment.

For this man.

A couple, likely in their fifties, also hand in hand, walked slowly past them, the woman's eyes locked onto Savannah's. Her lips curved into a secret smile.

Savannah knew her heart was in her eyes. This woman kept her eyes trained on Savannah as she walked past. The man leaned into her, kissed the top of her head, and though she only caught of glimpse of his face, she saw the love reflected there.

This.

This was her destiny. A sense of serenity settled over her. "I love you, too."

It was going to be a late night. Again, Savannah was disappointed that Noah hadn't planned better. It wasn't like him. A trip all the way to Las Vegas seemed like it warranted at least a stay over of one night. Nonetheless, her heart was bursting. Noah had just declared his love to her in front of God and a world of strangers. She truly couldn't keep the smile from her eyes.

When they reached the MGM Grand, they walked through the casino, passed the buffet, and toward the theater to the Joel Robuchon restaurant, decorated elegantly in black and white, replete with pink tablecloths.

As she followed the hostess toward their table, an odd tingle went up Savannah's spine as she heard women laughing ahead. Noah had reserved a table in the corner with a plush cloud-soft circular bench next to the cozy fireplace with a mirror above.

When the hostess stopped in front of a table, Savannah stopped. There were three people sitting at their table. She glanced at Noah who had a huge grin on his face.

Perplexed and confused, she turned back to the women.

Looked past the gorgeous blonde young woman.

To her sister.

And her mother.

Noah stepped forward. "Emily and Charlotte," he said with a nod. Then turned to take Savannah's hand. "Savannah, this is my daughter, Danielle."

Danielle stood up and hugged Savannah. Savannah then looked into lovely blue eyes that mirrored Noah's. She had the same goofy grin that her father was wearing.

"It's nice to meet you," Savannah said automatically.

Danielle laughed. "It's nice to finally meet you too."

"Mom? Emily?" Savannah said. "What are you doing here? I don't understand."

They look expectantly at Noah.

He squeezed her hand. "I thought it was time for everyone to meet," he said, then helped her slide into the circular booth. Noah and his daughter sat on the outside. Savannah sat between Noah and Charlotte.

Dinner was a blur. Savannah struggled to wrap her head around how both her sister and her mother had ended up in Las Vegas without her knowing about it. She always knew where they were. Her mother chatted with Danielle like they had known each other forever.

"Are you ok?" Noah asked, about halfway through dinner, his lips next to her ear.

"I think so. I'm just... astounded. Why didn't you tell me they would be here?"

"I wanted to. I wanted to tell you so much that it was hard for me to talk about anything else."

"That explains it."

"It's hard for me to keep a secret," he said.

She stared into his eyes. Frowned. "How can that be? When you're so full of surprises?"

He shook his head. "I can't explain it. I guess this was just really important to me."

Before she could further contemplate his statement, they were drawn back into the dinner conversation. They were discussing a show they had tickets for that evening.

Savannah frowned. So her mother, sister, and Noah's daughter were staying the night, but they were returning home tonight. The whole scenario made no sense.

She set down her fork. "We don't have tickets," she stated. With the table suddenly hushed, she continued, fighting to keep her voice neutral. "We're flying back to Alabama tonight." She lowered her eyes and bit the inside of her lip as she battled with the emotions warring inside her. Disappointment seemed to be at the forefront at the moment.

When no one spoke, she steeled herself and looked up. All three women were staring at Noah. Savannah turned her gaze to Noah. His eyes were closed and he was squirming.

Squirming? Noah Worthington?

She picked up her glass of wine and lifted it in a toast before swallowing a sip. A bubble of laughter spilled over her lips.

Noah Worthington was human. The man whose attention to details was legendary had truly botched this one.

He had brought her mother, her sister, and even his daughter to Vegas. They all had tickets and obviously were staying the night. But even though he had gotten them here all together, he hadn't thought about the two of them spending the night.

Now all eyes were on her. Eyes that questioned her sanity, but Savannah didn't care. She was going to savor the moment that Noah screwed everything up.

The server brought their ticket and Noah quickly handed the man his credit card.

He then reached into his bag, no doubt to retrieve his iPad to check the weather. Of course, they had to leave soon. Savannah's private amusement was rapidly fading.

But it wasn't his iPad that he pulled from his bag. "Since it's Christmas, I brought gifts for everyone," he said. He pulled out three flat blue boxes and handed one each to their family members.

Before Savannah had time to react, he pulled out a fourth box, this one square all around and handed it to Savannah. She recognized the trademark Tiffany's boxes. Noted that her box was different from theirs. But it should be, she told herself. They were family members. She was his… girlfriend?

Holding the box in her hands, she looked up at Noah, a million questions swirling in her head.

"Open it," he said.

The other three women already had theirs open. He had given each of them a silver bangle which they all promptly put on their wrists.

As they oohed and aahed over their gifts, Savannah sat,

silently, holding her little blue box with the white ribbon wrapped around it. Unshed tears glistening in her eyes. It didn't matter what was inside the box. It only mattered that she was here. With her family.

With Noah.

Realizing all eyes were on her again, she pulled the bow loose.

"Wait," Noah said, placing a hand over hers. "Let me." He took the box from her and removed the wrapping. Then he slid off the seat and knelt on one knee.

She swallowed thickly. Her mind refusing to function.

He took out a little blue box and lifted the lid.

Revealing a shiny, dazzling, diamond ring in a perfect Tiffany cut setting. He took her hand in his.

She gasped and lifted her eyes to his. Felt a tear drip down her cheek. Then another. She swiped at them.

What was it with Noah and tears anyway?

"Savannah Skye," he said.

Another tear.

"I've always loved you and I always will. I want to wake up with you every morning and fall asleep with you next to me every night."

She closed her eyes. Took a deep breath.

"Savannah," he said.

She opened her eyes and locked her gaze onto his.

"Will you marry me?" He reached out, wiped a tear from her cheek.

She didn't answer. She couldn't catch her breath.

Had anyone ever died while being proposed to?

"Savannah?" he asked, with a little laugh, and a nervous glance at her sister.

"Yes," she said, with a deep intake of air. "Yes," she said again, a smile breaking across her face.

Then she was in his arms and everyone at the table was laughing.

Noah slipped the ring on her finger. Put his lips against her ear. "This has been far too long coming. I don't want to waste any more time."

She nodded against his chest. Stared at the most beautiful engagement ring she had ever seen.

She was engaged!

To Noah.

The thought was almost surreal. Like he said, too long coming.

They gathered up their things and went outside.

"Where are you staying?" she asked her mother. It no longer mattered whether they stayed or left. As long as she was with Noah, nothing else mattered.

Her mother glanced at Noah before she answered. "The Bellagio."

She nodded, her hand in Noah's.

"We'll go back to the hotel with you," Noah said.

"Yeah," Savannah said, enjoying her own humor. "Our plane doesn't leave until we get there."

They all climbed into the limo and Noah opened a bottle of champagne.

"To us," he said, holding up his glass.

"I'm so glad you all could be here," Savannah said, then found herself fighting back tears again.

They clinked their glasses together and sipped champagne while until they approached the front drive of the Bellagio.

They all got out and went into the lobby.

Noah stopped, and turned to face Savannah. Held both her hands. "There's one other thing."

Savannah couldn't imagine what else Noah could possibly have on his mind. They had just gotten engaged. Perhaps he wanted her to move with him to Ft. Worth.

These were things she hadn't considered. She loved her house. She was thinking about going back to school.

She must have had that deer in the headlights look on her face.

"Savannah," Noah said. "Stop thinking."

She mentally shook herself. Smiled.

She was engaged to Noah Worthington.

"We're actually staying here tonight."

"I don't have…"

"I know," he stopped her before she could explain, again, that she needed her go bag.

"Your mother brought everything from her house. Your make-up. Some clothes."

Savannah looked her mother who merely shrugged. "It's what he wanted. I didn't think you'd mind."

Her thoughts were too jumbled for her to decide if she minded or not. Then it struck her. Champagne. Noah had drunk champagne in the limo and wine at dinner. He'd planned this all along. So much for Noah missing details.

"Ok," he said. "There's one other thing."

She laughed. She couldn't help it. "What?"

"Remember how we were never friends?"

"Of course," she said, smiling at the memory of the way he had kissed her on their first date.

"I don't want to be engaged either."

He'd gone mad.

Again.

"I don't understand," she said, feeling the weight of the diamond on her finger.

"I want to be married."

"Ok," she said.

"Now," he said, a mischievous smile on his face.

"Right now?"

"Sure," he said. "Everyone we care about is here."

Savannah looked at her mother and sister watching them expectantly. His daughter, a smile on her face.

Almost on cue, the wedding march wafted through the air.

I'm hallucinating.

"And," he said, taking a step back to look at her. "You're wearing white."

Savannah laughed. "What are the odds?"

"I think I hit the jackpot."

Noah had set up everything through the hotel and all the details had been handled.

She had flowers. There was a cake. A photographer.

The rest was a hazy jumble. They had skipped the whole friendship stage and they had breezed past the engagement phase.

Thirty minutes later, Noah's lips were on hers and she was Mrs. Noah Worthington.

And just like that, twenty years were gone in an instant.

"We did it," he said.

"I had almost given up on you," she said.

"Key word, my love," he said against her lips. "Almost."

The line to fly out of Vegas was long. They sat quietly waiting their turn for take-off. Savannah had run out of small-talk and Noah didn't seem particularly chatty.

Two days had passed since the wedding and Savannah still glowed when she looked in Noah's direction.

If she had thought they were close before, they were even more close now. Bonded in every way.

After sitting quietly for a few minutes, she asked, "When did you first know you wanted to be a pilot?"

"The minute my father sat me in the captain's chair of his private plane."

"Really? How old were you?"

"Four."

"You've got to be kidding. Four years old?"

"No kidding." He looked around. "It was at night sort of like this," he said. "Crowded."

"What was he thinking?"

"I don't know. Bored maybe."

"Are you? Bored?"

"Me? Never when I'm flying. But being a passenger can definitely get to be boring. Are you?"

She shook her head. Not bored. Concerned about Noah's suddenly quiet mood.

"You know what?" he said, unbuckling his seat belt. "You fly."

"What? No. I don't know what to do."

"I'll help you."

"I can't Noah. It's not safe."

"Of course it is. I have my own set of controls." He nodded toward the controls in front of her.

He reached over, unbuckled her belt.

They changed places and got buckled back in. Savannah's heart raced. Noah had indeed gone insane.

She was still holding her handbag. Looking around for a place to put it, she saw a side pocket. Her slim handbag slipped right in. She grabbed the wheel and held on.

Noah laughed.

"You don't have to hold it yet."

"Come on, Noah, you get us in the air first."

He must have seen the panic in her face because he acquiesced.

And got them safely in the air.

After the plane leveled out, he switched the control over to her.

"Your turn," he said.

Savannah's eyes widened.

"Put your hands on the wheel and turn ever so slightly."

She did. And the plane responded. "Oh no!"

"You did that. Now turn it back."

She gently eased it back on course. "Wow. Now what?"

"Now you just sit back and hope nothing weird happens."

"Noah!"

"If anything weird happens, I'm right here."

"Did your daddy let you fly?"

"Oh no. I was back in the back before takeoff."

She cut her eyes at him.

"That was different."

"Should we be watching for other planes on the… air?"

"An alarm will go off if radar picks anything up."

"Cars should have that."

"Agreed. But it wouldn't take long to be become desensitized."

"Hmm."

Her lips felt a little dry, so she reached with one hand for her handbag to get her lip-gloss out. Instead, her fingers brushed against a little flat box.

Keeping her eyes on the air in front of them – from driving habit probably, she pulled out the box. A blue Tiffany box tied with a white ribbon.

She stared at the box. Looked at Noah who watched her.

"Noah."

"I told you I was thinking about taking a wife."

She examined her hand. "I think you already did that."

He winked at her.

"So, what, the first girl who comes along… you'll be ready?"

"Merry Christmas, ma chérie," he said.

"Wait," she said. "When did you buy this ring?"

"I bought it in New York. The day of your presentation. While you were out shopping, I

went shopping, too."

"How do you know I was shopping?"

"I know you, remember?"

She laughed. "Who's this one for?"

He smiled into her eyes. "I think it might be for my wife?"

He opened the box revealing a silver bangle similar to the ones he had given her family and his sister, but this one was actually two, perpetually interconnected.

"I was thinking about that. I might have a condition about marrying you."

"You already said yes"

"You didn't give me time to think."

"All right. What's your condition?"

"That you not disappear on me again."

"I vow right here, right now, to never again go anywhere without letting you know."

She smiled. "That might be a little bit excessive. We'll have to figure that part out."

"I love you, Savannah Skye," he said, putting his arms around her into an embrace, nestling her head beneath his chin. "I have from the very first day we met. It was always you."

And he had always been the one for her. She'd been waiting for him her entire adult life.

And flying high above the world, with no one there but the two of them, she had a glimpse into their future. That life with

Noah Worthington would never be dull. It would be exciting and comfortable all at once.

And her heart had found its home.

And this time around…

This time it was forever.

THE END.

BESTSELLING AUTHOR OF BEGIN AGAIN
KATHRYN KALEIGH
Love
AGAIN
THE WORTHINGTONS
UNBREAK MY HEART SERIES

Love Again

THE WORTHINGTONS

CHAPTER

One

Claire Worthington believed that life moved in only one direction. Forward.

"Mom!" Danielle said excitedly as she approached Claire down the wide UCLA hallway. "My psychology class is so lit. The instructor is on fire."

Claire gathered up her iPhone and iPad, drew her handbag over her shoulders. She'd been waiting for two hours for her daughter's classes to end. "So... you like it?" Claire asked for clarification.

Danielle grinned. "It's gonna be awesome."

"That's great," she said. Claire glanced at her watch. She had just enough time to get Danielle to her counseling session at Resolutions Treatment Center, then they could have a quick lunch before Claire's meeting with a new artist coming in at two o'clock.

They walked together down the hall at UCLA, dodging

students hurrying to their next class, most of them looking down at their phones.

"He runs the Psychology Clinic, so he's gonna let us observe some sessions. Can you believe it? It's my first semester and I already get to observe."

"That's great, honey," Claire said. Ever since Danielle began mental health treatment last winter, she'd been dead-set on studying psychology. She'd been so disappointed that her hospitalization had caused her to drop out of her advanced classes in the spring, that Claire had pulled some strings and gotten her into summer classes at the university at the last minute.

Scheduling had been an utter nightmare ever since. Spring had been a process of Danielle finishing up high school in Ft. Worth and moving to Los Angeles. Fortunately, Claire already had a house in L.A. Considering everything that had happened in the last few months, the move had gone smoothly.

Since Claire had to attend mental health counseling with Danielle twice a week, Claire drove her to class those days.

"Grayson is even going to have an art therapist come talk to us so we can see what that's like."

Claire stopped and gazed at her daughter, causing the other students to flow around them.

"Mom, what?" Danielle had that panicky *Please don't let the other students find out I have parents* look on her face. "Come on."

Claire followed, but her brain remained frozen. The art therapy part was interesting and Claire wanted to hear more about it. Later.

Something else entirely had her attention, however, at the moment.

Grayson.

A name that was becoming more popular with babies born today, but quite unusual during Claire's generation. She knew because she'd looked it up.

Did she dare ask?

She had to know. "What's his last name?" she asked, holding her breath.

Danielle shifted her backpack and smiled as she checked an incoming text. "I don't know," she said, keeping her eyes on her phone. "Can we skip therapy today?"

"No," Claire said automatically, exhaling in frustration. Danielle asked the same question nearly every day. Today, however, her daughter was particularly glowing. The psychologist had warned her that Danielle would have fleeting moments of happiness. But that had been months ago. Surely at some point she no longer had to worry when her daughter was happy.

"What did he look like?" She asked.

"Grayson?"

"Yes. Shouldn't you call him Dr. or Mr. or something?"

Danielle rolled her eyes. "It's not the south, Mom. It's L.A." Then she stopped texting and looked up at her mother. "Cute," she said. "About Daddy's size. Your age maybe. I don't know. Do you want me to find out if he's married?"

"Heavens no!" Claire said, feeling the flush on her cheeks.

"Why do you want to know?"

"I had a friend in high school named Grayson. But it couldn't possibly be the same guy."

Danielle shook her head and attached her gaze back to her phone. "No way. He wouldn't have been your type. This guy just retired from the Air Force."

Claire clasped a hand over her mouth to keep from gasping. Grayson Moore had been in the delayed entry program and entered the Air Force the day after graduation. He'd promised to write, but he hadn't. Not even once. Not one letter. Not one phone call. It was twenty years ago, so they hadn't had cell phones. Well, Claire had a cell phone, but Grayson didn't. Grayson hadn't had email either.

She sighed as she steered Danielle, whose attention was glued to her phone, her fingers flying over the screen, toward the car. Things would have been so much different if they'd simply had cell phones back then.

The name and the Air Force part matched up, but a psychology instructor? Claire tapped her fingers on the steering wheel as she waited for traffic to move.

That didn't fit. Not even a little.

Danielle's therapy session was uneventful. Danielle seemed to be truly excited to be starting college. Her daughter had just gotten back from spending a week with her father Noah and his new wife. Claire and Noah had been divorced just over six months. Noah had gotten married the day after he and Claire had officially gotten divorced. Talk about not letting the ink dry.

But Claire was happy to have it over with. Now she didn't have to worry about the obligatory visits to Ft. Worth to be with her husband.

Claire had a house in L.A. and a growing business. She'd been growing her business for years, but her husband had no idea. He thought she was here sipping mimosas with her girl-friends.

Technically, she began to network before she even married Noah. By the time they were married, she was having business meetings several times a week. Throughout the early part of their marriage, Noah thought Claire was taking money from her father to supplement Noah's income. She never told him the truth. She'd been earning the money and never once touched her father's. Well, that didn't include the start-up money her father had given her, but Claire didn't count that since she'd paid it off in mere months.

After the session, she and Danielle drove back toward the university and had lunch at a trendy little restaurant set up in the middle of a greenhouse. Claire ordered a fried green tomato po'boy with avocados, and veggie bacon and Danielle ordered a shrimp po'boy. If the two of them had a favorite restaurant to go to together, it would have to be this one. It was called the York and Orleans and they both had favorite lunch items on the menu.

Claire was sending an email on her phone to a vendor to begin discussing wine options for an upcoming fundraising event. As she hit send, she noticed that Danielle had uncharacteristically set her phone down on the table and was staring across the crowded restaurant.

Though Claire glanced in that direction, she didn't see anything out of the ordinary.

Then she heard his laugh.

Every nerve cell in her body tensed.

And a memory from twenty plus years ago was awakened.

"Mom?" Danielle whispered. "It's him."

"It's who?" She whispered back, but her eyes were glued to the handsome man in the white shirt and black slacks three tables over. He sported two-day old stubble on his face and his hair was still thick and dark.

Tall, dark, and handsome.

That's always how she'd thought of Grayson Moore. Now he was even more handsome with twenty years of maturity on him. If she hadn't heard his laugh, she probably wouldn't even have noticed him. Well, she would have noticed him, but she wouldn't have recognized him.

"It's Grayson," Danielle said. "My psych teacher."

No. Way.

"Come on," Danielle said. "I'll introduce you."

Grayson was with another man, a student perhaps? Or a younger colleague? "No," she said, but Danielle was already standing up and walking toward his table.

Claire was in full panic mode.

This couldn't happen. Not like this. She got up and walked the other way. Toward the restroom. She needed a second. Just one second.

Claire Worthington didn't panic.

Grayson Moore recognized the student who stood at his table. He rarely did, especially after only the first day, but this particular student had been especially enthusiastic and there had been something about her smile that had caught his attention.

"Hi," she said with that smile. "I'm sorry to interrupt, but I'm in your psychology class. From today."

"Sure," Grayson said. "How are you?"

"I'm good. I'm really excited about the class, but... I think my mom knows you. Or something." The student was frowning

now and looking across the restaurant. "I was going to introduce you, but she… left."

"Your mother?" He looked past the girl, searching for
someone who looked motherly.

"Yeah. We're having lunch," The girl stood next to his chair,
searching the restaurant for her missing mother.

Grayson glanced at Bob, an applicant for a teaching position.
Shrugged as though to say *this happens sometimes.*

Bob seemed unaffected. In fact, he used the distraction to
finish off his sandwich.

"It's okay," Grayson said. "I can meet her next time."

He followed the girl's gaze toward the restroom and his eyes
locked on the woman walking toward them. His dream woman.

Literally. The woman walking toward them had the same
lithe movements as his high school sweetheart.

He knew, however, that it wasn't her. His high school sweetheart was blonde. And this woman was brunette. He looked
more closely at the student with her red bow shaped lips. Then
back at the woman walking toward them. He knew that smile.
"It's Claire," he said.

"Yeah," Danielle said. "That's my mother." She jerked her
head around to stare at Grayson. "Wait. How do you know her
name?"

Grayson couldn't answer. His tongue was tied up in knots.
The man who talked for a living couldn't put two syllables
together in his head to save his own life at this moment.

Claire stood at his table now, next to her daughter, and
Grayson knew why the student's smile had caught his attention.
It was her mother's smile. The one he had known so well.

Twenty years ago.

His eyes strayed to her lips and his neurons traveled down a path he thought had long been severed from his brain.

"Grayson," Claire said. "It's good to see you. You've met my daughter, Danielle."

His brain chemistry was scrambled, but he found himself reflexively returning her smile. Claire may be brunette now, but she was still the girl he'd loved in high school. "It's good to see you, too, Claire. Where have you been?"

"I stepped into the lady's room," she said, her eyes wide with innocence.

Grayson didn't buy the innocence. She knew he wasn't being literal. But he let it go for now. When her daughter wasn't standing next to her, he'd ask again and this time he'd add the words *for the last twenty years* to his question.

"My daughter has been raving about your class since this morning."

"I try to make things interesting," he said, trying to ignore the ringing in his ears. He was trying to wrap his head around Claire having a daughter. They'd talked about having children. Claire had wanted two – a boy and a girl. Grayson had wanted four. Did she have other children? Now that his brain was thawing, so many questions were beginning to form.

If Claire had a child, she was married. Claire Beauchamp was nothing if not traditional. He glanced at her ring finger. No ring. Divorced then. There was a simple diamond on her index finger. And a small diamond on a silver chain around her neck and larger diamonds in her ears. She wore a red pencil skirt with a white jacket cropped to her waist. Black pumps with red bottoms graced her feet. A Gucci handbag hung across her shoulders. Grayson had no doubt that the things she wore at this moment cost more than a month's salary for him.

That was the Claire he knew. *Where did you go?*

He wanted to talk to her. Needed to talk to her.

Claire dropped her daughter off at her friend's house and drove the thirty minutes to the gallery. She had plenty of time to get everything ready before the artist came in at 2:00. The fundraiser was in two weeks, so she had plenty of time. She had it down to a science.

She could only hope that the artist, Maine D'Court, had come through and had enough paintings ready to show. He'd promised her that he worked fast.

Claire wasn't sure that fast was necessarily a good thing in the art world, but it was probably like everything else. It wasn't the speed at which something was done, it was the perseverance.

Maine D'Court had come through. He had brought three paintings in addition to those he had promised.

Maine already had the paintings inside and set up for her look at when Claire got to the gallery.

She should have been elated. Could have been elated. Would have been elated.

If she hadn't just encountered the one man she had ever loved.

So, instead of elated, she was... edgy.

It was the only way she knew to describe the nerves tingling through her body.

She and Grayson had dated her sophomore and junior years

in high school. He was one year older, so when he graduated, he had joined the Air Force with a promise to see her soon.

That had been the last time she had seen him.

The night before he left for San Antonio, Texas. She still flushed at the memory of that night.

"So, Claire, what do you think?" Maine asked.

"They're impressive," she said, reining her thoughts back to the present.

He preened. Just a bit. But she saw it. "I'm inclined to celebrate," he said.

"That's a great idea," Claire agreed. "You should do that." Claire picked up his contract, turned to the signature page.

"You'll come with me," he said.

Claire smiled in an effort to turn around the anxiety that washed over her at his words. "Oh, no," she said, watching his expression change from friendly, excited artist to rejected man. If he pulled his paintings now, the whole fundraiser would crash and burn. There would be no mentorships. No scholarships. It would all be for naught. "I'll go next time. After the fundraiser. Right now I'm buried in paperwork and," she glanced at her watch. "I have to be up early for a meeting tomorrow." She lowered her voice. "And don't tell anyone, but alcohol gives me the worst possible headache you can imagine."

She sent up a silent prayer of thanks when he backed off, appeased, for the moment at least. He winked, clicked his tongue, and cocked a finger at her. "I'll hold you to that," he said.

Claire held her breath as he signed the contract. "Now, I have to get this to the fundraising attorney," she checked her watch again. "Before he leaves for the evening. We're on a strict deadline." She grabbed up her handbag, and, clutching the signed contract in her other hand, left him standing there in her own office.

Her heels clicked on the stairs as she raced down them and outside to her BMW sedan. She was in her car with the doors locked before she took a deep breath and pressed her hands against the steering wheel.

The paperwork could have easily waited until morning. Even Martie, her personal assistant, could have driven it over. Or they could have faxed a copy to lock in the contract.

She had just needed to get as far away from Maine D'Court as she could. Maybe tonight would be a good night to hibernate at home with some good undistracted rest and relaxation.

She sent Martie a quick text asking her to lock up. When Claire received an affirmative answer, she shoved the contract into her briefcase and headed home.

Claire parked in the garage, went inside, and greeted her silver Persian kitten. Charlie wasn't even a year old. He'd been her gift to herself after the divorce was finalized. She picked him up, and hugging him to her, took him into the kitchen to feed. She pulled the top on a can of kitten food and stirred it into a saucer.

Laughing at Charlie's barely audible meow, she ruffled his hair and watched him lap up the food.

She went upstairs, changed into her slim crop pants and a t-shirt. She went into her walk-in closet, keyed in the code to her wall safe, and took out a slim photo album.

She carried the photo album back downstairs, opened a bottle of Dakota Shy Cabernet Sauvignon, poured a glass, and curled up on her sofa.

Claire loved her house. She's chosen everything from the basic design to the doorknobs. She loved her over-the-top walk-in closet with shelves and drawers. She loved her kitchen with its huge windows overlooking a wooded back yard. She loved her fireplace with the plasma TV hanging on the wall over it.

She could open her iPad and close the shades on her windows, turn on her TV, and see if anyone was at the front door. All that technology blended seamlessly into a warm cozy environment. Her home was her haven – her safe place away from everyone where she didn't have to worry about saying the right thing or dressing a certain way.

Even when Danielle had friends over, she felt relaxed here. This was her space.

Charlie sat next to her on the floor and stared at her. She picked him up in one hand and put him on the sofa beside her. He slapped at the fringe on a throw she'd tossed across the back of the sofa, then curled into a ball next to her and fell asleep purring.

Claire sipped her wine, then taking a deep breath, opened the photo album. It had been a long time since she'd dared to open it up – probably fifteen years.

It was a photo album she'd started when she was sixteen years old. There were lots of pink hearts drawn with a felt tipped pin. On only the first page, Grayson smiled back at her.

Her heart skipped a little as she studied the picture of the two of them together. They looked so very happy with their arms wrapped around each other.

Claire had given up long ago trying to figure out what went wrong.

It had been so long – twenty years. Did it really matter anymore?

Seeing him today had brought butterflies back to her stomach. Butterflies she thought had flown years ago.

Danielle texted saying she was going out to dinner with her friends and would be home late.

Perfect. Claire had the whole evening to herself.

Claire flipped through the pages, allowing the memories to play through her mind. Some bringing a smile. Others bringing tears.

When the clock chimed seven o'clock, she closed the album and set it aside.

What were the odds that she'd run into Grayson Moore? Why today?

It doesn't matter. It's all in the past now.

And Claire Worthington kept her eyes on the future.

CHAPTER
Two

The event was going to be a huge success. Claire could feel it. And she had an instinct for these things. The wine was flowing freely and the artist was charming. Women would be falling over themselves to transfer money. Already, he'd sold three paintings. His artistic style was conservative. The kind an older woman would want displayed in her home. Not too trendy and not the kind that would have shock value.

A few new people had come in that Claire needed to greet.

As she watched, a group of four split, leaving one standing alone as she approached.

Her heart tripped up a notch as she approached him. He stood staring at a painting with splashes of purple and red. Claire's favorite out of the ones the artist had contributed. He stood with his hands behind his back, his legs a few inches apart. Dark hair curled at his collar.

She stood next to him. Stared into his handsome face. How was it possible he had gotten more handsome than he was at eighteen? He was in his prime now, she admitted, her lips twitching up.

"I wonder why he named it *Fireworks*," he said.

"How did you find me?" she asked.

He shrugged, shifted his attention to her. Studied her as though she, too, were a thing to admire. "It wasn't hard."

"You like art?" she asked.

"I admire anything with beauty. Where did you go, Claire?"

"I didn't go anywhere," she said, feeling the lump in her throat. "Why did you disappear?"

"I was in the Air Force. You knew where I was."

"Not even once," she said. "You didn't write. You didn't call. Not even once."

The pain she felt saying those words out loud were reflected in his own features. "Of course I did."

"No," she said. "I would have known. I was right here. Waiting."

"Claire," he said. "I called you every chance I got. The calls were refused. Every time."

"No," she said.

"I called collect. I didn't have any other way to call you."

She wasn't sure how to respond. Why would he say that? Grayson had never been one to lie.

"Did you read my letters?" He asked. "I sent you information on how to contact me. But you didn't."

"What letters?"

"I wrote you letters and mailed them, mostly every week, at first anyway."

"Real letters?"

He scoffed. "Real letters. With stamps."

"You must have had the wrong address."

He recited her parents' home address. Claire felt a little light-headed. She needed to sit down, but instead, she took a deep breath and steadied herself. "I never got them," she breathed.

"Claire," he said. He almost reached for her, but instead, put his hands in his pockets.

"I have to… um…" She glanced around. "I have to see to my guests."

She had to think. And she couldn't think with him staring at her that way. Like he wanted to pull her to him and kiss all the years away.

She turned and walked across the room, keeping her head high. Her imagination was a thing to keep a tight leash on. At least where Grayson Moore was concerned. She put a smile on her face as she approached two middle-aged women standing in front of a very expensive painting.

Weekly etiquette classes for the last years of high school had taught her nothing if not how to hide her emotions. Miss Baker's voice still resonated in Claire's head. *Never let them see you sweat. Or cry. Or have uncontrollable laughter. In fact, always be in control.*

Emotional control was so ingrained in Claire's psyche, she wasn't sure she could be any other way.

By the time the evening was winding down, only one painting was left unsold. It was Claire's favorite – the purple and red one. The one the artist had named *Fireworks.*

The artist, Maine D'Court, was ecstatic. They had agreed that he would receive a small percentage of sales, but mostly he was trying to establish a name for himself. If tonight was any indication, he was well on his way to success.

The members of the Enrich American Minds Foundation

were also elated. With the money earned tonight, they would be able to pick five high school students, mentor them through graduation, guide them into college, and provide tuition support.

Now the hard work started. Claire had to hire ten new mentors, two of whom would follow each student who was chosen.

Because of tonight, five students who never would have set foot on a college campus would now have the opportunity to become college educated, productive members of society.

Claire walked around the gallery, reminding her committee members about their meeting Monday afternoon. She stopped in front of the *Fireworks* painting and wondered why it hadn't sold.

"Is this the only one left?" Grayson's voice was like a familiar balm settling over her soul.

"Yes," she said without turning around.

"I like it."

She turned then and looked into those blue eyes that had haunted her dreams for years. "It's curious that no one bought it."

"How much?"

She lifted an eyebrow.

"How much for the painting?"

"You don't want to buy it," she said turning back toward the painting, though her heart was racing and every cell was tuned towards Grayson's presence.

"How much?" he asked again.

"You can't afford it."

She counted to ten before turning back to him.

"I'm not eighteen anymore," he said.

She smiled. That was an understatement. Very well. She'd play along. She quoted him a figure.

He reached into his jacket pocket and pulled out a checkbook.

She was pleased that she managed to keep her jaw from dropping.

Grayson prided himself on not flinching. There went two months' salary. This was retirement money, but still…

He'd heard Claire tell three different people that this was her favorite painting by this artist. She hadn't said that about any of the others, so he felt confident that it was the truth.

As he wrote out the check, he wondered if that was why no one had bought it. Perhaps no one had the heart to buy it out from under her.

Grayson wasn't buying it out from under her. He was giving her a one hundred percent success rate tonight.

And he planned to give the painting to her when the time was right.

"Is this where you work?" he asked as he handed her the check. Surely he'd earned a bit of information by donating.

"Yes," she said. "My office is upstairs."

"Nice," he said, sweeping his gaze around the spacious, modern, gallery. A wide staircase led upstairs to an open area. Offices, he assumed and meeting space. It was impressive.

"Thank you," she said, a smile settling over her features. He liked the smile better than her consternation.

"Does Danielle still live at home?" he asked.

"Yes," she said.

She was making him ask. "Do you have other children?"

"No, just Danielle."

There was no one else within earshot. He had so many questions but he couldn't tell if he was making her uncomfortable or not. But she was still standing there, so he could only assume she was willing to talk with him. Claire had always been good at keeping her emotions in check. He knew she'd been schooled to do that. She was the rich girl. The one with every possible door of opportunity in front of her. He had been just a regular guy. Joining the Air Force to serve his country.

He'd often wondered if she was part of what drove him to keep bettering himself. He knew she was the reason he never married. He'd had girlfriends, sure, even lived with one of them, but none of them had ever been marriage material for Grayson. Claire had ruined that for him. She had been the only one.

"Do you have children?" She asked, running her fingers along his check.

He shook his head. "No."

"Really? You wanted four."

I wanted four with you. "Things change," he said, the smile dropping from his lips. It was definitely better to talk about her. "And you wanted two."

"Things change," she said. Perhaps telling her about the letters, though she apparently hadn't gotten them, was helping to keep her here talking to him.

Maine D'Court approached, "Claire," he said, his voice silky.

"Maine," Claire said, shifting to include him in their conversation. "We just sold the last of your paintings," she nodded toward Grayson.

Grayson scowled. Had he really just given this man money?

This slim man with a ponytail of all things. The military man in him cringed.

"Is that so?" Maine said. "Well, I hope you enjoy it."

"I'm sure I will," Grayson said, stretching to his full height of six feet. Maine was at least four inches shorter.

"I'll have your check for you early next week," Claire said, turning away slightly. Grayson gave her points for gracefully dismissing the man.

"Great," Maine said. "Let me know when you're ready to get out of here."

"Get out?" she echoed.

"Yeah. You owe me a drink, remember?"

Grayson saw the flash of panic shoot through her eyes. She didn't want to go with him.

She looked directly at him, a smile on her lips. "Not tonight, Maine."

"You promised."

She shook her head. "I already have plans," she said.

Grayson felt his muscles tense. It had been a few years since he'd been in a fight. Might feel good.

"You promised," he said, shoving a finger at her.

"Hey," Grayson said, stepping in front of Claire. "The lady said no. When a lady says no, she means no."

"We had plans," Maine said, trying to reach behind Grayson for Claire's hand. She stepped back before he could touch her.

"No," Grayson said, stepping front of Claire. "The lady is with me."

Maine glared at him, then at Claire, before, muttering, he walked away.

"He sure knows how to win friends," Grayson said.

"Thank you," she said, turning her gaze to Grayson.

"He has some nerve, doesn't he?"

"I'm afraid so," Claire said. "But I think he's harmless."

Maine, however, didn't leave. He sat on the stairs leading up to Claire's office. And watched them, his expression surly.

"I hope you're right," Grayson said. The gallery was nearly empty now. "If you don't mind, I'll hang around until you get to your car."

"I don't mind. I have to go up to my office for a few minutes before I leave."

"I'll go with you," Grayson said. He was relieved that she wasn't one of those women who didn't want protection from men. Grayson never understood that. What those women didn't understand was that they may be smarter than most men, but they would never have the testosterone to match. It was like a man who thought he could go up bare handed against a lion. The lion would always win.

Claire was smart though. The smartest woman Grayson had ever known.

Maine watched them, said nothing as they went upstairs to her office. Grayson stood outside her door, bodyguard style while she gathered up what she needed to take with her.

Claire tossed papers into her briefcase. She planned to work from home this weekend, but she was having trouble thinking about what she need to take with her.

She was having trouble thinking about anything other than Grayson Moore standing outside her office door ready to protect her from an ardent admirer with an inflated self-esteem.

Had she been too friendly with Maine D'Court? She had promised to have a drink with him after the showing, but she hadn't meant right after on the same night. It had been intended as discouragement. Like *sure, we'll get together sometime and catch up* when both people knew that would never happen.

Claire tapped her fingers on the desk as she considered how she was going to get Maine D'Court out of her gallery without making a scene. It was because of him that tonight had been so successful. She didn't want to seem ungrateful. But it had been a business arrangement. He'd made a lot of money. Sold paintings he never would have sold. It was a win-win.

She was mostly cross with him because he was disrupting her thought process about Grayson. Grayson was the one she wanted to be thinking about. Not a narcissistic artist.

She gathered up her handbag and drew it over her shoulders. She was thankful Grayson was here tonight. She wasn't sure what she would have done about Maine D'Court. His persistence bordered on stalking.

Would she have to be afraid now? And afraid for Danielle?

As they walked back downstairs, side by side, Claire was struck by the familiarity of walking next to Grayson. He was a full head taller than she was. And, she readily admitted, she felt safe with him at her side.

Maine D'Court, however, was nowhere in sight. They did a quick search, but the building was empty.

Claire locked up with Grayson keeping watch. Their cars were the only two cars left in the parking lot. Maine D'Court, it seemed, had decided to go his own way.

Nonetheless, Grayson walked around her BMW and peeked through the glass into the backseat.

"Were you deployed?" she asked.

"You could say that. All in all, I spent about ten years overseas."

"Wow. That's a lot."

"I went to college here, though, at Stanford."

"Impressive."

"That's where you went, right?"

"I didn't go," she said.

"Oh," he said.

"I got married and started my business."

He gazed around, then pinned those blue eyes to hers. He was standing close now. So close, she could see the little lines around his eyes. Little lines that weren't there twenty years ago. "You never married?" she asked, her voice barely a whisper, dreading the answer.

"Nope. Hard to meet anyone when you're rarely home."

"Well, you were living overseas, right? And then college. Sounds like ample opportunity. A lot of soldiers get married while they're on tour of duty."

"I'm only interested in American girls. And college students were babies by the time I got there."

"Do you still see them that way?" she asked.

"Even more."

"That's probably a good thing since you're surrounded by college students all day long."

"Children," he said. "Are you going straight home?"

"I usually do."

"I'd ask if you wanted to get a dinner, but you already shot one guy down tonight."

She glanced at her watch. "It's a little late for dinner, isn't it?"

"I suppose so," he said, never taking his eyes off hers. "I hadn't noticed. I'm surely not going to ask you for drink."

She laughed. "Too bad," she said. "I would have gone." She slipped into her car and he closed the door.

She smiled as she drove away, enjoying the astounded expression on his face.

It took a full ten minutes for her heart rate to go back to a normal rhythm.

She'd never in a million years expected Grayson Moore to still be single after all these years. He must have women throwing themselves at him constantly. No one could look that good and be that gentlemanly and not have women after him.

He must have found out about her fundraiser through UCLA. Too late, she realized she should have asked. Ah well. Chances were good she wouldn't see him again unless she happened to run into him in Danielle's psychology building.

She had accounts to work on this weekend. And thank you letters to write. There was no time to dwell on the past. What was done was done.

Grayson watched Claire drive out of the parking lot and resisted the urge to follow her. Maine D'Court was probably harmless. More bravado than any actual threat. Still, it wouldn't hurt for her to be vigilant until she was out of his crosshairs.

But mostly, he stood there, letting her words echo through his mind, sending little shock waves of unexpected pleasure. *I would have gone.*

And then he'd let her slip right through his fingers again. He *had* called her. Not right away and then once he was in

Germany, using the phone became even more difficult. He mused that her consistent lack of response was most effective.

It had worked just like he taught in class. In fact, he sometimes used the example of trying to reach an old girlfriend as an example of extinction in his intro psychology classes. If she'd wanted to extinguish his attempts, she had certainly done it the right way. Absolutely no response. Not even once. However, just like he taught, he'd had spontaneous recovery. In textbook reaction, he'd shown up on her doorstep the day he got back from Germany. Her mother had told him she wasn't home. And suggested he not come back.

It had worked. He'd finally gotten the message. When a lady says no, she meant no. Still, there remained lingering doubt through the years. Doubt because he'd never actually spoken to Claire.

When his mother sent him the newspaper clipping of Claire's marriage to Noah Worthington, something in his heart had cracked. She could have at least told him.

Even though he moved on, he never found anyone he wanted to commit his life to. Claire had been it for him. His soul mate.

He'd come close a time or two, but something always interfered. When he didn't feel like blaming his lack of desire for marriage on Claire, he blamed it on the things he'd seen in Iraq and Afghanistan. Even without a diagnosis of PTSD, he knew it was normal to have difficulty with attachments.

Grayson hadn't even gone looking for Claire later on Facebook. If she was happily married, he certainly didn't want to be the one to create any doubt in her mind.

Now that he'd run across her and she was single again, all bets were off.

He drove the thirty minutes to his apartment near the university and went inside. He couldn't help imagining how Claire might see his place. It was clean, but a little cluttered. He had the basics – TV, sofa, small dining room table. The apartment had come furnished, so he hadn't had any input into the décor. It hadn't seemed to matter. Until now.

He grabbed a bottle of water and settled on his sofa with his computer. He logged into the university website and typed in Danielle Worthington. It was so very easy to find Claire's address. *It's not stalking.* He just needed her address so he could send her the painting. After he wrote down her address, he exercised self-restraint. For all of three minutes.

Then he typed the address in google maps. Nice neighborhood. Lots of trees and space. And not so very far from the university. He estimated he could be there in fifteen minutes if she needed him.

He logged out of the university website and laughed at himself. Even if she needed him, she had no way to get in touch with him. His phone number wasn't on his check. He even had doubts that he would see her again. He'd found her easily enough just by googling her name. She was well-known in the fundraising community. It looked like she'd done well adding art to her method. He was impressed that she'd branched out from the usual charities to one that was personally near and dear to his heart – higher education. Higher education often got lost in the shuffle, but what she was doing was awe inspiring.

It was funny, he mused, how their minds had converged so

many years after they'd disconnected. He was teaching college and she was raising money for students to attend. He was surprised she hadn't gone to college. She'd planned on it. But, marriage, it seemed, had taken precedence. There was no way to figure it out. He would have to talk with her to solve the mystery of her life.

She wouldn't have dinner with him, but she would have gone to have a drink with him. *If he'd asked.*

Claire had always been a mystery to him.

He had to tread carefully. He didn't want to repeat whatever mistake he'd made twenty years ago that had scared her away.

He'd start slowly.

He'd start with the painting.

CHAPTER
Three

Claire closed the lid on her computer and stretched. She'd been up since dawn and had been working nonstop for two hours. It had been a week since the fundraising event. She'd gotten tons of work done, but the week had been jam packed with meetings. So, as usual, she was spending Saturday morning working in her home office.

Feeling the need to stretch her legs, she got dressed in her tights, sports bra, and T-shirt. She laced up her running shoes and put in her earbuds. She went into her exercise room, turned on Taylor Swift, and hopped on the treadmill. She never warmed up. Warming up always seemed like a waste of time. She just took off running.

She was well into mile three when the doorbell rang. Danielle was still asleep and it was too early for any of her friends to be coming over. It was rare that anyone was up and about on a Saturday morning. Even the neighbors stayed to themselves.

She went to the door and peeked out through the glass. A courier stood there with a large package balanced against his legs. Oh no. Surely Maine D'Court didn't send her a painting. She'd put his check in the mail, so he should have it now. She'd even added in a bonus for having a one hundred percent sell out. Maybe that had backfired and encouraged him. She'd hoped he would leave her alone now that the fundraiser was in the past.

She couldn't leave the courier standing on her front stoop all day. She opened the door and he slid what could only be a painting into her foyer and propped it against the wall. "These usually go to the gallery," she said, "Are you sure you have the right address?"

The boy showed her the address label. She didn't recognize the return address and there was no name listed. If this had been the gallery, she would have thought someone was sending her an unsolicited sample of their work. But for it to come to her home address was creepy.

She thanked the courier and locked the door. Then she ripped the thick paper from the painting and sat down on the stairs.

It was the fireworks painting. The very same painting she had personally sent to Grayson on Monday.

Unless...

She checked the back for the sticker she always added to indicate that it was purchased for the purpose of charity. And breathed a sigh of relief. The sticker was there. For a moment, she had feared that Maine D'Court had painted another just for her.

But this...

Grayson had spent a lot of money to buy this painting. And now he was just giving it away. She dug through the wrapping for a note, but there wasn't one. Nothing.

She stood with her hands on her hips. He could have at least sent his phone number along so she could call and thank him.

She should really send it back to him. It was too much to accept. But the thought made her giggle. They would quickly spend more on sending the thing back and forth than he'd paid for it to begin with.

When she had quoted the price, she didn't think he would actually buy it. If she'd thought he was going to buy it, she'd have taken off her commission, but then once he had his check book out, it would have been an insult to suddenly lower the price as though he couldn't afford to pay. In truth, she had no idea how much Grayson Moore could afford to pay.

"Mom?" Danielle called sleepily from the top of the stairs. "I thought I heard the doorbell. Is everything alright?"

"Everything's okay, honey," Claire said, reaching to pick up the wrapping paper. Charlie followed Claire down the stairs and rolled around in the paper, sending them both into a spell of giggles.

"What is that?" Danielle asked. "Is that from the fundraiser?"

"It is." Claire had no idea what to do with the painting.

"Did you buy it?" Danielle asked.

Claire shook her head.

"Who did?"

Claire looked at her daughter. She couldn't lie to her. "Grayson," she said.

Danielle's eyes widened. "No. Way."

"Way," Claire said, pulling on some twine to entertain the kitten.

"But..." She studied the painting. "If he bought it, why would he send it to you?"

"He probably overheard me telling someone that I liked it."

"So... he bought it for you," Danielle said, her lips turning into a smile.

Claire shrugged. "I guess."

"Do you like it? Really?" Danielle asked.

"Yeah. I do."

"We should put it in the kitchen," Danielle decided. "We need some color in there."

"Let's take it in there and see," Claire said.

The two of them carried the painting into the kitchen and stood it against the wall Claire had left bare. Danielle had been right. It did add a splash of color to the room.

"Nice," Danielle said. "Now tell me why my psych teacher would send you a painting."

"I have no idea," Claire went to turn on the tea kettle.

"Mom," Danielle said in a voice much too old for her eighteen years.

Claire pulled two mugs from the cabinet. "Alright," she said. How much did she tell her daughter? The truth, but not everything. Just like with Noah.

"We dated in high school."

Danielle gasped. "You did not!"

Claire smiled as she sipped water.

"Wait," Danielle grew serious. "I know that look. Is Grayson my father?"

Claire coughed as the water went down the wrong way. "Heavens, no. Noah is your father, honey."

"That's good," Danielle said. "But if you married Grayson, I'd have two awesome fathers."

"I can't believe you just said that," Claire said, but the idea latched onto her own fantasies.

"Why not? He's so much fun."

"I haven't even seen him in twenty years."

"Looks like he noticed you."

Claire flushed. Only out of the mouths of children. Especially almost adult children who had been in intensive therapy for almost a year and had learned to say what they felt.

"You should call him," Danielle said.

"I don't have his number."

Danielle tugged on the twine and laughed as the cat leaped into the air to grab it. She looked back at Claire, a smile on her lips. "I do."

Claire hadn't thought of that. She could call Grayson at his office. Fortunately for her, it was Saturday, so he wouldn't be there.

"I have his cell number," Danielle said.

Claire nearly dropped the tea kettle. "What? How?"

Danielle shrugged. "It's on the syllabus."

"He put his cell number on his syllabus?" She asked as she poured water into their mugs for tea.

"Sure. It's no big deal. It's not like anyone will call him. They'll just send texts."

"I didn't know they did that," Claire murmured. Texting a professor seemed like such an invasion of privacy. Especially texting a man who didn't even have a cell phone the last time she knew him.

She took a deep breath. "I could text him."

"Are you kidding? Mom. You can't text a thank you for a gift like that. I know how much your paintings go for. Seriously?"

"You're right."

"You're scared."

"I am not," Claire said. She so was.

"I'll get you the number," Danielle said, with a mischievous smile. "But you don't have to call him if you don't want to. I'm sure you'll do what's right."

It was so strange to hear her own words coming back to her from the one she'd said them to so many times before.

Danielle's phone rang. Claire recognized the ring tone Danielle had picked for her father. Noah called his daughter several times a week. Danielle's suicide attempt had been a wake-up call for all of them.

She took her tea and sat at the little table in the kitchen nook and watched the birds flutter around the bird feeder. The bird feeder she'd forgotten to fill.

The housekeeper was coming today. She'd put it on her list. Claire needed a shower before she called Grayson.

And, yes, she would call him. It was the right thing to do.

Claire called at eleven o'clock to thank him for the painting. She said she would text a picture over once she had it on the wall. It might be awhile.

She said she and Danielle were about to have lunch and go to the mall. One of Danielle's friends was coming along.

Grayson enjoyed the easy conversation between them. Unfortunately, it was all too brief.

He hadn't known if she would call. He hadn't given her his phone number on purpose. He didn't want it to be too easy… or too obvious. He also knew that his cell phone was on his syllabus. The only way she would get it would be if she talked to Danielle about him. It meant she told Danielle who'd sent the painting. It was important that Danielle be included in this new relationship with Claire.

Claire and Danielle were a package deal now. He knew that up front. And he wanted to make sure Claire knew he knew it.

He closed the textbook he'd been reading. He was distracted now and there was no way he was going to be able to concentrate. He saved Claire's phone number in his phone, put on some shorts and his running shoes and headed out for a jog.

Jogging cleared his head when nothing else would. He jogged down the sidewalk to the park and let his mind wander as he joined the Saturday morning families out for some sunshine. It was hot, but nothing like the south where he'd been stationed the last couple of years. San Antonio was hot. After lunch, jogging was prohibitive, to say the least. But here the weather was nice comparatively.

Claire said she never got his letters. He had the address right. What could have happened?

Her parents had seemed to like him well enough. But with him out of the way, it was hard to say what had happened. He'd googled the Worthington family after his mother had sent him the article about Claire's wedding. The Worthington family of Ft. Worth was wealthy to say the least. He couldn't blame Claire's father if he'd managed to arrange a marriage for her with someone of wealth.

Grayson certainly couldn't have offered her the lifestyle she was used to. He came from an upper middle-class family. He was doing okay now with his retirement from the military and his salary from the university. But still, he couldn't put himself in the wealthy category.

It was fortuitous that Claire was divorced now that he was back in town. It was even more fortuitous that Claire's daughter was in his class. Grayson had only been teaching for one year, starting last fall. The only way it could have been weirder was if she'd shown up in his very first class.

Grayson had learned a long time ago not to push things. If something was going to happen, it would happen. If he tried to push it and make it happen, it would only turn out badly.

He'd shown up at Claire's fundraiser, he'd bought the painting, and he'd sent it to her.

It was time to back off.

He wasn't putting the ball in her court. That wouldn't be fair. She'd done nothing to deserve that kind of treatment. Especially when she didn't know the rules.

But he would lay off for a while. Let things simmer. She was newly divorced. She didn't need him pushing at her.

Besides, August 3 was his last day in Los Angeles. Grayson would have finished his one year visiting professorship and had accepted a one-year full-time teaching position at Robert Morris University in Pittsburgh.

Four

Claire went upstairs knowing she would find her mother in the sitting room on the third floor of her home. Since her father had died three years ago, her mother had happily retreated from the hectic society life and spent her days mostly reading and sometimes sending emails and Facebooking with old friends.

The small sitting room, twice as large as most apartments, was not only spacious, but serene. Her mother had a flair for decorating that led to a calm atmosphere. Claire wondered how long it would be before her mother sold the large, cumbersome house where she had lived so many years with her husband and move into a smaller, more manageable place. Of course, with a live-in housekeeper, a cook, and a variety of other hired help, Claire mused that it probably didn't matter much. Her mother could live on the third floor of the house and the rest of the house would sustain itself. She even had a personal assistant who paid the bills and handled the business side of running a household including shopping for staples.

Claire had a personal assistant, too, but the girl, Martie, mostly handled business administrative work. And errands. Claire hated errands. The driving. The in and out of the car kind of errands. She had a weekly dry cleaning delivery service and basic food delivery, so Martie really had a limited number of errands.

"Claire," her mother smiled and stood up to hug her. "Did Danielle come?"

Danielle and Betty had been fast friends since the day Danielle came into the world.

Claire supposed it was a natural since Claire spent so much time working and Betty kept her during the weekdays when Danielle wasn't in school.

"She's got her afternoon yoga class and then she's going out with some friends."

"Aw," Betty sank back into her chair. "Tell her to come by when she has time."

"You know you'll see her this weekend."

"It's never soon enough," Betty said. "What brings you out here on a Tuesday?"

Her mother wanted to cut to the chase then. "I wanted to talk to you about something."

"All right. Would you like something to drink?"

Claire shook her head. "I have water."

"What's on your mind?"

"Do you remember Grayson?"

Her mother's face went blank. How could she not remember Grayson? Claire had been going to marry him.

"Of course," Betty said.

"He said he called."

Betty didn't even pretend not to know what Claire was talking about. Betty looked away, seeming to gaze at a bouquet on her desk.

"Did he?" Claire asked, her voice soft.

"He did. He called collect a few times. I didn't take the calls. Then he stopped."

"Mother. Why did you refuse his calls?"

"He was military," her mother said, turning back to face Claire. "You would have been part of another lifestyle. I didn't want that for you."

"Another lifestyle?"

"The military. I didn't think you would fit in."

Claire scoffed. "Shouldn't I have been the one to decide that?"

Betty sighed. "Probably. But I knew you weren't in a place to decide. You were too in love."

"Mom." Claire leaned forward in her chair. "What's wrong with love?"

Betty leaned away. "Do you remember I had a sister?"

"Of course. Aunt Mary. She died when I was… six? I was in first grade."

"Yes. She was older than I was. 8 years older. She was in love with a boy in the Army. He was drafted and they were married immediately." Betty took a deep breath. Kept going. "She got pregnant. Her husband was killed over there. In Vietnam. It broke Mary's heart. She took her own life and that of the child."

"Oh no," Claire pressed her fingertips against her forehead. Remembered all the forms she'd lied on. In both Ft. Worth and here. *Has anyone in your family ever committed suicide?*

She'd answered *no* on each and every one. How many staff

members had mentioned that suicide runs in families? "What didn't you tell me?" she asked and looked up at her mother, knowing the hurt was naked in her eyes. "Danielle…"

"I thought that if no one knew, it would be better."

"But when Danielle…"

"I know. I didn't say anything. I know they say it runs in families. But my therapist told me that it wasn't genetic. It was learned through environment. He said it was better if I didn't say anything."

"Danielle doesn't stand a chance."

"No! Don't think like that."

Claire straightened in her chair. Lifted her chin. "What does this have to do with Grayson?"

"Oh." Her mother fiddled with the handle on her desk drawer. "Every time I thought about the Army, I got sick to my stomach. Still do."

"So you punished me?"

"When Grayson said he was going into the Air Force, I couldn't stomach the thought of you being part of that world. I couldn't stand the thought of you living your life in misery."

"But you encouraged me to marry Noah." Claire said. Would her mother get the implication that she'd ended up in misery after all.

Her mother paled. "Yes," she uttered.

Claire shook her head and turned away. She fought the host of conflicted emotions that threated to overwhelm her.

"Was it really that bad?" Betty asked.

"No," Claire admitted. "It wasn't that bad being with Noah. We hardly ever saw each other. But, Mother, you kept me away from Grayson."

Her mother slowly reached for the bottom desk drawer handle and pulled it open. "I was going to wait and let you find these after I was gone." She reached into the back of the drawer. "But I have a feeling you need these now." She pulled out a two-inch stack of letters tied together with a ribbon and set them on the edge of the desk in front of Claire.

Claire stared at the stack of letters – at her name and parents' address scrawled across the front. And Grayson's name at the top. The letters were unopened. A weight sat in the pit of her stomach. A weight that carried regret and sadness. As the emotions settled in her gut, they released a new emotion.

Hope.

"Hi."

Grayson was in the middle of a department meeting when Claire called. They were discussing the summer advising schedule. None of the full-time faculty really wanted to be there. As the visiting faculty member, Grayson was sure he'd draw the short straw anyway, so when Claire's name came up on his phone, he stepped out.

"Is this convenient?"

"Sure," he lied. It had been just over two weeks since he'd sent her the painting.

"I won't keep you long. I was just wondering if you'd like to meet." She paused. "For that drink."

"Sure," he said. "When?"

"How about tonight?"

He had so much to do this weekend, it was going to be

impossible for him to even come close to catching up. "Okay," he said. "Want me to pick you up?"

"No," she said. "I'll meet you. How about D'Vine's at seven o'clock?"

"I'll be there," he said.

He went back into the conference room and he was the only one smiling through the rest of the meeting. He ended up taking the most summer office hours, but not even that could spoil his good mood.

After the meeting, he googled the address for D'Vine's before swinging by his apartment for a quick shower and change of clothes.

He got to the D'Vine lounge at six and found a bistro table toward the back so he could watch the door for Claire. He ordered some bread and a glass of wine while he waited.

He'd almost given up on hearing from Claire. He'd been toying with the idea of calling her. To take her up on that comment she'd made about having a drink with him. He certainly wasn't going to let her go that easily. In fact, his resolve to not push at her had been quickly fading.

There had been something in her voice when she'd called that he couldn't put his finger on. She sounded… serious. If he'd been contacting her, he would have worried that she wanted him to leave her alone. She'd sounded that serious. Right now, he was thankful he hadn't pushed at her.

Other than that, he was at a loss. Perhaps she was a much more serious person than before. When they dated in high school, she'd always had a smile in her voice. Except for the day before he left. In retrospect, sleeping together the night before he shipped out probably hadn't been the best idea.

He'd often wondered if that was why she didn't take his calls or answer his letters.

He'd done the math. Danielle was definitely not his child.

She walked in the door fifteen minutes early. It was going to take awhile to get used to her being brunette. She carried herself with different kind of confidence she'd had in high school. In school she'd been a bubbly majorette. Now she was a confident businesswoman.

He stood up so she would see him. She smiled and walked toward him. His attraction for her had never dimmed. He wondered how much his life was about to change with just this one meeting.

He held the bar stool while she climbed up, then sat next to her. "What would you like to drink?" he asked.

"A glass of chardonnay," she said.

He ordered her drink and another one for himself. They sat in silence for a couple of minutes before she lifted her gaze to his.

"I finished reading your letters," she said.

A jolt of surprise and trepidation shot through him. Surely she wouldn't hold something he'd written twenty years ago against him.

"But... you said you never got them."

"I didn't. But my mother did."

It had been her mother all along. He'd suspected her father, but it hadn't really occurred to him that her mother might be the one against him.

"She decided I wouldn't make a good military wife," she scoffed.

"Wow," he said.

She lifted her eyes, wide with unshed tears. "I'm sorry," she said.

"You have nothing to be sorry about," he said.

A single tear dripped down her cheek. He reached out and gently swept it away with a finger. "Don't be sad," he said.

"Your letters," she said. "What you wrote was so very heart wrenching. You must have been devastated when you didn't hear from me."

"You could say that," he said. "But it was a long time ago. Time heals."

She took a deep breath. "Yeah."

"You must have been deeply hurt when you didn't hear from me."

She nodded. "I was. My parents convinced me that I would never hear from you again and that I should move on."

"They made sure you didn't hear from me," he said.

"It was a terrible thing they did."

The server brought their wine. Claire sipped, then set her glass down.

"I don't hold it against them, he said. "They were only looking out for you."

"Ha. Sometimes it's better if parents don't interfere." She rested her hands on the table, running her fingertip along a crack in the wood.

He reached out and put his hand over hers. "You have Danielle," he said. "And the future is bright."

Claire wondered that either of them was willing to talk to the other. He believed that she hadn't responded to his letters while she believed he hadn't bothered to write or call. All this happened when they were most vulnerable. They had been young and had just slept together for the first time.

Both of them stabbed in the heart. But twenty years had passed. And Grayson was right. Time did heal. If it didn't heal, it did at least dull.

Had they been given a second chance? Claire wondered.

"Danielle said you recently retired from the Air Force. Have you been in this whole time?"

"I did twenty years. I won't say I loved every minute of it, but I got a college degree out of it and a nice retirement."

"You said you spent a lot of time overseas."

"A lot."

"What was your job?"

"I was a PJ," he said, then clarified. "Pararescue. Search and rescue."

"Impressive," she said.

"It was different."

"I can't even imagine."

"I wouldn't want you to. In some ways, your mother was right. The military is no place for having a family."

"Maybe," she said, still lost in the haze of his letters.

"Does the painting fit with your décor or is it a sore thumb?"

"It fits," she said, tapping her wine glass with a well-manicured fingernail. "Unfortunately, it's still sitting on the floor."

"It is kind of big," he agreed. "Would you like me to hang it for you?"

"Sure," she said. "But I don't want to impose."

"It's not an imposition, I promise," he assured her. "Have you eaten?"

"I had a snack," she said.

"Me too. Want to get dinner?"

She searched his eyes. Seemed to contemplate her answer. "Okay. I can do that," she said.

He laughed. "Nothing like a little enthusiasm."

She chuckled with him. "I'm sorry. I'm not the best of company right now. I just read two year's worth of letters from an old boyfriend."

"Prolific little guy wasn't he?"

"Maybe he should have been a writer," Claire said.

"I do write my share of research papers."

"A little different, I hope."

"A whole lot different."

She took a second sip of wine. "I'm sure your papers are well written."

"Yeah." He, too, sipped his wine, set down the glass, and kept his eyes down. His forehead was creased right in the middle. Worry lines that were in the process of etching a permanent home.

Even now, after twenty years, she knew him well enough to know something was troubling him. "What's bothering you?" she asked.

He shook his head. Glanced at her, then scoffed, and held her gaze. "I need to tell you something."

"That sounds ominous," she said and braced herself for whatever it was that had him in knots. Perhaps he had a terminal illness or perhaps he was gay. Whatever it was, she had a feeling it didn't bode well.

"It's about my job," he said.

She relaxed a bit.

"I have a master's degree in social work which allows me to teach psychology, but it's hard for me to find a full-time teaching position."

"I'm listening," she said.

"This job at UCLA is what they call a visiting professorship which is a nice way to say I get to work full-time but only for a year. I've managed to land a full-time teaching position."

"Congratulations!" she said.

"Thank you," he said.

"But…"

He scrubbed a hand across his chin. "It's in Pittsburgh, Pennsylvania."

Claire kept her emotions in check. On the outside. On the inside, her little bubble of hope burst, splattering her dreams and sending her thoughts down a familiar path from twenty years earlier.

They'd been sitting outside, at the park. It was early Spring, so the weather had been cool. Claire had been content, sitting there on a blanket, reading, with Grayson stretched out beside her. She'd thought he was sleeping.

"I'm going to be leaving soon," he had said.

"What?" She'd put her book aside and looked down at him. His eyes were closed.

"For Basic Training."

What felt like a knife had stabbed through her heart. She still remembered that feeling. She knew he'd joined the Air Force, but was hoping that he wouldn't have to actually go anywhere. "Where?" She asked.

"San Antonio."

She remembered staring straight ahead. Telling herself not to react. She'd been schooled in keeping her emotions in check.

But he was going away and there was nothing she could do to stop it.

The same feelings washed over her now. Grayson was going away and there was nothing she could do to stop it.

"When do you leave?" She asked, the déjà vu clogging her throat.

"August 3."

She swallowed, allowing the sadness to wash over her. It would pass.

But she needed to get away. She slipped off the bar stool, grabbed her handbag, and straightened her jacket. "I 'um. I need to go," she said, simply.

She rushed outside, dodging people, she barely saw. The only thought that consumed her was the need to get away.

She got into her car and sat, staring blankly ahead.

The tears threatened to spill from her eyes. Something wasn't right. She hadn't felt this intensity of emotion even through her divorce.

There had been only two times in her life that she'd felt this way. When Danielle attempted suicide and the day Grayson left over twenty years ago.

Grayson paid the check and walked out onto the street.

When he'd entered the Air Force all those years ago, he'd been excited. He'd expected to finish up boot camp, then tech school, then get Claire, marry her, and take her wherever he went next. Six months at the most away from her.

Such was the innocence of youth.

He'd done everything he knew to do at the time to keep her. But he'd been so wrapped up in his career. Once he'd become pararescue, he hadn't had the time to think about much of anything else. The job had consumed his life.

He couldn't shake the feeling, however, that he'd let Claire slip through his fingers.

In the back of his mind, he'd always thought he would someday come back to her and whisk her away. He supposed to be honest with himself, he'd imagined her waiting for him.

All that had changed when he'd gotten the newsletter article about her marriage. He'd thrown himself into work even more then.

He'd gotten a Silver Star and a host of other awards. Awards that didn't mean anything at the end of the day. He'd been awarded for doing his job.

And now what did he have to show for it?

What he didn't have was Claire.

And now history was repeating itself. His job was taking him away from her.

And just like last time, he wanted to spend as much time with her as he could before he left.

It was selfish, yes. But he was drawn to her.

Now that they were adults, there would be no parents keeping them apart. They had cell phones. He could text her and know that she got the message. Or he could pick up the phone and call her.

It wouldn't be like last time.

He got into his car and buckled up. He couldn't let her slip through his fingers again.

Seeing her was a sign. A sign that they still had a chance.

He typed the address that he had memorized into his GPS and headed toward her house.

As he went through the gates into her community, he was reminded that he may have a Silver Star awarded by the President of the United States, a master's degree, and a respected job in the community, but he would never live in her world.

He pulled into her circle drive and sat. This is where he could walk away. Go on about his life and let her go on with hers. It was the easy, uncomplicated thing to do.

Or... he could get out, walk up to her door, and complicate things for both of them.

Grayson groaned. He'd never chosen the easy way to do anything.

The least he could do was to hang the damn painting he'd bought for her.

Five

Claire went straight to her bathroom and washed her face. She hated the way she'd left Grayson. It was so uncharacteristic of her.

But she'd needed to get away.

It was as though she was reliving the whole thing all over again. His whole leaving her behind again.

It had been so long ago, yet it seemed as though it was happening again.

It didn't matter that she now knew he had written her letters and tried to get in touch with her. Her heart remembered only the pain.

She changed into casual pants and T-shirt. She never should have asked him to meet her for drinks.

What was in the past was in the past.

She knew better than to walk backwards. Walking backwards always led to bumping into something. Someone always got hurt.

Focus on today.

Focus on what she could control. Not what she couldn't. He was moving away.

Again.

He had shown up in her life again just long enough to give her some closure. At least now she knew. She knew he hadn't just abandoned her.

If anything, she had abandoned him.

Maybe she should have tried harder.

She thought about Danielle.

Would she be willing to lie to her own child as her parents had lied to her?

If she believed it was for Danielle's good, she might.

Danielle had had several boyfriends over the last couple of years, but no one serious enough to consider marrying.

Perhaps her mother had been right to keep her from marriage at such a young age. It was something she could have believed if her mother hadn't turned right around and practically shoved her at Noah.

Claire had liked Noah. He was handsome and charming.

And if it hadn't been for Grayson, she probably would have fallen in love with him.

Instead, she'd kept her emotional distance and poured herself into starting her business.

It was how she'd coped with Grayson's leaving her behind and, as she believed, not even trying to contact her after she'd slept with him.

As she went downstairs, her doorbell rang.

She peeked through the one-way glass on the door and her pulse rate quickened.

Grayson stood there, his hands in his pockets, and concern on his face.

Taking a deep breath and releasing it in a sigh, she opened the door. And they stood looking at each other.

"I promised to hang that painting for you," he said.

"Yes, you did," She stepped back and a smile tugged at her lips.

He came inside and she closed the door. "Claire. I…"

He lifted a hand, but she turned away. "It's back here," she said.

Her blood pounded in her ears. She stopped in front of the painting and swiped at her hair. If she'd known Grayson Moore was going to be here, in her house, she wouldn't have changed into her crop pants and or washed the make-up from her face.

After seeing the painting propped there against the wall, he turned and swept his gaze around her kitchen.

Though she was proud of her house and loved the choices she'd made in designing it, it mattered very much to her what Grayson thought.

"Nice," he said.

"Thank you," she said.

"Whoever did the design did an awesome job."

"That would be me," she said.

He turned his focus back to her. "You?"

"Yeah," She felt the heat rise in her cheeks.

"You're full of surprises," he said, his voice husky.

She bit her lip. "I have a hammer," she said, opening a kitchen drawer with an impressive array of tools – hammer, screwdriver, level, nails, measuring tape, and even a laser level.

"Let me see what you have in there," he said, quickly

becoming intimate with the contents of what she thought of as her tool drawer.

He took the hammer and found a couple of sturdy nails. "Do you have a pencil?"

"Of course," She grabbed a pencil from her kitchen desk and handed it to him.

"You want it about here?" He asked, after measuring the height of the painting.

"That looks good. Centered."

"Hold these nails," he said. She held out her palm as he placed the nails in her hand. His hand hovered there, his knuckles against her palm, sending little shock waves through her. It was the first physical contact they'd had in over twenty years.

His gaze glued to hers, he released the nails and pulled his hand away.

Her nerves tingled. And she couldn't think. He measured and marked, then took the hammer and after a few quick strikes, had two nails in the wall. He picked up the heavy painting and easily slipped the wires over the nails.

He stepped back, straightened the painting. "How's that?" He asked.

She blinked and forced herself to focus on the painting. "It's perfect," she said. Even if he'd hung it upside down, it would have been perfect in her eyes at that moment.

"Do you need me to do anything else?" He asked.

Kiss me.

The thought came out of nowhere and jarred her out of her trance. "No," she said. "Thank you for doing that."

"It was the least I could do after buying the thing."

Claire chuckled. "As Danielle says, it adds a splash of color to the room."

"Has he bothered you anymore?" he asked.

"Maine D'Court? No."

"Good. I was afraid I was going to have to embarrass him."

She laughed. "Would you like some hot tea?"

"Sure," he said.

Grayson settled on Claire's sofa with a cup of hot tea in his hands. He'd never had hot tea in his life. Claire's place was spotless. There was no way he could let her go to his place now. He had papers and books strewn everywhere.

She looked relaxed. She was wearing casual gray pants that looked like a cross between sweat pants and tights with a light pink T-shirt. She'd scrubbed her face free of make-up before he got there leaving her smelling like soap.

He didn't want to leave. He just wanted to be near her. He'd ask to dinner, but she looked like she'd already settled in for the evening. With two sisters, he knew better than to even bring it up.

"Do you want to order a pizza and watch a movie?"

She pulled her feet under her and smiled. "Sure." Her kitten, Charlie, had exhausted himself running and playing and was curled up in her lap.

How many nights in high school had they had gotten pizza and watched a movie? It was the most normal thing he could think of.

She'd told him Danielle was out with friends and wouldn't be home until much later.

She picked up her iPad and clicked on the screen. "Do you still like Hawaiian pizza?" she asked, looking up at him.

"Yeah. Good memory," he said.

Smiling, she made a few more clicks. "The pizza should be here in about fifteen minutes." She clicked some more and the TV came on displaying the image on her iPad. "What would you like to watch?" she asked.

Grayson was impressed. "You pick," he said.

"All right." She pulled up a series called *The 100*. "I've been thinking about starting this series. Danielle has been watching it and loves it. I've been needing to catch up so I can watch it with her or at least talk with her about it."

"Sounds good," he said. "Let's do it."

She was curled up on her side of the sofa and he on the other side. She had her feet tucked under her and a pillow hugged under her chin.

It was comfortable. Almost familiar. Except she should have been sitting next to him with his arms around her.

But she was skittish. She'd run away from him twice already. Once in the museum and once at the lounge. Maybe three times if he counted the York and Orleans where they'd met. He was fairly certain she'd seen him and ducked into the restroom while Danielle walked over to introduce her.

He didn't blame her. Couldn't blame her. They'd been something like star-crossed lovers the last time around. He was glad they'd gotten to straighten out the misunderstanding. They'd been kids with her parents doing what she thought best for her daughter. Life had moved forward.

This was either a second chance to begin again or a chance

for closure. He wasn't sure which one yet. He was leaning toward the second chance to start over.

When the doorbell rang, they both got up to go to the door to get the pizza.

"Hi Gregory," Claire said.

"Hi Mrs. Worthington." The delivery boy glanced at Grayson, then tried to look behind Claire. "Is Danielle home?"

"No, sorry. She's out tonight."

"Oh, well," he glanced at Grayson again. "Tell her I said hi."

"I will."

Grayson pulled some tip money out of his pocket and handed it to Gregory. "Thank you, sir," he said.

After Gregory left, Grayson carried the pizza into the living room while Claire went to the kitchen to get plates.

"You know you're getting older when the pizza delivery guy calls you sir," he said when she came back with plates and two bottles of water.

"Wait until you have a child," she said. "Then you really get used to it."

Grayson didn't respond. He focused on sorting through the pizzas. "You're still vegetarian," he said, noting her cheese pizza.

"And sometimes vegan," she said.

"Vegan is hard," he commented.

"Yeah. It's not so bad here, but in Ft. Worth it's almost impossible to be vegetarian, much less vegan."

"Beef country."

"You have no idea."

"How long have you had this place?" he asked.

"A couple of years. I started building it while Noah and I were still married. He didn't even know it."

Grayson filled his plate, sat back and took a bite. "This is good," he said. "You must have felt like you were living a double life."

"I did. Most people wondered why I would do that. Why I would have a life without Noah even knowing about it."

"That is something to wonder about," he said.

"It wasn't that Noah was too busy. We're all busy. I think it's just because he wasn't here. He was gone more than he was home."

"Still," Grayson said. "It seems like it would have been worth a conversation."

"We had a strange relationship, Noah and me. It was more of an arranged marriage than a marriage made in love."

"I kind of wondered about that. But you had a choice. Right?"

"Of course. But everyone wanted me to do it. And..." she took a bite and kept her eyes down.

He finished her sentence for her. "And I wasn't here."

"Pretty much," she said.

"You kind of have a trend going."

"Ha. Not a good thing."

"I'm sorry," he said.

"Not your fault."

"But it was about me," he said. "So, I'm sorry."

"I forgive you," she said, meeting his gaze.

"And I forgive you," he said, a mischievous grin on his face.

She smiled. "So, what, we just play it all over again? Hang out until you leave?"

"I don't know," he admitted. "I guess we just see what happens."

She considered. Nodded. "Might be better if we not repeat that last night."

She remembered. Of course she remembered. A woman always remembered her first time. As did a man.

"Deal," he said. "Do you like the show?" He asked, deliberately changing the subject.

"I do. Boys aren't very smart."

"I've always said girls are smarter than boys."

"As a rule, I agree."

"I believe it," he said.

They finished their pizza and Claire carried pizza boxes while Grayson carried plates to the kitchen and began putting them in the dishwasher.

Claire's phone rang. She frowned and answered. Her face went pale. "Where did you say?" She asked.

"Is she okay?" Claire closed her eyes and swayed a little, steadying herself with a hand on the counter. "I'll be right there."

"What is it?" Grayson asked.

She shook her head. "Danielle was in an accident."

Claire was trembling. She needed to find her handbag, but she couldn't remember where she left it. She paced to the living room, then back to the kitchen before she remembered that she kept her purse upstairs in the closet. She raced upstairs, grabbed her purse, and raced back down.

Grayson stood there, keys in his hand. "Come on," he said, taking her hand. "I'll drive."

Claire started to protest. The words formed on her lips, but she couldn't get them out loud. She let him lead her to his car and help her inside.

"Where?" he asked.

She told him the address and he took off driving. "Tell me what happened," he said as he drove.

She sat tensed on the edge of the seat. "I don't know. There was a car accident." She bit her thumbnail. "They said she was okay."

"We'll be there in a minute," he said.

Claire knew it would be more than a minute. It had been less than a year ago – last fall, that she'd ridden in the ambulance with Danielle after she drank too much vodka and took too many pills. Claire kept her Xanax locked in a safe now and rarely took it. She'd rarely taken it anyway. She'd only filled it because the doctor had insisted it would help with sleep. But Claire didn't like being knocked out. She liked being in control. If Danielle needed her or even her mother, she wanted to be alert in an instant.

Had Danielle tried to hurt herself again? She seemed to be doing so well. Her doctors seemed pleased with her progress. They'd told her that some adolescents go through that sort of thing, then never have any other problems. It was all about being aware. Being aware of signs and triggers. And getting help right away.

Claire hadn't seen any signs. And there hadn't been any triggers. Except for Danielle starting college, but she was excited. Claire was pretty certain about that.

"Hey," Grayson said. "I'm right here. You're not alone."

She brought her attention back to the moment. Focused her gaze on Grayson. "Thank you," she whispered.

He reached over and took her hand in his. "They said she was okay." He glanced at her reassuringly, then put his eyes back on the traffic.

They rode in silence the rest of the way to the hospital.

"I'll let you out," he said, dropping her off at the door to the ER. "I'll find you," he said as she jumped out and sprinted toward the doors.

Claire ran to the desk and asked for her daughter. The receptionist tapped on the computer, asked for Claire's name and then promptly ushered into one of the exam rooms. When she stepped through the door, Danielle was sitting on the edge of an exam table. "Mom!" She said. Danielle was being examined by a young male doctor.

Claire ran to her and squeezed her hand. "What happened, Baby?"

"I was riding with some girls across campus and we were hit by another car."

Claire felt a tear spill down her cheek. Her baby wasn't safe anywhere. Not even at school.

"She has a clavicle contusion," the doctor said.

"It means she has a bruised collarbone," Grayson said. All eyes turned on him. "Right?"

"Yes," the doctor said. "I'm going to wrap this bandage around you. You need to try and not move your arm more than necessary for about two weeks."

"What does that mean?" Danielle asked. "Not more than necessary?"

"It means take it easy," the doctor said, glancing at Grayson and fastening the ends of the bandage.

"I'll wait outside," Grayson said.

"No," Claire said, reaching for his hand. She needed his strength.

"Mom," Danielle said, "I'm okay. But I do need to get dressed now."

"We'll be right outside the door."

She stepped outside with Grayson and he pulled her close. She fit just like she remembered. Just under his chin. He held on tight.

"What does it mean? A bruised collarbone?" she asked against his chest.

"It means she didn't break her collarbone which is certainly a good thing. It means she's going to be in pain and have some swelling. She can use ice for the swelling, but she'll need to keep it in a sling to keep from moving it around too much. She should be back to normal with a week or two."

"It doesn't sound too bad."

"You might want to keep her home in the bed or on the sofa for a few days especially while she takes pain medication."

"Okay," she said, taking a deep breath.

"Is there something you haven't told me?"

"I wouldn't know where to start," she said.

He pushed back and lifted her chin until her eyes met his. "Start with Danielle," he suggested.

"Last Fall she attempted suicide."

"Oh Claire," he said, pulling her against him again and stroking the back of her head.

It felt good to have someone to lean on. "She needs to call her father," she said, trying to push back.

He held tight. "She can call on the way home. Or in the morning. Claire. She's okay."

He felt her nodding against his chest. "On the way home. Noah will want to know." *Unless he's flying and doesn't have phone service.*

The doctor left and Claire went back to help Danielle get dressed.

"Grayson came with you," Danielle observed.

"He did."

"How did that happen?" Danielle asked.

"He came over to help me hang the painting."

Danielle grinned, then groaned when she moved her arm wrong. "The doctor wrote a script for pain pills, but I'm not going to take them."

"Why not?"

"I don't wanna be a pill head."

Claire hid a smile. Perhaps all that therapy had done some good.

"Is Grayson coming back with us?" she asked.

"He drove me here, so yes."

"Good."

"You're enjoying this," Claire observed.

Danielle shrugged. Groaned. "It's cute."

Cute. Claire rolled her eyes, but as they got Danielle up and into the wheelchair, her eyes teared up. The memory of her daughter on life support was too fresh.

As soon as they hit the door, Grayson grabbed the handles

on the wheelchair. "Some students will do ANYTHING to get out of going to class."

Danielle laughed and some of Claire's tension dissipated. Danielle was okay, she repeated to herself. She'd been in a minor accident. She hadn't tried to hurt herself again.

"Are you kidding?" Danielle asked. "Your class is my favorite."

"Well, we'll see how you feel after you finish that first test next week."

"I'm going to ace it. Especially now that I get to miss therapy and yoga. I get to miss yoga, Mom," Danielle said.

"Yes, you do. For at least two weeks."

"That's like three hours a day I can spend studying."

"Probably more like three extra hours a day to sleep," Grayson teased.

Danielle yawned. "Good idea."

Once they got back home and got Danielle into her bed, Claire walked back downstairs with Grayson.

"That pain medicine knocked her out," Claire said.

"It's good for her to get some sleep."

"Is it going to be very painful?"

"Hard to say. It depends on the swelling."

They reached the front door. "I'll come by tomorrow after class to check on her."

"Okay," she said as he pulled her against him into a close hug. They stood hugging as the minutes ticked past. When the grandfather clock in the foyer tolled the midnight hour, Grayson pulled back. "I'll see you tomorrow," he said and slipped out the door.

Claire locked the door and leaned against it.

It was only a hug.

But it had been like coming home.

Grayson stood in the middle of the supermarket riddled with indecisiveness. What did one give an 18-year-old college student as a get-well gift? As a college professor, he needed to know these things. Too late, he realized he should have asked the student worker in the office.

He went up to the customer service counter and asked the young girl working there. "What kind of gift do you recommend to give a college student who's recovering from an accident?"

"It depends on what she likes."

"I don't know her all that well," he said.

The girl raised her eyebrows. "A flower?"

"She's my girlfriend's daughter," he clarified.

"What does she like?"

"All I know is she's a college student. Oh. And she has a kitten."

"Some cat toys? And an Amazon gift card?"

"Perfect!" He said. He located the pet aisle and started with a round blue pet bed. He put in some stuffed rats and a collapsible wand with something shiny on the end. He threw in a couple cans of canned cat food and moved to the gift card section. He picked a one-hundred-dollar amazon gift card.

Satisfied with his selections for Danielle, he started toward the checkout, passing the florist on his way. Going with impulse, he chose a single get well balloon and had blown up for purchase. The florist rang up his purchase and helped him arrange the cat toys with the gift card sitting in the middle, wrapped it with cellophane and tied it with bright blue ribbons to match the balloon.

Pleased with his purchase, Grayson took it out to the car and drove the short distance to Claire's house. He was getting used to the area and didn't feel quite so intimidated anymore. He noticed that one of Claire's neighbors needed to clean his gutters and another had a foot-high ant hill encroaching on his sidewalk.

The people may have bigger, nicer houses, but they still had the same problems as everyone else.

Claire met him at the door with her phone to her ear. "Sorry," she mouthed.

"For Danielle," he said, indicating the cat bed.

Claire put her hand over her phone. "She's in the living room." She walked toward the kitchen. "Surely we can reschedule," he heard her saying.

"Hi there," Grayson said, stopping at the living room door. Danielle was sitting on the sofa with her arm in a sling and a pained look on her face. Charlie was on his back swatting the fringe on the throw. "I brought you and Charlie something."

He set the package on the sofa next to her.

"You can sit," she said.

"How's your shoulder?"

"It hurts," she said. "What did I miss today?"

"Nothing," he said, holding out his phone. "I recorded it for you."

"Seriously!"

"Yeah, let's keep it between us, okay?"

"Sure."

He handed her his phone. "You can send it to yourself," he said.

She took his phone and a couple of seconds later, hers chimed. "Thank you." She tore the cellophane off and snagged the gift card, putting it on the end table next to her before unwrapping the collapsible pole with the shiny thing on the end of it.

She bobbed it in front of Charlie and he went wild chasing it wherever Danielle swung it.

She giggled and Grayson laughed.

"What are you two up to?" Claire asked, coming into the room.

"Look, Mom. Grayson brought toys for Charlie."

"I see," she said, turning a warm gaze in Grayson's direction. "How thoughtful."

"What's going on?" he asked.

"Danielle, would you like some tea?"

"Sure," Danielle said, giggling at Charlie's antics.

"Let's get some tea," Claire said, motioning for Grayson to follow her. They went into the kitchen and Claire turned on the teakettle.

"I love it that I can be here with her, but I had a major

committee meeting set up for tomorrow. It's going to take some work to get everything rescheduled."

"Then don't," he said. "I can stay with her."

"It's likely to go late into the evening."

"All the more reason for me to be here."

She pressed her fingertips against her forehead. "Really? No," She turned off the tea kettle. "I can't ask you to babysit."

"Claire," he said. "She's not a baby. And you didn't ask. I like Danielle. We can hang out and watch movies."

She poured water into three mugs. He smiled when she didn't even ask him if he wanted any.

"Okay," she said. "Are you sure it's not an inconvenience?"

"I wouldn't offer if it was."

She stirred and turned to him.

"I know you're a package deal now," he said. "I'm good with that. I actually like it. You and Danielle need my help. Let me help you."

"Okay," she said. "Can you grab one of these?"

He picked up two mugs and they carried them into the living room.

"I need to call Martie," Claire said, leaving them.

"Sure."

"Can you stay?" Danielle asked. "Mom and I are going to watch *The 100*."

Grayson grinned. "If you Mom says it's okay."

"Are you kidding," Danielle said. "Mom's crushing on you."

Grayson sat on the other end of the sofa and grinned. "Seriously?"

Danielle laughed. "You two are like teenagers."

When Claire got off the phone and joined them, they ordered

Chinese take-out and binge watched *The 100*. Claire pulled a footstool up and sat between them in the middle of the sofa. She slipped her feet out of her sneakers and propped her bare feet on the stool. Grayson followed suit and pulled off his shoes. He propped his feet, with his white socks, on the foot stool. He was distracted the whole time they were watching TV by his feet being only inches from hers.

Geez. He had to remind himself that they weren't teenagers anymore. He was quite content to just sit next to her, their feet almost touching.

Though he was enjoying their time together, he was looking forward to saying goodnight.

After she noticed Danielle falling asleep, she suggested she go to bed. She followed Danielle up to bed to help her put on her pajamas. Then she came back downstairs to tell Grayson goodnight.

He'd been answering emails on his phone. Students were starting to stress now that their first test was coming up.

"I'm glad you stayed," Claire said.

"Thanks for letting me. I had a blast."

"You're sure about tomorrow?" she asked.

"Stop asking. I'm looking forward to it. You don't mind if I cook in your kitchen, do you?"

"Of course not. Enjoy yourself."

He rubbed his hands together. "Danielle's vegetarian, too, right?"

"As far as I know."

"That's okay. I have some vegetarian tricks up my sleeve."

He pulled her into a hug. She started to pull away, but he pulled her closer.

He didn't want to let her go. Ever.

But this time when she pulled away, he kissed her on the forehead and squeezed her hands. "I'll see you tomorrow," he said.

Claire was happy she could make the committee meeting, but she wanted to be somewhere else. She wanted to be home, with Danielle and Grayson. They were there in her kitchen. Without her.

She clicked on her phone to check the time again. They were interviewing mentors today. She should have delegated it. But she liked to keep a tight rein on her company.

Old habits were hard to break. If she was going to start having some semblance of a personal life, she had to become more comfortable at delegating.

Her mind was wandering anyway.

She kept thinking about being in Grayson's arms. The feel of his lips on her forehead. Wanted more. So much more.

"Do you want stir-fry or spaghetti?" Grayson asked, putting the sacks of groceries on the counter. "I brought stuff to make both."

"Spaghetti," Danielle said. She sat at the breakfast table nook, with her headphones on listening to her lectures. She hit pause. "It's really hard to keep up when you're not there sitting in the classroom."

"I agree," he said. "That's why I refuse to teach online classes. I took an online class once. And it was a joke. I learned absolutely nothing."

"I should be able to go back to class Monday," she said.

"Three days from now." He nodded. That should do it. "You would have only missed two days. Not bad. Only a week's worth of material during the regular semester. But," he stopped and waited until she looked up. "You can only come to class if you let your mother drive you."

Danielle scoffed. "That's not a problem. I'm not one of those people who thinks if you don't drive, you aren't grown up. I can be grown up and not drive. In fact, I think I'll move to New York when I get out of school so I never have to drive."

"Where did you get that idea? It's almost un-American."

She laughed. "Savannah talks about New York and how she wants to live there."

"Who's Savannah?"

"That's Daddy's wife."

It took Grayson a minute for his mind to wind its way around that piece of information. So, Claire's ex-husband had already remarried.

"Well, in that case, you can come to class on Monday."

She smiled and put her earbuds back in her ears.

Grayson chopped onions, bell peppers, and black olives. He found a large stove top pot and mixed in whole tomatoes, tomato paste, tomato sauce, three cans of cream of onion soup. He added the onions, bell peppers, black olives, and a host of Italian spices. After it simmered for awhile, he added in some grated parmesan cheese. While it simmered some more, he grated some mozzarella and poured some red wine into the pot.

He heated water in another pot for the pasta.

While he waited, he opened his MacBook and answered emails from students. He enjoyed the peacefulness of the kitchen, Danielle engrossed in her studies at the kitchen table, the view of the backyard, shaded by trees.

And more than anything, the knowledge that Claire would be home soon. He glanced up at the painting that she'd chosen, and that he'd bought and hung. His contribution to the house.

Charlie came into the room, sat in the middle of the kitchen floor, and started to meow.

He looked at Danielle. She took out her headphones. "He's hungry," she said.

"What do we feed him?" he asked.

She started to get up. Winced and sat back down. "It's in the pantry. There," she pointed, holding her shoulder. "There are little plates there, too, for him."

Grayson opened the cabinet and took out a can of kitten food and a plate. He dumped the food into the bowl and set it in the floor.

Charlie howled.

Danielle laughed. "You have to mash it up and put warm water on it."

Grayson did as she said and put the plate back in the floor. Charlie stopped meowing and lapped up the food.

There. Crisis solved. Now they could get back to their peaceful evening. He laughed at himself. He even liked the cat.

He turned everything off on the stove to wait for Claire and went back to his emails.

The doorbell rang. He and Danielle looked at each other. She shrugged.

"Want me to go see who it is?" he asked.

"Sure. I'm not expecting anyone."

Grayson went to the front of the house and opened the front

door. A man, about his size, stood with his back to the door, one hand on the front porch post. Though he turned with a smile on his face, his smile quickly turned to confusion.

"Can I help you?" Grayson asked.

"I'm Noah."

Noah. Noah Worthington?

Danielle's father. Claire's ex-husband.

The pieces fell into place as the two men stood looking at each other. Grayson had a definite advantage. "I'm Grayson," he said. "Claire's… friend." He held out his hand.

Noah shook his hand, though he watched him warily.

"Come in," Grayson said, stepping back. "We're in the kitchen."

Noah followed him through the house.

Danielle looked up and saw Noah following him. "Daddy!" She said, standing up, wincing in pain.

Noah came across the room and hugged her gently. Then he stepped back and examined her sling. "Does it hurt?"

"Not so much," she said. "Only when I move it."

"I'm so glad you're okay, Baby," he said.

"Mom and Grayson are taking good care of me," she said.

"Grayson."

"Grayson is Mom's friend from high school," Danielle said.

"We met," Noah said. "Where's Claire?"

"She had a meeting," Danielle said. "We're going to eat when she gets home."

Danielle's phone chimed. "She'll be here in ten minutes."

Noah glanced at Grayson. Neither one said anything.

Danielle shoved her books aside.

Grayson put the angel hair on to cook. "Three minutes to

dinner," he said to no one in particular. "We have plenty Noah. Can I get you something to drink?"

"Sure. But I can get it."

"No problem."

Noah poured a glass of wine for himself. "Want some?" he asked Grayson.

Grayson declined. Noah sat at the kitchen table next to Danielle.

While father and daughter talked, Grayson heated the sauce and drained the noodles. He set out plates and silverware on the counter. Everything was ready, but Claire would have to take it from here.

A few minutes later, Claire came into the room. "I'm home," she said, brightly.

"Hi Mom," Danielle said. "Noah's here."

Claire's expression went blank. Grayson wondered if Noah had a habit of making surprise visits.

"I see," she said. "Hello Noah."

Grayson watched their interaction. It was stiff. He wondered if it was because he was there. "Look," Grayson said, "Everything is ready for dinner," he said. "I can take off. Give you guys some privacy."

"No!" Danielle said.

"Don't even think about it," Claire said. "That's not even an option."

"I don't mind, really," Grayson said.

"I'm the one who should be leaving," Noah said. "I shouldn't have popped in uninvited. I didn't know…"

He didn't know anything had changed with Claire, Grayson thought.

"No one is leaving. Both of you are being silly," Claire said. "Let's eat at the table. Noah, you set the table while Grayson and I get everything ready."

Noah took the plates and silverware to the dining room.

"I am so sorry," Claire whispered to Grayson. "He just does that. He just shows up without calling."

"It's okay," Grayson said. "I understand. He's Danielle's father."

"Still," she chewed her bottom lip. "I don't want you to feel awkward."

"I don't," he said, taking her hand. "Claire," he said, sweeping a strand of hair off her cheek. "I don't expect everything to change just because I'm here. I know you and Danielle have a life. I'm just grateful you let me be a little part of it."

Her chin trembled. "Thank you," she said. Then she seemed to shake it off and smiled. "This pasta smells delicious. I can't wait to try it."

"But..." he said. "There is one thing."

"What is it?" she asked. He heard the little catch in her voice.

"I promise to never show up unexpectedly."

He heard the relief in her laugh.

Claire was nearly undone. Her ex-husband and her high school sweetheart were here in her home at the same time. Having dinner.

And same said high school sweetheart was the guy she was currently crushing on.

She had to get herself in check. This would not do.

She'd nearly cried in front of Grayson.

Claire never did that.

Always in control.

It's what she had been taught. She was good at it.

But somehow all bets seemed to be off where Grayson was concerned.

Danielle seemed to be unaffected. Her father and her mother's guy friend over at the same time.

Maybe Danielle was unaffected because she had friends with unusual dynamics. Claire and Noah had been married longer than any of Danielle's friends' parents.

That was it, she decided. She took a deep breath and focused on enjoying the pasta Grayson had cooked for her and Danielle.

She was a little surprised that Noah had stayed. *Am I supposed to get used to this?* Would Noah be bringing his wife next time?

She shrugged. Stranger things had happened.

He loved Danielle beyond anything else. It was very important that she do everything she could to keep them all connected.

Besides she and Noah were going to be better as friends. Already, she could tell. She liked that there were no expectations when she saw him. No pretending required. And really, their relationship was the same now as it had pretty much ever been.

Seeing him didn't cause her heart rate to quicken the way it did when she saw Grayson. When she'd walked into her kitchen and saw both of them there, Noah sitting with Danielle and Grayson standing over the stove, she had been drawn to Grayson. Hands down.

She'd loved Noah. He was the father of her daughter and he

was a good man. But she was... had been... in love with Grayson.

She carefully set down her glass of sparkling water and straightened the napkin in her lap.

She would have to think more about this. Later.

Right now she needed to keep her edge. Danielle was telling Noah about her classes. Specifically, how much she loved her psychology class.

Grayson beamed.

"Honey, tell them about what you're taking this Fall," Claire said.

She rested her chin on her hands and watched her daughter interact with the men at her table. Just as she had thought earlier, Danielle seemed to have no problem with both of them being there. It was a most interesting situation.

Perhaps Danielle wouldn't mind having two fathers.

She pulled herself out of her fantasy world.

Grayson would be leaving soon, so that was just that. A fantasy.

But Claire had schooled herself well on living in the present.

And she suddenly realized that she, just as Danielle, honestly didn't mind having both of the men there at the same time.

"What do you do?" Noah asked Grayson.

"I'm a professor of psychology."

"He just retired from the Air Force," Danielle added.

"The Air Force?" Noah seemed surprised. "What did you do?"

"Pararescue."

"You jumped out of a few good planes," Noah said.

"Quite a few," Grayson said. "Do you parachute?"

"Oh no. My goal is keep the plane in the air, land smoothly, then step onto the ground."

The men laughed. "A good goal to have," Grayson agreed.

"My wife," Noah started, then stopped, glanced at Claire.

Claire shrugged.

"My wife, Savannah," Noah continued. "would love to talk to you. She's studying psychology and she's especially interested in studying traumatic experiences."

"I know quite a few men who went through them," Grayson said, easily, but Claire noticed the tension in his face. He took another bite, then set his fork down.

Danielle must have noticed, too. "Hey Dad," she said. "Did you know that we have something called mirror neurons?"

"What's a mirror neuron?" Noah asked.

"We have neurons in our brains that are activated when we watch someone feel something. So, when we see someone cry, our similar neurons are activated and we feel empathy for them. We essentially feel what they feel." She glanced at Grayson. He gave her a quick nod.

"That sounds neat, honey. Sounds like you're learning a lot."

"I am! Grayson has been teaching us all about biology and how the brain and body are connected."

"I'm proud of you, Danielle," Noah said.

"Your daughter is doing really well in class," Grayson said.

"I guess I'll know after my test next week," Danielle said. "It's a lot of material."

"I always say that intro psychology is the hardest psychology class," Grayson said. "You have to learn a little bit about all the different fields of psychology. There's a whole class on physiological psychology and you have to learn about the basics all in one chapter. Then you have to learn about the history of psychology and one on psychological disorders. You get a glimpse of everything and have to learn new terminology about everything."

"Even statistics," Danielle said.

"It sounds rigorous," Noah said.

"It is," Grayson agreed. "As long as she puts in the work, she'll be okay."

CHAPTER
Seven

After dinner, Noah and Danielle went into the living room to "hang out," as Danielle put it. Grayson and Claire hung back to clean up and do the dishes.

Grayson was feeling a bit restless. "I'm gonna head out," he said.

"What? Why?" Claire said.

"It's late and I've been here since early afternoon. I've to get home and start making a test for next week."

"It's because Noah is here," Claire said.

"Sort of," he admitted as he put plates in the dishwasher. "But not in a bad way. I just met him, so I need to give you guys some time to adjust. I'll stay longer next time."

She stood holding the dishcloth, her mouth curved in that lovely little smile that he loved. "Okay," she said. "But next time, I do the cooking."

He took a step toward her. Took her hand and kissed her palm. "Or… maybe I'll take you out to dinner next time."

She smiled. "Sounds even better," she said.

"I'll say goodbye, then head out," he said.

She nodded. Then turned back to wipe at the counter. Everything was back in its place. It was as though he'd never been there.

He said goodbye to Danielle and Noah before slipping out the front door and bounding down the stairs to his car.

He sat for a minute, watching the house. He hadn't been completely truthful with Claire. It was hard to be there with Noah. Knowing that, even though they were divorced, Noah belonged there more than Grayson did.

Noah and Claire had a history. And they would have a reason to stay in touch. Danielle.

Grayson could deal with that. He liked Noah. Noah seemed like a good guy.

Grayson knew himself well enough to know what had gotten under his skin. It was talking about, even briefly, his time overseas. It only took a comment or a random reference to put his mind back there. And he used a lot of energy to keep that from happening.

He started up the motor and headed to his place. He did need to work on putting together the psychology exam for next week. But he also needed some time alone. Some time to settle himself.

Grayson fell asleep on the couch watching reruns of *Game of Thrones*.

Some time later, after being jarred awake, he knocked his phone on the floor as he grabbed for it.

He didn't recognize the number and didn't even know what time it was. He swiped to answer.

"Grayson?" The woman's voice was upset.

"Yes," Grayson sat up. A flash of fear shot through him. He hadn't spoken to either his mother or his sister lately. He pulled the phone away to glance at the unknown area code.

"This is Alex Taylor."

Grayson rubbed at his eyes. He didn't recognize the name. He squeezed the phone waiting for her to go on.

"I'm calling about my brother, Timothy. I don't know where his phone is, but he had me save your number in case I ever needed anything. I'm sorry to call so late."

Timothy Taylor. His best friend. "Is he okay?" Even as he said the words, he knew she wouldn't be calling if everything was okay.

"No," Alex said and her voice broke. "They took him to the emergency room. It's bad."

"What happened?" Grayson was awake now, but he couldn't process what she was saying. He'd just talked to Timothy, what, two weeks ago. Maybe three.

He'd gotten a new job and was about to be granted visitation to see his kids again.

"He shot himself." He heard her sobs through the phone line.

"What? When?"

"I don't know," she sobbed. "It was earlier today or last night. I don't know. I talked to him yesterday. He sounded kinda weird, so I came over to check on him this evening when he didn't answer his phone. The cops just left."

"Are you at his house?" he asked.

"I'm on my way to the hospital."

"Do you need me to come?" he asked.

"Would you? There's nobody but us. I don't know what to do."

"Okay. I'll see when I can get a flight to Houston and call you back. Is this your cell phone?"

"Yes," Alex said. "Thank you."

"Call me if you know anything."

He hung up the phone. And sat staring at it while he tried to process what he had to do. Timothy and he had a pact. They'd agreed to take care of each other's families if anything ever happened. They had also agreed to call each other if things ever got so bad they couldn't deal with it.

Then a memory stabbed him in the gut. Timothy had sent him a text last week. Grayson had been in the middle of class. Grayson scrolled back through his texts. Last Tuesday. *Call me when you get a minute.*

Grayson hadn't responded.

It wasn't Timothy who had broken the agreement. It was Grayson.

The guilt stabbed him like a knife. He had to get to Alex. He had to be there for Timothy. It was 9:45. He had to get online and find a flight. He had to pack.

He had to call Claire before it was too late.

He dialed her number before he changed his mind and before it got any later.

"Hello," she answered.

"Claire. Are you still awake?"

"Yeah. I'm just reading."

"I have to get to Houston," he blurted.

"Why?"

"My best friend's in the hospital. He attempted suicide and

his sister called me." Grayson stood up and went toward his bedroom. He dragged his suitcase from the closet.

"When are you leaving?"

"I don't know. I've got to see when the first flight out is. I called you first."

"You need to leave now?"

"Yeah. They just took him to the ER. His sister is all alone."

"Hold on," she said. "Let me call you right back." The phone went dead in his ear.

Grayson tossed his phone on the bed along with his suitcase. He opened his iPad and looked up flights out of L.A.

Claire called back. "Can you be at the airport in two hours?" she asked.

"I think so." It was thirty minutes to the airport. That was about an hour to pack. He could do it in thirty.

"I'm going to text you a phone number. After you park your car at the airport call this number. Noah will take you to Houston in his plane."

"No," he said. "I can't let him do that."

"Of course, you can. It'll be impossible for you to get out tonight. Noah can have you there in no time."

"I couldn't ask…"

"You didn't. I did. And don't try to pay him."

"It's not about the money." He said. How could explain that it was more about how he felt about Claire?

"Then go pack. I'll text you the number. Call me in the morning when you know something about your friend."

"Okay," he said.

"I'll be here when you get back. Good night, Grayson," she said.

"Good night."

Before he could say anything else, she hung up the phone.

Grayson went into the bathroom and washed his face. This was a side of Claire he didn't know. Calm and decisive. He liked it.

While he was in the bathroom, he tossed his toiletries into his shaving kit and carried it back to his suitcase.

Timothy better pull out of this, Grayson thought. Because *you owe me one, buddy.*

"Noah, are you sure you don't mind?" Claire asked.

"I was heading that way in the morning anyway," he said, as he locked in the flight on his iPad.

"But you haven't slept."

"I'll get a room in Houston and sleep before I head up to Ft. Worth tomorrow."

"Thank you," she said.

"Thanks for coming to check on me," Danielle said.

"I'm just glad you're okay, kitten," he said.

"When can you come back?" Danielle asked.

"When do you want me to?" he asked.

Danielle scoffed. "Tomorrow."

Noah kissed Danielle on the top of her head. "You know I would," he said. "How about if I call you tomorrow." He glanced at Claire. "I guess I'd better start calling before I show up."

Claire laughed. "Then you wouldn't be you."

"Sometimes that wouldn't be a bad thing."

"I'll walk you to the door," Claire said.

"Danielle said you know Grayson from high school," Noah said when they were out of earshot of their daughter.

"We dated," she said.

"And now?"

"I don't know. Nothing can come of it."

"Why not? You seem to have a good thing."

"He's moving away in a couple of months."

"That's too bad," he said. "He seems like good guy."

"He is."

"And you like him."

Claire smiled and realized that, yes, she did like him. Even after all this time. She'd never stopped liking him.

"Maybe you can change his mind," he said.

Claire shook her head. "I don't think so."

"There's always hope," he said. "Look at me."

Noah was the eternal optimist. Especially since he'd gotten back together with Savannah. They had been college sweethearts. Ever since they'd gotten back together, Noah had been an insufferably happy romantic.

He swept his thumb under her chin. "I'll take good care of him," he said.

Claire had learned a lot about Noah when they'd gone through therapy after Danielle's suicide attempt. She learned that he'd never gotten over Savannah.

Claire, however, had never mentioned Grayson. In fact, she'd managed to talk about herself as little as possible. She'd only talked about work and, as a result, Noah had learned something about her.

They'd come out of Danielle's crisis with a new respect for

each other and a friendship they'd never had before. She liked that they were no longer at odds.

After Noah left, Claire curled up on the sofa with Danielle and they watched the Hunger Games together until Danielle started to fall asleep.

"Come on, Sweetheart, let's go to bed."

Danielle stood up and winced.

"Do you need some medication?" Claire asked.

Danielle shook her head. "I have to get up tomorrow and study. It makes me sleep too much."

Claire helped Danielle change into her pajamas and tucked her into bed.

She went to her computer and began putting together an ad seeking her next artist. It was her tried and true method of dealing with emotions.

Grayson didn't make it in time. When he got to the ER and asked for Timothy, the nurse had pointed him toward a woman curled up in the corner, sobbing.

"Alex?" he said, going up to her.

She lifted her face, her eyes swollen. She nodded. And began wailing.

"Hey," Grayson said, kneeling next to her and taking the woman he'd never met, the sister of his best friend, in his arms.

When she finally quieted, heavy in his arms, he wondered if she'd passed out. "Hey," he said, nudging her gently. "I'm gonna get you some water and a cloth for your face."

He shifted her to rest her head on a chair. Grayson escaped

and went straight to the nurse's station. He asked for water and a wash cloth. And information.

Timothy had died about an hour ago from a self-inflicted gunshot wound.

"We need to contact the VA." he said.

"We'll take care of it, sir," she said.

He took the water back to Alex. She was sitting up now. He handed her the wet wash cloth, but she just held it. He took it back from her and washed her face.

"What do I do now?" she asked, her voice hoarse.

"I'll take care of it," he said. "Is there someone I can call for you?"

She looked into his eyes and the tears started again. "There's no one," she said. "Just you."

Grayson sat next to Alex and put his elbows on his knees. His friend Timothy had given twenty years of his life for his country. He was a decorated veteran with no one to grieve for him except his sister and his best friend.

Now he was a statistic. One of the many who fell victim to suicide.

Grayson had slept a little on the three-hour flight to Houston, but he was emotionally drained.

How had things gotten so bad with Timothy? How had they gotten so bad that he'd chosen a permanent solution to a temporary problem?

Grayson knew there were far too many similarities between himself and Timothy. Grayson, too, had no family other than his mother and sister. The parallels sent a shiver down his back.

What would he do if he found himself Timothy's shoes? May God protect him from that.

Grayson did not want to spend the rest of his life alone.

With no one to call if he fell into the depths of despair.

With no children to keep him alive. Children were the number one protective factor against completed suicide.

Grayson had never given much thought to having children. Not since Claire.

Perhaps it time to think about it again.

Claire had received only three messages from Grayson since he'd left in the middle of the night Friday. One was as he'd promised saying he'd arrived safely. The second was that his friend had died. And the third was that he would let her know when he was headed back. All three messages had come through at various times of the day Saturday.

It was Thursday and he still hadn't contacted her again. She couldn't help wondering what he'd gotten into. Danielle said that their test had been postponed and someone else had been teaching their class for 4 days now. Danielle was not happy. She said all they did was take notes and she missed Grayson's entertaining teaching style and examples.

Patience was the one thing Claire was good at. Noah had unintentionally schooled her well in that. She'd basically learned to see him when she saw him.

If she and Grayson had been in a relationship, she told herself, she would have called him. No more waiting and wondering.

But they weren't in a relationship. And they weren't going to be. Less than two months and he would be on his way. It wasn't wise to get too attached.

Reattached.

Claire turned off her computer and stood up. She stretched and checked the time. It was time to meet Danielle for lunch. Then counseling.

She checked her phone. No messages.

She grabbed her handbag and, as she walked through the gallery, glanced at the two new paintings that had come in for her review.

Neither one particularly drew her to them. Not enough to bring the artist in.

She would put out another ad.

Danielle didn't have much to say at lunch. After four days of not having Grayson teaching her psychology class, her interest in the subject had waned. They both spent much of their time at lunch on their phones.

After lunch, they got into the car to drive to the mental health clinic.

"Do you want to drive?" Claire asked.

Danielle lifted her shoulder in its sling.

"I know," Claire said. "But do you want to? It's been ages since you've asked to drive. You should be used to your antidepressants by now."

"No," Danielle said, scrunching her nose.

"I thought all teenagers wanted to drive."

"Driving is retro. I'm gonna have a driver when I go to work."

Claire laughed. "Really? How are you going to afford this driver?

Danielle shrugged and resumed texting. "I don't know. I'll probably just live close to work and walk."

Claire moved into traffic and considered her daughter's statement. Danielle's father had the same aversion to driving. Perhaps Danielle inherited this from Noah. In Noah, it manifested in wanting to fly everywhere. Danielle didn't want to fly, but she didn't want to drive either. Her daughter preferred to keep her eyes glued to her phone.

Generations were changing, Claire mused.

Her phone chimed indicating a text message. Claire's hand reflexively moved to pick up her phone. She glanced at her daughter and put her hand back on the wheel.

And sighed.

Perhaps she couldn't blame Noah after all. Perhaps Danielle was just a product of her time. Maybe, Claire thought, she should get a driver.

Her fingers itched to check her message, but she made it all the way to the mental health parking lot before she grabbed her phone.

It was text from Grayson. *I'm back in town. Catching up. Teaching tomorrow. Dinner tomorrow night?*

She followed Danielle into the clinic with a little spring in her step that had been missing all week. They sat in the waiting area and Claire sent back a quick text. *Okay.*

She didn't want to seem overly enthusiastic, but the smile on her face had Danielle looking at her sideways.

"You heard from Grayson." Danielle said.

Claire bit her lip to hide the smile that threatened to spread across her face.

"You did!" Danielle said. "Is he back?"

"He'll be in class tomorrow."

"Thank goodness," Danielle said. "I don't think I could stand another day of those boring lectures."

"You do know, that most college professors do just that – lecture?"

"Danielle?" Dr. Lee called from his office door.

Claire and Danielle went into his office and settled onto Dr. Lee's couch. He sat across from them and smiled. "You both look rather happy today."

"Mom's crushing on my psychology professor," Danielle said.

"Danielle," Claire said, her cheeks hot. "I am not!"

"Well, technically he's her old boyfriend from high school, but they haven't seen each other for like twenty years."

Dr. Lee studied Claire. Smiled. "I've never seen you look this happy," he said.

"Things are going well," she said. "At the foundation."

Dr. Lee glanced at Danielle who shrugged. "It's okay," he said, turning back to Claire. "to have some happiness in your life."

"I have happiness," she said.

"Good," Dr. Lee said, then turned back to Danielle. "What's going on with you, Danielle?"

As Danielle talked about her classes and her new boyfriend - that Claire hadn't known about - Claire, reflected about what Dr. Lee had said.

Did people really think she wasn't happy? Was she happy? Had she ever been happy?

She was happy. They had been right, she did have to admit. She was crushing on her old boyfriend. And…

Claire realized she had been happy in high school, her

sophomore and junior year before Grayson left for the Air Force. In fact, her fondest memories were there. With him.

History, it seemed, was repeating itself.

In more ways than one. She'd known then that he would be leaving for the military. And she knew now that he was leaving for a one year teaching position. He'd said he was coming back then. This time he hadn't said that.

This time he wasn't making any promises.

We're not in a relationship this time.

"Claire, are you alright?" Dr. Lee asked.

Claire jerked herself out of her reverie and smiled. "Yes. I'm good."

"Danielle was just asking if she could have her guy friend come over tomorrow."

Claire looked at Danielle who was watching her expectantly. "Of course. She doesn't have to ask me that."

"You'll have to go pick him up, Mom. He lives on campus and he doesn't have a car."

"Do you want to go get him?" Claire asked.

Danielle held up her bum shoulder.

"Right. Of course. I'll drive you to pick him up." So tomorrow, Claire contemplated, she would be double-dating with her daughter.

The rain set in the next day. The weather channel described it as a rare westward monsoon thunderstorm.

Grayson juggled his umbrella, three pizza boxes, and a single red rose he'd picked up for Claire. It would have been a perfect day to get delivery, but Claire wanted to try a new pizza place that didn't deliver.

Grayson didn't mind picking up the pizza. He just needed to find a way to keep everything from getting soaked.

When he got to the safety of the front porch he was soaked, but somehow he'd managed to keep the pizza and the flower dry. Mission accomplished.

Claire opened the door and burst out laughing.

"I'm sorry," she said, biting her lip. "It's not funny. You're soaked."

"I'm glad I could provide humor to your day," he said.

She took the pizza from him and set it on the table in the

foyer. He took the rose from under his jacket and handed it to her. A host of emotions ran across her face, the strongest being surprise.

"Oh. Wow," she said, closing her eyes as she inhaled its scent.

He didn't ask. Didn't want to know. But he could only imagine that it had been quite some time since anyone thought to bring her a flower. Even something so simple as a rose bud.

When she opened her eyes, she had so much unguarded emotion, it caught him off guard. "You're beautiful," he said.

Again, surprise.

And he felt so much regret for the girl he'd left behind all those years ago.

If he knew then what he knew now, he would have found another career. He would have found a way to stay with Claire.

He vowed to himself in that moment to do everything he could to make it up to her.

"Is Claire's boyfriend here?" he asked.

"They're in the living room playing a video game. Thank you for getting the pizza. If I'd known it was going to rain, we would've gotten delivery instead."

"I don't mind the rain," he said. "And anything for two beautiful girls."

"You're soaked," she said.

"Yeah," he ran a hand along his jeans. He'd gotten wet getting the pizza, then again getting from his car to Claire's door.

"Let me put those in the dryer for you."

"I don't have any other clothes."

"Some of Noah's are still upstairs in a box. I'll grab you some sweats and a t-shirt," she said and before he could answer, she dashed upstairs. About two minutes later, she was back.

"You can change in the bathroom right here," she said, indicating the half-bath on the way to the kitchen.

Grayson took the clothes into the bathroom and after drying off with a towel, pulled on the sweatpants and shirt. He refused to give any more thought about wearing her ex-husband's clothes.

After changing, he took the wet clothes and handed them to her. She put them in the dryer, then they took the pizza into the living room and Danielle introduced them to Joey.

"Joey's in our class," Danielle said.

"Sure," Grayson said, hoping he hid the fact that he had no idea. The college freshmen all looked alike to him. Until he got to know them, of course. It was one of those unfortunate things that went along with aging.

"Are you two ready for your test on Monday?" he asked.

They looked at each other. "We're going to go upstairs and study after we eat," Danielle said.

Claire rolled her eyes and looked at Grayson. "We did a lot of studying in our day, didn't we Grayson?"

Grayson was so caught off guard by her statement, it took him a minute, then he burst out laughing. "I blame our *studying* on that C I got in Calculus. But your mother was a different story. No matter how much we studied, she still managed to pull off A's every time."

Claire blushed. He had caught her by surprise, too, it seemed.

"You started it," he said, with a wink.

"Well, why don't we eat this pizza before it gets cold. Grayson had to brave the thunderstorm and rain to get it here."

The youngsters only needed one invitation.

After they ate, they were true to their word and headed off upstairs to study.

"Some things never change," he said.

"What? Their studying?" Claire asked as she stacked plates. "I much prefer them *studying* upstairs than being out somewhere doing drugs."

"That's an excellent point. And I agree completely."

"Hey," Claire said. "Have you noticed that young people don't care about driving and cars anymore? Or is it just Danielle?"

"No. I've noticed. With a couple of exceptions, they don't go to malls either."

"I think it's because they aren't motivated to go anywhere. They can do everything on their phones."

"Almost everything," he said, teasingly, indicating the giggles coming from upstairs.

"It's been awhile…" she said.

"Since you've seen anyone?"

"Ha. There have only been two for me."

"Two? Two men?"

She kept her eyes down as she put the pizza boxes in the garbage disposal. "You. And then I married Noah. I've only been divorced for less than a year."

She straightened and raised her chin. Did he imagine the ever so slight quiver of her chin? "And you? Are you seeing anyone?"

"I like to think I'm seeing you," he said.

Her eyes widened and she turned away to wash her hands in the sink. With the dish cloth in her hands, she turned back to face him. "Are we doing this again?"

He was blindsided by her question. Were they? "No," he said. Her eyes widened. "Claire." He did the only thing he could think of to do. He closed the distance between them and drew her into a hug. She put her arms around him. And he just held her to him.

"I don't know how to answer that question," he said, murmuring against her ear.

"I know. You don't have to," she whispered.

"No. I think I do. It's only fair." He pulled back and took her hand. "Let's go sit, okay?"

They went into the living room and sat next to each other on the sofa. He held her hands in his. So soft.

"I didn't think I'd ever see you again," he said. "I thought you were happily married. So I left you alone."

She nodded and lowered her gaze. "It's okay."

"No," he said, lifting her chin until she met his gaze again. "I can't just bust in here and upend your life again. Not when I'm about to leave again. That isn't fair."

"Grayson..."

"No." He shook his head. "It's not fair to you. But the thing is, I can't help myself."

"So... what do we do?" She asked.

He let go of her hands and sat back, scrubbed at his face. "I have to go. I signed a one-year contract."

"I'm not asking you not to go."

"I know. I'm not saying that."

"What are you saying?"

"I'm not sure," he said. "I guess I'm saying that if we are doing this again, I'll do my part differently."

"You did everything right."

He scoffed. "No. I didn't. I was more focused on my career than staying in touch with you."

"Grayson, how can you say that? You wrote me all those letters and you called."

"All I had to do was get an email address."

"You didn't know. You were young."

"Still."

"Grayson," she said, sliding closer to him. "What my mother did was wrong. She knows that. We have to let go of the past."

He lifted his gaze to hers and put his fingers on her cheek. He ran his thumb along her bottom lip. Her lips parted.

"Claire," he said and put his lips on hers.

When Grayson's lips touched hers, it was like a lightning bolt shot through her body. Her lips remembered.

Her heart remembered.

The years disappeared and they were back in her parents' house, making out on the couch again.

Everything shifted and she knew nothing would be the same again.

It didn't matter that Grayson was leaving again.

Just like it hadn't mattered that he was leaving all those years ago. In fact, the knowledge that he was going away made it all the more sweet. All the more to be savored.

A warning went off in her head.

Was that why she'd slept with him before? Because she knew he would be leaving and she wouldn't have to deal with it?

No.

She shifted back and her eyes fluttered open.

"We can't," she uttered.

"I know," he said. "the kids."

"No. We can't," she said again, a little louder this time.

"I'm sorry," he said. "I thought…"

"I do." She shifted and stared at the fireplace. "It's different now. We aren't kids."

"And I'm leaving again," he said.

"Yeah," she said, turning back to him. "You're leaving again."

"We have two months," he said.

She shook her head. "No."

"Claire. Let me have another chance. Like you said, we aren't kids. We can talk every day. We can visit all the time. Until I can figure out something."

"I won't leave L.A." She'd left L.A. once before. Her home was here. Her dream home. That she had designed from the ground up. Her business was here. Her contacts. The only time she'd been unable to visit was when she had been pregnant with Danielle. She'd been miserable and had redoubled her efforts to establish her business here. She was an L.A. girl. Through and through. "You have to know that up front," she said.

"Fair enough. I understand."

"And I won't sleep with you until… well… until… it's right."

He laughed. "That's not what I'm after. I mean, it is, but it's not all I'm after. I enjoy you, Claire. Just being with you.

"No pressure, then?"

"None. The opposite of pressure." He held up his hands.

She laughed, glad to have the tension broken. "What's the opposite of pressure?"

"I'm not sure. We'll have to figure that out."

"That should be interesting," she said.

"We'll have the anti-pressure relationship," he agreed.

She looked at him for a minute. "What does that even look like?"

"I don't know. I think we'll have to invent it."

"Okay."

"Come here," he said, pulling her into a hug.

She tucked her head under his chin and pulled her feet onto the sofa and wrapped her arms around him. He smelled so good. Like soap and rainwater all mixed in together. It reminded her of the time they'd been caught in the rain on the Santa Monica beach. They were supposed to be at the library, studying. But it had been such a beautiful Sunday afternoon. One minute they were enjoying each other in the sunshine and the next, after ignoring the dark clouds and coming in just a little too late, they'd been running along the path to their car.

"Do you remember Santa Monica?" she asked.

"We laughed the whole way back to the car."

"I thought my mother was going to kill me when we came in the house drenched."

"You should have heard my father when I tried to explain about the mud inside his car," Grayson said.

"Oh," She shifted to look up at him. "You never told me."

"It was no big deal. I just cleaned it up and was grounded for a week," he said.

"Ah. That explains a lot."

"Yeah, well, I stayed grounded a lot."

"It was my fault," she said.

"Yes, it was." He squeezed her. "But I wouldn't have traded a single minute of it."

"I'm sorry to interrupt, but…" Joey said.

Claire jumped to a sitting position. "What is it Joey?"

"Danielle asked me to come get you."

"What's wrong?"

"She um… fell… off the bed," His face was beet red. "I think she might have hurt her shoulder."

Claire was up running up the stairs in a heartbeat with Grayson at her heels.

"Danielle?"

Danielle sat on the floor holding her arm. Claire knelt next to her. "We were playing with Charlie," she said. The kitten sat on the bed, innocently licking his paws.

"Where does it hurt?" Grayson asked, kneeling next to them.

"My shoulder."

"This is where you bumped it," Claire said.

"It's probably just bruised again," he said.

"I think I broke it."

"Can I look," Grayson asked, looking from Claire to Danielle.

Claire nodded. Danielle said "okay."

Grayson gently removed the sling and pressed his fingers against her shoulder.

She winced.

"I'm sorry," he said.

"It's okay," Danielle kept her chin high.

"It's not broken," Grayson said.

"Are you sure?" Danielle asked. "It hurts like a… hurts like crazy."

"Pararescue," Grayson said. "Remember?"

"Right."

"Okay, let's get you off the floor and up on the bed. Joey, will you help?"

Joey moved forward. "What do I do?"

"Just let her grab your arm. Never pull on her."

Danielle grabbed Joey's arm and with Grayson supporting her back, she got to her feet and back onto the bed.

"How did you get into pararescue?" Joey asked.

"I went into the Air Force," Grayson said.

"Awesome. And you jumped out of airplanes?"

"All the time."

"Maybe I should do that."

Grayson laughed, but locked his gaze onto Claire's. "Maybe you should see where this thing with Danielle is going first."

Danielle groaned. "We don't have a thing."

"We could have a thing," Joey said.

"Do you need anything, else, Danielle?" Claire asked. "Grayson and I are going to go back downstairs."

"No. I'm good. Thanks, Grayson."

"No problem."

Claire and Grayson left them discussing the possibility of *having a thing*.

Grayson grimaced. "I think I might have overstepped."

"No," Claire said. "Let them have that conversation. Maybe someone should have mentioned something to us."

"Yeah. We're the old wise ones now."

"Ha. It's an unknown hazard of parenting."

"And teaching."

"I imagine there are a lot of similarities."

"Except I get to leave them behind when I go home at night."

"That's when the fun starts," she said.

"Danielle likes baseball?"

"Yeah, how did you know?"

"Well, she has a poster of the Dodgers on her wall and a couple of baseballs on her dresser where most girls have Barbies."

"It's something she and her father used to do together."

"Used to."

"They still go, but not as often."

"That's too bad."

"It's okay. She's into college now. I should see if your clothes are dry."

"Is that a hint?"

She rolled her eyes. "I'll be right back."

Claire left Grayson in the living room and went to the laundry room. His clothes were dry. She looped his jeans and shirt over her arm and carried them back out to him. "You can wear what you have on home if you like."

Grayson chuckled. "You are telling me it's time to go."

"No. You can stay, but you'll see a grown woman fall asleep on the couch."

He smiled and ran a finger over her chin. "I'm tired, too. Are you busy tomorrow?"

"I have to take Danielle to visit my mom, then I'm free."

He ran his finger over her bottom lip.

She took a step back. "'Do you want to come with me?" she asked.

"Whoa. I don't know."

She smiled. "You have to face it some time. Better sooner than later, don't you think?"

"I don't know, Claire. Sometimes it's best to put off today what you can do tomorrow."

CHAPTER
Nine

Grayson picked up his dry cleaning, dashed through the supermarket for basics like sodas and bread, then filled up his car with gas. Saturdays were for errands and getting everything ready for next week. The Air Force had taught him nothing if not discipline.

He didn't mind working hard. In fact, while other people were standing around complaining about not having enough time to do things, he was off doing them.

He subscribed to the work hard play hard club. He worked hard, then he tucked work away and played. He was good at compartmentalization.

Teaching college was turning out to be different, however, and he found it be taxing. His work was bleeding over into his play time. It was part of society's culture. Take the good with the bad, he mused.

Unfortunately, when a student emailed or texted, they expected an answer right away. Even on the weekends. And with their first test coming up on Monday, the questions were coming like wild-fire. It hadn't helped that he'd been out nearly a whole week.

He stopped at Starbuck's for a coffee, sat outside, and while sipping his coffee, did a quick check-up of messages. Then he sat back and watched people for a few minutes. Some people were obviously heading to work, but most were like him. Running errands and starting their weekend off with a jolt of caffeine.

One couple, in their twenties, caught his attention. They were giggling with their heads bent close as they ordered and waited for their coffee. He couldn't help but wonder if he'd made the wrong decision by entering the Air Force like he did. Not that regretted his military service. He'd do that part all over again. Even knowing that he'd sometimes have nightmares and intrusive memories. Nothing four weeks in the VA hospital in Little Rock hadn't helped him get under control. But maybe he should have married Claire first. Their lives would have been different. He would have been gone, so she still could have had the career she had today. The only thing that would have changed was that they would had a life together. A family.

Grayson was still grieving the loss of his friend. But in truth, he was grieving more the tragedy than anything else. He knew the statistics. He knew that veterans took their lives everyday. Suicide wasn't just a military phenomenon, but these men and women had only been doing their jobs – serving their country. The resulting post-traumatic reaction was a travesty.

He tossed his empty cup in the trash and shook off his thoughts. He couldn't rewrite the past. Still, he couldn't help thinking that there should be more that he could do to help his fellow veterans.

Grayson had three hours before he was supposed to meet Claire at her house. Then the three of them were going to Claire's mother's house.

He could think of plenty of things he'd rather do than face Claire's mother. He hadn't done anything wrong. She was the one who had hidden his letters and phone calls from Claire. He could only imagine that he was the last person she wanted to see.

Arriving back at his apartment, he put away his dry cleaning and his groceries. He decided to change clothes again, opting for a white button-down shirt in place of the casual polo shirt he'd put on that morning.

With some time left, he turned on his computer and went to the veteran's administration website to look around. There were lots of social worker jobs, but no openings.

He came across one of his buddies from grad school, Bob. He and Bob had taken every class together.

He found Bob's email address and dashed off a quick email before heading out the door to pick up Claire.

They were waiting for him. They'd been sitting on the sofa playing Words with Friends back and forth.

Claire was cute in a mid-thigh length flared skirt, a t-shirt, cropped sweater, and white canvas sneakers. Danielle had on jeans and a sweatshirt.

Claire seemed a little nervous. He asked her about it.

"I didn't tell my mother you were coming. In fact, I haven't mentioned you since she gave me the letters."

"Oh. Well. That's comforting. Nothing like busting up on the one person who tried successfully to get rid of me."

"It wasn't you. She likes you. It was the lifestyle that scared her. She'll be fine now."

"Easy for you to say."

Danielle looked up from her phone. "You'll like Grandma," she said. "She's really a kind person. I've never heard her speak unkindly of anyone."

"That's comforting," Grayson said. "Thank you for telling me."

"No problem," Danielle said, putting her gaze back on her phone.

The twenty-minute ride to Betty Beauchamp's house was mostly silent. Danielle was texting. Grayson and Claire were lost in their own thoughts.

He parked at the curb and they walked up the sidewalk, Danielle in front.

Betty was waiting at the door. Danielle, according to Claire, was the one person who could lure her from her rooms upstairs without complaint.

Betty, Grayson, reflected, looked good physically, but there was a sadness about her.

They hugged and talked about Danielle's shoulder before Betty turned to Claire. Claire hugged her mother, then turned to Grayson.

"Mom," she said. "This is..."

Her mother interrupted. "Grayson." Smiling, she reached out and took his hands in hers. "It's so good to see you again."

"It's good to see you, too, Mrs. Beauchamp."

"Let's go inside, shall we? I made lunch."

"Are you sure she didn't know I was coming?" Grayson whispered as they followed Betty and Danielle into the house."

"I didn't tell her," Claire said.

"Danielle," Grayson said.

Claire shrugged. "Maybe."

Betty had made tuna sandwiches. They sat at the kitchen table eating tuna sandwiches and chips while Danielle chattered to her grandmother about her classes, her shoulder, and Joey.

After they ate, Betty and Danielle went out back to fill Betty's bird feeders.

"You'd never know they talked every day," Claire said.

"Really? Every day?"

"Yep."

"Nope. I thought it must have been at least a week."

Claire laughed. "The two of them are thick as thieves."

"Must be nice," he said. "To have someone that close."

"I never did."

"Yeah. Me either," he said.

"You never talked about your grandparents."

"Nothing to talk about. My grandfather was military, so they lived in Germany while I was growing up. I saw them maybe one time."

"That's unfortunate. What about on the other side?"

"Died before I could get to know them."

"Same thing on Noah's side. I mean his mother's still living, but they weren't close."

"Was Danielle close to your father?"

"She was. I think that's part of what led to her suicide attempt."

"She seems good now," Grayson said.

"She's great. At first, they said we should watch her when she was too happy, but now they agree that she really is okay."

"That must be a relief."

Claire blew her hair out of her eyes. "You have no idea," she said.

"You said she's spending the night?" he asked.

"Yeah. We have the rest of the day to ourselves."

He grinned. "That sounds irresistible."

She raised a delicate eyebrow.

"Actually," he said. "I was thinking. The Getty is having an art exhibit that you might like if you haven't seen it. It's 18th Century Europe."

"Ooh. I haven't seen it. But I want to."

"Want to go?"

"Yes!" She jumped up. "Let me tell them we're leaving."

He chuckled and sighed with relief. He'd avoided a conversation with Claire's mother. Perhaps she subscribed to Claire's policy about letting the past stay in the past. Keep moving forward.

When they got to the Getty, it was crowded. As they hiked to the front of the museum, he took her hand. She had a little spring in her step and could have easily passed for someone in her early twenties.

Now that he'd found her again, he never, ever wanted to let her go again. He would have to take the job in Pittsburgh. It would be unprofessional to leave them without someone to fill in. But after that, he would have to find a way to get back to her.

Claire would not be single long. She was absolutely adorable. She was beautiful, smart, funny, and a great mother. He wondered if she wanted to have more children.

They reached the counter and he bought them two tickets to the museum.

Maybe it was her smile. Or her lithe figure. Or both. Whatever it was, Claire turned men's heads.

Claire had spent countless hours here studying art.

She knew every crook and cranny of the public part of the museum. She even knew some of the private administrative parts, though it had been nearly twenty years since her days as a volunteer. She'd absorbed everything about the place.

She'd considered going to school to study art, but the more she learned, the less she thought it would be worth her time to invest in a degree. She had learned what she needed to know hands on.

She still wondered sometimes, if she'd made the right decision, especially when someone asked her where she studied. It was a question she rarely got now that she was successful. Perhaps the word had travelled.

She loved sharing her love of the museum with Grayson. She loved holding his hand as she navigated her way through the halls.

She also loved the way he looked at her. His attention never strayed. She could tell he scanned the crowds. Figured that was his military training. She would have expected no less. But his eyes stayed on her, especially when he wore that look of interest.

He'd always had that look for her. Since they were in high school.

Now that she was older, she knew how rare that was. That it was a gift. Very few people were fortunate to have someone who looked at them like that. Especially someone who looked like Grayson.

Tall, dark, and handsome.

She felt safe with him. No one was going to bother her while she was with him. Maine D'Court had come closest, but as soon as Grayson stepped up, he had stepped back. With her fingers looped in his, there was no question that they were together.

They stopped to admire a painting of two lovely ladies and he shifted to stand behind her, wrapping his arms around her.

She closed her eyes. Just for a minute. And enjoyed the feel of him against her.

"You can see the brushstrokes," he said.

Her eyes fluttered open and she focused on the painting. "It's beautiful," she said.

"I went to the Louvre when I was in Europe," he said.

She pulled away to look into his eyes. He released her. "I had no idea you liked art."

"I guess I had a little early influence," he said, sheepishly.

She thought back to their early days. Her eyes widened. "We did come here," she said. "I'd forgotten."

"On more than one occasion."

"If I recall, you weren't that into art."

"I was young. And getting ready to go into the military. I probably had some notion that it wasn't manly to like art."

She laughed. "I'm glad you saw the error of your ways."

"I actually like the architecture most of all. But I appreciate the art."

"I know what you mean. I'm drawn to the art, but I appreciate the sculptures for what they are. There's a difference."

They moved along to the next group of paintings. They spent the next two hours meandering through the museum, in no hurry. She could think of no place she'd rather be than there, at the museum, with Grayson.

It was nothing short of a small miracle that they have found each other again.

"Did you ever think we'd see each other again, much less get back together?"

"I wondered all the time. If I'd know you were divorced, I would have already looked for you."

"If you'd looked for me, you'd have known," she said, her lips bowed prettily.

"You're quite right."

"So how were you planning on finding out?"

"I'm a man. I didn't have a plan."

She laughed. "I thought you were happily married long ago and living with your wife and three kids."

"You remembered. I'm impressed."

"Why wouldn't I? I was planning to be that wife." She said the words before she thought. She bit her lip and fervently wished she could rewind and make the words go away.

"I was planning on you being that wife, too," he said.

She smiled, no longer thinking she'd said the wrong thing.

They walked a few feet. "So, we're back together?" he asked, a mischievous glint in his eyes.

She felt her cheeks heat with a blush. She had said that. "I just meant. Together. Like this."

"Do you want to be back together?" He asked.

"Do you?"

"I never wanted to be apart," he said.

"But you've had other girlfriends."

"You got married."

"Point well made. You never wanted to get married?"

"I toyed with the idea a few times, but no. I never dated anyone that I wanted to marry."

"Hmm."

"Hmm. What?"

"Nothing," she said. "I just thought you would have."

"Maybe I was waiting for you."

"Whatever," she said, moving away from him. "You weren't even looking for me."

"Waiting and looking don't have to be different things."

She leaned over a rail and wondered about the appeal of the painting in front of her. She often wondered about the appeal of paintings. Why some had mass market appeal and others didn't. It seemed to be whatever elicited emotion. Not about how well it was painted.

"The past is past," she said.

"Agreed."

"I'm hungry."

"Want some popcorn?"

And just like that, Grayson mused, they fell back in step. It had been surprisingly easy. Take the girl to a museum.

He laughed to himself. Not just any girl.

Claire.

Claire was the only girl he knew who would find going to the museum to be an entertaining afternoon. He knew girls that liked the casino. That liked to go shopping. He even knew a girl once who like to target practice.

But Claire was one of a kind.

In more ways than one.

She was the girl who always had his heart.

He got them popcorn from the concession stand and they walked outside through the gardens snacking on popcorn.

"Tell me about the Air Force," she said.

"That's something you don't want to know about."

"Why not?"

"Okay. I spent a lot of time jumping out of airplanes."

"Not just for the sake of jumping."

"At first it was. While we were training. Then after we were deployed, it was for rescue purposes."

"So, you also learned a lot about treating injuries, too."

"Yeah, that was a big part of it. And learning to treat injuries in less than ideal conditions."

"You liked it?"

"There's nothing else like it. The adrenalin is addictive."

"Do you want to go back?"

"No. It's for the younger guys. I'm too old now. I stopped after ten years and went back to school. Then I had to do another three years as an officer. But my days of jumping into danger ended a long time ago."

"Good."

"Good?"

"I don't like thinking about you being injured."

"The young guys don't even think about that part. We thought we were indestructible."

"I guess there are a few good things about getting older," she said.

They stopped and sat on a bench. Watched a butterfly flit about. Claire held out a hand and it landed on her fingertip.

"They say butterflies are a reminder to focus on the here and now," Grayson said.

Claire glanced at him out of the corner of her eye. "Then the butterfly is my mascot."

They sat quietly while the butterfly sat on Claire's fingertip. She shifted slightly, but it stayed. "I've never had this happen," she said. "Have you?"

"Never."

He leaned over and pressed his lips against hers.

She closed her eyes for the briefest of seconds. When she opened her eyes, the butterfly was gone.

"Here and now," she said, feeling the sadness in her eyes.

"Don't be sad," he said. "Our here and now is full of promise and happiness."

She smiled into his eyes. "Yes," she said. "Yes, it is."

They went back inside the museum, but decided they'd had enough for one day.

"Would you like to have dinner?" he asked. "I know a good little Italian place nearby."

"Yeah," she said. "That would be nice."

When he said *little Italian place,* he meant little. The place had red and white checkered table cloths, but the wait staff wore black tuxedos. It was an interesting combination of quaint and fancy.

After they ordered pasta, Claire brought up the obvious. "Do you have a place to live in Pittsburgh yet?"

"I have a couple of possibilities," he said.

"You went there for an interview?"

"I did. One of the professors is taking a year to go live and work in Japan, so he was the one who showed me around the city."

"I've never been there. Is it nice?"

"Surprisingly, yes. It's very pretty. After we left the university area, he took me downtown. We drove through a long tunnel. When we came out on the other side, the city was there, right in front of us. With the river right there below us."

"Don't they have more than one river?"

"There are three right there that come together."

"I never paid any attention to it. But it sounds intriguing."

"I thought so, too," he said.

"You must be excited."

"I was," he admitted. "But not so much now."

Their entrees arrived and they sat quietly enjoying their food for a few minutes.

"This is really good," she said.

"I'm glad you like it."

"Claire," he said. "If we can make it work for just one year, not even a year, just until next May, I can try to come back here. I can find something else."

She nodded, but kept her eyes down.

He kept talking. "I wouldn't go, but I don't have anything else here now and they're counting on me. The guy who's going to Japan said they hadn't had all that many applicants. Granted, that was March, but still, it sounds like they really need me to cover for him. He said if he can't find someone to cover for him, he can't go."

"Do you know why he wants to go?"

"I think he has a girlfriend there. He wants to bring her back here, but she can't leave yet. I didn't ask too many personal questions."

"I admire you for wanting to help him out," Claire said.

"I'm a sucker for a sad story, I guess."

She looked back up at him. "I guess so."

"We can do it, right? Am I missing something?"

"No. We can do it."

"You're hesitant."

"It just feels like déjà vu," she said.

"It does. Doesn't it? I'm so sorry for that. I'll so make it up to you."

"Okay," she said.

After dinner, he drove them back to her house and walked her to the door. They stood at the door for a moment.

"I'm going to just go inside," she said.

"Okay," he said, confusion on his face.

She tiptoed up to kiss him on the cheek. "Thank you for a lovely day," she said, then he turned and kissed her lightly on the lips. She went inside, leaving him standing there looking befuddled.

Claire closed the door behind her and leaned against it. She closed her eyes and pressed her fingertips to her lips.

It had been so easy to fall back into being a couple with Grayson. Too easy.

So easy it frightened her.

Then came the reminder. He was leaving. Again. Soon.

She locked the door and pushed away from it. She went into the living room and flopped down on the sofa.

People did long-distance relationships all the time. All. The. Time.

It wasn't like she didn't have the money to visit him. It wasn't about the money.

It was about all the evenings she would spend alone.

All the mornings she would wake up alone.

She'd spent nearly twenty years of her life in that kind of relationship.

It was not how she wanted to spend the next ten, twenty, or thirty years.

He said he could try to come back after a year. Try.

Once he was away, it became easier to stay away. He'd be lured by the next opportunity.

She knew. She'd been through it before.

It was different with Noah being a pilot, but there were too many similarities to what Grayson was proposing.

She couldn't ignore it.

Perhaps she should lay low for a bit. Play it cool. Stay away.

She scoffed.

She could no more stay away from Grayson Moore than a moth could stay away from a flame.

She could, however, disappear for a bit.

Pushing herself off the sofa, she went into her home office, turned on her computer, and sent the necessary emails and made the reservation

CHAPTER
Ten

When they had gotten back to Claire's house, Grayson hadn't been sure how to proceed. He'd opened the car door for her and walked her to the door.

She'd meant to kiss him on the cheek, but he turned and caught the kiss on his lips. Their lips barely brushed against each other, but it was enough to leave him wanting more.

Then he waited while she went inside. After he heard the door lock click, he turned and went back down the sidewalk to his car.

He sat in his car, gripping the steering wheel and watched her door. She'd been quiet since they'd talked about his moving.

She'd brought it up. Something he hadn't been going to. He was going to focus on the moment.

He'd enjoyed spending the day with her. It had been easy to forget about their real world problems and just be together.

But now he was at a loss as to how to proceed.

Should he give her some space? Or should he go up and knock on her door?

It was gut-wrenching to think that they had less than two months to spend together before he went away for a year. And here they were spending it apart.

Shoring up his resolve, he got out of the car and started up the sidewalk. A dog barked in the neighbor's yard and he jumped. Stopped.

Claire's downstair's light went off. He watched until the light upstairs come on. He couldn't see inside because she had closed the curtains, but the upstairs light was muted compared to the bright light downstairs.

He couldn't knock on the door now. It would be in poor taste to do so when she was getting ready for bed.

He sighed and turned around.

He would call her tomorrow.

The next morning, he sent her a text message. It was a simple *good morning* with a smiley face.

No response.

He dragged himself to his coffeepot and poured his second cup.

He had PowerPoint presentations to prepare.

He went back to his desk and sat down.

Maybe she was still asleep.

Danielle would be at orientation all day, so maybe Claire had turned her phone off.

He opened the textbook and began a new file on personality disorders.

Maybe she went out to work in her yard. Did Claire work in her yard?

Or did she hire her yard work done?

There were so many things he didn't know about her.

He googled images for borderline disorder. Copied a couple into the file.

Maybe she went for a jog.

Did she jog?

He checked his phone again. It showed her message was delivered.

He turned his phone over and went back to work. He managed to get through two personality disorders before he checked his phone again.

By the time he got through all ten, he'd talked himself into calling her. It was almost noon. Maybe she wanted to have lunch.

He dialed her number, but it went straight to voicemail.

He hung up.

Today was not going to be a good day.

If she was avoiding him, he needed to let her be.

Even with the possibility that something had happened to her, he couldn't very well just show up at her house. He'd promised he wouldn't do that. He could see already that was a promise he was going to have to break.

Too antsy to sit still, he gathered up his dirty clothes and turned on the washing machine. Then he changed his sheets.

And took out the garbage.

It had been all of twenty minutes.

Today was definitely not a good day.

He went to the kitchen to make a sandwich, but too late, realized he had nothing edible. Nothing but stale bread.

He pulled on a pair of jeans and a t-shirt, picked up his keys and drove to the supermarket.

It didn't take long to fill up his cart. He made sure he had plenty of food. Just in case someone stopped by.

After he checked out and loaded his car, he decided maybe he should drive by her house just make sure she was okay. He wouldn't stop. He'd respect her privacy.

He pulled up to the curb on the street in view of her house, but he had no way to tell if she was home or not. As always, her garage door was closed. Since it was daylight, he had no way of knowing if her lights were on.

Feeling a bit like a stalker, he drove away.

He drove home, put his groceries away, and decided he needed to clear his head.

He left his phone charging on his nightstand and, grabbing his keys, went out the door. The apartment complex was adjacent to a little woodsy park.

He walked among the trees a bit before finding a bench and sitting. No one else was out and about this afternoon. He supposed it was too warm for them, but after living in Texas, he enjoyed the weather.

Grayson needed to give Claire some space. She'd made that apparent. In his experience, a woman would ignore him for only one of two reasons. Either she wasn't into him or she hadn't decided yet. And really, he'd never experienced that second option, so he was tacking it onto his list to give Claire the benefit of the doubt.

He took a deep breath. He needed to be cool.

The ink was barely dry on her divorce papers. She'd been married and divorced. She'd had a child. And that child had been troubled recently. Those things would shift a person's perspective on life.

He'd been in the Air Force. He'd experienced traumatic experiences including watching people die. A lot of people. Good people. Men fighting for their country.

They weren't the same people as they had been in high school.

Besides, Claire ran in different social circles. She'd been married to a successful pilot and she'd established herself as a successful entrepreneur of not only an art gallery, but also a charity foundation.

He was a social worker teaching college kids.

Claire was a woman who made decisions with her head, not her heart. Grayson wasn't a logical choice for her. The hormones that had connected them in high school may no longer be there or even more likely weren't strong enough for them as adults.

Especially since he was going away. Again.

Either way, he had to resign himself that she may not be invested in him this time around.

Some people couldn't, for whatever reason, reengage in a previous romance.

His resolve strengthened with a determination to let her contact him, he walked home.

He took his phone off the nightstand.

There was a message from Claire.

His heart skipped a beat.

I had to go out of town for a few days. I'll let you know when I get home.

He sent back a quick response. *Is everything okay?*

She responded immediately. *Yes. Don't worry.*

Don't worry. What was that supposed to mean?

He had about a thousand questions. Where was she? Was she alone? What was she doing? Why hadn't she mentioned that was planning to be out of town?

Remembering his resolve to play it cool, he stuck his phone in his back pocket. He went to his little home office desk and opened his computer. He heart sank when he saw that he had twenty-three emails from students.

He sat his phone on the desk and sat down to get to work. Before opening the first email, he sent a simple text to Claire. *Okay.*

Whatever it was she had to do, he had to leave her to it.

He had a presentation to prepare and emails to answer.

Claire took a taxi to the Metropolitan Museum of Art. She'd gotten caught in the early morning traffic of Manhattan. She didn't mind.

New York had such a different feel from L.A. New York had so much energy in such a small space.

She loved it.

She'd sometimes thought about renting a small apartment here, but the hotel was the more logical choice and had all the comforts without the headaches.

She paid the driver and stepped out in front of the museum. There was something about a museum that she found inexplicably heady.

Today was no different. It had been almost three years since she'd made the trip over to New York. She'd been trying to find the time to come back for quite some time.

After talking with Grayson and getting tangled up in her thoughts, she knew it was the perfect time for her to get away.

Danielle was stable and busy with school and a new boyfriend. The divorce was behind her. She could take a few days and immerse herself into art.

She had no meetings set up and no one in the art community knew she was here. She was dressed as a tourist and planned to spend the day merely meandering through the museum, going wherever her eyes led her.

After wandering for a couple of hours, she stopped and had lunch in the little café, then wandered some more. Before she even realized it, several more hours had passed and she needed to head back to the hotel.

Her mind was racing with ideas for her next show, so she barely noticed the traffic. She made a few notes on her phone.

She went back to her room and ordered a salad. Like L.A., there were plenty of vegan choices in New York.

While she waited for her dinner to arrive, she went to the balcony and stepped outside. The sun had set and Times Square was lit up in all its glory. She was high enough that the sounds were slightly muted, but still distinctive.

This was something she would love to share with Grayson. The thought came out of nowhere and caught her off guard.

A sudden wave of loneliness swept over her. She'd been so engrossed in the museum all day, that she hadn't thought about him. At least not consciously.

But now that she was here, at the end the day, she missed him.

Room service brought her salad and panini along with a complimentary bottle of champagne. She almost refused the champagne, but instead set it next her on the little table while she ate. "Why not?" she said aloud. If Grayson was there, they probably would have gone out to dinner. But even if they'd decided to stay in, it would have been so much better to have him here.

She opened the champagne and poured the bubbly liquid into a glass watching the play of bubbles.

She checked her phone. Pulled up the text messages from Grayson. Other than to say *okay*, he hadn't texted since she'd told him not to worry.

Maybe jetting off to New York like that without telling him hadn't been the best idea. She'd just needed to get away. To think.

Her phone buzzed in her hand. It was Martie.

"Hello?"

"Sorry to bother you," Martie gushed. "But two new paintings just came in from a new artist."

"Are they any good?" she asked.

"They're stunning."

"Wow. Really? What's the artist's name?"

"Paul Bache."

"Thanks for telling me," she said.

"I just couldn't wait to tell you."

After they hung up the phone, Claire sipped the bubbly champagne.

Martie usually took new artists in stride. Maybe she was becoming more invested in the art world.

She picked up her phone and sent a quick text – *Send a picture.*

She took her wine glass and her phone and went to sit on the balcony.

A few minutes later, her phone buzzed again. She opened the text and a picture of Grayson popped up. He was on a balcony also, only it was dark behind him. Maybe a wooded area? She zoomed in, but couldn't tell. He had a sexy little sideways smile on his face.

Why would Martie send a picture of Grayson? Were they together?

She felt sick to her stomach. Had he gone to the studio looking for her and ended up going out with Martie?

Why had Martie sent her that picture instead of the painting?

Martie had seen him come into the studio to see her. Hadn't she?

She paced back inside and, scrolling through her messages, tried to make sense of the situation.

She stopped pacing. Oh. No! She had accidentally sent the picture request to Grayson.

She set the glass of champagne on the nightstand and climbed into the middle of the bed. This is why she never drank more than a sip or two. The last time she'd had a couple of drinks, Danielle had been… created.

She ran her hands over her face. Glanced at the bottle of champagne. She'd barely touched it.

She went to Martie's text thread and asked for a picture of the painting.

Martie said she'd send it tomorrow. She'd already left for the day.

Claire sighed. What to do about Grayson.

He sent another text. *Do I get a picture of you?*

She gasped. Uh oh. She opened her camera app and held the camera out for a selfie. Should she smile or look serious? She tried a couple of poses and examined the pictures. Taking a deep breath, she sent him a picture.

He wrote back. *Where are you?*

New York

There was silence on the other end of the phone

Are you serious? He wrote back. *Why?*

Why indeed? *I needed to go to some museums.*

She laid back on the bed and waited.

I see. You didn't want to tell me?

No. She sent back.

Do you want me to come join you?

Claire giggled. Right. *You have to work tomorrow.*

So? He wrote. *So do you.*

Guess I won't be there.

Can I call?

She stared at the phone. No. She didn't need to talk to him right now.

I can't talk right now.

Are you alone?

She rolled onto her stomach. *Yes.*

Have you been drinking?

How could he possibly know that? *Why do you ask?*

You're being… funny.

I'm always funny.

Ha. Can I call? He asked again.

She didn't answer this time. She left her phone on the bed and went to the refrigerator for a bottle of water.

The phone rang while she was drinking water.

She stretched across the bed and picked up the phone. "Hello."

"Well hi."

"Hi," he said. "So you're really in New York?"

"Sure."

"And you didn't want to tell me."

"I couldn't."

"Claire. You can tell me anything."

"Okay," she said.

"Right?"

"I was afraid."

His voice was serious. "I will never. Ever. Do anything to hurt you."

Her giddiness faded into tears. "It might be a little late," she said, her voice hoarse with unshed sobs.

"That was an accident. We were kids and didn't have any control over it. We aren't kids now. We're in control."

She inhaled deeply. Regained control of her emotions. "You're right," she said, her voice steady now.

"Claire, please don't run away from me again."

"I wasn't running away," she said, though she knew that was exactly what she had done.

"I want to be part of your life."

"You are part of my life."

"I want to be the part where you at least let me know when you're going to New York. Even if you don't invite to go with you. I understand that you sometimes need time alone."

She took a deep ragged breath. Did she dare let herself care about him again? Did she let him care about her? "Okay," she said.

He laughed. "Okay? What?"

"Okay. I'll tell you next time."

"Fair enough."

"Grayson? Are you sure you want to go down this route again?"

"I'm one hundred percent sure."

"Why?"

There was silence on the other end of the phone.

"I'll tell you when you get back."

"All right," Claire said.

"Please be careful over there."

"I will," she said.

"I'll talk to you tomorrow," he said and they hung up the line.

Claire sat on the hotel bed, holding her phone.

It had been such a long time since someone actually cared where she was and what she was doing. Sure, her daughter kept up with her, but that was different. Danielle didn't necessarily want to spend time with Claire, even though she wanted Claire to be there for her.

And Noah. Well, Noah had a tendency to do his own thing. She couldn't blame him, either, since that had been their agreement going in.

And despite the coldness of their marriage, Claire had never, not once, cheated. Although after their legal separation went into effect, they had both agreed that it was okay to date others, Claire hadn't been interested. She'd thrown herself into her work even more. And that was the time Danielle had needed her parents there for her. Claire had to give Noah points for dropping everything and being there every day for Danielle.

Claire found herself in an interesting spot. She had only been with two men in her life. She was divorced from one and the other wanted to resume their relationship after twenty years. Did people even do that?

It went against her keep moving forward policy.

Or did it?

Her thoughts were winding around themselves and she was getting tangled up in her own ideas.

She put on her pajamas and crawled under the blankets. She would have to think about this tomorrow.

Tomorrow was another day.

Grayson, too, got ready for bed, even though it was still early.

He looked at the picture she'd sent him and laughed to himself. She obviously had no idea there was an open bottle of champagne behind her. As far as he knew, Claire didn't drink alcohol. She'd played it cool by having a sip or two, but she never drank more. She was much too in control of herself.

The fact that he'd caught her drinking was an anomaly. Finding her in New York hadn't even occurred to him.

He'd been shocked when she asked him to send a picture.

He could only explain it by her use of alcohol.

He must have really gotten under her skin for her to run all the way across the country from him.

She didn't say anything about work or meetings. And she probably would have told him if she'd had a planned trip.

Now that he knew where she was and that she was safe, his resolve to let her have time to sort things out was even stronger. At least she was far away from the likes of that Maine D'Court artist.

Tomorrow was exam day. He had to get up early to make copies. He would have to think about setting up online testing next year. There was no reason not to update his classes. Giving tests online would be much more efficient.

Since everything was ready for tomorrow, he went online and bought three tickets to Saturday's Dodger's game. It was time to add a little excitement to their lives.

Claire spent the next day at the Museum of Modern Arts. She got there in time for a seven thirty guided meditation session. She grabbed a mat and made herself comfortable in front of Claude Monet's *Water Lilies*. While relaxing her mind and clearing her thoughts, she wondered how something like this would go over at her studio. She'd put Martie on setting it up for a trial basis. It would get some people inside her studio who otherwise would probably never set foot inside. Maybe she could go a step further and host a yoga class. The more comfortable she could make people feel coming through her doors, the more clients she could culture.

This idea alone was worth the trip over.

That and having a conversation with Grayson that she probably never would have initiated face to face.

She blushed a little at the memory that she'd accidentally asked him to send her a picture. That was something she never would have done. She could only imagine what he must have thought.

After the meditation session, a man who looked vaguely familiar approached her.

"Claire Worthington?"

She didn't answer. She wasn't here in a business capacity. She was wearing jeans and canvas sneakers. No one was supposed to know she was here.

"I'm Allen Samuels. We met at a fundraiser here a few years ago."

"Right," she said. She recognized him as someone she'd met before. "You're with…"

"I'm with Dolls for Rags Foundation."

She remembered him then. Danielle had gotten a group in her high school involved in doing some fundraising for them. She'd spoken with Allen several times on the phone. He was about ten years older than she was and she'd always found him a pleasant man to work with. He wasn't bad to look at either.

"Of course," she said. "I remember you now. My mind was somewhere else."

"Understandably," he said. "I'm sorry to interrupt like this."

"I don't mind," she said.

"I've been meaning to call you about a collaborative project, so you can only imagine how surprised I was to see you here. It's almost like I conjured you up."

Claire laughed. "Perhaps you did."

"Do you want to get coffee?" he asked. "Or maybe lunch."

"Coffee sounds good, but I don't think anything is open yet," she said. In truth, she wanted to get the meeting with him over with so she could resume her wandering.

"I think they open for coffee for the meditation crowd."

They went to the Terrace and found a table next to the window with a clear view of the skyline and street below. Claire ordered a cappuccino while Allen ordered coffee.

"What did you have in mind?" she asked.

"Right the point, I see. Alright. I'm thinking of expanding Dolls for Rags out your way."

"Great. How can I help?"

He stretched out his legs and sipped his coffee. "I'm looking for a partner."

The hairs on the back of Claire's neck tingled. She'd never had the need for a partner. Never wanted to have a partner.

"You seem to be doing quite well on your own," she said.

"I am," he agreed. "But you see, my wife died recently and I'm just not enjoying the work like I used to."

"Oh," Claire said, burying her expression in her coffee cup.

"I know. It sounds like a sad story, so I won't bore you with it. But..." he waited until she looked up and met his gaze. "I heard through the grapevine that you're divorced now and I thought maybe we could become friends."

Claire bit her lip to keep from laughing out loud. It was the oddest proposal she had ever been presented with. Was he asking her to become a business partner or a romantic partner?

"I'm not sure what you're asking me," she said.

"Ah hell, I'm not either. But I've always been attracted to you. And we obviously share interests. I guess I was hoping we could work together or play a bit. Or both."

Claire laughed out loud. She couldn't help it. To his credit, he laughed with her.

Allen's... proposition was flattering. She'd known him for

some time. He had a stellar reputation in the art community. She'd always found him attractive.

Now that his wife had passed away, he was doubtless considered an eligible bachelor.

Ideally, he was a perfect match for her. Same social standing. Same interests. Similar career goals. Age appropriate.

Yet, she couldn't stop thinking of a certain Air Force veteran with gorgeous blue eyes. He'd kissed her ever so lightly the night before she'd run away from him. He'd kissed her and awakened so many memories that intertwined with the unexpected longing for more. So many feelings that she had been overwhelmed.

"I'm flattered," she said, biting her lip to stop laughing. "But I'm here for a sort of personal pilgrimage."

"I understand," he said, holding his hands up. "No pressure." He picked up a little square napkin and wrote his name and phone number on it before sliding it toward her. He winked. "In case you change your mind."

He stood up and held out his hand. She placed her palm against his and he kissed the back of her hand.

She felt absolutely nothing, aside from a little discomfort. Her gaze darted around the room, but no one seemed to be paying them any heed.

"Until we meet again," he said.

"Take care of yourself, Allen," she said and meant it. He was a nice guy.

As he walked away, she folded the napkin and tucked it in her handbag. She turned her gaze back to the view as she finished her coffee.

Claire had been well-schooled in controlling strong

emotions. She was quite good at keeping her feelings under control. Danielle had been the one exception to that for the most part.

The other exception had been Grayson. When they'd been together, she'd felt overwhelming love. Then, after she didn't hear from him, that emotion had turned to despair. She'd hidden it, of course. She'd hidden it so well, that she'd convinced herself that she was over him. And had ended up married to Noah.

She watched as a pigeon landed on a neighboring rooftop. Even here in the midst of the city, nature still ran its course.

She took a deep, ragged breath. It was natural to have feelings. Human.

Her parents had been wrong in sending her to etiquette classes. Well, perhaps they hadn't been wrong. There was certainly some merit in having control of strong emotions.

There was also merit in having feelings.

Claire had loved Grayson. She had never stopped loving him. Neither of them were to blame for what had happened to keep them apart all those years ago. Perhaps it had been divine intervention. They were who they were because of what happened. And because of Danielle, she wouldn't go back and change what had happened for anything.

The fact that they'd found each other again after twenty years was a major miracle in itself. They hadn't even been looking. It had been fate. It had to be.

Moving forward, she had no reason to deny herself what she felt for Grayson. In the great scheme of life, a few weeks with Grayson could be worth more than twenty years with someone else. If it led to a long-distance relationship, so what? She wasn't giving anything up.

Sure. She would be giving up the option of dating someone like Allen Samuels. But she didn't care about Allen Samuels. Or any of the other guys who might be out there.

There was only guy she cared about.

Grayson Moore.

And it was quality, not quantity.

She wanted to go home. Right now.

The streets of New York were alive with millions moving about.

She was in awe that there was only one person on this earth that she wanted to be with right now.

She closed her eyes as the emotions washed over her.

She was here. She may as well spend the day in the museum. She'd fly out in the morning.

She smiled at the way she instinctively went practical. Years of training and practice didn't disappear in an instant.

She sent a quick text to Grayson. *See you tomorrow?*

He wrote back in an instant. *Sounds perfect.*

She grinned. Thanks to modern technology, things were already different this time around.

When Claire answered the door the next evening, Grayson was in awe. Claire was wearing those yoga-type pants and a long t-shirt over them. She had on white canvas sneakers that she wore just about everywhere except to work. She had on no make-up and her hair was pulled back in a ponytail.

He'd never seen her look more beautiful.

It had to be the smile she wore. Unlike most of the time they'd spent together, she didn't have that air of suspiciousness about her. Her smile was all over her face. But mostly he noticed it in her eyes.

"You're beautiful," he said. She always was, but this was different. More relaxed. And open.

"I'm sorry," she said.

"Sorry for what?" he asked. What could she possibly have to be sorry about?

"I'm sorry I ran away."

He laughed. "I'm the one who should apologize. I'm the one who scared you away."

"I shouldn't be skittish," she said.

"It's cute."

"Come inside," she said and he followed her back to the kitchen. "I was just about to put something in the oven."

"Do you want some help?"

"Sure," she said, handing him her kitchen shears. "You can open this jar of artichokes and cut them into little pieces."

Grayson tested the lid. "I see why you wanted me over here. To open this jar."

She laughed. "Guilty."

"Do you have an old knife or screwdriver?"

He could open the jar, but didn't dare use what was no doubt expensive silverware in her collection.

She opened a drawer and pulled out a screwdriver. "Will this do?"

"Perfect." He rapped it in three places on the top of the lid and it popped open with a simple twist.

"I never can get that to work," she said.

"It's all in the wrist."

While he cut up artichokes, she buttered a deep casserole dish, added two packs of cherry tomatoes, and stirred in some crushed townhouse crackers. She added a few more pats of butter along with some sun-dried tomato vinaigrette salad dressing. "I never said it was exactly healthy," she said.

"Looks a lot healthier than how I usually eat," he admitted.

She added in spices and stirred in his artichokes, then put the whole thing in the oven.

"It looks good," he said. "What's it called?"

"I call it my sun-dried tomato dish," she said.

He took a step toward her and she didn't back away. He took another step and was now in her space. He tucked a strand of hair behind her ear and looked into those gorgeous green eyes. As he bent close, she closed her eyes and tilted her head up. He placed his lips next to the corner of her mouth. Her intake of breath was ragged. He put his arms around her and pulled her against him.

"Oh," he said. "I brought you something." He'd nearly forgotten.

"What is it?

He reached into his pocket and pulled out the tickets to the baseball game. "Tickets for Saturday's game," he said, fanning the three tickets.

"You got three," she said.

"Of course. You don't think I'd leave Danielle out, do you?"

She grinned. And wrapped her arms around him. "You're awesome."

Her phone rang. "It's Martie," she said.

"Go ahead," he said. "I'll just answer some student emails on my phone."

Claire wandered down the hall as she talked to her assistant. Grayson hadn't been exaggerating. He only thought he had a lot of emails to answer before the test. Turns out he was even more inundated after the test.

He couldn't understand why a student who hadn't had the time to prepare for an exam wanted to ask for more work. He politely stated that he had a policy against extra credit and let it go. While he typed, he sat down at Claire's breakfast table. After he finished answering all his emails, he set down his phone and waited.

His gaze wandered to a note pad where she had scribbled notes about yoga and meditation classes. Intrigued, he read over her notes. Her ideas were spot on.

Get people in. Get them comfortable.

And they become customers.

He heard her say the word *yoga* to Martie. Claire was one of the most driven people he had ever met. She didn't just talk about doing things. She did them.

He flipped the page, wondering what else she had come up with during her two days in New York museums. And there, tucked beneath the page was a napkin. A man's name and a phone number was scrawled across the napkin. The handwriting was definitely not Claire's.

Allen Samuels.

Hearing Claire wrapping up her conversation, he dropped the paper to conceal the napkin and picked up his phone. As she came in his direction, he stood up.

"That was Martie," she said. "We're starting up a meditation class."

"That sounds interesting," he said. Actually, it was fascinating, but he couldn't think past the buzzing in his ears. Had Claire picked up a guy while she was in New York?

While she checked the dish in the oven, she chatted about how she'd come up with the idea for the class. "I wish I'd thought of it myself," she said. "But I don't think there's anything wrong with building on an idea," she said, straightening to face him. Her face was alive with excitement.

"There's nothing wrong with it," he said. "I admire your grit in making things happen."

Some of the excitement faded from her expression as she watched him. He scrubbed at his face. "I need to borrow your restroom," he said.

He turned and strode to her restroom. He closed the door and stood there, inhaling deeply.

This was not good. He didn't want to be the guy who put a downer on his girl's ideas. Just the opposite. He was supportive. He loved her idea. He just couldn't get the thought of her meeting someone in New York out of his head.

Maybe he didn't really know her. He only knew who she used to be. Or what she appeared to be. He didn't know the circumstances of her divorce. He hadn't asked and didn't think it was his business.

Was Claire the kind of girl who went off and met guys on a whim?

His gut said no.

He splashed cool water on his face. In truth, they hadn't talked about their relationship being exclusive. Did adults even do that? In high school, they'd said they were "going together." When did they get to the point of not seeing other people? He'd just assumed they were exclusive.

Perhaps he had no right to do that. Perhaps it needed to be stated. Talked about. Considered.

It had been a couple of years since he'd had a steady girlfriend. He couldn't even remember how they'd gotten to point of being steady. Or if they even had. He'd liked her, but he couldn't remember worrying too much about what she did with her own time.

Again, he had a tendency to make a lot of assumptions.

But not with Claire. He didn't want to mistakenly make assumptions. And he surely didn't want her going to New York or anywhere for that matter picking up men.

"Grayson, are you alright?" Claire asked from the other side of the door.

"I'm okay. I'll be out in a minute."

Whatever it was, he couldn't go all Neanderthal on her. He didn't know how she was coping with his leaving again.

He had to take it slow and let the relationship build. When the time was right, he'd bring it up and they could agree to be exclusive. Whatever people called it these days.

He would most definitely bring it up before he left for Pittsburgh.

Feeling much calmer now, he found her in the kitchen getting plates from the cabinet.

"Are you sure you're alright?" she asked. "You looked a little unwell for a minute."

"Yeah," he said. "I'm good. I'm probably just need to eat something."

"It's ready," she said.

"Great. Here," he said, reaching for the hot pad. "Let me get that out."

Some of the suspiciousness was back in her eyes. He kicked himself for that. She filled their plates with the tomato casserole and they went into the living room, and settled on the couch to eat.

"Wow. This is really, really good," he said, after the first bite.

She chucked. "You sound surprised."

"You're the one who self-professed not to do much cooking."

"Just because I don't do it much, doesn't mean I can't," she said with a mischievous smile.

"I'll have to remember that about you. You're a woman of many hidden talents."

"That's right," she said.

"Want to tell me about other hidden talents?" he asked. Even as he said the words, he knew he was headed down a path he'd told himself he wouldn't go.

"Oh no," she said, teasingly. "Discovery is the best part of the process."

"Is that so?" he asked.

"It is. Besides, think about how little I know about you," she said. "I haven't even been to your place. I don't have any idea how you live."

"It's nothing to get excited about," he said. "I promise."

"Maybe not, but you know everything about me. You know my decorating style. I don't even know what color hand towels you have."

"Hand towels?"

"Yeah. You know. Basic stuff."

He thought about his little apartment. And compared it to her fancy house. Once she saw how he lived, she may lose interest in him. He didn't and couldn't live the way she did. She had done a nice job of distracting him from the mysterious Allen Samuels. He may as well get it over with. His philosophy was to snap it off like a band-aid. If she didn't like that part of him, it was a good time to find out.

"Alright," he said. "Tomorrow then."

"Tomorrow then what?"

"Tomorrow I'll cook dinner for you at my house."

She looked at him sideways. "Okay," she said.

"Hey," he held up his hands. "It was your idea."

"So we're seeing each other three days in a row."

And he thought he was quick to cut to the chase. Seeing each other. That didn't sound quite as committed as going together.

He shrugged. "Unless you have something already planned." He sat back. "I shouldn't have assumed."

"No," she said. "I don't."

"We can wait. Take a break."

"No," she said. "I don't want to take a break."

"Claire," he said. "If you have something else going on, just tell me."

"I don't have anything else going on."

"If there's someone else in New York... it's okay."

She huffed out a breath. "There's not anyone in New York. I just needed to clear my head. That's all. I didn't even get out except to go to two museums."

He shouldn't ask about it directly. If he did, he'd be admitting that he'd looked through her papers. But... if he didn't ask about it, it was going to eat at him.

. . .

After dinner, Claire put their plates in the dishwasher. She couldn't figure out what was going on with Grayson.

He'd been different since she took the call from Martie. Was he jealous of work? He shouldn't be. He'd spent the time answering emails from students. Did he think Martie was someone else? Another man, perhaps?

"You know Martie's a girl, right?" She said suddenly, whirling around to face him.

"Of course," he said. "I met her, remember, at your fundraiser."

"Right," she said. Wiping off the cabinet. Still. Something was off. "That was Martie who called earlier."

"I know. You told me."

"Do you want to watch TV?" she asked.

"Sure."

They went into the living room and turned on the television. Whatever it was, it wasn't bad enough that he wanted to leave, but it was bad enough that he was acting distant.

"Was everything okay with your emails?" she asked.

"Yeah. Just normal questions from students."

"Then what's bothering you?"

He just stared at her.

"I'll get us some water," she said, standing up. She started toward the kitchen, then stopped and stood squarely in front of him. "I know something's bothering you. Since I talked to Martie. But I can't figure out what it could be."

"Something is bothering me, but I can't figure out how to tell you."

She crossed her arms. "That's better. Maybe you should just spit it out."

"I'm worried that you met someone in New York."

"Okay, maybe you should spit it out in such a way that it makes sense to me."

He inhaled deeply, locked his gaze on hers. "Alright. While you were talking to Martie I sat at your table and happened to see your notes about the yoga classes. I think it's an awesome idea, by the way. After I finished my emails, I was thinking about your classes and I read your notes." He paused. Waited.

"Okay," she said.

"I saw the phone number for Allen Samuels," he said.

"What phone...?" She must have left that napkin in her papers from her trip. He was worried about that? She snorted. Then bit her lip.

"What?"

"You should have just told me."

"I didn't want you to think I was snooping."

"I'd rather think you were snooping than acting all funny."

"Okay," he said.

"Allen gave me his phone number. He asked me to call him about a business deal. Then he started to hit on me. So I told him I wasn't interested."

"You kept the number."

"He's a business colleague whose wife recently passed away. I think he's going through some stuff."

"I see."

"Grayson, you have to tell me these things. You have to tell me what's bothering you and not keep it inside."

"You're right," he said.

"You teach this stuff, right?"

"I do. But helping others do it is a whole lot easier than doing it myself."

"Don't worry, okay?"

He stood up, pulled her close, and wrapped his arms around her. "Okay, my love, I won't worry. But I have an early meeting in the morning and I need to look over my notes for tomorrow's classes."

"You're leaving," she said against his shoulder.

He nudged her back a bit, and she saw the smile playing about his lips. "Don't worry, okay?"

"Ha. Point taken."

She walked him to the door. He kissed her goodnight. A gentle kiss on the lips. More. She wanted more. But he kissed her on the forehead and then he was gone. "Lock the door," he said as he stepped out.

She locked the door and set the alarm before she went back to sit on the couch and hugged a pillow to her.

It was early, but she should have heard from Danielle already. She sent her a text asking for her ETA.

Might sleep over at Joey's. Do you mind?

Yes. Instead she typed. *No. Just let me know.*

A couple of minutes later Danielle wrote back. *See you tomorrow.*

Another evening to herself. Her interactions with Grayson had felt off. That was the only way to describe it. The evening had started off well enough. Then after she'd talked to Martie, things had changed. He said it was because he'd found Allen Samuel's phone number. Surely he hadn't really been worried about that.

Then she remembered seeing a text come through on her ex-husband's phone. She still remembered the words. *Looking forward to our trip.*

He'd explained it away. It was a female pilot. Michelle maybe? Noah said they had a flight together – the first one in some time. He explained that Michelle tended to blur boundaries.

But more than the words and the explanation, she remembered the feeling. Just thinking about it brought that sick feeling back to the pit of her stomach. It was the kind of thing that never went away.

She got up, went into the kitchen, and found the napkin with Allen's phone number. She balled it up and tossed in the trash. She should have done that to start with. She'd thought they could work together. But Allen wasn't in a place to do that right now. Maybe later. If so, he could contact her. She wasn't hard to find.

There was nothing else she could do about it now. She just needed to give Grayson time. Time to believe her.

Keep moving forward.

CHAPTER
Twelve

Grayson drove straight home. He felt unsettled. He'd wanted his renewed relationship with Claire to be clean. That was the beauty of starting over. At least it should have been.

Instead he found himself worrying about things that probably didn't mean anything.

Probably.

The downside to starting over was the other side of the coin. He expected everything to slip into place without the normal getting to know each other stage. He was finding out that even with starting over, that phase couldn't be skipped.

It was going to take some time to blend their lives back together. That job in Pittsburgh loomed over his head. Like an angry deadline. He felt like they had to cram all the preliminary requirements to a long-term relationship into the few weeks before he left.

That was unrealistic. He needed to get his head straight.

The next morning after class, everything went off the tracks.

He had to stay through the afternoon to help out with advising. It wasn't his day, but being the low man on the totem pole meant he had to take up the slack. Then the department chair called a meeting at the last minute.

It baffled him that the other faculty members didn't seem to mind the last minute request. One of the ladies even brought brownies.

The meeting did nothing but put Grayson in a foul mood. He had planned on getting home in time to clean his apartment before Claire came over. And he needed to go by the supermarket.

By five o'clock, they were still discussing the merits of changing their program requirements.

Grayson stepped out for a restroom break to send Claire a message. *Stuck in a meeting. Can we reschedule for another night?*

She responded quickly. *No problem.*

The timing on this was not good.

Claire stepped out of her heels, sat down hard on the bed, and blew her bangs out of her eyes.

"Great," she said out loud. "Just great."

She'd left the museum early and stopped by the Blow Dry Bar. Her hair felt light, bouncy, and straight, with just a little flip on the ends.

She wanted to be mad, but she'd had it happen too many times before. How many times had Noah's flight been delayed? She couldn't even remember.

She unzipped her dress, but stopped when she caught a glimpse of herself in the mirror.

Another evening at home. Alone.

It seemed to be the way of things.

But the way of things didn't have to be.

She zipped her dress back up and put her shoes back on. Grabbing her handbag, she headed back downstairs.

She didn't have to go to New York. There was an exhibit tonight at the Natural History Museum that she'd been thinking about going to. If she left now, she could make it.

As she was backing out of her driveway, her phone buzzed. It was Martie asking her to stop by the gallery. *I need help with something. If you aren't busy.*

Claire sighed. Why did Martie always think she was available? Probably because she was. She wrote back, *I'll be right there.*

And why indeed was she always available? *I'm a business woman first,* she always told herself. The gallery was on the way to the museum. She could swing by, then head to the museum. She put her phone in her bag and set it on the seat beside her.

As she pulled onto the street, her phone buzzed again. "You'll just have to wait, Martie," she said out loud. "I'm on my way."

Grayson sat in the meeting, listening to the other faculty members go on and on about things no one could possibly really care about. He checked his watch.

He'd made a promise to Claire.

No faculty meeting was worth breaking a promise to the woman he loved. What kind of message would he be sending if he didn't show up tonight?

After the way things went last night, ditching out on her tonight was the worst possible thing he could do.

After five weeks, he would probably never even see these people again. Maybe at a conference. Maybe.

He fidgeted in his chair. Checked the time on his phone again.

He wouldn't do it.

He wouldn't cancel out on her like this. He didn't have time to clean his apartment or go to the supermarket, but that didn't mean they couldn't see each other.

He typed a message. *Since I didn't make it to the supermarket or have time to pick up my dirty socks, if I bring pizza, can I come over?*

He waited. Staring at his phone as though staring at it would cause her to respond. He waited five minutes. Ten. The faculty members droned on and on. Fifteen minutes and no response.

His decision made, he got up and quietly walked out of the meeting. As the door closed behind him, he heard them still talking, not a hitch in the conversation.

He got into his car and drove straight to Claire's house. He hated her garage. He couldn't tell if she was home or not. Since she hadn't answered his text, he decided not bring pizza.

He rang the doorbell. Waited.

Then he walked around to the backyard to see if there were any lights on. The house was dark. She definitely wasn't home. Unless she was asleep.

When she was home, the house was lit up like a baseball stadium.

Walking around aimlessly, he noticed there was a garage window. It was small, and over his head, but since he was in the backyard anyway, he decided to see if he could take a peek into the garage.

He had to drag a chair over from the patio and climb into it. He imagined the trouble he would be in if Claire came home and found him lying in her back yard, mangled from falling off a chair.

While peeking into her garage.

Of course, it could be days before she found him. He'd never known her to go outside much. She might notice him one day when she was taking out the trash.

At any rate, she wasn't home. The garage was empty.

Climbing down without mishap, he dragged the chair back to its rightful place.

He should go home. And try to call again tomorrow.

He wandered back around to the front of the house.

He would wait.

Since he was parked in her driveway, he realized she would know he was there. That was a relief. At least if he'd fallen in her backyard, she'd have known to go looking for him.

He went to the front steps of the house, sat down, and waited.

His stomach growled. Maybe he should have gotten the pizza after all. At least, then he would have something to eat. He thought about having something delivered, but somehow it seemed that would dilute the whole gesture of waiting for her.

He checked his phone. Answered some more emails. Did they never end? He sent one word answers – yes and no. At least they couldn't complain that he didn't answer in a timely manner, even on a Friday night.

He was reminded of one of his professors in graduate school, an older man nearing retirement who proclaimed email to be evil and the Internet to be the downfall of civilization. At the time he'd pitied the man. Now he understood completely. Unfortunately, the professor had been forced into retirement when he refused to teach online classes.

He reclined against the steps, his elbows propped behind him, his legs stretched out. He decided he should use the time to think about what he would say to Claire when she got home instead of worrying about old professors or student emails.

As the sun set and darkness settled over him, Grayson decided that grand gestures were sorely overrated.

He'd promised he wouldn't show up without calling first.

Perhaps he should try calling.

He quickly dismissed that idea and decided to stay the course. It would be much harder to ignore him if he was standing in front of her. Besides, there were exceptions to every promise.

By the time Claire had resolved Martie's dilemma, it was too late to make it to the museum.

Martie rarely had a dilemma she couldn't handle, but when one of the paintings had arrived with a rip in the top right-hand corner, she'd panicked.

"What do we do?" Martie asked, searching Claire's face.

"Did you call the artist?" Claire asked.

Martie's eyes widened with another wave of panic. "No way," she said.

"I'll call her," Claire decided.

When Claire got off the phone with the artist thirty minutes later, they'd decided to meet in the morning to assess whether the painting could be salvaged.

"Was she upset?" Martie asked.

"No, I mean, sure a little," Claire said, "but she understood that it wasn't anyone's fault. These things happen."

"It just had to happen to us."

Claire laughed. "Yes. It figures, doesn't it?"

It was getting late, so they locked up together, and Claire headed home.

When she pulled into her driveway, she had to slam on her brakes to keep from hitting the car parked in her driveway.

It looked like Grayson's car. Her heart did a little flip of anticipation, followed by a spurt of trepidation. Grayson said he was working late tonight. He wouldn't be here if he was working late.

The next thought was Danielle. She was supposed to be at her grandmother's house.

Claire dug her phone out of her bag and saw that she only had the one message. The one she had thought was from Martie.

Which she now saw was from Grayson. Something about dirty socks and pizza.

She lifted her eyes from his message and saw him standing on her front porch.

How long had he been waiting?

She got out of her car and walked toward him. He slowly walked down the stairs, his hands in his pockets. As she got closer, she could see that he looked tired. And a little frustrated.

She would be frustrated, too, if she'd spent the evening waiting on someone's front porch.

They didn't say anything as they walked toward each other.

Then his arms were around her, her face buried against his chest.

This. This was what she'd been searching for.

It was Grayson all along.

Not just today. Or last week.

But twenty years.

Since the night he'd kissed her and left her in her own bed to sneak down the hallway and out the back of her parent's house.

She remembered lying in the bed, her heart breaking. She'd cried that night. She'd cried like she'd never cried before while her body ached with new sensations.

After she'd finished crying, she'd focused on the promises he'd made. Promises to write. And call on the phone.

They'd be together again soon. He'd see her on leave.

That was the last time she'd heard from him for twenty years.

It hadn't been his fault. She knew that now. But even knowing it, the sting was still there.

Now with his arms around her, some of that sting was beginning to heal. His touch soothed and comforted hurts that were buried so deep, they'd become part of her.

"I love you," he said against her ear.

She gripped him tighter, her hands fisting in his shirt and blinked back the tears, but she couldn't hold them back. The tears fell silently, dampening his shirt.

She didn't think it was possible, but he held her even more tightly against him.

Then he reached down and, putting an arm beneath her knees, picked her up and carried her up the front stairs of her house.

When they reached the door, he slid her to her feet. She reached out and touched the door knob to unlock it. He pushed it open and followed her inside. And waited while she locked the door from the inside.

Then he took her hand and led her to the sofa. He sat and pulled her into his lap. He kissed her forehead, her eyelids, then the corner of her mouth.

Then his lips were on hers and everything else faded away – yesterday and tomorrow. There was only right now. In this moment.

When they came up for air some time later, Grayson said, "I'm starving. Do you have anything to eat?"

Claire laughed. "I'm starving, too. Let's check the refrigerator."

Claire sat on a stool at her kitchen counter while Grayson grilled egg, cheese, and tomato sandwiches.

"It's a cross between an egg sandwich and a grilled cheese," he said.

"I think I have some potato chips," she said, going to the check the pantry.

"Not exactly vegan food," he said.

"As long as it's vegetarian, I'm good," she said.

He flipped the sandwiches over, then stepped over to kiss her on the nose. The gesture made her smile.

He was the only person who had ever kissed her on the nose. She remembered the first time. He was a football place kicker and she'd been a majorette. It was during a particularly close Friday night game.

She'd been standing on the sidelines in her little red uniform. The crowd was cheering as Grayson kicked and made the field goal, leading their team to a last minute victory. Grayson had walked across the field straight to where she was standing and in front of the crowd, cheering for his winning field goal, he'd kissed her right there on the tip of her nose.

The crowd had gone wild.

That kiss had been a famous moment at their high school. Someone had taken a picture and it had been displayed in the high school office. As far as she knew, it was still there. The tall football player and the petite majorette had a made a touching picture of high school sports and innocent young love.

"Do they still have the picture up?" Grayson asked as he pulled two plates from the cabinet.

Apparently, his thoughts had gone down the same path as hers.

"As far as I know."

"We were supposed to get married and have a house-full of kids," he said.

"I know," she said, "everyone thought it."

He took their plates to the table. As they sat next to each other, his eyes locked onto hers. "It's not too late," he said.

"What?" She laughed and took a bite of her sandwich.

"It's not too late."

"Really? You want to have a house full of kids? Now?"

"Well," he said. "Maybe not a house full. But I wouldn't mind having maybe one." He bit into a potato chip. "Or two. Or maybe three."

"Ha. Obviously, you've never been through childbirth."

"I never wanted children with anyone else."

She searched his eyes. Those beautiful blue eyes. And was speechless.

He shrugged and bit into his sandwich. "I'm just saying," he said a few seconds later.

"You're serious," she breathed.

"Eat. We'll talk about it later."

"Oh no. You can't say something like that, then just let it sit there," she said, but bit into her sandwich anyway. "Yum," she said. "This is really good."

He now had a smug look on his face. "I'm a really good cook," he said. "And as my sister can attest, I can change diapers, too. And I do so willingly."

"Are you auditioning?" she asked, amusement playing about her lips.

"Just watering some of those seeds," he said.

"What seeds?"

"Those seeds I planted back in the day. When I was a hot football star and you were a sexy little majorette."

She grinned. "You're still pretty hot."

"And you're still pretty sexy."

They finished eating and cleaned the kitchen together.

"What did you do with Danielle and Charlie?" he asked.

"Danielle is spending some time with her grandmother and she took Charlie with her. I may have to get another cat to keep me company when she's not here."

He dried his hands on the kitchen towel and pulled her to him. "I can keep you company."

She laughed as he kissed her ear.

"You are trouble, Grayson Moore."

"You like trouble."

"I must," she said.

"Then you're saying you like me," he said, kissing her face.

"Yes," she giggled. "I like you."

"That's good to know," he said, kissing her on the lips now. "I should go," he said.

"Uh huh," she said but he had her off balance and she couldn't think.

He took her hand and led her toward the door.

"Danielle is still going to the game with us tomorrow?"

"She wouldn't miss it for the world," she said.

"Good. I'll pick you up at five."

"Make it four so we can pick up Danielle," she said.

He kissed her again and walked out the door.

Before she could lock the door, he was back.

Her face broke into a smile as he kissed her.

"I have to move your car," he said. So much for romantic notions.

Thirteen

Grayson moved Claire's car aside, then backed his up to the road. He then pulled hers into the garage. After the garage door was safely closed, he used bringing her key around as an excuse to kiss her again.

He didn't want to leave. He wanted to stay and devour her.

But he knew it wasn't the way to do it. He'd professed his love and she'd remained silent. She was still coming around.

Grayson felt confident that she would. But first she had to reconcile their long-distance relationship. He knew better than to rush her.

He had no doubt that he wanted to marry her. He'd never had any doubt. He'd put the notion aside when she'd married Noah, but the minute he found out she was divorced, he'd known he had never stopped loving her and she was the only woman he ever wanted to marry.

There was just the minor problem of logistics. He had to go

and she wouldn't go. Couldn't. She had too much invested here. A lifetime.

Grayson felt fortunate that he didn't feel ties to L.A. Hadn't felt ties, he corrected, until Claire walked back into his life.

He had to tamp down his sense of urgency to be with her and make up for lost time.

He stepped into his empty apartment and sighed. It wasn't much, but he had to live here a few more weeks. The next time Claire asked to spend time at his apartment, he would have no reason to hesitate.

He had too much energy to sleep, so he went into the kitchen, took out a box of black garbage bags and began the excavation process. He was moving soon, and unlike all the times he'd moved before, he wasn't going to take more than a few personal items other than clothes with him.

He started with the kitchen, throwing out old cans of food he was never going to eat and spices he'd had forever. From now on, he'd only be cooking with fresh food.

About midnight, he collapsed on the bed and napped a few hours before getting up early the next morning and resuming his house cleaning. He was a man on a mission.

He was ruthless in his closet as well. Everything except the necessities had to go. He must have hauled two dozen bags to the dumpster. The more he threw out, the more he wanted to throw out. It was most liberating.

Even his books. He chose six books he wanted to keep. The rest went in his car to take to campus to put on their give-away table.

He stopped when he came across an Apple iPad box in the

back of his closet. The box itself had changed over the years, but the contents had not.

He sat on the edge of his bed and opened it up. There was copy of the picture when he had kissed Claire on the nose at the high school football game. He didn't even know if Claire had been given a copy. His coach had given him this one. There was their photo from senior prom. He looked a little goofy in his burgundy tux, but she had been lovely in her pink dress.

He'd kept every note she'd written him in high school. It was from the days before text messages, so he had a stack of scraps torn from her notebooks. One simply said. "hi."

There was one, though, that had been written on blue paper. He carefully unfolded it and read the words she had written so very long ago:

Dear Grayson,

I wish you didn't have to leave, but I know you have to. You have to do your duty for our country. When you get back, I'll be here. I only ask that you stay in touch with me. Let me know what you're doing. What you're thinking.

And I need to know that you're safe.

I love you with all my heart. I always will.

He refolded the letter into its well-worn grooves. This letter had gotten him past countless battle wounds. Wounds that weren't visible to anyone who looked from the outside. The only way to see these wounds was to dip deep into his psyche. Knowing that Claire was there waiting for him even though she never wrote back had been enough to keep him going.

He only had to do four years and he would be out.

He'd gotten the letter from his mother with the newspaper

clipping tucked inside only two days before he had to sign his discharge papers.

By the time he went into the office to meet with his superior, he'd made up his mind. He now had no reason to get out of the Air Force. He could make a good career in the military.

After that, he couldn't bear to look at the letter, but he couldn't bear to get rid of it either. So, he'd tucked it away in the shoe box he carried around with him.

After the shoe box started falling apart, he stuffed it all in a sturdy Apple box.

But it had been a really long time since he'd taken the time to pull the notes and letters out and read them.

She'd asked him to stay in touch with her. Nothing more. Nothing less.

And despite his best efforts, he'd failed to do just that.

This time when he was gone for a year – not four years – he would make sure he stayed in touch. He would call her every day and he would text throughout the day. He'd tell her what he was doing. In fact, he would start that habit right now.

Hi. He texted. *How is your day going?*

Running errands. She wrote back.

He smiled. This was going well already. *I've been cleaning my apartment.*

Ugh. I would not want to trade.

Still ready at 4:00?

Yes. Time for me to head home. She wrote.

He sent back a smiley face emoji and went to get into the shower.

. . .

Claire put up her groceries and got into the shower. She hummed to herself as she washed her hair. Nothing in particular, just a catchy little tune she'd heard on the radio while she was out doing errands.

She'd been pleasantly surprised to hear from Grayson in the middle of the day.

Perhaps this thing with them had possibilities.

After her shower, she put on a pair of jeans, a T-shirt, and layered with a light sweater. She put on her favorite white canvas sneakers.

Just as she finished her make-up and put on her earrings, the doorbell rang. Grayson was right on time.

As he drove to her mother's house, he told her about how he'd gone through his apartment and purged everything he didn't need.

"I did that before I moved into my current house. I can't stand to live in clutter."

"It's a good thing I got it done before you came over," he said, a horrified look on his face.

She laughed. "I don't judge. Have you seen Danielle's room?"

"Actually, yes," he laughed.

They didn't talk about the fact that he would be leaving soon or that his real motivation was probably getting ready to pack up his apartment.

Claire thought maybe if they didn't talk about it, it wouldn't be what their relationship centered around.

They pulled into her mother's circle drive. "This is a huge house for one person," he commented.

"I know. I wonder if she keeps it for Danielle. Danielle loves the swimming pool."

"I bet she does," he said.

Grayson tried to ignore the trepidation he felt at driving up to Mrs. Beauchamp's house. It was the same house Claire had grown up in.

And he was still a little afraid of Claire's mother.

When they went inside, Claire went upstairs to help Danielle with something.

Grayson was left to follow Betty to the kitchen.

"How are you, Grayson?" Betty asked.

"I'm good." He was a soldier. He sucked up his fear and surged forward.

"Danielle tells me you're going to be moving across the country soon."

"Unfortunately, yes."

"Sounds a little familiar," she said.

Grayson winced. This was why he was afraid of Betty.

"I'm only going to be gone for a year," he said.

Would you like something to drink?" she asked.

"Water would be great, thank you," he said.

She handed him a bottle of water. "Grayson," she said. "I apologize for what I did. I overstepped my boundaries when I hid your letters and calls from Claire."

"It was a long time ago," he said as they sat at the kitchen table.

"Nonetheless, I wouldn't blame you if you never forgave me."

"I forgive you, Mrs. Beauchamp. It changed the direction of our lives, but Claire and I are who we are now because of it. And Claire has Danielle. Even I wouldn't change that."

"You're a kind man," she said. "I'll always regret the way I wronged you and Claire, Danielle notwithstanding."

"It means a lot for you to say that," he said.

"If it matters, I'm fully supportive of you now. I know how much Claire cares for you and I'll do everything I can to make up the wrong I did to you both."

"Mrs. Beauchamp."

"Please call me Betty," she said, putting a hand over his.

"Betty," he said. "Claire and I are working this out between us and I want you to know, from the bottom of my heart, that I forgive you."

"You're a good man, Grayson Moore. I truly hope that you and Claire can make a go of it this time."

Claire stopped at the kitchen door when she heard their voices. Their conversation brought tears to her eyes.

She blinked back the tears and took a deep steadying breath. With a smile on her face, she walked into the kitchen. "What are you two up to?"

"Just catching up," her mother said.

"You look so serious. And here we are getting ready to go to my very first baseball game."

"You're kidding?" Grayson asked.

"Nope," she said. "I've never been."

"I'm glad you told me," he said. "I'll make sure you have the whole experience."

"I'll get Danielle so we can get going," she said. *And give them time to finish up their conversation.*

They ate peanuts and Claire even sipped a beer. Danielle and Grayson ate hot dogs. This was after they had eaten Mexican food at the restaurant on their way to the stadium.

There was so much energy at the game. Claire hadn't expected that. On television, the game always seemed to move so slowly. She'd never actually been to a live baseball game. That had been Danielle and Noah's thing.

Grayson had gotten them really good seats. They were close enough – in the lower level directly behind the dugout - to actually see what was going on.

Danielle obviously enjoyed it. She'd even put her phone in her jacket pocket. Danielle and Grayson talked lingo while Claire listened, watched the game, and watched the crowd.

And reflected. She was glad that Grayson and her mother had talked. She felt like things were smoothed over with them now. Her mother seemed to accept that Grayson was back in her life and she didn't seem to have a problem with it.

On the contrary, she seemed rather contrite about what she had done and she appeared to welcome Grayson back.

It was one less thing preventing Claire from completely forgiving him and moving forward with their relationship.

"Mom look!" Danielle said, pointing to the screen.

As Claire looked, the image zoomed in and she was looking at herself and Grayson. Grayson was watching the screen, too. In the next instant, there was a heart drawn around them the word kiss over their heads.

Grayson turned and putting one hand behind her head pulled her to him and kissed her nose. Then he pressed his lips against hers and pulled her close into a kiss that could in no way be G-rated. The crowd cheered.

He pulled back and smiled into her eyes. Over the pounding in her ears, she heard him say those words again. "I love you."

And this time, she said them back.

Fourteen

The next few weeks went by in a blur. Claire and Grayson became attached at the hip when they weren't working. When they were at work, they texted throughout the day.

They quickly got into a rhythm. Work during the week, evenings spent at her house, mostly, though sometimes at his. They cooked together, watched movies, and TV, and sometimes they just sat quietly and read, cuddled up together on the sofa.

On the weekends, they got out, had dinner, went to museums, plays, even an airshow. Sometimes Danielle went with them and sometimes they went alone.

Either way, they forged their way as a couple.

Claire stood at her bathroom counter running a flat iron through her hair. They had two weeks left together. She tried not to think about it, but she couldn't stop herself. It was almost like being on a mental countdown.

She hated it.

She didn't, however, tell Grayson.

Grayson showed up a little after five o'clock. When she opened the door, he handed her a red rose.

"It's beautiful," she said, taking it from him. Smiling, she took it to the kitchen and slipped it into the vase along with the one he'd brought her yesterday. She slid the vase back to the center of the kitchen table.

Then she was in his arms.

"I was thinking," he said.

"Uh oh."

"What? You like most of my ideas," he said.

She laughed against his chest.

"Okay," he said, "running in the marathon wasn't my best idea."

"Hey, I did the best I could."

"You might like this idea better. It's something I've always wanted to do."

"Tell me," she said, under the pretense of being skeptical. In truth, she'd been impressed with his creativity at finding things for them to do.

"This weekend," he said, nuzzling her neck.

"Yes?"

"We could rent a car and drive up to San Francisco – along the coast. And we could fly back."

This was unexpected. They hadn't left the area. In fact, they hadn't even spent the night together. "And what would we do in San Francisco?"

"We could ride bicycles across the Golden Gate Bridge and spend the weekend at Sausalito."

A weekend with Grayson in Sausalito. Alone. A whole weekend. "Okay," she said.

"Really?" he took her hands in his and grinned.

His smile was contagious. "Sure. Why not? It sounds like fun."

"So… can you leave in the morning?"

She almost automatically said no. But there was nothing going on at the gallery this weekend. Nothing going on tomorrow. Martie could handle the routine. Danielle was busy doing her own thing. "Yeah," she said, surprising herself. "I think I can."

"Cool," he said. "I'll make reservations."

While Claire boiled water for pasta and washed salad greens, Grayson sat at the table and, using his iPad, made reservations to rent a car and flight reservations to get them back on Sunday.

"I think the drive down will be nice," he said, "but I'd rather spend the morning on the island than driving back."

"I agree. It's a good idea."

There were four hotels in Sausalito. He picked the Cavallo Point Hotel. This one looks like it has the best view," he said, holding the iPad so she could watch the video.

"It looks really nice," she said. "I've only been to San Francisco a couple of times, but I always flew and I never got to the bridge."

"I've been once, but it was a quick drive and I always wanted to get back and bicycle over."

Biting her lip, she drained the pasta. This was Grayson's last weekend before he left for Pittsburgh. He had been crossing items off his bucket list for the last few weeks. There was no way he could maintain this level of activity week after week. Going to Sausalito was a big one.

He'd said he would be coming back here after the year was up, but something told her he didn't really believe it.

"It'll be fun," she said. "As long we can take breaks. I haven't ridden a bicycle since I was a kid."

He hugged her. "We can go as slow as you want to. I just want to spend time with you and make you happy."

She wanted to tell him that they could stay right where they were and she would be perfectly content. But he seemed to have his heart set on making the trip. She lifted her face to kiss him. "It'll be fun."

"Let's see if I can get a reservation," he said.

While he was online, his phone buzzed. He let it go to voicemail.

"Do you need to answer that?" she asked.

"Nah. It's probably a student." But when it buzzed a second time indicating voicemail, he picked it up and checked it. "Students usually text…" he said. Then grew quiet as he listened to the message.

"What is it?" she asked when he put his phone down.

He shook his head. "Odd. I just got another job offer."

"What? How? I didn't know you'd had any other interviews."

"In San Antonio. I interviewed with them back in April."

"You should call them back."

He picked up his phone and paced toward the living room. She could hear him talking as he paced.

He hung up the phone and came back to the table and opened his iPad.

"Well?" she said.

"The person they had hired had to pull out at the last minute, so, since I was their second choice, they called me."

"You told them you had a job, right?"

"Right."

San Antonio wasn't significantly closer than Pittsburgh. Anything outside of L.A. and it didn't matter.

Five minutes later, he had a room reserved. "I think this room has a good view," he said. "I'm surprised they had anything available."

"Me too," she said.

After dinner, they snuggled a few minutes on the sofa, but they were both eager to start packing. Claire had to call Martie and Danielle to let them know she would be out for the weekend. This was different from her *business trip* to New York. In fact, she couldn't remember the last time she'd been away for a weekend for fun.

As she talked on the phone getting everything set up, she stared at her clothes trying to decide what to take.

After she hung up the phone, she quickly filled up her suitcase with everything from jeans to a sundress to casual pants. When she got to her pajama drawer, decisions became a little trickier. She usually slept in shorts and T-shirt. She wasn't out to seduce Grayson and even if she was, she didn't own anything that would fall into that category.

She had a pair of cotton pajamas she'd only worn once. They were conservative enough that she would feel comfortable in them. And not feel like she was trying to be seductive.

Not that she would mind. They had somehow made a tacit agreement not to go too far. The other time, they had been kids with raging hormones and delusions that marriage would follow.

Now, they were complicated adults. Even with tentative plans to stay together, both of them knew, at least Claire knew, that everything was uncertain right now. It was best if they didn't complicate things with sex.

Having done everything she could do tonight, she decided it would be best if she was well rested. She could finish packing in the morning.

Although she'd been a little reluctant about the trip, she woke early the next morning with a sense of excited anticipation. A whole weekend alone with Grayson.

The very idea quickened her pulse. The fact that it was their last weekend together before he left next week made this trip seem all the more bittersweet.

He pulled into the driveway at eight o'clock in a rented SUV. When she opened the door, he swung her around in a hug that swept her off her feet.

It was like they were two kids getting away for the weekend.

He took her suitcases to the car while she locked up. Danielle had Charlie at her grandmother's again, so there was nothing to worry about.

They chatted about everything and nothing as they headed north out of town. He took Highway 101 – the scenic route. It would take a little longer to get there, but Claire deemed the view of the coast well worth the extra time.

It was late afternoon when they checked into the hotel. Grayson had been right. They had an awesome view of the bay.

The room had only one bed – a king bed. Something neither of them said anything about.

"What are we doing first?" Claire asked, as she unpacked her suitcase, wondering if she should change.

"I thought we'd just walk around, get something to eat," he said.

"I should be able to wear this?" She ran a hand along her jeans.

"Sure. Looks perfect."

She added a light short cardigan, and after freshening up, came back to stand next to him at the window.

"Are you okay?" she asked.

"I'm great," he said, pulling her against him.

"It was a beautiful drive and I'm glad we did it," she said. "but I have to admit I'm glad we're flying back Sunday."

"I agree," he said. "It's always fun to start out on a trip, but going home can sometimes be something of a downer."

Claire laughed. "I know what you mean."

"Ready?" he asked.

They drove downtown and parked. Claire had never been to Sausalito. It was a quaint little town with some tourist shops and restaurants and lots of tourists walking about. They found a restaurant on the water. It had white table clothes and servers all in black. Grayson had been relatively quiet since they'd gotten to the room.

Grayson knew they needed to talk. He knew he'd been putting it off for several weeks, but time was running short.

"Can I order you a drink?" he asked, when the server stopped at their table.

She hesitated a moment. "Sure. I'll have a cosmopolitan."

Grayson order a martini. "We'll have to ride the ferry back after we bike over to San Fran."

"I hear the ferry is nice," she said. "Nice views of the bridge."

The server brought their drinks. Grayson held his up in a toast. "To us," he said.

They clinked glasses and Claire sipped her pretty pink drink.

"Something's bothering you," she said.

"Yeah," he agreed. "And if it isn't bothering you, we've got a problem."

She set her drink down. Sat up a little straighter. "You're leaving next week."

He nodded. "I'm thinking we should talk about it."

"We should," she said.

But they didn't. They sipped their drinks. Grayson was glad he'd ordered a drink. He'd been dreading this conversation.

"You might as well spit it out," Claire said.

He chuckled. "I guess there isn't much to say."

Claire rolled her eyes. "Grayson Moore you're not going to get away with that line."

He laughed. "You're right. So… I've got some money saved to fly over at least once a month."

Claire put her hand over his. "Grayson no."

"You don't want me to visit?"

"Of course, I do. I just didn't think about…. I don't want you to spend your savings on the flights. I could buy…"

He cut her off. "No. Don't even think it. I won't come if I can't pay my own way."

"Okay," she said, sitting back. "Then I can come there."

"That's kind of the same thing. I can't let you spend your money coming to see me."

"Then I guess we'll be talking on the phone a lot."

Claire swallowed the lump in her throat. If Grayson was going to be difficult, then this move wasn't going to go as smoothly as she had hoped. "Why don't we think about it and talk about it on the way home? I don't want to ruin our trip."

He finished off his drink and nodded.

"I'd like to walk around and get Danielle a T-shirt," Claire said, to lighten the mood.

"Sure," he said, but his smile was tight.

Claire had been through enough counseling with her ex-husband and her daughter to figure out that tension was running high between them right now because neither of them wanted to admit that they probably would see each other only occasionally after this weekend.

She'd been putting off allowing herself to think about it, but that was no longer an option.

We have this weekend, she told herself. The best thing they could do was to make the most of it. Focus on the here and now.

During dinner she chatted about the museum and how well the meditation and yoga classes were going. She chatted about the next fundraiser coming up in September. And tried to ignore the unpleasant thought than Grayson most likely wouldn't be there for it.

As she talked, she braced herself for this being their last weekend together. Period.

If he was worried about money, she wouldn't let him come

visit and she wouldn't visit him. At the end of the academic year, they would see where they were.

If he came back to L.A., he came back. If he didn't then she couldn't hold it against him. He had a career. A career that was in a lot of ways she'd never considered, was a lot like the military. He could request a certain location, but he had to be prepared to go wherever the next job was. He might very well end up in Georgia or Maine. There was no guarantee there would be anything open in L.A. The fact that he'd taken a one-year temporary two years in a row wasn't a good sign.

She couldn't very well ask him to do anything different. That would be like asking her to do something besides her gallery. It was in her blood. She had no choice.

After dinner, they walked downtown hand-in-hand and wandered through the shops. She kept her negative thoughts to herself. As a result, they had very little conversation. She bought Danielle a T-shirt that smelled like coffee – on purpose. The coffee beans were baked into the material.

It didn't take long to go through the shops, so they drove back to the hotel.

Claire disappeared into the bathroom to wash up and put on her pajamas.

When she came back out, Grayson was sitting in a chair patiently waiting for her.

"Come here," he said, patting his knee.

He squeezed her against him. She wrapped her arms around him and held on.

He picked her up and carried her to the bed, tucking her beneath the covers. Then he went around to the other side of the bed and climbed in. He lay there for a minute staring at the ceiling.

Then he shifted over, took her in his arms again, and put his lips on hers.

They fell asleep kissing.

When Claire woke the next morning, her first response was panic. She was wrapped in a vise-grip. When she realized she was wrapped in Grayson's arms, she relaxed.

The morning sun was peeking through the gap in the curtains. She had no idea how late they'd stayed up kissing. But her lips were swollen.

One thing hadn't changed. She couldn't get enough of kissing him.

She maneuvered her way out of his arms and went to get into the shower. Today was going to be a challenge for Claire. Her idea of exercise was yoga. On a mat. In an air-conditioned room.

She'd ridden a bicycle as a kid, but truly, it had never been her thing. She'd quickly gotten bored with riding around the block.

Fortunately, riding across the Golden Gate Bridge was a far cry from riding around the neighborhood. And anything she did with Grayson was good. Well, running the marathon had been the exception to that rule.

After they got dressed, they went downstairs for coffee and breakfast. Grayson seemed less tense today. Some of his excitement was back.

When they got to the bicycle rental shop, she was the one who was a bit nervous and he was ready to get going.

The man at the shop gave her a rubber band. "What is this for?" she asked.

"It's to tie your pants to your leg so they won't get caught in the spokes," Grayson said.

Oh boy. There was so much she didn't know.

When they got on their bikes, she was a little wobbly.

"I don't know about this," she said as they rolled out of the parking lot.

He laughed. "Come on, Claire, you can do it. Let's get to the trail, then we'll stop and rest."

As they rode a few minutes, she became a little steadier, but didn't care for riding along the traffic. The cars rushing by made her nervous. She didn't know when she would fall. She couldn't help imagining hitting a rock and tumbling over – right in front of a car.

"Grayson," she said. "Don't they have a trail or something?"

"It's up ahead. Don't worry. They're used to cyclists. They won't run over you."

"I'm glad you're so confident," she muttered under her breath and heard him laughing.

Fortunately, they made it off the streets and to the trail without mishap. Going uphill, however, proved to be quite strenuous.

Before they got on the bridge, they stopped and rested.

"You can tell I've never done anything like this before," she said, taking out her water bottle. "Somehow I pictured us just hopping up on the bridge and riding across. I didn't think about having to get all the way to the bridge."

"I didn't do a very good job of preparing you," he

commented. "But," he said. "I brought trail mix." He pulled out a package of nuts and dried fruit from his back pack.

"I wondered what you had in there," Claire said.

"Always prepared," he said. "I have a first aid kit, too," he said with a wink.

She rolled her eyes. "I thought you were confident about this thing."

"I am confident, but, you know, things happen."

"It's a beautiful day," she said. The sky was clear blue and the weather couldn't have been more perfect for an outdoor activity. The trail to the bridge was crowded with other cyclists as well as people walking.

When they rode onto the bridge and the bay unfolded below them, she caught her breath. "Wow," she said, steering to the side of the trail and stopping. Grayson, following her, rolled up beside her and stopped.

"Yeah."

The skyline of San Francisco was in the distance, but it was the bay below that was truly magnificent.

They began their ride on the bridge and the wind whipped up. Claire wondered if it was going to topple her over.

"Are you okay?" Grayson asked, coming up alongside her.

"Yes," she said.

As they went around the first pylon, the wind was so strong she had to get off her bicycle and push it. She stopped to gaze below at the churning water below. "Wow," she said.

He came close enough to kiss her. "I'm glad you're with me," he said. "What do you think?"

She smiled. And squeezed his hand. "It's so much higher than I expected. I love it."

"Did you notice?" he said, indicating the water below. "They added netting so no one can jump."

"That was a good idea. I wonder if they've had to use it."

"I'm sure they have."

When they got to the other side of the bridge, Claire was exhausted. Her legs ached. They stopped for a few minutes to admire the view back toward Sausalito.

But… it turns out they had a long way left to go. They had to ride to Fisherman's Wharf to catch the ferry back.

Four hours later from the time they'd rented their bikes, they made it to Fisherman's Wharf. They found a place to leave their bikes so they could walk around a bit and get lunch.

They stopped at a busy café on the wharf and settled in for lunch.

"So, I was thinking," Grayson said. "Since it's such a pretty day, we should ride our bikes back across the bridge."

She made a face. "You go ahead. I'm taking the ferry."

He laughed.

"I think that was one of the most awesome things I've ever done," she said.

"Truly?"

"Truly."

The server came and Claire ordered a soda. After she left, Grayson said, "I think I'm going to fall out of my chair."

"What?" she asked, innocently.

"Claire Worthington ordered a soda."

"A monumental achievement calls for a celebration."

"How long has it been?" he asked.

She shrugged. "I don't know. Fifteen years. Twenty. Maybe more."

"It's got to be more. Because I've never known you to drink a soda."

She laughed. "I guess I can still surprise you."

"You surprise me every day," he said, taking her hand and kissing her knuckles. "I'm so going to miss you," he said.

His words sent a stab into her heart. They'd gotten close these past few weeks. They'd seen each other every day.

"Hey," he said, seeing her expression. "We'll still see each other."

"Not every day," she said.

"No, not every day."

Her heart ached. "It won't be the same," she said.

"I think I finally discovered the secret to getting you to open up to me," he said.

"What's that?"

"Get you so exhausted you can't control your emotions."

"You might be right," she said. "Exhausted and hungry."

They ordered sandwiches and Claire sipped her soda through a straw. "I'd forgotten how good a coke could be," she said.

"It's good to live a little, isn't it?" he said.

She had a feeling she knew where his mind was going. They'd been here before.

"No," she said.

"No, what?" He asked picking up a French fry.

"Whatever it was you were thinking."

"I was thinking that when we get back to Sausalito, we should have ice cream."

"Right," she said.

They ate in silence a few minutes.

"So, really, what do you think I'm thinking?" He asked.

"I think you're thinking that since you're leaving, we should live a little. You know."

"We are living a little."

She decided to let it go. Maybe she was imagining things.

"I think you're the one with dirty thoughts," he said.

She nearly spit out her coke. "Ah ha," she said. "Your mind did go there."

"Yours went there first."

"Is that so?"

"In the last hour, yes. It's true. But overall, probably not so much."

She laughed. "I'm gonna miss you, too."

"I hope so," he said. "But I'm planning on…" He stopped and gazed out the window of the café.

"Planning on what?" she asked.

He turned back and gazed into her eyes. "I don't know how to ask you this."

She set down her glass, overcome with trepidation. He looked so serious.

"What is it?"

He squeezed her hand. "I don't know what it's called anymore."

She frowned. "Give me a hint."

"We called it going together."

"You're talking about an exclusive relationship?"

"Yes," he said. "that."

Relief washed over her, followed by worry. She wasn't sure if he wanted to see each other exclusively or if he wanted to see others. She went with the latter. "You want to see other people."

"What? No! I don't even want to talk to anybody but you."

Relief. It washed over her like a balm.

"So…" he said. "Will you be my girl?"

"I thought I was your girl," she said, a smile playing at her lips.

He kissed her – a brief peck on the lips, but his face lit up. "So, that means we can make last minute plans and not have to worry about it."

"Grayson," she said. "You've had that since the day Danielle reintroduced us."

They got their bicycles on the ferry along with about one hundred other people and made their way to the top level to find a seat. Claire was physically exhausted.

The Golden Gate Bridge was to their left. It was majestic and Claire as in awe that just that morning that had ridden bicycles across it. The fog was coming in now and the bridge was partly obstructed by it.

Grayson nudged her. "See there," he pointed toward the bridge. "We should have ridden back across it."

"I think you would've had to carry me. My legs feel like rubber."

"I'd carry you," he said.

She laughed. "It's a long way. Even for a soldier."

He laughed, too. "You're right. But for you, I'd do it."

She felt safe with Grayson. She believed that he really would carry her if he needed to. It was almost like her heart had been on hold – waiting for him to come back. Why hadn't she known that? Why hadn't she looked for him?

Life. Life was the answer. Life always moved forward.

But once in a lifetime, the lucky ones got a chance to start over and do the important things again.

She was one of the lucky ones. And Grayson was one of the important things.

She squeezed his hand.

He smiled into her eyes. "I love you," he said.

"I love you, too," she said.

As the ferry took off across the water, the wind racing in her face, she didn't know if the tears were from the wind or from the rare moment of blissful happiness.

The water was choppy, but Grayson put his arm around her and held her close.

"Let's take a picture," he said, taking out his camera and holding it out at arm's length. Leaning their heads together, they smiled for the camera. Then smiled at each other. Grayson snapped the pictures.

As they looked at the images, Claire said, "I think you should take them over. Maybe later after we've had a shower."

He laughed. "We can take some more." But he didn't delete and she was too tired to care.

It was an ordeal getting their bicycles – Claire had never seen that many bikes piled together in one place. She'd stood back and let Grayson find them among the throngs of people searching for their own bicycles.

They rode them back to the bike shop and turned them in. Then they had to walk back to the SUV before they could finally drive to the hotel.

Claire got into the shower and let the hot water run over her exhausted muscles. How could she feel so spent and so content at the same time?

She dried her hair with the blow dryer and waited while Grayson showered.

While she waited she lay on the bed – for just a moment and that's when her legs really began to ache.

When Grayson came out, she said, "I don't like to complain, but my legs hurt. I mean it hurts like a toothache."

"Here," he said, taking pillows and putting them beneath her legs. He went to his toiletry bag and brought her two aspirin and a bottle of water. "Take these."

He sat down beside her as she took the medication.

"You don't hurt?" she asked.

"No," he said, "but remember I have the advantage. Years of P.T."

"I'd never make it," she said.

"You'd be surprised. So tomorrow, we'll do it all over again."

"You've gone insane."

"Maybe a little. Did that help?" He asked, gesturing to the pillows.

"No," she said.

"Maybe I can help," he said.

He started with her feet and massaged his way up to her calves. "Is this where it hurts?"

Claire mumbled something that he took to be a yes. He knew this kind of pain, though it had been a long time. He'd be sore tomorrow, but sore was preferable to this deep muscle pain that she was experiencing.

Her skin was smooth as silk and when he glanced at her face, her eyes were closed in sensations of bliss.

He could seduce her now. He had no doubt about that.

But he wouldn't do that.

He'd done that once. Twenty years ago and the regret still ate at him. He never should have seduced her the night before he'd been shipping out for basic training. But they'd been kids and it was how they'd shown their love for each other. It was how they'd been trying to bind themselves together.

But not this time. This time he knew they would see each other again soon, but he wasn't willing to take the chance that history could repeat itself.

He loved her too much to risk hurting her again.

Her phone buzzed. He reached over, picked up her phone from the nightstand, and held it out for her. She cracked one eye open.

"It's text," he said.

"Danielle?"

He glanced at her phone. "I don't think so."

"You check it. I'm too tired.

He read the message. *Hi Claire. Did you read my proposal? Let me know what you think and I can schedule a visit.*

"It's from someone named Allen."

"What does he want?" She muttered against the pillow.

"He wants to come visit."

"Later," she said. He chuckled, but there was more to this story that he would have to find out later when she wasn't drunk with sleep. He set the phone aside, his brow furrowed with worry.

As he massaged her calves, she fell asleep. He climbed into bed and, pulling her into his arms, slept next to her.

CHAPTER
Fifteen

Claire sat outside Dr. Lee's office and waited while Claire had her therapy session. It was Tuesday and she was thinking about tonight. Grayson was planning to leave Thursday morning. That gave them two more nights together before he left. They had talked about it and after their trip to San Francisco, they both wanted to just stay home and enjoy the quietness of each other's company.

To distract herself, she was reading a novel by Isabella Quinn called Forgotten. Lost in the fictional world, she didn't see the door open and Danielle come out.

"Mom?" Danielle said. "Dr. Lee wants you to come in."

Claire closed her iPad as fear shot through her. "Is everything okay?" she asked as she gathered up her handbag. She thought Danielle was doing so well. She knew that Danielle's relationship with Joey had cooled, but Danielle always had boyfriends who came and went. Her issue had never been related to that.

"I'll wait out here," Danielle said as Claire hurried into Dr. Lee's office.

"Claire," he said. "Sit down."

"Is something wrong with Danielle?" she asked.

"No, no. Danielle is doing quite well," he said. "It's you I want to talk about."

"Me? Why?"

"Danielle tells me your boyfriend is moving away soon."

"Thursday," she said.

"This is the same man who abandoned you in high school."

"He didn't abandon me exactly."

"No, I understand," he said. "It was all a misunderstanding. But it felt like abandonment." He paused a moment. "For over twenty years."

Claire took a deep breath.

Dr. Lee was right, of course. "We probably shouldn't be talking about me," she said.

"I know. It's hard to talk about yourself."

Claire laughed and shifted in her chair. She'd come here for Danielle. Now Dr. Lee was wanting to delve into her brain.

"I'm okay," she said.

"I'm sure you are" he agreed. "I'm just wondering how you're coping with all this."

She pressed her hands together. "We're still going to see each other."

He nodded.

"I know. We planned to see each other last time, too, but we were kids. We weren't in control of things that happened."

"You feel in control now," he said.

Claire shifted again. "No. Not really."

"But you're okay with him leaving."

"I'm not okay with it. I just don't have a choice."

Dr. Lee nodded again. And waited. "You're very brave," he said.

"I'm not brave," she said.

"You seem brave to me."

"Do I?" she asked with a little laugh. "Because I'm not brave at all."

"You do a good job of hiding your fear."

She nodded. "I was trained to not show emotion."

"That can be a good quality to have at times."

"And not at others. I know."

Dr. Lee sat quietly studying her. "Is there anything you'd like to discuss with me?"

Claire shook her head. "No, but I appreciate your concern."

"Can I give you some unsolicited advice?"

"Of course."

"Don't keep it all bottled inside. Find a way to let yourself feel. Not all the time, just during a time that you choose. When you're alone. I think you'll find that you can cope much better if you let yourself feel emotions from time to time."

Claire nodded. "I do. I do feel emotions with Grayson."

"That's good." Dr. Lee took his glasses off. Claire had watched him enough with Danielle to know that it was a sign he had something significant he was about to say. "Have you found that you've been able to forgive him?"

"Yes," she said.

"But do you sometimes have lingering doubts that maybe history is replaying itself all over again?"

"Yes," she said. How had he known that? She hadn't told anyone.

"That's a difficult thing to get past."

"It is. But it's possible." Claire wasn't sure if she was telling him or asking him.

"It takes a lot of faith and a lot of strength. I admire you for being able to start over with someone who hurt you so much."

"He didn't hurt me on purpose."

Dr. Lee smiled. "Again, I admire you for being willing to give Grayson a second chance. He's a very lucky man. And I think I can safely say that Danielle likes him. She thinks he'd make a great stepfather."

Claire laughed nervously. "That might be a little difficult living so far apart."

Dr. Lee just nodded.

After Claire left Dr. Lee's office, she turned to Danielle. "You told Dr. Lee about me and Grayson."

"I tell him everything."

"I see."

"He's really easy to talk to," Danielle said.

"Uh huh."

"I guess you have to get used to somebody getting into your business."

"I think you're right," Claire admitted as they walked together down the hallway toward the door to the parking lot. "You know, I never told you, Danielle, but I really admire you for how you've opened yourself up this past year and let people help you get past those feelings of hopelessness that you were feeling."

Danielle grinned. "Thanks. I admire you, too."

"Why?" Claire asked.

"Why? For everything. You're so successful. And you let Grayson come back into your life without even a hitch. I think that means you really love him."

"I do love him," she said, the admission warming her heart. Other than Grayson, she hadn't told anyone else. Not even Danielle.

"No," Danielle said, as they climbed into the car and closed the door. "I mean you must REALLY love him."

Claire smiled. "I do." Then she grew serious. "Does that bother you? I mean… Daddy."

"Are you kidding? If you and Grayson get married, that means I would have the two most awesome dads ever."

Claire sat quietly on her sofa, reading her novel as she waited for Grayson. She'd gotten used to their routine – dinner together every night. They didn't even talk about it anymore. It was just understood. Instead, they talked about where they would eat or what they would cook. What they would watch on TV – a series like *Game of Thrones* or a movie.

Sometimes they just sat quietly and read.

It was going to be lonely without him here in the evenings.

When the doorbell rang, she went to answer it. He was earlier than usual.

When she opened the door and saw him standing there,

leaning against the post, with one hand behind his back, her heart melted.

She held out her hand.

"What?" he asked.

She smiled, but kept her hand out.

He reached out and took her hand in his.

She laughed and reached behind his back, but he twisted away and laughed with her.

"I know you have it. I have eleven in the vase. So tonight makes twelve."

"Uh oh," he said, feigning horror. "I knew I was forgetting something."

She reached behind him again, but this time, he let her grab the rose that she had known would be there.

"You've spoiled me," she said.

"You think so?"

"Yes."

"You haven't seen anything yet."

"Is that so?" She took the rose inside and added it to the vase on the kitchen table. There were twelve now. He'd started bringing her one every night, excluding the time they'd spent in San Francisco. He'd even managed to make it work with them being out for two nights. It occurred to her that he must have been planning that trip longer than he'd let on.

Maybe he wasn't as spontaneous as he led her to believe.

She turned and he was standing behind her. He swept her into a hug. She put her arms around him and her fingers dug into his shirt.

He backed away to study her face. "Are you still sore?" he asked.

"No," she said. "But I'm thinking maybe I need to add cycling to my workout. So I'll be ready next time for whatever you come up with. Marathons. Bike rides."

"You never know," he said.

"Nope. I never know." She settled her head back against his chest and told herself he wasn't gone yet. "So how far in advance do you plan these activities?"

"That, my lovely, is a secret I'll never reveal."

"Ah. Secretive and mysterious."

"You'll never be bored with me around," he said, nuzzling at her ear. "What do you want to eat?" he asked.

"I thought we'd make a fried green tomato po'boy."

He laughed. "That's different."

"I have them all the time for lunch with Danielle." She bit her lip. "I've never made one though."

"Do you have all the ingredients?"

"I'm always prepared," she said.

"Okay," he said, taking her hand and pulling her with him to the kitchen. "I'm starving."

She laughed. "You're always starving."

"It's true. You've found me out."

Later that evening, Claire and Grayson were curled together on the couch like a couple of kittens. Charlie was there with them, coaxing Grayson to rub under his chin. He was getting bigger and Claire pointed out how big his little paws were getting.

"So..." Grayson said, "I don't think you ever answered me."

"Hmm. About what?"

"About having another child."

"That's not something that can be easily answered."

"Danielle told me that Noah's wife is expecting. You two are about the same age, aren't you? And it's her first."

"I think she might be a little older. And, yes, Danielle told me that, too."

"Well?"

"Our situations are different."

"You're so avoiding answering me," he said, kissing her earlobe.

"Oh no. You're leaving tomorrow."

"What?" he asked innocently.

"We are so not going down that road again."

"Don't worry. When I ravish you, I don't plan for us to leave the bed for a week."

"A week, huh?"

"Yep. I just can't decide between a cruise or holing up in a mountain cabin."

"The cabin sounds nice. But it sounds like we're gonna need room service. Besides, I've already done the whole honeymoon cruise thing. It's overrated."

"See there, I have you already planning our honeymoon."

"You're kinda sneaky, aren't you? I didn't know you were such a planner."

"You have no idea how much work goes into being spontaneous," he said.

"You're right. It's much easier to plan things."

"Are you sure I can't talk you into driving with me? We can stop off at the Grand Canyon and spend a couple of nights."

"I thought you didn't allow time for sight-seeing."

"For you, I would be late."

"Not a chance," she said. "You'll be fired before you even get there."

"I've got until Monday."

"You know I would, but I've got that fundraiser Saturday. It's been planned for months."

"And you've only known me for weeks," he said.

"Yet somehow it seems like years," she said.

They laughed, then sat quietly with the television playing a movie neither of them were watching.

"So, I'm thinking I'll call you every night," he said.

"Okay."

Grayson didn't want to leave. Once he walked out that the door, he ran the risk of destroying the fairytale life they'd created.

A year – even nine months – until next May was a long time.

So much could go wrong.

He may not be able to find a job back in L.A. He could live off his retirement from the military, but Claire would expect more out of him. He needed to have another career.

To be successful and make her proud.

Besides, he'd seen too many good men crash and burn after retirement. It was crucial for a man to keep working. He couldn't risk ending up psychologically disabled.

But he had to leave. He had a long day of driving tomorrow.

He held her close. He would be back.

It's a temporary separation.

He needed to believe that.

A long-distance relationship was one thing. A long-distance marriage was another thing entirely.

I'll make it work.

He had to believe it.

"You should go," she said, sitting up.

"I don't want to."

"Good. I don't want you to either." She stood up and tugged on his arm. "Come on."

"I should have known you'd kick me out eventually."

"It had to happen."

"Come on," she said again, "I'll walk you to the door."

At the door, they held on to each other as the seconds ticked past.

Until she nudged him again. "Go," she said. "You need to be well rested. I don't want to be the reason you fall asleep at the wheel."

He kissed her softly. "I'll see you soon," he said. "my love."

Her eyes were closed. Charlie meowed and stood up to put his front paws on Grayson's jeans.

"He's saying good-bye, too," Claire said, picking up her kitten and holding him to her.

"Be safe," she said.

Grayson turned and went out the front door. His eyes stung from unshed tears.

This was one of those things in life that felt so very wrong.

He'd set a course for himself that he longer wanted to follow. But he had no choice. He had to honor his commitment.

A soldier followed through.

He listened until he heard the door lock and her alarm beep into place.

Then he went down the sidewalk, got into his car, and backed out of her driveway.

His heart ached. He needed to get this over with so he could get back to her.

Claire went to the kitchen and, after feeding Charlie, sat at the little table and slid the vase with the roses toward her. A couple of the roses were already dead.

Soon, they would all be dead.

But she would keep them, she decided.

She would keep them because they represented so much planning and thought that Grayson had gone through for her. A rose a day for two weeks giving her a dozen roses.

They represented the love that he had shown for her this summer.

She could only hope and pray that they hadn't gone from high school sweethearts to a summer romance.

She wiped at the tears at her eyes before they could fall from her lashes and pushed the roses back to the center of the table.

She had to trust that whatever was supposed to happen would. She got up and headed upstairs, Charlie scampering at her heels.

Time only moved forward.

Claire woke at her usual time. She'd left the curtains open in her bedroom so the soft morning sunlight was streaming across her face.

She stretched. Everything was as it should be. Danielle had come home late, but was tucked safely in her bed. Claire knew because she'd waited up. Danielle thought she'd gotten lost in the novel she was reading on her iPad, but in truth as soon as Danielle stuck her head in the door to say goodnight, Claire had been out.

But as her brain came more awake, she knew that everything wasn't as it should be. Grayson had left last night. And although they had ended their early evening with kisses and promises to stay in touch, it was going to be different. They'd seen each other every single day for the last few weeks. Now they would merely have phone calls and perhaps at most, monthly visits.

Claire couldn't help comparing this separation with the one twenty years ago. They'd been kids then. She wasn't even out of high school. They'd had sex their last night together before he shipped out. Sex for the first time.

This time they hadn't had sex, but they had been attached at the hip.

They'd been more physically intimate last time and more emotionally intimate this time.

Claire climbed out of bed and got into the shower. She did her best thinking in the shower, but not today. Today she was unable to sort through the emotional tangles in her head.

Today was the first day of trying to get her life back to normal.

She'd known going in that Grayson would be leaving. Knowing that had made their time together bittersweet. She wasn't the teenager anymore. The one who believed that anything was possible.

She knew that them having careers on opposite sides of the country wasn't going to work out. Relationships couldn't work that way. Sure, it would be exciting for a little while to visit and see each other. She'd go to Pittsburgh and see some snow.

But if anyone knew how hard it was to stay connected in a long-distance relationship, it was Claire. She'd lived with Noah, her ex-husband, but he'd been away from home more than he'd been there. Even if she'd wanted to have something deeper with him, it would've been next to impossible with that physical distance.

Time moves in only direction. Focus on the future.

She got dressed for a meeting with her board of directors. Woke Danielle to say good-bye before she left home. Stopped on her way to work for a latte at Starbuck's.

Kept her attention on the moment.

Halfway through her meeting, her phone buzzed with a text from Grayson.

I miss you. I hope your meeting is going well.

How much longer would he know her schedule?

It wouldn't be long. He'd get caught up in his own world. The excitement of his new job.

She shook off the feelings of negativity.

Day by day.

That's how she'd get through it

It's how she'd gotten through it last time he'd left and it was how she'd gotten through her marriage with Noah. Then her divorce.

One day at the time.

She picked up Danielle and they went to the York and Orleans for lunch.

"What's wrong, Mom?" Danielle asked, minutes after they had sat at their table.

"Nothing," she said.

"It's okay to miss Grayson," she said. "I miss him, too."

Claire forced a smile on her lips. "We'll see him soon," she said.

"Of course, we will," Danielle agreed.

Claire asked Danielle about her upcoming orientation for Fall classes and listening allowed her to sit quietly and focus on her daughter.

That night Danielle spent the night at the university for orientation, so Claire had the house to herself for the first time in a long time.

The timing probably wasn't the best. It allowed Claire time alone to think. A mixed blessing.

She sat on the sofa with Charlie nestled close to her and looked through the photo album from twenty years ago. She'd been a teenager when she'd put it together, but now the same feelings were back. The same feelings she'd felt the last time Grayson left.

She closed the photo album and opened the photos on her phone. Smiled at the pictures of the two them interspersed with pictures of the three of them. Claire and Grayson. And Danielle.

It was the same. Yet different.

Her phone rang and Grayson's picture appeared on her screen, jarring her out of her thoughts.

"Hey, where are you?" she asked.

"Albuquerque, New Mexico."

"Really? Wow. I thought you might want to stop and see the Grand Canyon."

"No. I couldn't do that. I'll wait until I'm with you."

"Grayson..." she said.

"I miss you."

She squeezed her eyes closed tightly. "I miss you, too."

It was the same. Why was it so different?

"Grayson," she said again.

"What is it Claire?"

"What were we thinking?"

"We were thinking that we have something special and we can make it work."

Silence.

"Claire?"

"Yes?"

"Have you met someone else already? Is it that Maine D'Court guy? Is he there?"

Claire laughed and felt better than she had felt all day.

"Please say no," he said.

"No," she said, a tear slipping down her cheek. "What about Allen?"

"Who?"

"Allen. The guy who's coming for a visit."

She laughed. "I turned down his proposal."

"Promise?"

"I promise."

"Good. We're good then."

When they hung up the phone, Claire hugged her cat to her and cried into his fur. "I don't think I can do it, Charlie," she said and rubbed the tears from his fur. Once Grayson arrived safely in Pittsburgh, she would tell him. She would tell him she couldn't do this whole long distance relationship thing.

Grayson got up early the next morning and like every morning, the first thing he did was check his phone. His screen saver was Claire's picture. He opened up his phone and scrolled to his photos. Holding his finger against his favorite photo to animate it, he watched the two of them smile and kiss on the ferry with the Golden Gate Bridge behind them. He'd never seen her look so beautiful as she did in that wind-swept exhausted moment. Her defenses had been down and the love she felt for him was in her face.

He put his suitcase in his car, and filled up his tank with gas. The further away he got from Los Angeles and Claire, the more anxious he became. He had an odd sensation that the tie that bound them would break if he got too far away. Pennsylvania seemed like such a long way away. Maybe he should have sold his car and flown. If he'd flown, he'd be there by now and he wouldn't be dealing with the prolonged sensation of getting further and further away from her.

Within the hour, he was struggling to see the road in front of him. The morning sunlight in the desert was blinding. It took all his concentration to keep his car on his side of the highway.

He decided to stop at a waffle house for breakfast to take a break. Perhaps if he took a break, the sun would shift and it would be less hazardous to drive.

As he waited for his eggs and bacon to arrive, he turned off his cell phone and turned it back on. His service had been spotty since he'd hit New Mexico.

He had a phone message from yesterday.

He played the message as his food arrived. Then played it again.

His face broke out into a wide grin.

And the weight of the world fell off his shoulders.

It was already nine o'clock in Pittsburgh. He quickly ate his breakfast, then replayed the message.

He then called the department chair in Pittsburgh who had hired him.

After a few minutes of conversation, he realized that he'd just made someone else's day.

He needed to make another phone call, but he had to wait two hours. He got back in the car and this time, the sun was at his back. He turned on his music and sang along to a James Taylor song.

That evening, Claire worked late. When she finally got home, she was too exhausted to worry much about dinner. She sent out for Chinese and turned on the TV while she waited. Everything was on autopilot for her next fundraiser. It had been a very productive week. She had nothing pressing to do at the moment.

She needed something to keep herself from thinking. She dragged herself off the couch and began putting clothes in the washer. It was time to do some cleaning.

The Chinese place usually took about an hour because it was a little bit of a drive for the delivery guy. But Claire always gave him a big tip, so he didn't mind driving out her way.

She hadn't been watching the clock, but when the doorbell rang, she instinctively knew it was about time for the delivery guy to arrive.

She went to the door and opened it without peeking outside first.

No one was standing there. Pulling the door to behind her to keep Charlie from following, she looked left, then right.

Grayson must have been pacing on her porch. He was walking toward her.

"Now what if I'd been a serial killer," he said, stopping a few feet in front of her.

"Grayson?" Her mind struggled to link the pieces together.

She hadn't heard from him all day, but last night he'd been in New Mexico. On his way east. To Pittsburgh.

Now he was standing here on her doorstep.

Perhaps she was imagining things.

While her brain was in lockdown, he took two steps and pulled her into his arms, sweeping her feet off the ground.

He twirled her around, then set her down.

Her blood was flowing again.

"What are you doing here?" she asked. "You're supposed to be heading the other direction."

"I love you, Claire."

Her heart skittered and she smiled. "I love you, too." She waited a heartbeat. "Is your phone broken?"

He laughed. "Nope. But my heart was breaking."

"I don't understand. You came all this way just to tell me that. Are you going to be late?"

"Nope. Not taking the job."

She stared at him. Her brain trying to make sense of it all. She rubbed her palm against the side of her head. "Wait. You said you had to take this job. You couldn't let down the university in Pittsburgh."

"Maybe it was something about driving alone through the desert for hours, but I had an epiphany."

"What kind of epiphany?" she asked, not bothering to keep the skepticism out of her voice.

"I'm not the only person who needs a job right now. There's a whole line of people who'd like that job in Pittsburgh."

"I'm sure. But…"

The Chinese delivery guy drove up to the curb.

"Are you expecting someone?" Grayson asked.

"Yes," she said, keeping a straight face.

"I see." He took a step back.

Claire was a little surprised at the pain on his features until she realized he thought the delivery guy was another guy coming over.

"Grayson," she said.

He shook his head. "It's okay. I shouldn't have assumed."

"Grayson," she laughed.

"Here's your delivery, ma'am."

"Thank you, Robert," she said, signing the receipt and adding her tip.

"Have a great evening," Robert said, heading back toward his car.

Grayson just watched her.

"Come inside," she said.

"I'm a little tired," he said.

"It's okay. Come in. Eat some Chinese food with me. And tell me how you ended up back here."

He smiled. "I hit the wrong button on my GPS."

"Ha." They settled into the living room and opened the boxes of food. "What happened with the teaching job? Did they cancel or something?"

"No. I canceled on them."

"But you said."

"I know. I had a sense of obligation, but after I called the department chair, she assured me that they had a list of people waiting. They had given me preference because I'm a veteran."

"Out of a list of equally qualified people."

"Exactly."

"You turned down the job?"

He nodded.

"Help me understand."

"First I need to ask you something."

"Okay."

"Do you think I could borrow your guest room for awhile?"

"Of course. While you look for another job?"

"I already have another job."

"Oh." Her heart sank. He wasn't going to Pennsylvania, but he would be going somewhere else instead. She set down her fork with a sudden loss of appetite. She'd been so happy to see him, she hadn't realized that he must going to take the full-time position in Texas. What was it about Texas and her men anyway? Noah had been from Texas. He was living in Alabama now, but he still had a business based out of Fort Worth. Now

Grayson was going to be living in Texas. Where was it? San Antonio? It didn't matter. It was Texas and not here.

"Claire," he said. "I'm staying here."

She shook her head. Grayson wasn't inclined to be unemployed while he looked for a job. She couldn't allow him to do that. Even if it meant he had to move to Texas.

"I can't let you be unemployed," she said it out loud. "Even if it means moving to Texas."

"They already filled the position in Texas."

"You can't not work," she said.

"Claire," he said again. "Look at me."

She looked up. Met his gaze. Took a deep breath.

"I'm going to work for the VA."

The VA. He'd said that was a possibility for the future. That it was really hard to get a job there. "But..."

"I know. I said they wouldn't hire me because they rarely have openings. But they did."

"They hired you?"

He nodded.

"Here? In L.A.?"

"Yep."

"For good. Permanently?"

"Yes," he said. "I got really, really lucky."

"This is like... a miracle."

"Fate is keeping us together this time."

"Wow," she said. Then she threw her arms around him. He pulled her into his lap and held her tightly to him.

"There's nothing keeping us apart anymore," he said. "Except maybe the Chinese delivery guy."

Claire started laughing. Then she couldn't stop. "I can't

believe you thought I'd have a guy over already," she said through giggles.

"I don't ever have to worry about that again." He waited a beat. "Right?"

"You don't have to."

"Claire," he nudged her back to look into her eyes. "I know how much you love this house."

She nodded. She didn't want to leave here.

"That means you'll have to invite me to stay here with you."

"I'll think about it," she said.

His expression sobered. "It'll be awkward if you don't want your husband to live here with you."

"I don't have a husb…" She stopped talking and stared into his eyes. "Anymore…"

"Do you think you could tolerate another one?"

"I'll think about it," she said, swallowing the lump in her throat. She was overcome with emotion. Emotion that threatened to spill over and consume her.

"One who's around all the time, especially in the evenings and weekends."

"I don't know," she said, biting her lip to keep her face from splitting into a ridiculous grin.

"Think hard," he said. "Because you're about to have to make that decision."

"What do you mean?"

"I like you, so I'll warn you. You're about to be proposed to." He dumped her off his lap onto the sofa and before she knew what he was doing, he was kneeling on the floor. "Claire Beauchamp…" he said. "Worthington…." He started over. "Claire… Will you marry me?"

She couldn't hold it any longer. Her face split into that ridiculous grin. "Yes!" She slid onto the floor with him.

He pulled her against him and they ended up lying side by side on the floor, arms wrapped around each other.

He swept the hair from her face and lifted her hand. Kissed her knuckles. "Tomorrow," he murmured. "Tomorrow we'll go shopping and get something to put on this finger." He kissed her ring finger and she thought her heart might burst with happiness.

Then he was kissing her. Suddenly he stopped and looked into her eyes.

"Will Danielle be back tomorrow?" he asked.

"Yeah. Why?"

"I was thinking we could find a Justice of the Peace tomorrow."

Her eyes widened. "Tomorrow?"

"I don't want you to have a chance to get away this time. Besides, I don't have anywhere to live, so I need to lock this thing down."

"You're such a romantic," she said.

He grinned. "Let me show you just how romantic."

Then his lips were on hers again.

Claire's befuddled mind worked to make sense of all that was happening. Grayson was back. For good. And tomorrow she would be his wife. Then her emotions trumped her thoughts.

And she was lost in his kiss.

No matter how they got here.

Life moved in only one direction. Forward.

THE END.

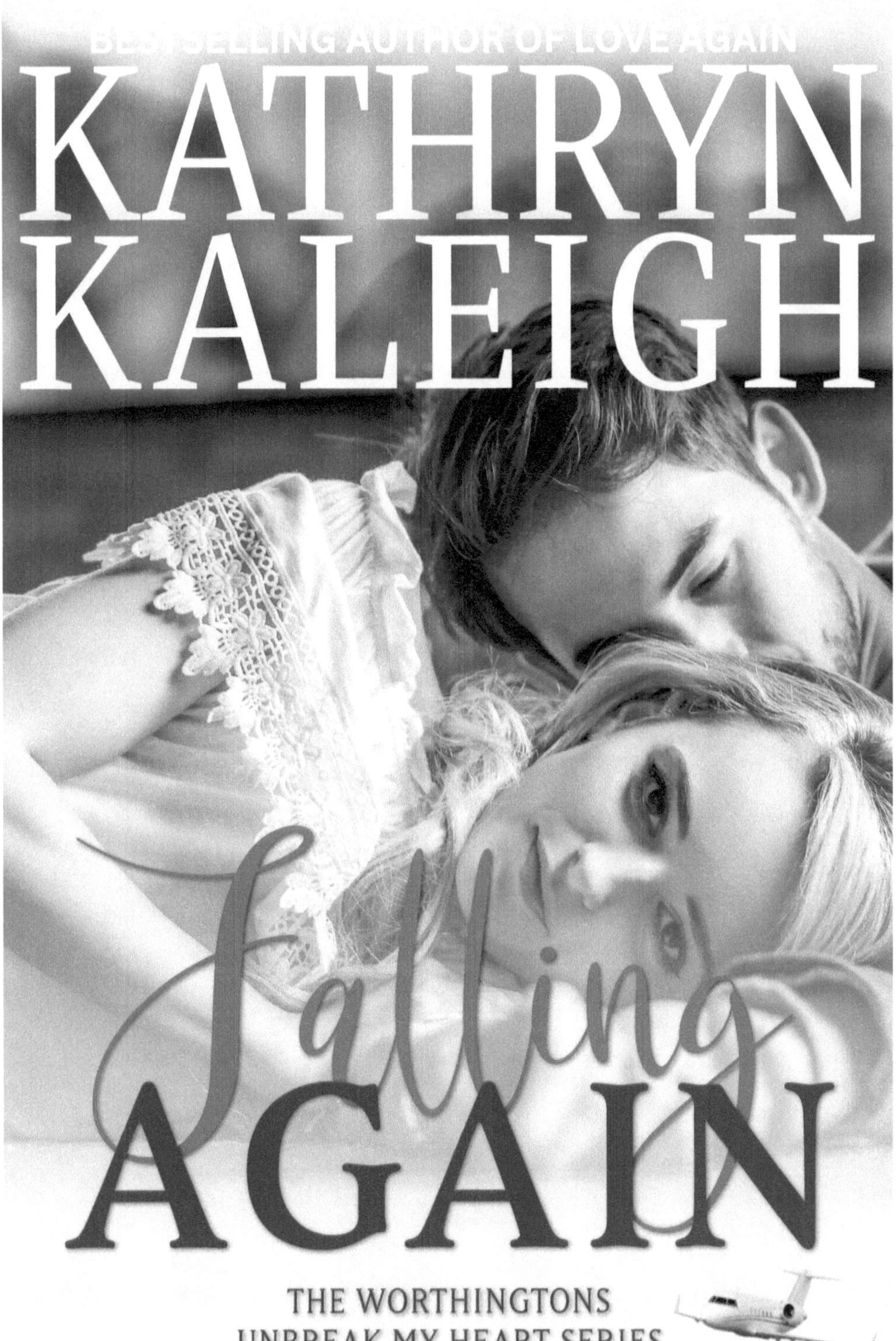

KATHRYN KALEIGH

Falling AGAIN

THE WORTHINGTONS
UNBREAK MY HEART SERIES

Falling Again

THE WORTHINGTONS

CHAPTER

One

At the moment, Danielle Worthington was having a hard time believing in true love, much less happily ever after.

After unclipping the camera from the tripod, she adjusted the camera's shutter speed and photographed the models in front of her. The models were *posing* as a happy couple. They wore jeans and t-shirts to portray a casual, relaxed look, and stood in front of an historic wooden house with a white picket fence at Sam Houston Park.

They were depicting the American Dream.

Their smiles looked true and their affection genuine, but Avery and Jacob could barely stand the sight of each other.

Jacob put his arm around Avery and pulled her close. They gazed at each other, their faces only inches apart. Danielle went up the stairs and stood on the other side of them. She took more photos. They were such a cute couple.

"I've got enough casual," Danielle said. "Go get dressed up, guys."

As Jacob and Avery turned away from each other, their smiles turned to scowls. At least they were professional enough to pretend to like each other during the shoots.

Danielle glanced at her phone. She had two hours to get back to her office in time to meet her father for lunch. A wave of anxiety swept over her in anticipation of that meeting.

She took a deep breath and swallowed the nausea. Her father loved her no matter what. *Right?*

He'd always been there for her. There was no reason why he wouldn't be there for her now.

Avery and Jacob were back within minutes. Avery was now wearing a red party dress, and Jacob was wearing a black tux.

They made such a beautiful couple.

Danielle's heart did a little summersault as an image of *that* night flashed through her mind. The night that she had worn a floor-length red dress, and Joey had worn a black suit. Danielle had felt like a princess that night. She'd thought they were in a fairy tale.

The fairy tale hadn't collapsed at midnight, but at six a.m. the next morning. That girl, whatever her name was, had been surprised that Joey wasn't alone. In fact, that was the only satisfaction that Danielle took from the whole fiasco.

Now she saw her relationship with Joey for what it had been all along: a sham, just like Avery and Jacob. She'd fallen for an illusion.

Never again.

After taking several more photos, she could tell that they were getting tired, and she needed to rest too.

Walking back to the parking lot, she enjoyed the warmth of the Houston sun. She'd lived here for six weeks now, but already she had found that she liked the friendliness of the people and the warmth of the weather.

A Los Angeles native, Houston wouldn't have been her first choice. She had an affinity for New York, though she'd only visited there once with her stepmother, Savannah, whose love for the big city had been contagious.

Nonetheless, Danielle was content with Houston.

Except for one small detail.

When she got to the parking lot, she had to call an Uber. Houston was definitely a driving town, and Danielle would be content if she never had to drive.

After the Uber driver picked her up, she noticed an American flag decal on his rearview mirror. Seeing it was like taking an instant punch to the gut.

Her ex-boyfriend, ex of five weeks and four days, was in the Air Force, stationed here in Houston. They'd been on-again-off-again for several years. When he'd suggested she move to Houston, she'd thought they were moving forward. Together.

Unfortunately, she'd been moving forward alone. Danielle had subsequently implemented a self-imposed dating moratorium. It hadn't been hard to do since she was in a strange town and knew absolutely no one other than coworkers. And since they all worked independently, she really didn't know them either.

She'd found a furnished apartment to rent, a job, and left home for the first time.

Okay, she admitted to herself that there were other factors involved. One, her mother had just gotten married a second time, this time to her high school sweetheart, so moving out of the house was long overdue. And second, Houston put her a little closer to her father, who lived in Alabama and had a charter flight company in Fort Worth.

Though she hadn't seen him in nearly two months, he was flying down today to take her to lunch for her birthday. Today, she would tell him that she and Joey had broken up, and she was living alone in Houston. And again, the thought made her queasy. Odd. She'd never been nervous about seeing her father before.

Maybe she'd picked up a virus.

Samuel Johnson was not a shopper by nature. In fact, he considered himself a man of very minimal needs: basic clothing, an iPhone and iPad, a uniform for work, and a reliable truck. Oh, and an airplane. In fact, the airplane was first on his list, but it was such a basic thing, he rarely even thought about it. Sort of like air.

As a result, standing in the Apple store in Highland Shopping Center trying to decide whether to buy an iMac, a MacBook, a MacBook Air, or a MacBook Pro had him so completely out of his element, that he couldn't process.

Get her a good Apple computer and put it on the company credit card. What the boss requested, the boss got.

Especially when the boss was Noah Worthington of Skye Travels. The man who was paying him for two weeks *before* he even started work to give him time to relocate from Houston to Dallas.

The store wasn't busy this morning, and Tom, one of the

blue-shirted employees, stood patiently waiting while Samuel considered his options.

"Do you have any questions?" Tom asked.

Samuel nodded. "Which one should I get?"

Tom laughed. "What do you need it for?"

"I have no idea."

"No problem," Tom assured him.

"It's not for me. It's for… my boss's daughter."

"Ah." Tom's eyes widened knowingly. "What kind of work does she do?"

"I have absolutely no clue."

"Oh boy."

"Yeah. Oh boy indeed." He knew her name and the fact that her father was a pilot and owner of Skye Travels, so she couldn't be very old. "I know today's her birthday."

"Well, if she works at a desk, you should probably go with the iMac. If she travels, you can't go wrong with any of the notebooks."

"Her father's a pilot."

"Too bad it's not for him." Tom scratched his chin. "Can you ask him?"

Samuel glanced at his watch. "Not likely. He should be in the air."

"I don't suppose you could ask her?"

Samuel shook his head. "Not even a chance. It's a surprise."

"We have a fourteen-day return policy."

A ray of hope opened up, and it was as though the weight of the world fell from Samuel's shoulders. "Which one is more expensive?"

"The MacBook Pro."

Samuel tapped the keys on the notebook computer. But the images on the MacBook Pro drew his attention. "I like that one," he said more to himself than to Tom.

"It's a great computer. It just came out."

Samuel glanced at his watch. *Always go with your gut.* He knew not to overthink things. *Go with your first reaction unless you have compelling evidence not to.* The wisdom drilled into him as a pilot never failed to spill over into other parts of his life. Besides, if he didn't make a decision and get moving, he was going to be late.

CHAPTER

Three

Two hours later, Danielle looked up from her computer at a knock on her open door. A man holding a large box, half as tall as he was, stood in her doorway.

He wasn't wearing a uniform, so he didn't appear to be a delivery guy. Besides, the box was wrapped in what at first glance appeared to be blue birthday wrapping paper, not shipping paper.

A birthday gift? No one here at the office knew it was her birthday.

She glanced at the time on her computer. She had a male model coming in to interview at three o'clock. Maybe he was early. She could get that out of the way while she waited on her father who was characteristically late. No doubt he would blame it on the weather or other flight delay problems.

"You're early," she said.

Confusion crossed his features. *Adorable.* Oh yes! He was hired before he even got inside her office. He was tall and toned with clean-cut features. It was hard to find an attractive male model without a beard these days. And those bright blue eyes were going to light up her camera.

"I try to always be on time, if not early," he said.

Too bad she wasn't doing audio. His smooth voice would be perfect.

"Come in," she said. "I'm meeting someone, but he's late. We can go ahead."

He came inside, shifting the box. "Where do you want this?" he asked.

"What is it?"

"It's an Apple computer. But I think it's supposed to be a surprise."

Danielle glanced at the smaller Apple computer sitting on her desk and salivated just a little.

Who all knew she wanted a new, larger, computer? Her mother, Claire, her father, Noah, and her ex-boyfriend.

"Just set it here, on the floor," she said, indicating the space beside her desk. The relief was evident on his face as he set it down. Danielle didn't see a card attached.

I'll have to come back to this.

"Sit," she said, nodding toward the empty chair in front of her desk.

After he sat, she laced her fingers under her chin and allowed herself to gaze into his eyes. "How long have you been a model?" She asked.

"I'm not a model."

She smiled as she considered the possibility of exclusivity. She could be the only graphic artist with his handsome face on book covers. "So... no experience?"

He frowned and shook his head. "Not with modeling."

"It's okay," she said quickly. "You don't have to have experience."

He grinned and leaned back in his chair.

Okay, maybe he's a little too relaxed.

"Maybe we could--" Her phone buzzed. It was a text from her father.

Is Samuel there yet?

She wrote back. *Who is Samuel?*

I sent him to bring your birthday present.

Danielle looked up at the man sitting across from her. Her hopes for exclusivity crumbled.

Is it a computer? She texted.

Silence.

"Are you Samuel?" she asked, looking up at the man sitting across from her.

He nodded.

Where are you? She texted.

Stuck at the airport in Dallas. Thunderstorms.

"When was he going to tell me that?" She asked, rolling her eyes.

"I'm not sure," Samuel said.

Danielle scowled at her phone. *Who is Samuel?* She typed again.

My newest pilot.

Why is he here?

In the process of moving. I took advantage of him being in Houston.

Danielle blew her bangs out of her eyes and ran a hand through her hair.

She glared at Samuel, who wasn't smiling anymore. "You're a pilot," she said, unable to keep the accusation out of her voice.

"Right now I wish I wasn't," he said, straightening in his chair, one hand on the chair arm. "I can go," he said.

Don't go. "Wait," she said.

He sat back, watching her expectantly.

"You work for my father." She made sure to keep her voice calm.

"I started yesterday. Today, he sent me to buy your birthday present."

She smiled. "That's my father." She glanced at the box in her floor. "Who wrapped it?"

"I did," he said.

"That seems like a lot to ask."

"Oh," Samuel said. "He didn't ask me to wrap it. He just asked me to pick it up from the Apple store and drop it off here. He said he didn't have time to pick it up before he met you for lunch."

She melted a little at the thought of this man – this handsome stranger – picking up wrapping paper for her gift and wrapping the computer himself.

"He's not coming," she said.

"It's storming in Dallas," he said.

"Yeah," she said, checking her phone. No messages. She shoved it aside.

"Do you have alternate plans for your birthday lunch?" he asked.

She sighed. "I'll just order something and have it delivered. I might use the time to set up this computer."

"I can take you to lunch."

Her eyes widened. The old Danielle Worthington would have jumped at the opportunity to have lunch with a pilot who looked like a model.

No. The new Danielle was under a dating moratorium. *Maybe I should go to AA. Hi, I'm Danielle. I haven't had a date in five weeks, four days, and ten hours.*

Lunch technically wasn't a date.

I'm Danielle. Please help me.

He was waiting for an answer.

"I'm--" *I'm normally not this daft.* "I can't," she said.

He was frowning again. "But… it's your birthday. Surely you want company."

"I do, but--" *You're too tempting.*

The wave of nausea came out of the blue. It lodged in the back of her throat, and she knew without a doubt that she was going to be sick. She held up a hand. "I'm going to be sick," she said. *I should not have skipped breakfast.*

She slipped out of her chair onto her knees and, turning her head just in time, threw up into the wastebasket.

As she hunched over the wastebasket, gagging, she felt Samuel pull her hair back and hold it. He handed her a Kleenex, and she wiped her mouth.

It was one of the most mortifying things she'd ever had happen. So much for impressing the handsome pilot – that she would not, absolutely would not, go out with. Or even out to lunch.

"Thank you," she said. "I'm better now."

He put a hand under her elbow to help her up. After she was safely back in her chair, he placed a hand on her forehead. "No fever."

"You're a doctor now?" She asked.

"No, but when I was five-years-old, my mother decided to give me two little sisters."

"Wow. I don't envy either one of you."

"You don't like children?" He asked, pulling the plastic bag from her trash can and tying it up.

"They're okay. Just not for me."

"I'll be right back," he said, leaving the room and taking the plastic bag with him.

Danielle leaned back and closed her eyes – just for a moment. Then she pulled a mirror out of her handbag and quickly checked her appearance.

This was not good. First of all, she was rarely sick. But that wave of nausea had been overwhelming. This was November. Was there a bug going around? She'd felt okay… Then she remembered the nausea this morning while they were shooting. She was definitely coming down with something.

And second, it was not cool to throw up in front of a hot model pilot. Even if she wasn't dating right now, and she wasn't, she could not be throwing up in front of him and having him hold her hair.

She groaned. And sighed. He'd held her hair.

And checked her for fever.

It was good thing she wasn't open to dating.

Samuel came back into the room and placed a package of saltine crackers on the desk in front of her as he sat back down in the chair.

"What?" She asked.

"They're good for nausea," he explained. When she just

looked at him, he reached over, opened the package and held it up for her.

She pulled a cracker from the sleeve. "Where did you get these?"

He shrugged. "My truck." He set the crackers back on her desk.

Danielle nibbled the end off the cracker. "You keep crackers in your truck?"

"My mom has me keep some with me in case I forget to eat."

Danielle finished the cracker and reached for another one. She swallowed a bubble of laughter. He was a mama's boy. It was cute.

"Your mother's pretty smart. I feel better."

"Good." He grinned. "Let's go get something to eat, then we can get this computer set up."

"But…"

He shook his head. "There's no way I'm leaving you now. You don't get to throw up on your birthday, then eat by yourself."

He must think she was pathetic. "I had plans."

"Yes, I know. Your dad. But he can't be here right now." Samuel lifted an eyebrow and smiled at her. "And since I work for him, I'm your alternate lunch escort."

It's not a date. It's an alternate lunch escort. He was right. She did need to eat. And it was kind of pathetic to be eating lunch alone on her birthday.

She wasn't going to tell him that her plan for tonight was to have pizza delivered to her apartment. Alone.

CHAPTER
Four

Samuel Johnson was not impulsive.

He also hadn't dated anyone since Jessica, his girlfriend of four years, had been killed in Afghanistan two years ago. So for two years, he'd kept his heart guarded.

At twenty-five, he wasn't easily impressed. He kept his head down and his heart in the sky. As a pilot, the only place he felt at peace was in the air. That's where he felt closest to Jessica. With Jessica in Heaven, it was his way of staying close to her.

Ironically, his focus on flying these last two years had given him a marketable edge. He hadn't planned on ever leaving Houston, but when he was filling out applications, he'd run across an ad for Skye Travels. He wasn't sure why Noah Worthington even advertised. His company was legendary.

When Noah had called him to interview and then offered him a job on the spot, Samuel had hesitated. He'd put Noah off for two weeks. He was pretty sure that no one ever put Noah Worthington off, certainly not for two weeks.

But in the end, he couldn't resist the offer to work for Noah, even if it meant leaving Houston. Technically, he was already on the payroll. He had to take one flight up to Dallas to meet with Noah this week, but otherwise, he'd spend the week packing and getting everything ready to move. Not a bad way to spend the first week on the job.

Until this morning. This morning, Noah had called and asked him to not only pick up a birthday present for his daughter, who just happened to live in Houston, but also to deliver it to her.

Samuel found the whole thing a little perplexing. There was no way that Noah Worthington thought he was going to fly out of Dallas today. Legend had it that Noah was better at forecasting than most meteorologists.

He was also well-known for his stubbornness. Samuel supposed that his daughter's birthday wasn't something he would give up lightly. If there had been a way for him to get here, Samuel had little doubt that he would have done so.

Samuel had been surprised to learn that Noah had a daughter living in Houston. He had heard that he had an ex-wife living in California and a current wife living in Alabama. Samuel hadn't paid much attention to whether or not he had children.

He had a daughter all right. Samuel was nearly speechless as he watched Danielle gingerly nibbling on a cracker. She was beautiful, and he could most definitely see where she could be from California. Her long hair was a swirl of pale lavender and brunette. And it was soft. When he'd held her hair back while she was throwing up, he'd been in awe at the softness of it.

If he hadn't known better, he would have thought she was

pregnant. He almost laughed out loud at the idea. That definitely didn't fit his first impression. She'd even suggested she didn't want children.

"Are you better?" He asked.

She nodded and gave him a half-smile. It was the same expression he'd seen on Noah's face.

"Good."

"I'm so sorry." She swept her hair up and dropped it across her left shoulder. "I feel mortified."

"No need to apologize." He kept his gaze on her mesmerizing green eyes. "Remember. Two little sisters."

"Maybe so, but I'm not your sister."

Thank goodness for that. It had been a long time since Samuel had been this attracted to anyone. About six years, to be precise. He remembered the day he'd met Jessica like it was yesterday. Jessica was nothing like Danielle. Jessica had been jogging in Houston Park with no makeup and her natural-brown hair pulled back in a ponytail. She'd been friendly.

Samuel had been playing Frisbee with his golden retriever, Jack, when the Frisbee landed right at Jessica's feet. Samuel had always thought it was divine intervention. Laughing, she'd picked it up, and tossed it back toward Samuel. Jack had stopped to look at her, barked once, then turned around and went after the Frisbee.

"Thanks," Samuel had called out as she waved and jogged away. Three days later, Samuel and Jack had been sitting on a park bench waiting for her. When she saw them, she stopped right in front of them and bent over, hands on her knees, as she caught her breath.

"We're not stalking you," he'd said.

"I'm not worried," she said. "I'm lethal with my hands."

"I can't stop thinking about you."

She'd laughed. And that had been that. They had dated for two years. Then Samuel had proposed, and they'd been engaged when she was deployed to Afghanistan.

Samuel had done everything by the book. He'd had his life with Jessica planned out.

Only Jessica had been returned to him in the belly of a plane, a flag draped over her coffin.

Samuel had done little more than go through the motions for the next two years. He'd all but shut down his life, everything but flying. He stayed in the air as much as possible. When he was flying, he didn't have to worry about the world.

Or other people.

Jessica had been practical and no-nonsense. Down to earth. He never knew if the military did that to her, or if she was drawn to the military as a result of her personality. Maybe it was a little bit of both.

Now he was sitting here in front of a girl who appeared to be the exact opposite of Jessica. A girl with lavender streaks in her hair. A girl wearing perfect makeup, skinny tights, and a dark gray sweater dress.

And in the mere minutes since he'd met her, she'd thrown up in her wastebasket. Not exactly a very romantic start.

Nonetheless, Samuel was enchanted.

Samuel stood up and waited while Danielle gathered up her handbag and logged out of her computer. "Pappa's Burgers is just down the street," she said, almost salivating as she craved a shrimp po'boy. No need to tell Samuel that she had eaten lunch there every day for the last two weeks. "Can you drive?"

"Sure," he said, following her out of her office.

There was also no need to tell him that she didn't have a car. There was a city bus stop on the corner near her office. The bus stopped just walking distance from Pappa's Burgers.

As he fell into step beside her as they walked through the open lobby to the elevator, she couldn't help but notice that he was a head taller than she was. He was a good height for her. Not that she was interested.

The dating moratorium was firmly in place.

They got into the elevator and went down from the fourth floor to the first. He held the door for her as they walked through the almost-deserted first-floor lobby to the front door. The security guard nodded as they walked past.

When they got to the parking lot, she followed him to a charcoal gray Toyota Tacoma pickup truck. Danielle smiled to herself. One thing she'd learned a long time ago. True Texas boys drove pickup trucks. He held the door as she climbed inside.

Samuel's truck smelled new and was spotless inside. He went around and got into the driver's seat. "Pappa's Burgers, right?" He asked, giving her a smile that sent tingles down to her toes.

"Yes," she said. "Do you know it?"

"Are you kidding?" He asked as he pulled onto Westheimer Road. "It's a Sunday tradition in my family."

"Seriously?"

"Yeah. My parents, my brother and his wife, my sister and her husband, my youngest sister, and both sets of my grandparents eat there for Sunday lunch all the time."

"That is so special. I'm jealous. My dad and his family live in Alabama, and my mom and her family live in California, so I don't think my entire extended family has ever been in the same restaurant at the same time."

"How sad," he said.

"Yeah," Danielle agreed, feeling her eyes tear up. It was odd, because it had never bothered her before. It was just life as she knew it.

They pulled into the little parking lot, and before he jumped out, Samuel glanced at her and said, "wait here."

He came around and opened her door. Then he held his hand out to help her climb down from the cab. She put her hand in his, and he latched on to steady her. Her eyes met his ocean blue ones, and she forgot she was supposed to be moving. Her hand felt small in his, and a sensation of being in safe hands washed over her.

She swallowed, and with a slight tug on her hand, he guided her from the truck.

When her feet were on the ground, he released her hand. *This is not good. It's not a date. He's a lunch escort.*

They went inside and stood in line to place their order. It wasn't crowded today. There were only three people ahead of them.

"I'll be right back," Danielle said, dashing toward the restroom. *I must have been drinking too much water lately.* After washing her hands, she put on some clear lip gloss and ran a hand through her hair. The colorist at Visible Changes had gotten her hair exactly right, brunette with a few tasteful purple highlights woven throughout. They'd called it a mermaid balayage. It was Danielle's first time to have hand-painted high-lights, and she absolutely loved it.

By the time she got back to Samuel, he was waiting at the counter to order. The guy behind the counter smiled. "A shrimp po'boy with coleslaw?" He asked.

Samuel glanced at the menu on the wall. "That's not on the menu," he pointed out.

"It's okay," she said, feeling her cheeks flush that the guy had remembered what she'd ordered every day for the last two weeks. "They make it for me anyway."

"Huh," he said. "Make that two," he told the checker.

They got their sodas and found a booth near the back, next to the windows.

"How long have you lived in Houston?" He asked.

"Six weeks," she said, sipping her cola. "And you?"

"My entire life."

She frowned. "How are you working for my dad in Dallas and still living in Houston?"

"Unfortunately," he said, "that's about to end. I've got about one more week before I have to move."

"Oh," she said, not bothering to keep the disappointment from her voice. Despite her dating moratorium, she could still enjoy his company. Samuel seemed like someone she wanted to keep close.

"The real question is," he said, narrowing his eyes. "With your mother in California and your father in Dallas, how did you end up in Houston?"

That was a door she didn't want to walk through. She decided to stall a bit before answering. "My dad actually lives in Alabama with his second wife Savannah."

"I know," Samuel said. "But still, he has a business in Dallas – or technically Fort Worth – either way, they aren't here."

"Yeah," she said, biting her lip. "That's kind of a long story."

"I don't have anywhere else to be," he said, settling back in his seat, his eyes focusing on her. Danielle felt the heat rise in her cheeks again. Despite her dating moratorium, she was not immune to having a handsome man's undivided attention.

The server brought their sandwiches and French fries, giving her a moment to think about how much she wanted to reveal.

He took a bite of his po'boy. "This is really good," he said. "I think they used to have these on the menu."

"That's what they told me." She nibbled on a French fry and

took a deep breath. "I'm in Houston because my boyfriend was transferred here," she said.

He narrowed his eyes and watched her.

"We broke up five weeks ago," she added, feeling a need to set that straight. She didn't want Samuel to think she had a boyfriend. Not that it mattered either way, she reminded herself. Was that relief she saw flicker across his features?

"Wait. You've lived here for six weeks, and you broke up five weeks ago?

"Technically five weeks and four days ago."

She could see him doing the math in his head, but he let it go. "You moved from California?"

She nodded.

"That must be quite a change."

"It's a huge change," she admitted, biting into her sandwich and closing her eyes. She was addicted to these things.

"Are you going to be moving back?"

"I don't know yet. I have a job here. A job I really like."

"There's a chance you might get back together with your boyfriend?" He asked.

"Ha. Never. Not a chance." Was she supposed to ask about his dating status? It was hard to know how to keep this from feeling like a date.

It already feels like a date.

"Why did you break up?"

She shook her head, shrugged, and looked into those blue eyes.

"I know it's none of my business," he said. "But you came a really long way to be with him. For what? Three days?"

"I don't know. We'd been together on and off for about five

years. I thought it was going somewhere, you know. But it turns out he didn't."

"He cheated," Samuel said.

Danielle's eyes widened. "How did you know?"

"Two sisters," he said with a grin.

"Right. Two sisters."

"If you're so close to your family, why are you leaving?" It occurred to her that he might be moving because of a girlfriend. Or maybe a boyfriend.

"It's a great opportunity to work with your father. He's legendary, you know. And it's not like I have anything else going on."

"No girlfriend?" She asked, unable to resist.

He shook his head.

"A boyfriend?"

He laughed. "I'm heterosexual."

She laughed back and he stared at her. "That's good to know."

"Why is that good to know?" He asked.

"Well," she said. "You know. So I know how to talk to you. If you like boys, I don't want to ask you about girlfriends, and if you were gay, well, you know."

He laughed again.

Danielle was intrigued. Joey hadn't laughed with her in a long time, and she hadn't even realized it until this moment. In retrospect, there were so many clues that he was no longer into her.

"I'm glad we got that sorted out," Samuel said.

She smiled. "Me too."

Suddenly, she couldn't eat another bite. "I'm stuffed," she said.

"You barely ate anything," he pointed out.

"I know. I do that sometimes. I'm still a little queasy from… you know… earlier."

"Yeah," he said, finishing off his sandwich. "Are you gonna get that to go?"

She shook her head. "No thanks."

He reached over, picked up the other half of her uneaten sandwich and proceeded to eat it.

Danielle laughed.

"This is too good to go to waste," he said. "How did the checker know what you wanted to order?"

"I ordered it yesterday," she said. There was no need to tell him that she'd ordered it not only yesterday, but every day for the past two weeks.

"We'll have to get it again," he said.

Danielle sat back in her seat and squeezed her hands together under the table. This was dangerous territory. He used the word *we*. Danielle was nothing if not well-versed in the language of relationships.

She and Joey had been on and off for several years. Danielle always dated in between – during the "off periods."

This was more than an "off period." This was more of an exclamation point. *The end* to their relationship. Catching him cheating on her when she'd just moved all the way out here, alone, to be with him was more than she could take.

Hence, the moratorium on dating.

CHAPTER
Six

Samuel came from a large family with lots of traditions, and one of those traditions was that birthdays never went unnoticed and certainly no one was allowed to spend one alone.

Since Danielle was new to Houston, he was fairly certain that she didn't have plans for the evening.

"What do people do for fun in California?"

"People?" She grinned at him.

"Okay. You. What kinds of things do you do for fun in California?"

"I've spent a lot of time in museums and art galleries. My mom owns an art gallery."

"Do you go to museums because you like it or because it's expected?"

She seemed to consider. "I guess because I like it. But I'm not really sure. It's just what I do. No one's ever asked me that before."

"Really?" He sat back, stretched his arm along the back of

the booth. "Let me ask a different way. If you could do anything you wanted on your birthday, what would it be?"

"I'd want to be whisked off to Disneyland to have dinner at the Magic Kingdom."

He mentally calculated the distance between Houston and Anaheim and then Houston and Orlando. "I could actually make that happen."

Only a pilot's daughter wouldn't find that statement odd. "You asked." She shrugged.

"Disney World is closer."

She laughed. "I've never been to Disney World." She sipped her soda. "Why do you ask?"

"Since you just moved here, I'm assuming you don't have plans for your birthday tonight."

"I do actually have plans."

"Oh." Good. He didn't have to rescue her. "What are you doing?"

"I'm going to have pizza delivered and binge watch *Hart of Dixie.*"

"There are so many things wrong with that answer."

"You don't like pizza?"

"Of course I do. What's *Hart of Dixie?*"

"It's a series on Netflix about a New York doctor who moves to the south to practice medicine."

"I can see where you'd like that."

"Plus, I'm sure my mom and dad will call."

Samuel shook his head. "I can't let you do that."

Her eyes widened. She hadn't been shocked that he could fly her to Disney World, but she was shocked that he wouldn't let her spend her birthday alone. Nonetheless, she took it in stride. "What do you suggest then?"

"I sounds like I can either take you to Disney or a museum."

She laughed. "It'd be hard for me to go to work tomorrow after a late flight. And, to be honest, I really don't feel like going to a museum."

"What else do you like? Bowling? Sky diving? Dancing?"

"Ha. Since I had planned to have pizza delivered and watch TV, you can probably guess that I'm actually rather boring."

"I seriously doubt that."

"Well, not very adventurous either."

"Danielle, you have a tendency to sell yourself short. You picked up and moved to Houston from California without knowing anyone other than the one person you'd probably rather not think about right now."

"Yeah." She stared out the window for a minute. "I like movies." She turned back to smile at him.

Samuel grinned. "Then since you won't let me fly you to the Magic Castle, can I take you to a movie?"

"It's not a date." Danielle rolled her eyes.

"It's okay if it is." Danielle could tell that her mother was smiling, even through the phone.

"I'm on a dating moratorium."

"Right."

"Oh and Mom." Danielle walked to her window and stared at the traffic below. "Since Dad didn't make it for lunch, I still haven't told him about breaking up with Joey."

Her mother was silent for a moment.

"Mom? Did you tell him?"

"It's not like I talk to him every day. In fact, I haven't spoken to your father in weeks."

"Good." She blew out a breath of relief. "I need to tell him myself."

"I understand. Enjoy your evening out. It's been a long time."

Danielle turned and saw Samuel getting off the elevator.

"Mom. He's here. I have to go." Her pulse jumped into over-time, and she suddenly wished she'd had him pick her up at her apartment so she could have showered and changed. Fortunately, she kept heels at the office, and she'd slipped into them. *It's not a date.*

"Happy Birthday, sweetheart."

"Love you, Mom."

Danielle closed her cell phone and slipped it into her pocket.

Samuel stopped at her door and grinned at her. He held a little gift bag in his hand. "I brought you something."

"Aw. You didn't have to do that."

"I promise. It's nothing." He handed it to her. "Nothing like the Apple computer I brought you this morning."

She took the gift bag. Her father *had* sent Samuel to buy her computer. "Hmm."

"Do you want to set it up? We have time." He nodded toward the computer, now unwrapped but still sitting on her floor.

"Okay." She reached into the gift bag and pulled out a book. *Things to do in Houston.* She looked up and laughed. She hadn't seen him take two steps toward her.

He was standing much too close. Close enough for her to gaze into his sky-blue eyes beneath soft lashes. He smelled good; clean and earthy. Sandalwood? Her gaze strayed to his kissable lips curved up at the corners in a smile.

"I... um..." She took a step back. Held the book to her chest.

"It's a welcome gift." He didn't move. "To Houston. In case you're interested in what there is to do here."

"Thank you." She swallowed, her mouth suddenly very dry.

"Do you have scissors?" He nodded toward the computer box.

Spurred into movement, she went behind her desk and opened three drawers before she found a pair of scissors. She handed them to him and watched as he slid it through the seal. She was obviously the only one affected. This was not a good thing.

"Did you decide on a movie?" He pulled the computer from its box.

She shook her head. "I've been on the phone."

After setting the computer on her desk, he pulled his phone out of his front pocket and after a couple of clicks, handed it to her. "I have an app. This theater is the one closest to us."

As she scrolled through the movies, he said. "I don't mind romantic movies." He took the plastic off the computer and plugged the cord into the back.

By the time she could focus enough to choose a movie, he had the computer set up.

"How about this one?" She handed the phone back to him.

"Looks good to me." He glanced at the screen. "We have time for dinner."

"Sure."

"Where do you want your computer?"

She'd already decided how to rearrange her desk, so she quickly pointed out where to put the computer.

"Ready?" He asked.

She grabbed her handbag and jacket. "Yep. All good."

After she locked her door, they went to the elevator and rode down in silence.

"Are you in the mood for anything in particular?" He held the elevator door while she stepped through.

"I saw a Cheesecake Factory at the Galleria."

"Cheesecake Factory it is."

He opened the door on the passenger side of the truck, and she put one foot up on the running board. Her other foot wobbled a little. This was going to be a little difficult in heels.

"Can I help?" Samuel asked, again standing near.

She laughed. "Yes. I think so." She reached out to put her hand on his arm, but he picked her up by the waist and set her on the seat. "Oh. Thanks."

He went around to the driver's side and hopped in.

"I'm not used to trucks." She wasn't sure if it was normal to have trouble climbing into the cab or not.

"It's okay. It's a Texas thing. What do you drive?"

"I don't."

He glanced doubtfully in her direction, then put his eyes back on the road.

"Help me understand."

She smiled. "I have a car in L.A., but I never drive it. To be honest, I'm not even sure what it is. It's something my father bought me. I drove him to the airport once."

"You don't drive?"

"No." She laughed.

"I've never met anyone who didn't drive."

"You have to be kidding."

"No. Maybe it's just here, but growing up, getting our driver's license and something to drive is what we all look forward to."

"Yeah. I'd rather do something else."

He pulled into the Galleria parking lot and drove up to the valet. "Like what?"

"What do I do? Make phone calls. Text messages. Read. Anything."

He got out of the truck, shaking his head. "I'll come around."

The valet already had her door open, but Samuel stepped to her, put his hands on her waist, and set her on the ground. She tried to ignore the voice in her head that pointed out just how sexy it was to have a man pick her up like that. "Thank you."

The entranceway was crowded. He took her hand and led her through inside the restaurant. His hand was firm, yet gentle. She could have easily pulled away, but she enjoyed the feel of her hand in his.

They were seated downstairs in the bar area.

"Would you like a drink?" He offered.

"Just water."

"You sure? I don't mind."

She shook her head. "Water's fine."

She ordered four-cheese pasta, and he ordered fettuccini.

"Thanks for getting me out of my apartment." Danielle said, sipping her water. "But I really would have been okay."

"I'm sure you would, but I would never have forgiven myself for letting you spend your birthday by yourself. In my family, it's not allowed."

"That's nice. My mother always did something, but my dad was often flying."

"Pilots do tend to put flying ahead of everything else sometimes. I don't think it's on purpose."

"I don't either."

Danielle caught a clear whiff of grilled meat as a server went by, and the nausea slammed through her again. She put her hand over her mouth.

"Are you okay?"

"I need to get to the restroom."

"It's over there." He pointed, then stood up. "I'll go with you."

He grabbed her handbag off the seat and escorted her to the restroom. She wasn't sure she would have made it without his help leading the way. But she did. And she was sick.

Eight

Samuel stood outside the restroom door and waited for her.

An older woman came out. "Is that your girl in there?"

"Yes."

"There's no one else in there if you want to go in. I can watch the door."

"Thank you." He rushed into the restroom and found her kneeling over a wastebasket. He held her hair. Then, when she was finished, he got her a wet towel.

"Better?"

"Yes. How did you get in here?"

"Someone's watching the door. If you're okay, I'm going to step out."

She nodded as he helped her stand up. "I'm good now."

A few minutes later, she rejoined Samuel in the hallway.

"Do you feel like eating? We don't have to stay."

She looked up at him. "Actually I'm really hungry now."

They sat at the table, and Samuel quietly studied her. That

was twice in one day that she'd thrown up. Twice that *he* knew of. He wouldn't be insensitive and ask if there were other times. And now she was fine. Hungry even.

And he had a flashback to his sister's pregnancy. She'd done the exact same thing.

Danielle pregnant?

She smiled at him.

He didn't know her well enough to know. But even if she was, he still wanted to spend time with her. To get to know her.

He was enchanted.

Danielle was humiliated. But she had enough of her mother in her to hide it behind a smile.

When the food came, she ate half of it, then couldn't eat any more. But that wasn't unusual. It was actually more than she usually ate.

After dinner, they collected his truck from the valet, and he drove them the short distance to the theater.

He watched her closely, and she didn't blame him. She'd only met him today, and already she'd thrown up twice.

He was a perfect gentleman on their non-date date. He bought popcorn and one Coke.

"Maybe this will keep your stomach settled." He handed her the Coke. She sipped and took a small handful of popcorn.

"Do you mind?" He waited for her to shake her head before he took the Coke and sipped. From the straw. The same straw she'd just used.

Now was decision time. She only shared straws with guys

she was willing to kiss. When he handed the Coke back, she smiled and put her lips on the straw. She saw him smile out of the corner of her eye.

The movie started shortly. After they put away the soda and popcorn, Danielle tried to focus on the movie. They sat comfortably, like two friends, but Danielle was acutely aware that she was sitting next to him.

She had to keep reminding herself that it wasn't a date. He was just a guy taking pity on her for being alone on her birthday.

Toward the end of the movie, Danielle relaxed and her eyes grew heavy. On top of everything else, it would not be good to fall asleep.

She managed to stay awake, but as the credits rolled on the screen and they stood up, she swayed.

Right into his arms. "Whoa. What happened?" He steadied her back on her feet.

"I don't know. My legs were weak. I was so sleepy."

"You probably wore yourself out being sick all day."

"Probably." Though she didn't feel sick at the moment. Just very, very exhausted. And achy all over.

"I should get you home."

"I think that's a good idea."

Danielle was quiet as they walked out to his truck, and he helped her inside. She gave him directions to her apartment, but otherwise, had little energy for conversation. It was nearly eleven o'clock, and sadly, she admitted to herself that she was usually sound asleep long before this time every night.

He walked her to her door and waited as she unlocked the door and opened it. She stopped, with one foot inside her apartment and one still outside, and turned to him. "Thank you." She smiled into his lovely blue eyes. "Thank you for making this a wonderful birthday."

As she closed the door and locked it behind her, she thought to herself, *I'm not even thinking about kissing him.*

CHAPTER

Ten

There were some things a guy should never ask... or suggest. Growing up with two sisters and a mother in the house, Samuel had picked up a few pointers.

Asking a girl you'd just met if she was pregnant was specifically on that list. Asking a girl who obviously didn't know she was pregnant was not specifically on the list, but he was pretty sure it was contraindicated.

As he stood in line at the corner CVS with a box of Premium saltine crackers in one hand and a bottle of lime-green Gatorade in the other, he wondered how she could possibly not know. He'd heard of girls not knowing they were pregnant, but they were usually girls who were significantly overweight. Danielle was maybe one hundred ten pounds. If she didn't know she was pregnant, it couldn't possibly be long before her clothes started to get a little tight around the waist.

Maybe he should just wait.

In the three days he'd known her, she hadn't done anything

that would harm a fetus. She didn't drink alcohol, or smoke cigarettes, or do anything else that would be considered harmful behavior.

Nonetheless, he had two nieces and one nephew, and he had heard more details from his two sisters, who had gone through pregnancies, to know that there were things that needed to be done.

He paid for the crackers and went out to his truck. He was doing everything he could to make sure Danielle ate regular small meals and kept her in crackers to help with the nausea. But she needed to go in for a medical evaluation and she needed to start prenatal vitamins.

He steered his truck out into the traffic to head back to Danielle's office. *I'm not a doctor. Having nieces and nephews does not make me an expert. Leave her alone.*

Feeling good about his decision, he walked across the parking lot and into the building. Besides, it wasn't like she was his girlfriend. She'd said she was never getting back with her ex. *Once a cheater, always a cheater.* But if they were having a baby together, that could very well change things.

Samuel did not want to get in the middle of that. If Jessica had gotten pregnant with their baby and some other guy tried to get involved in it, Samuel would have had to break his jaw. It wouldn't have mattered if they were broken-up or not. The baby would still be theirs – something they made together. What kind of guy would let the mother of his child just walk away?

Samuel's resolve and good intentions lasted another twenty seconds – until he walked into her office and found her sitting on the floor next to the trash can. Her face was pale and her eyes wide as she looked up at him.

"I don't feel so good," she said.

Even if she wasn't pregnant, something was definitely wrong. "I need to get you to the doctor," he said.

She shook her head. "I'll have to call my doctor in Los Angeles, then get my dad to fly me over."

Even to Samuel, a pilot, Danielle's way of thinking baffled him. It obviously didn't even occur to her to see a doctor in Houston; Houston was home to some of the best doctors in the country.

He smiled to himself. Was this what he had to look forward to with his own child? Did the daughter of a pilot automatically think of flying as the first option for transportation?

He cleared his throat to keep from laughing. Danielle didn't even have a car. She used the city bus system and Uber.

"I can get you in to see a doctor here."

"I don't have a doctor here," she said, as he helped her off the floor and into her chair.

"My sisters go to the Houston Women's Clinic. I can call and get you an appointment."

She didn't say anything. She just watched him with those huge green eyes. *I pushed her too far.* He opened the box of crackers and tore one of the sleeves open. He smiled as he held it out to her. "It's just an offer," he said.

She took a cracker, chewed, and leaned back with her eyes closed. "That might be a lot easier," she said. "I don't really have the energy to make the trip to L.A. right now."

"Do you want me to see if I can get you in tomorrow?" he asked, slipping his cell phone out of his jacket pocket.

"Sure," she said, rubbing her temples. "I didn't know I was going to fall apart at age twenty-three."

He laughed. "I don't think you're falling apart."

She sniffed and sighed. "I think I'm coming down with a cold, too."

Samuel located the phone number of the clinic and dialed. He told himself that his deception was warranted. She doubtlessly thought she would be seeing a primary care physician. He would play dumb when she found out she was seeing an obstetrician.

CHAPTER
Eleven

Danielle was miserable. She felt like she was coming down with a cold. She was nauseated and throwing up. And she was exhausted. She needed to work on a book cover for Isabella Quinn, but she had zero energy, much less any creativity.

Samuel had dropped her off at her apartment, so now that she was alone, she collapsed on the sofa and, curling her feet beneath her, pulled a throw off the back of the couch and closed her eyes.

She wondered, again, if her father was secretly paying Samuel to watch out for her. He said he was on her father's payroll, but here he was hanging out with her. He couldn't possibly be bored enough to want to spend time with a girl who was always either being sick or complaining about feeling sick.

She would go to his doctor and get something to get past this, then she would be better-able to fight her growing attraction and attachment to this man.

Samuel was nothing like Joey. She'd met Joey when they

were just freshmen in college. That had been ages ago. Her step-father, Grayson, had inspired Joey to join the military, and she had watched him become a different person. Unlike most guys, the uniform had not been good for Joey. He'd be gone weeks without calling while he was stationed here or there, and they had drifted apart. He'd dropped out of college, and they'd grown even further apart. But then, just when she'd moved on and put him behind her, he'd show up again.

Joey had a certain charm that she wasn't immune to. He would use *we* language and talk about getting married. Danielle considered herself trendy when it came to fashion and hair color. She was the first to jump on the mermaid hair color trend, and she did yoga at least once weekly. She enjoyed her mother's artsy friends. They were so different from Claire, her very tradi-tional mother, that Danielle had been fascinated – like a moth to a flame, she'd studied them and learned about the art world. Not the history of art, but modern art, what attracted people to a painting. Things like that.

She'd switched her major from psychology to fine arts. She had enough of her mother in her to take on a second major, marketing, and so far, the combination was serving her well in the real world of work.

Her downfall had been Joey.

He'd crooked his finger, and she'd followed. *Come join me in Houston. We'll have so much to do. It'll be fun.*

She should've known better. She knew him well enough to know that *come join me* did not translate into *come be with me and be my girl.*

At least not in the sense of any depth. He wanted her to be his girl, alright, for just about three days.

Then he'd recruited a young eighteen-year-old into his bed.

Danielle wasn't shocked. She pretended to be. But she knew he'd been playing around on her ever since he put on that uniform and went off to basic training in San Antonio. A girl could tell those things.

Instead of being shocked, she'd been repulsed.

She wondered now why she suddenly developed repulsion toward her on-and-off boyfriend of five years. Perhaps it was the detail of walking into his apartment and finding him in bed with a young girl, kissing her on the stomach.

Still… not a complete shock.

There were rose petals tossed all over the room. Rose petals? Joey had never used such a romantic gesture with Danielle. Not even once.

When she stripped it down to the bare bones – and Danielle had taken plenty of time to dissect her feelings – it wasn't finding him with the girl. It was finding him with the girl in the very same bed where they had made love the night before.

The. Very. Same. Sheets.

And rose petals?

He'd told Danielle that he loved her. He always did that when they were intimate. He would tell her when he thought she was asleep.

And that was the one detail that tripped her up every time. Because he told her when he thought she was asleep, she believed him.

She believed that even though he wasn't ready to commit, that he still loved her more than anyone else.

She'd thought he would commit eventually.

The old Danielle, back when she was a teenager, hadn't been

very good at coping. In high school, while her mother had been out at a gallery event, and her father had been with his new girl-friend, Danielle had been alone after a breakup with a boy she'd particularly liked. His name was Richard, and he'd completely swept her off her feet. She had thought they were going to get married. He was five years older and was a pilot she'd met through her father. She'd had enough sense to never tell her father those two details. Even after weeks of family therapy, she kept those details to herself. In retrospect, she'd sensed it was rather Freudian. She hadn't known about Freud at the time, but she had known that her father didn't need to know.

Nonetheless, in a moment of desperation, she'd taken her mother's Xanax and mixed it with her father's bourbon. That had led to intense individual and family therapy during a mental health hospitalization. It was not a time in her life that she ever wanted to repeat.

She'd lost track of the number of boyfriends she'd been through since then, Joey not included. She suffered through many breakups, but none of them had taxed her coping skills like the one with that pilot. He had been her first sexual experi-ence, and her last, until that night with Joey five weeks ago.

All in all, Danielle's adventurous spirit with clothes, hair, and even in some ways, her career, didn't cross over into her world of relationships.

She dated. A lot. But she rarely crossed that line. With Joey, she'd still been young and vulnerable when their relationship started. She couldn't explain why she'd kept going back to him.

But just because she'd slept with him, didn't mean she couldn't let him go.

Over. With.

She was over Joey.

Somehow the process of being over her long-time on-off boyfriend had led to her needing to take a break from all men.

She hadn't decided how long this self-imposed hiatus was going to last. There was currently no expiration date.

So here she was, vulnerable from her breakup with Joey, when Samuel waltzed in with his innocent sweetness.

Such was the story of her life. Joey had waltzed in when she was vulnerable from her brush with suicide, and Samuel waltzed in after her discontinuation of what she now knew was a toxic relationship with Joey.

Only this time, she was better at coping. If she just didn't have this cold. Or virus. Or whatever it was that was making her sick. She'd felt *off* since that morning nearly six weeks ago. She'd gotten up while Joey was still asleep, gotten dressed, and while it was still dark outside, slipped outside and taken an Uber to her apartment.

As the Uber pulled up to her apartment, she realized her phone was on Joey's bar, so she'd gone straight back to get it.

That's when she'd discovered the whole Joey the scumbag episode.

She'd decided to just calmly get her phone leave.

She hadn't looked back. She had gotten into the Uber that waited for her and gone straight back to her apartment. On the drive back, she'd blocked Joey's number, then on second thought, deleted his number from her phone.

Danielle woke the next morning on the couch and reached for her cell phone on the coffee table. She blinked against the sunlight streaming in through the patio doors. Since she was on the tenth floor of her apartment building, she didn't bother closing the blinds at night. She liked the view of the city lights below.

It was eight o'clock. She'd been asleep for nearly fifteen hours. Samuel would be there to pick her up at eleven. She needed to shower and get herself together. Sitting up, she groaned. It was never a good idea to sleep on the couch. Every muscle ached from sleeping so long on the uncomfortable couch.

Fifteen hours! How was that even possible? She stumbled to the bathroom to take a shower. The hot water on her aching muscles helped. After stepping out of the shower, she tied the towel around her and walked to the kitchen where she had left the package of saltine crackers Samuel had given her.

Her doctor's appointment was at one o'clock. That gave them time for a quick lunch.

Unfortunately, right now, the very thought of food left her feeling ill.

Samuel knew it was Noah calling before he even looked at his phone. His new boss had a special ring tone.

"I know I promised you this week for moving," Noah said as a greeting. "But can you make a quick run for me?"

Oh no! "Today?"

"Yeah," Noah said.

"I can't."

There was silence on the other end.

Samuel made the quick decision to appeal to Noah's emotional side. "I promised to help Danielle with something."

He heard what sounded like a sigh on the other end of the phone. "Well, can it wait until tomorrow?"

"No. Tomorrow's Saturday. I can fly tomorrow if you need me to."

"It needs to be today," Noah said.

"I'm sorry," Samuel said. "I can't let Danielle down."

"Alright," Noah relented. "I'll see if I can get someone else."

"Great. If I'd known ahead of time…"

"We talked about this Samuel," Noah said. "You have to be available at a moment's notice."

"It's your daughter, Mr. Worthington. It's important."

"She's okay?" He asked, alarm in his voice.

"She's okay," Samuel said. "But I'm picking her up at eleven for an appointment. If I'm not there, she'll have to take the bus."

"Yeah," he said, his voice softening. "She has an aversion to driving."

"She told me she never drives."

"She told you the truth. Her mother and I tried giving her a car years ago. It sat in the garage. I think she took it out once when I insisted she drive me to the airport."

Samuel laughed. "Maybe she prefers flying."

"Maybe." Noah hesitated. "Take care of my girl. I'll find someone else for the flight."

Samuel hung up and sighed with relief. He hadn't said anything that wasn't true. He'd merely sketched around the truth. It was the right thing to do anyway. It wasn't his place to disclose Danielle's business. But if Noah sent him off flying today, Danielle wouldn't make her doctor's appointment, and his gut told him she'd put off going altogether.

Glancing at the time, he showered, shaved, and put on a pair of jeans and a polo shirt. It may be November, but it was warm today in typical Houston weather.

He reminded himself, on the drive over to pick up Danielle, that he was doing this for Noah. His employer's daughter needed help, and since he was on the payroll, he was honor-bound to take care of her.

When he pulled up to the door of her apartment building, Danielle was standing outside waiting for him.

She was wearing a flowing lavender dress splashed with a bouquet of flowers and a little matching sweater. She looked incredibly feminine. His heart stuttered just a little as she smiled at him.

He pulled up and got out of the truck, meeting her on the passenger side. She was wearing flats today, so the top of her head barely reached his shoulders. He opened the door and helped her climb inside. When she put her hand on his arm before stepping into the truck, she looked up at him and smiled.

The flash of attraction was unmistakable. He not only wanted to take care of her, he wanted to know what it felt like to kiss her.

These were feelings he'd thought he'd buried with Jessica.

His boss's daughter was not the one for him to be having these thoughts and feelings about. If they were going to resurface, they needed to resurface with someone else.

Once she was inside the truck, he closed the door and pulled himself together as he walked around to the driver's side.

"Where would you like to eat lunch?" he asked.

She grinned sheepishly. "Pappa's Burgers?"

If he'd learned one thing, it was to never question a woman's food cravings – pregnant or not. "Alright," he said. "Pappa's it is."

He saw her expression of relief out of the corner of his eye.

As they waited for their shrimp po'boys to arrive, Samuel said, "You look like you're feeling better."

"I am," she agreed. "The crackers help."

He smiled. "I'll tell my mother. She'll be happy to know that her insistence that I keep crackers in my truck paid off."

Danielle chuckled.

"Did you find out what happened to that model you were expecting?"

"No," she said. "Sometimes they get cold feet." She shrugged.

"Really? That's odd."

"It's kind of an odd business."

"Do you work for yourself?"

"Sort of, but not really. Sort of like you and my father, actually."

"How so?"

"I work for a company called 'Show Don't Tell Book Covers.' They do all the advertising and handle the office. I make my covers and submit them to the office manager, who posts them on a website. I make a percentage."

"Why not just do it yourself?" Samuel sipped his soda.

"Because I'm new at it. A lot of designers spin off their own companies."

"So once you get established, that's something you might think about doing?"

"Maybe. What about you? Are you thinking about starting your own company?"

He waited while the server dropped their food off. Then dipped a French fry into ketchup before tasting it. "I don't know. I'm not sure I want the overhead." He met her gaze. "As you may be aware, airplanes are rather costly."

She chuckled. "I suppose there is quite a difference between buying an airplane and buying a computer. I'd still have to hire models though, just like he hires pilots."

"I guess we have similar business models." He took a bite of his sandwich. It was good, but he truly hoped she got around to wanting to try something new for lunch, sooner rather than later.

Then he caught himself. It had been so easy to just slip into a routine with Danielle. They'd meet for lunch, then work around her office until she was ready to go home, then he'd drive her to her apartment building and drop her off. She hadn't invited him up, so their activities had been restricted to lunch and afternoons.

It was for the best.

She was the boss's daughter.

Samuel was smart enough to know better.

But her being the boss's daughter was a double-edged sword. He needed to keep his distance, but he also needed to watch out for her.

He had a feeling Noah had no idea how much Danielle needed watching after. She ate half her sandwich, just like yesterday. He picked up the other half and finished it off. He only shrugged when she smirked at him.

"You know, I was thinking." She smiled at the waiter when he stopped at their table.

"Can I get you a hand-made milkshake?" The waiter asked hopefully.

Her eyes lit up. "Hmm. That sounds good. What do you think, Samuel?"

"Sure," he agreed, pushing his empty plate aside. It was a good thing he had a high metabolism.

She ordered a chocolate milkshake, and he ordered vanilla.

"You said you were thinking about something?" Though he'd thought it was a little unusual at the time, he now found the little swirl of lavender highlights in her hair quite charming.

He liked the way her eyes lit up when she had a new idea.

"I feel better today. I haven't thrown up at all. Maybe I don't need to go to the doctor."

"Oh no." This was not one of her *good* new ideas. "The way you've been sick all week, you should get checked out. Just to make sure."

She wrinkled her nose. Then sighed. "All right. But only because you're going in with me."

Samuel coughed as the Coke he was swallowing went down the wrong way. Oh no! This was not going to backfire on him like this.

There was no way he was going to go in with her to see the gynecologist.

"Are you okay?" She reached out and touched his hand as regained his composure.

He held up his hand. "I'm good."

The waiter brought their milkshakes.

She sipped. Wrinkled her nose again. "I think this one is yours." She pushed her glass to him and traded.

Samuel picked up the glass and stared at the straw a moment. Her lips had just been on this straw. He had a rule. Never drink after anyone unless he was willing to kiss them. Sucking on this straw was going to be almost like kissing her. They'd shared a soda during the movie, and that had led to him thinking about kissing he even more.

Without thinking about it any further, he took a deep sip of the milkshake.

"Do you like it?" She asked.

He closed his eyes and let his breath out slowly. When he opened his eyes and looked into hers, he knew he was in more trouble than he'd thought.

CHAPTER
Thirteen

As Danielle sipped her milkshake, she studied Samuel over the top of her glass. He had suddenly started squirming.

"Are you okay?" She watched his eyes dart to hers, then to the traffic outside the window.

"Yeah." He looked back at her. "I'm good."

"I'm glad you're going in with me," she said.

He scrubbed a hand across his chin. "I'm not sure that's a good idea."

"Why not?" She was curious now. What was making this guy uncomfortable? Ever since she mentioned him going in with her, he'd avoided eye contact.

"That might not be a good idea."

"Why not?" She asked.

"I don't know you all that well."

She scoffed. "We've had lunch together almost every day this week. I think we know each other well enough. I mean..." She set her glass down and realized with a measure of embarrassment that she'd already drank half of it. "'Besides... I've thrown up in front of you. I don't think it gets much more intimate than that."

He coughed again. Then managed to look into her eyes again. "I think it can get much more intimate."

Now it was her turn to squirm. Well... when he put it like that...

"It's not like I have to get undressed or anything."

He was studying the traffic again. Sipping his milkshake. "You never know," he muttered against his straw.

He glanced at his phone. "Speaking of appointments, I think we better get going."

"We haven't finished our milkshakes," she pointed out.

"We'll get them to go." He motioned for the server and within minutes, they had fresh milkshakes in paper cups.

"I don't know what's wrong with me," she said against her straw. "I don't normally eat desserts."

"We'll see what the doctor says," he said, ushering her toward the front door.

"I have to make a quick stop," she said before she darted into the restroom.

Staring at her reflection as she washed her hands, she wondered what a mess he must think of her. She threw up all the time. She ate like a bird one minute, then a starving person the next, and she went to the bathroom all the time.

A thought darted at the edge of her consciousness, but she pushed it away. A virus. That's all it was.

Fourteen

The minute she walked through the door, Danielle knew the Houston Women's Clinic was not a doctor's office for colds and viruses. It was a female clinic in every sense of the word.

Samuel hadn't said much on the drive over. *He knew.* He knew he was bringing her to a gynecologist. Surely, he didn't think she was seeing a primary care doctor here? If he did, he was desperately misinformed.

"Have you been here before?" She stepped into the elevator and waited while he pressed the button. With his lack of hesitation in guiding them to the fourth floor, she already knew the answer to her question.

"Yes." He glanced at her, then stared at the elevator door. "My younger sister got divorced shortly after becoming pregnant, so I came with her to all her appointments.

"Ah-ha!"

He turned and looked at her quizzically. "Ah-ha what?"

Danielle got in line to check in. "You knew," she hissed. She took the clipboard from the clerk, and he followed her to a secluded area of the waiting room.

"I knew what?" He nudged her elbow when she quietly began writing in her name.

She looked up beneath her lashes. His gaze locked onto hers now. She squinted, unsure how she felt about the fact that he had brought her to a gynecologist when she'd thought he'd made an appointment for her with a family doctor.

"Samuel." She stood the clipboard on her knees. Nodded toward the waiting room. There were no one but females, and two of them were clearly pregnant. She leaned toward him. Whispered. "Do you think I'm pregnant?"

He ran his hands along his thighs, keeping his eyes straight ahead. "I don't know."

She lowered her head and focused on the paperwork, letting her hair cascade around her face. She bit her lip as she filled in her address and date of birth.

He turned back to her. "Is it possible?"

She bit her lip and focused on family history. Nothing to report. All were healthy.

Is it possible?

That was the question that had been darting around her mind all morning.

She had to admit that, yes, it was possible.

The other question was whether it was likely.

She turned the page and signed her name at the bottom of the form.

Without looking at Samuel, she stood up and took the clipboard to the reception desk. Then she turned and went back to sit next to Samuel and began digging in her handbag for her lip gloss.

She felt him staring at her. Waiting.

Waiting for her to reveal whether or not she'd been sexually active. And pregnant. If not pregnant, she had some kind of terrible disease. Even as she sat there, avoiding answering Samuel's pointed question, she felt sick. Again.

She heaved a sigh. And turned to face him.

At least he was looking at her again. "I don't know," she shrugged.

He scowled. "How can you not know?" He sat back, a knowing expression forming on his face. "If you don't know, that means it's possible."

"I don't know can mean a lot of things," Danielle said as her phone chimed, indicating a Facebook message. It was from Isabella Quinn, her author client who was waiting for a cover. Her only author client at the moment.

She read the message and rolled her eyes. "That's never going to happen."

"What?"

"The author wants the couple on her cover to be kissing."

Samuel laughed. "So? It's a romance cover."

"Jacob and Avery can't stand the sight of each other, much less to kiss."

"You said they worked well together, they'll just see it as a normal part of their job. Like any actor."

"You're right," she said, messaging Isabella back. *We have another shoot tomorrow. I'll make it happen.*

"Danielle Worthington." A nurse called her name.

Danielle stood up and held out her hand to Samuel. "Come on," she insisted.

He didn't move.

"It's okay," the nurse said. "We welcome husbands."

"I'm not…" Samuel began, but blew out his breath and took her hand.

Danielle smiled at the nurse as she went through the door and followed the nurse to the exam room.

Samuel had been here before.

But it was not a place he wanted to be with Danielle.

His mother would call it *improper*. Danielle was about to take off her clothes and be examined.

For pregnancy.

And he'd only known her for four days. She was his boss's daughter.

There were so many things wrong with this scenario, his flittering brain cells didn't know which wrong to light upon.

He forced himself to listen as Danielle described her symptoms to the nurse. He'd brought her here after all. It was the least he could do.

She turned and smiled sweetly at him. "Did I miss anything?"

He shook his head and wondered if he looked as uncomfortable as he felt.

"Everything off," the nurse said, slid the curtain closed, and stepped from the room. The curtain that separated Samuel from Danielle.

"Do you want me to step out?" *Please say yes.*

"Don't you dare leave me," Danielle said from the other side of the curtain.

He heard rustling as she began to undress. How long would it be before they had the results of the pregnancy test? She would have to do blood work. A couple of days?

She hadn't answered his question. The paradox was, that by saying she didn't know if she was pregnant, this told him that she could be.

There were many implications involved in this situation.

"Are you still here?" Danielle called as he heard her step onto the exam table.

"I'm right here," he answered. The thought of her sitting on the other side of the curtain wearing nothing more than a paper dress nearly sent him into a tailspin.

I shouldn't be thinking about her that way. She's Noah's daughter. My boss's daughter.

"Samuel?"

He knew that tone. She was going to be sick. *I shouldn't know this.*

"I'm going to be sick."

The words spurred him into action. He looked around for a trash can, but didn't see one. He only had seconds. Walking backwards, he went to the other side of the curtain.

And found the trash can. He slid it next to her and used his foot to open the lid.

He had made it in time.

He held her hair while keeping his gaze on the wall. Out of

habit, he put a hand on her back and nearly jerked back as his fingers touched bare skin. So soft.

The doctor came in just at that moment.

"Oh my," she said.

Grateful to have the distraction, Samuel looked at Dr. Neal. He recognized her from bringing in his sister. She was young, probably mid-thirties, and always had a smile on her face.

The doctor moistened a towel with water and handed it to Danielle to wipe her face. "Has this been happening a lot?" she asked.

"A little," Danielle said.

"All the time," Samuel said.

He looked at her then, wearing her paper gown, her hair flowing around her, one hand holding the wet paper towel. His heart tripped over itself. He took the towel from her and gently wiped her mouth.

"Thank you," she whispered, when he finished.

"Let's take a look," Dr. Neal said.

Samuel ducked back behind the curtain and pulled out his phone. Their voices were muted, and he checked his email to distract himself from listening in to what they were saying.

"How's your sister?" Dr. Neal asked, as she stepped out from behind the curtain.

"She's great," Samuel said, more than a little surprised that Dr. Neal remembered him.

"Take good care of this one."

"I will," Samuel said. "Thank you."

"Only a couple more days before you know if you're going to be a daddy."

CHAPTER
Sixteen

Danielle pulled her shirt over her head. The door closed, and they were alone again.

"Are you okay?" Samuel asked from the other side of the curtain.

"Yeah," she said. "I'll just be a minute." She hadn't realized just how nervous she'd been. Even after the examination, she really didn't know anything more than she had when she came in.

She could hear him pacing while she slipped into her sneakers and tied the shoelaces. "What now?" he asked.

"Bloodwork."

"Right."

Fully dressed, she stepped from behind the curtain. He stopped pacing and faced her. His hair was all over the place and his shirt was... crooked. She laughed. "You look like a mess."

"Thanks." He straightened his shirt. "You look... beautiful."

She bit her lip and tried to ignore the little thrill that shot through her at his unexpected words. "I guess I don't have a virus."

"Did she say anything?"

Danielle shrugged. "She'll call with the bloodwork results."

"Good. Hey. Why did she say that?" He opened the door and held it while she walked through.

"Why she said what?"

He shook his head. "Never mind."

Danielle hadn't corrected Dr. Neal's assumption that Samuel was the father of her possible baby.

She took the prescription for prenatal vitamins and shoved it into her handbag. She hadn't answered Samuel's question, but, yes, it was possible that she was pregnant.

The fact that she and Joey had been intimate the very night before she walked in on him with that girl was like running sandpaper over a paper cut. It hurt like hell, and she didn't want to even think about it.

They got on the elevator and went downstairs to the packed lab area.

If she was pregnant with Joey's child, he would never know it. She wanted nothing to do with him. And she was pretty sure he would want nothing to do with the child… or with her.

"Danielle?" Samuel touched her arm. "They called your name."

She stood up, but instead of going to the lab door, she waited for him. When he didn't stand up, she tugged on his elbow.

He chuckled and followed her to where the nurse waited. "I don't think I'm supposed to go back there," he said.

The nurse shook her head. "They try to get out of it all the time."

"It's good to know it's not just me."

She sat in the chair, pulled up her sleeve, held her other hand out to Samuel, who stood next to her. She scrunched up her face. "Ouch!"

The nurse chuckled. "I haven't even started."

"I know," Danielle said. "But I don't like needles."

"Not many do."

As the nurse stuck the needle in her arm, she clenched Samuel's hand.

"This is going to be fun. If, you know…" he said.

She glanced down at her arm to the blood flowing through the tube. He followed her gaze.

Then Samuel passed out on the floor.

Samuel was fairly certain he would never live it down.

He pulled the blanket over his head and decided it was a good day to sleep in. It was Saturday, and he had nothing to do. No plans. Not even with Danielle.

Danielle.

She was working today.

He groaned.

How was she going to get to the photo shoot location?

She would ride the bus. Like she always did.

Or use Uber.

He hated the thought of her riding the bus or even using Uber. It was supposed to be safe, but still…

He threw off the blanket and made his way to the shower. He stood under the hot water until it began to cool.

Who was he kidding? He wasn't about to stay away from her today. He smiled to himself. Not even the embarrassment of literally passing out at the sight of blood could keep him from wanting to see her.

She hadn't laughed at him. She'd done nothing but show concern. Nonetheless, it had been embarrassing to wake up on the floor after passing out.

That wasn't exactly the image he wanted to portray. He heated a cup of coffee and sent her a text. *Need a ride to the park?*

Two minutes later, his phone chimed with a response. *Already there.*

Did you take your car? He added a smiley face emoticon.

Ha. Yes. The one in L.A.?

He ran a hand through his still-damp hair. She was exasperating. Probably a lot like her father. He hadn't considered it until now, but with the exception of yesterday when he'd taken her to the doctor, most of their time together had been spent doing her work.

Samuel hadn't known very many women quite so driven to achieve.

Impressive.

He popped two pieces of bread in the toaster while he tied his boots. He couldn't very well leave her stranded out there. Not when he had a perfectly good truck.

As he maneuvered through the Saturday morning traffic, it occurred to him that he hadn't set foot in an airplane in over a week. He hadn't gone that long without being off the ground since… well… ever. At least not since he'd gotten his pilot's license.

And he'd barely even thought about it.

In fact, he'd thought about little other than Danielle since he'd met her.

He parked his car and walked to the little white house where he knew she'd be. It was a perfect day to be outside. The temperature had just enough of a nip that he was glad he wore his blue jean jacket. Red and gold leaves from an oak tree skittered about his feet. Fall was hands-down his favorite time of year. The new school year brought new beginnings. Anything was possible.

He knew something was wrong before he could even hear what they were saying.

The male model, Samuel couldn't remember his name, was pacing.

Samuel was pretty sure pacing didn't make the best photos.

When he was in earshot, he stopped, and, stepping off the path, stood next to a tree, watching the interaction.

The male model paced back and faced Danielle. Samuel's nerves went on alert. It had been awhile since he'd been in a physical scuffle. Not that he made a habit of fighting. Only twice, to be exact, and both in college, but he wasn't opposed to tackling anyone who threatened someone he cared about.

Cared about. He'd have to think about that later. Danielle had her hair pulled back today and she wore a bright blue pea coat. Her skin glowed with the crisp fall air.

"I won't do it," Jacob said.

Danielle stood her ground, one hand on her hip and the other holding her camera. "Okay," she said. "Just pretend."

Jacob shook his head, turned away. Samuel relaxed a little.

Avery, who stood a few feet from Danielle, glared at Jacob. "He won't do it," she said.

"It's just a job," Danielle said. "It's not like you have to like each other."

Jacob turned back and glared at both women. "You know what," he said. "I don't even need this job. I don't have to be here, and I don't have to do this. I quit." He turned on his heel and walked away.

The girls watched as he strode down the path that led to the park's exit. Samuel got back on the path and approached them. "Hey," he said. "What's going on?"

Danielle turned, and he saw the frustration on her face. "Jacob just quit."

"Why?" Why would he walk off a job where all he had to do was stand around and be photographed with one pretty girl by another gorgeous female?

"He didn't want to kiss me." Avery rolled her eyes.

"Right," he said. Danielle had mentioned something about the author she was working with needing a kissing scene. He'd forgotten about that. Danielle's doctor's visit had distracted him from thinking about anything else. "Just find someone else, right?"

Both women stared at him.

"Surely it can't be that hard to find someone who'll kiss Avery."

They looked at each other and after a beat, they both burst out laughing.

"It can't be just anyone," Avery pointed out.

"The author is going to flip," Danielle said. "She loved the chemistry between Avery and Jacob."

"If she only knew," Avery muttered.

"Now we have to start over with a new model."

Eighteen

Danielle studied Samuel. He hadn't shaved today. He had just enough shadow to give him that certain bad-boy look that she found irresistible. The same thought occurred to her that she'd had when she first saw him. *He would look good on a book cover.*

Women would definitely drool over him. Not that she was drooling. Well, maybe just a little.

Maybe she could talk him into posing – just for this author. Not that he would want to be a model. She knew enough about pilots to know that they were single-minded. In fact, she wondered why he was here and not off flying somewhere.

He caught her looking at him, and his eyes widened. He shook his head just enough for her to know that he knew what she was thinking.

"Samuel," she smiled sweetly. "Let me take a few pictures of you and Avery and send them to the author."

Now he was shaking his head in earnest. "I'm not a model."

"You don't have to be a model. You just have to let me photograph you."

"To be on a book cover," he glanced at Avery. "with her."

"Seriously," Avery crossed her arms. "Do I have a wart on my nose or something today?"

Danielle tore her gaze away from Samuel long enough to respond. "You're beautiful Avery. He's just being difficult. And Jacob… well… you would know better than I what's going on with him."

Avery rolled her eyes. "Yeah. You don't want to know."

"It's hard working with someone you have a history with." Danielle shrugged.

Avery had a stunned look on her face. As if everyone couldn't see it. Danielle turned back to Samuel. "Maybe I could take a couple and text them. If she says no, it's a moot point."

Samuel glanced at Avery and seemed to consider. Danielle swallowed a flash of regret. Samuel with Avery together in a photograph, much less on a book cover for all of eternity. Maybe this wasn't such a good idea after all.

She was about to open her mouth and say they would look for other options when Samuel said. "Okay."

"Okay? You'll do it?" Her emotions were all over the place. In that moment, she truly hoped she was pregnant, so she could blame it on that. She didn't want to admit that although it would help her out professionally if he said yes, she had truly hoped he wouldn't do it.

Avery was gorgeous, and Samuel was handsome. They were going to make a great couple. How could the author not want them on her book cover? Together.

She nodded and let professionalism win. "Go stand next to each other on the porch."

Lifting her camera, she watched them through the lens. Avery was looking at Samuel, but Samuel was watching her, not Avery.

"You have to look at Avery," she said.

Samuel turned his gaze toward Avery. *Good.* She took several pictures. Zoomed in. They did look good together. Avery reached out and put an arm on Samuel's.

Danielle was going to be sick. Right now. She lowered the camera and turned around.

By the time she was hurling the contents of her breakfast, Samuel was there, holding her hair. "Thank you," she murmured.

Danielle sat on the porch steps. *If I'm not pregnant, I have something terribly wrong with me.*

"Are you okay?" Avery asked. This was the first time Danielle had been sick around her.

"I think I must have a virus," Danielle took a tissue from her handbag and wiped her mouth.

"I'll get you some water," Samuel darted away.

"I hope I don't catch it," Avery said.

Danielle didn't answer. She didn't tell Avery that she wasn't contagious.

Within minutes, Samuel was back with water... and crackers.

"Let's take a break, Avery. Come back at one o'clock. By then I should have an answer from the author." Danielle pulled up the pictures, picked out three, and sent them to the author.

"No problem," Avery said, gathering up her backpack and heading down the path to her car.

Danielle nibbled a cracker and sipped from the bottle of water.

"Better?" Samuel brought over her tripod.

She nodded. "Thank you."

He sat down beside her. He rubbed her back, right between her shoulder blades. *No. I will not be attracted to Samuel. I can like him, but I'm not attracted to anyone right now.*

A dating moratorium. She might even be pregnant. Not a good time to be crushing on her father's new employee. A pilot at that. A pilot that was helping her out by posing as a model with her best girl model.

The nausea had passed, but she was still feeling unsettled. Seeing them gazing at each other had been too much. Had it been the possible pregnancy or just seeing them together? She really needed to get that question answered. Maybe she would get an over-the-counter pregnancy test on the way home and take that. She needed to know what was going on with her. Just so she knew how to interpret all these emotions going on with her.

When she was around Samuel.

Suddenly, a little golden retriever puppy was racing toward her. The puppy jumped into her lap and began licking her face. Danielle laughed.

A little girl, about five, was running toward her with her mother right behind her.

"Rex!" The little girl ran up to Danielle.

The puppy jumped out of Danielle's arms to nip around the little girl's heels. She squealed in delight.

The woman, winded, caught up with them. She smiled at Danielle. "Thank you so much."

"You're welcome, but I didn't do anything."

"My daughter loves this puppy." She held up the harness. "I don't know how he managed to get loose."

"He's adorable."

The woman knelt and wrangled the dog back into his harness. "Do you two have children?" Her daughter danced around them.

Danielle glanced at Samuel and shook her head.

"Well, don't wait too long. The older you get, the harder it is to keep up with them."

"I would imagine It's hard at any age."

The woman held her daughter's hand with one hand and the puppy's leash with the other. "Again, thank you for helping."

"Bye!" The little girl grinned and waved as she walked away.

"Cute." Danielle said. "Do you have any pets?"

"My mom has a couple of cats, but no, I don't. Do you?"

"I have a cat at my mom's. His name is Charlie. I miss him terribly."

"Maybe your mom can bring him for a visit."

"Maybe." Danielle stared after the girl with the dog.

Samuel glanced at his watch. "Want to get some lunch?"

"Sounds good." Anything to distract her from the direction of her thoughts.

They walked together down the path to his truck. "Do you mind stopping by the drug store when you take me home?"

"Of course not."

Her phone beeped. "She's already responded."

"That was fast."

"Yeah, unusual." Danielle slid open her messages. Looked up at Samuel. "She loves it."

"You don't seem happy about it."

Danielle shrugged. "I've put a lot of work into the images with Avery and Jacob. I even had a mock up done. I didn't know she was gonna want them kissing."

"Why wouldn't Jacob kiss Avery?"

"I don't know details, but they have a history."

"Still… if he's kissed her before…"

"I guess kissing is intimate for some people."

He gave her a lopsided grin. "I thought kissing was intimate for everyone."

Her face flushed. "Maybe he didn't want to risk opening up old feelings. Or maybe he just really doesn't like her."

"Guess we'll never know."

She took a deep breath. "So now you get to kiss Avery."

He stopped walking. She took two steps and turned back. He looked a little stunned. "What? You didn't put this together?"

"I guess I hadn't thought it through. It was kind of sudden."

Danielle took it as a good sign that he hadn't been looking forward to kissing Avery. In fact, she liked it that he didn't look any too happy about the whole situation.

By the time they reached his truck, she had a little bounce back in her step.

Nineteen

Samuel did not want to kiss Avery. First of all, she was too young. Second, she was blonde. And third, he didn't know her.

And fourth, she wasn't Danielle.

He surely didn't want to kiss her in front of Danielle. Something about that felt distinctly off.

He hadn't kissed anyone since Jessica. So that meant it had been years since he'd kissed anyone.

The whole train of thought just about sent him into a tailspin.

Since they were on the other side of town, and neither of them were familiar with the area, they found a little Mexican restaurant. Being the first ones there, they picked a booth in the back.

Danielle leaned back and put her feet on his bench. Who was going to rub her feet? From being around his sisters, he knew that pregnant women needed their feet rubbed. Often.

Danielle was going to be a single mom. And she was an only child. He didn't know a lot about the rest of her social life.

"When you moved from L.A., did you leave behind any friends?"

She shook her head. "Between work and my family and boyfriend, I didn't have any time left over. Besides," she shrugged. "I've never really been the type to go out with girl-friends."

She was similar to Jessica in that way. Jessica hadn't had girl-friends either. With her being in the military especially, all her friends were male, but she didn't go out either. Unless she was with him.

So far, that was the only similarity he'd discovered between the two girls. Danielle wore makeup and painted her nails. Her hair was highlighted in a trendy fashion. Jessica never wore makeup and never even went to a nail salon that he knew of. She kept her short hair pulled back most of the time.

"What about you?" She asked. "You have a guy friend that you hang out with?"

"Nah. My family keeps me occupied when I'm not flying."

"Speaking of. Aren't you supposed to be packing and getting ready to move to Dallas?"

"I'm packed," he said, "but don't tell your dad. He gave me two weeks, and I'm going to stay here as long as I possibly can."

"There really weren't any jobs in Houston?"

"There was a teaching job open, but I can't see myself teaching others to fly. I'd miss being in the air by myself."

"You sound a lot like my dad. He's only happy when he's flying. Or with his new wife Savannah." She wrinkled her nose.

"You don't like her?"

"Oh yeah. She's great, and my dad has been in love with her

since the day they met at college. But it's just weird thinking about him being with someone."

"I'm lucky, I guess. My parents have stayed together. As far as I know, they're happy together."

"You are lucky. My parents didn't like each other very much. Their marriage was a business arrangement." He made a face. "I didn't know this until after they got divorced. I just knew that my father was rarely home, and when he was home, I did things with him. We rarely did things as a family. It was almost like they were divorced, but living in the same house."

"Yuck."

"It was life as I knew it. I didn't know it was supposed to be any different."

"Your ex, what's his name?"

"Joey." She scowled. "But ex is a good name for him."

"Are you going to tell him about the baby?"

"If there's a baby," she corrected. "No. Absolutely not."

"I'd want to know," he whispered.

"But you're different. You're more settled."

"Are you saying I'm boring?" He scooped a chip into the salsa and tasted it.

"Of course not."

"It's okay. I know I am."

"It's better to be boring than to be a cad." Her face flushed.

There was still some heat there. She pretended to be over this... Joey... but there was some unfinished business. How was she going to cope with having her ex's baby? A man whose name she couldn't even stand to speak.

Joey would find out about the baby. He supposed it was possible that if they never saw each other again, he might not know, but it would be better for Danielle if she chose how he found out. She needed to pick the time and place, and Samuel needed to be with her.

He'd read somewhere that the number one cause of death for pregnant women was murder. Men like Joey, who most likely didn't want a child, could be unpredictable.

He would bring this up after she heard from the doctor.

Right now, he had to figure out what to do about this predicament involving kissing Avery.

"I changed my mind."

Danielle folded her arms and glared at Avery. "What? What's that supposed to mean?"

"It means no. I'm not kissing..." She gestured toward Samuel. "him."

"What's wrong with him?" Danielle studied Samuel, looking for something she'd missed. Other than his squirming at the moment, she saw absolutely nothing she didn't like.

Avery shrugged.

Danielle put a palm against her forehead and closed her eyes. This was a train wreck that she never saw coming when she got up this morning. It was a beautiful fall day. Perfect for photographing. "What am I supposed to do?" She asked, mostly to herself.

"You kiss him."

Danielle opened her eyes. She looked first at Avery, who wore a smug expression, then at Samuel, who had his eyebrows scrunched together. Her gaze went to his lips. And it was as though Avery's words had breathed life into the most wonderful idea. "Okay," she said and hoped her voice didn't sound as breathy as it felt. She cleared her throat and pulled her gaze from Samuel's lips.

She glanced down. She had on tights and a short skirt. Her jacket was short with a longer shirt layered beneath. Not so very different from what Avery wore. She could work with this.

"You'll have to take the pictures," she handed her camera to Avery. She'd have to do some serious Photoshopping, but this was doable.

The author liked Samuel, so maybe she wouldn't notice that the female model had changed. She'd just put the kissing couple – them – on the cover and send it to her.

Avery went into photographer role. "Let's do some warm-up shots first."

Danielle chuckled as Avery mimicked her.

Samuel wore a baffled expression. "So now *we're* the cover models?"

"Sure. Why not?"

"Why not?" He took her hand and led her halfway up the stairs of the white house. They waited while another couple walked around behind them.

"So we just look at each other?" he asked.

"That's a good start."

"I can do that."

"Try to look happy," she said and took her own advice, putting a smile on her face. Her mother had passed along many of the skills she'd learned in finishing school. Danielle knew how to look happy even in the most uncomfortable of situations.

As she gazed into Samuel's blue eyes, she heard the click of the camera, then she got lost in his eyes, and the rest of the world faded away. Her heart rate went into overdrive.

He took her hand and pulled her closer. Then he put his arms loosely around her. She put her hands on his chest and leaned her elbows against him. Her head tilted up. He was a full head taller than she was. A perfect height. He smelled good, like deep, rich masculinity.

They were close enough that she could feel his breath against her forehead. Her lips parted as he moved toward her. He kissed her forehead.

She swayed toward him. He pulled her closer, and her arms went around his neck. He kissed her cheek. The corner of her mouth.

Danielle thought she heard Avery moving around with the camera, but she didn't care if she took any pictures or not. Right now all she wanted was to feel his lips against hers.

He ran a finger along her bottom lip. Danielle shivered.

Then his lips were pressed against hers.

And she felt the spark all through her body.

He kissed her top lip. Then her bottom lip. Then the edge of her mouth again.

She wanted more. But he pulled away, leaving her feeling bereft.

Then he whispered in her ear. "We can do this later when no one's watching."

She opened her eyes and smiled. That was a lovely idea. More. Later.

Avery continued to snap photos while they smiled at each other.

"Okay, that's a wrap," Avery held the camera out toward Danielle. Danielle tore her gaze away from Samuel and took the camera.

"You two need to get a room," Avery said and bounced down the steps. "Call me if you need me Danielle," she said over her shoulder.

Danielle was blushing. She felt it all the way to her hairline.

"Do you think we made some good photos?" he asked.

"I'll have to look at them." How could he go from that kiss to having coherent thoughts? Her brain was fried. Just one kiss. Perhaps a moratorium wasn't such a good idea. She was like a person dying of thirst.

He took her hand and led her down the path to his truck. After he helped her inside, he smiled at her, and her heart did a somersault.

She was in serious trouble.

Twenty~One

They were mostly silent on the drive back to Danielle's apartment. She asked him to wait while she ran into the pharmacy.

That kiss had knocked his socks off. He wanted to see the photos, but he didn't want to seem weird about it. He would ask to see them later.

Right now, he had to figure out how to proceed. Now that he'd kissed her, kissing her again was all he could think about.

Would it be presumptuous to think that he could kiss her again? They'd kissed for a photo. He'd never done that before. He didn't know the protocol.

Was he to pretend like it hadn't happened? Protocol or not, that was never going to happen. Maybe he should wait and give her time to think about it; or not give her time to think about it.

His thoughts circled around until she came back with a small bag, and he decided to follow her lead.

He always walked her to the door, so he did that.

"I need to get to work on this cover." She gripped the bag in one hand as she unlocked the door with the other.

"Sure. Let me know how it turns out."

She smiled over her shoulder. "I will. Thanks for the ride today."

Then she was inside her apartment with the door between them.

He huffed out a sigh.

How could she go from that kiss to just walking away?

CHAPTER
Twenty~Two

Danielle locked the door and leaned against it. She took deep breaths like her counselor had taught her until her heart rate was back to normal.

She hadn't trusted herself around Samuel. One kiss and all rational thought had left her brain. She needed to get away from him before she threw herself at him.

She really did need to work on the cover. She was hoping the author either wouldn't notice or wouldn't care that Avery was missing from the image. She could take some more with Samuel later if need be.

But right now, she wanted to take the pregnancy test.

She went into her bedroom and curled up on the bed. She read the directions all the way through, then set the test aside. According to the directions, she would have to wait until morning. Apparently, pregnancy tests were more accurate when taken first thing in the morning. It was so tempting to ignore that little detail, but she put it aside and went into her home office and uploaded the pictures from today's shoot. She needed to do the serious work at her larger office computer, but she could at least start looking at the photos, in case they needed to do another shoot.

Avery may not be a photographer, but the photos that she took weren't half bad. She'd captured some really good images.

As Danielle scrolled through the photos, her heart rate increased again. She wanted to devour Samuel, and that was evident in the images.

It was surprising though that he obviously wanted to devour her, too. That kind of desire couldn't be faked. Especially not by someone who had absolutely no training in modeling or acting.

There was one particular image that jumped off the screen. His lips were pressed against her top lip and his hand pressed against her jaw. She hadn't even realized he'd touched her face. That was the image she was going to use.

She saved it to her screen and sat back. They looked good together. Really good.

And they had a connection. Or at least she had felt a connection.

To be fair, she hadn't given him a chance one way or the other. Then she remembered the words he'd whispered in her ear. *We can do this later when no one's watching.*

She scrolled back through their photos. She definitely wanted to do more of that sooner than later. Surely her moratorium had been going on long enough. Maybe it was time to come out of it.

She jumped when her phone rang, and her mother's picture popped up on the screen.

"Hi honey." Her mother sounded quite chipper. Not a good sign. "I'm coming into town next week. Can you have the guest room ready?"

CHAPTER
Twenty~Three

Pappa's Burgers for family dinner. Of all the places in Houston they could have picked for this week's gathering, they picked Pappa's Burgers.

Samuel parked his truck in the crowded parking lot and found his family gathered in the private room. Everyone was there. His older sister and her husband, his younger sister, his brother and his wife, and both sets of grandparents. Both of his sisters had brought their toddlers, too, rounding out four generations. His younger sister had brought a date, so that left Samuel as the only single person there.

Since he was the last one to arrive, he took the only seat left, right between his grandparents. The conversation went along as usual until their food arrived.

That's when the eldest of his two grandmothers, Veronica Johnson, leaned over and whispered near his ear. "When are you going to start bringing a lady friend with you again? We all miss Jessica, but it's been two years."

At least she had the decorum to not broadcast her comment to the whole table. The topic of his dating was one topic he did not want to get his sisters started on. "I'll look into that," he whispered back. "Maybe next time."

Veronica's face brightened. "I hope so. It saddens me to see you here all alone."

He glanced around the table. "I'm not lonely. I have my family."

"Yes, but it's different when you have that special someone with you."

Danielle's image was all he could think about. He halfheartedly tried to think about Jessica instead, but he couldn't shake the image of Danielle.

In the week since he'd met Danielle, she'd managed to consume his thoughts. She was the last thing he thought about before he went to sleep and the first thing he thought about when he woke up in the morning. Now he wanted her here with him at his family dinner.

He hadn't brought a girl since Jessica. Hadn't even wanted to.

"Tell me about her," Veronica said.

"Who?"

"The girl who has you preoccupied."

Samuel laughed. "We're just talking."

Grandma patted him on the hand. "That's a good place to start."

Samuel had one more week. Just one more week before he was supposed to be moved to Dallas to start flying for Skye Travels. For Danielle's father.

Talking to the boss's daughter wasn't the smartest thing he could do. The way he wanted to kiss her was definitely off limits.

It would be smart for him to go ahead and move now, before things went any further. To get her out of his mind. So he could at least have a family dinner without her hijacking his thoughts.

It had been bad enough before he'd kissed her. Holding her hair while she was sick. Helping her set up her computer. Taking her to lunch every day. Walking in the park with her. Listening to her talk. Learning that she hoped she never had to drive.

Then there was that kiss. It wasn't like he hadn't thought about kissing her. Oh, he had thought about kissing her plenty.

If only she weren't the boss's daughter, he'd scoop her up so fast, it'd make both their heads spin.

Perhaps Noah would be understanding. What was the worst thing that could happen?

Besides, if anyone was going to be hurt, it would be him. Danielle already had her hooks in him.

He hadn't seen her or talked to her since he'd dropped her off at her apartment yesterday afternoon. Maybe he should see if she was still talking to him before he planned out their future.

CHAPTER
Twenty~Four

Danielle was deep into Photoshopping the photo of Samuel and her. It had been rather odd at first, working with a picture of herself and the guy who sent her heart into overdrive. After a while, though, she had gotten into adding background images and fonts, and it had become just another cover. For the most part. Every now and then, she'd take a moment to relive that kiss.

She hadn't heard from Samuel since he'd walked her to her door Saturday. She hadn't exactly been encouraging. She wouldn't blame him if he didn't come back.

She checked her phone again. No texts.

She could text him, of course, but, again, her mother had trained her well. *If you want the boy, you have to let him pursue you. Chasing is built into their DNA. If there's no chase, there will be no chance for a relationship.*

She'd thought her mother was ridiculously old-fashioned

until her stepfather, a psychologist, had reluctantly agreed with her. Their situation was a little different because they'd dated in high school, but he agreed that he'd never once stayed with a girl who pursued him.

So Danielle sat on her hands and waited. Samuel seemed like an old-fashioned kind of guy, so it didn't seem odd to follow her mother's code with him.

She glanced up with a smile on her face when someone knocked on the door. It was time for Samuel to show up so they could go to lunch.

It wasn't Samuel at her door.

It was Joey.

She hadn't been sick all morning. In fact, she was thinking that maybe she'd gotten over whatever it was that she had. But seeing Joey standing in her doorway had her gauging how quickly she could get to the trashcan.

"Hey Danielle," he said.

She didn't answer.

"I just wanted to bring by your birthday present."

"Birthday present?" She scowled at him.

"Yeah. I had gotten this for you and thought I'd drop it by."

He set a blue gift bag on her desk.

"My birthday was last week."

"I couldn't remember exactly when it was."

Danielle folded her arms. The home pregnancy test had been inconclusive – a complete waste of time and money. *I pray that I'm not pregnant. If I am... and the father of my child doesn't even know when my birthday is...* She reined in her thoughts. "I can't accept it." She put her attention back on her computer. She stared at it, unseeing. Joey had interrupted her whole chain of creativity.

"Okay," he shifted his feet. "I'll just leave it anyway, since I bought it special for you. Do you want to get something to eat?"

She looked back up at him. "No. Joey. I do not want to get something to eat with you. I want you to leave and never come back."

"Surely, you don't mean that. We go way back."

"We may go way back, but we aren't going forward."

"Can't we at least be friends?" He gave her that smile that he used when he was trying to be charming.

"I don't want to be your friend. I don't want you in my life."

He held up a hand. "Okay. Don't get all riled up."

She shook her head. She wasn't *riled* up. She was just feeling quite firm on not wanting Joey anywhere near her.

She pointed to the door. "Go."

"Alright," he said, backing out.

As she watched him leave, she saw him pass Samuel in the open lobby. She still felt nauseated, but she could tell it was different. It really was from seeing her ex.

"Who was that?" Samuel glanced over his shoulder. "Never mind. That was your ex, wasn't it?"

"Is it that bad that you can tell?"

"You look like you're going to be sick."

"I just might."

"What's this?" Samuel pointed to the bag Joey had left on her desk.

Danielle rolled her eyes. "I don't know. He said it was a birthday present."

"A little late for that."

"I know. Right?"

"What is it?" He peeked inside.

"I don't know. I told him I didn't want it."

"Mind if I look?"

"You can have it."

"I doubt that." He pulled out a robe.

Danielle groaned. "Seriously? He brought me a robe? Here." She held out her hand and took the thin robe in her hands. "Old Navy," she said, checking the tag.

Samuel scoffed. "You don't wear Old Navy."

She laughed. And in that moment, it was determined. Her moratorium was over. She was crushing hard on Samuel Johnson and could no longer punish him just because he came into her life after Joey was in it. He'd known her all of one week and already he knew more about her than her ex-boyfriend ever did.

"I'm glad you're here." She handed the robe back to Samuel.

He stuffed it back in the gift bag. "Why? So I can get rid of this thing? What would you like me to do with it?"

She shrugged, a smile playing about her lips. "Trash can is back here."

He balled up the bag and deftly tossed it in.

"Good shot."

"I'm more than just a pretty face for your novel covers," he said.

Danielle laughed.

"When do I get to see?"

She minimized the cover she was working on and pulled the

photo before sliding the computer around so he could see. "Here's the photo I picked."

"Wow," he breathed.

"Here are the other pictures." She scrolled through the photos.

"Can I get a copy of those?"

"Really?"

"Yeah. I've never been in a photo shoot before. And I've definitely never been photographed while kissing. It's kinda… um…"

Danielle smiled. "I know. It's hard to describe, huh?"

"That's an understatement."

She sent copies of the pictures – the dozen or so that she'd picked out to keep herself - to his cell phone. "There you go."

His phone chimed. "Thanks. Let me know when I can see the cover."

"I will. Even if this author doesn't want it, I'll definitely be able to sell it."

"I'm glad I could help out."

"I've never been on a cover either. It's weird."

"Does this author sell a lot?"

Danielle shrugged. "Moderate. Not a name you would recognize, but she does okay."

"Just curious how many people will see us."

"Women all over the world will be swooning over our cover."

He laughed. "You're feeling better today?"

"Yeah," she blew her bangs out of her eyes with a sigh of relief. "I think I may be over what it was I had."

He raised an eyebrow, but didn't say anything. He sat in the chair on the other side of her desk and stretched his long legs out. Then he grinned at her.

She grinned back, and a little shiver traveled down to her toes. Her hands trembled a little, so she put them in her lap. "What?" She asked.

"I love watching you work."

She lowered her eyes. She lifted her fingers to the keyboard, then put them back in her lap and looked up at him. "I don't think I can work with you watching me."

"We could… do something else."

His words sent her thoughts down a very naughty path. Very bad. She replayed the kiss they had shared on Saturday. "Like what?"

He glanced at his watch. "We could get some lunch."

Relief and disappointment washed over her. "Okay."

"You might want to bring your coat," he nodded toward her coat hanging on the coat rack. "The temperature's dropping today."

"Really?" Her face brightened. "Maybe it'll snow."

He laughed. "Not likely, love. This is Houston."

As she reached for her coat, the bottom fell out of her stomach. *Love?* Surely she heard him wrong. He took her coat and helped her into it.

Pulling her hair from the collar and letting it fall down her back, she smiled into his eyes. He was looking at her now with an intensity she hadn't seen with him before. She licked her lips.

"You're beautiful," he ran his thumb beneath her chin and she trembled. She longed to feel his lips on hers again.

Her phone vibrated in her pocket. She pulled it out. "It's Dr. Neal."

"That was quick," he took a step back, but kept his eyes on hers while she talked.

Danielle listened to the nurse, thanked her, then put the phone back in her pocket.

"I'm pregnant."

Twenty~Five

A host of unexpected emotions washed through Samuel. The first thought was that he had been right. The second was an image of Joey walking past him in the lobby. That led to a wash of anger.

Then came a stab of regret. He wanted to be the father of Danielle's child.

He quickly set aside his own emotions and put his focus back on Danielle. Her face was blank.

"You knew." Her voice was quiet.

He shrugged. "Sisters." He drew her to him into a hug and tucked her head beneath his chin. He held her tightly, and she clung to him. They stood that way in silence as the seconds passed.

He had one week. One week before he had to move to Dallas. He had an apartment reserved with Air BNB for the next two weeks. He wasn't ready to commit to a lease in Dallas. He knew nothing about the city – which area was best to live in. Which area would be a peaceful commute to the airport.

In one week, he would be leaving Danielle on her own, to face an unexpected pregnancy with a man she no longer wanted in her life. He needed to talk to her. To find out what she wanted.

"Come on. Let's get out of here." He took her hand and led her out of her office, through the lobby to the elevator.

They went outside and got into his truck without talking. He didn't ask, he just drove to Pappa's. They were early, so they took a quiet booth in the back.

"How do you feel?" He asked, prepared to get crackers.

"I don't feel sick at the moment. I haven't all morning."

"That's got to be a good thing."

"You have no idea how miserable it is. And humiliating."

"Danielle." He held out his hand and she put hers in his. Their fingers locked loosely. "What do you want to do?"

Her eyes widened. "You mean, do I want to have the baby?"

"Do you?" He couldn't begin to imagine what it would be like to carry the child of someone he didn't love.

She took a deep breath. Looked around and squared her shoulders. "Yes."

He nodded. "Okay then." If she could deal with it, then he would learn to accept it. No matter the biological father, the baby would still be hers.

She pulled her hand away and pressed her fingertips against her forehead. "I have to tell my parents."

He nodded.

"I may not survive that."

He chuckled. "They're your parents. Surely, they'll understand."

"My father, yes. My mother, not so much. Image is very important to her. I'm going to be a disappointment." She was quiet for a moment. "Maybe I should have an abortion."

"Danielle." She looked at him. "Do not have an abortion because you might embarrass your parents."

She shuddered out a breath. "You're right. My mother is coming for a visit this week. I'll get it over with. Actually, it's really convenient that I live here. None of her associates in L.A. have to even know."

"It's hard to hide a child forever."

"Not forever. Just long enough for them to get used to the idea."

"It's a lot for you to get used to, too."

"Yeah. I never saw myself being a single mom."

"You should meet my sister. She's a single mom."

"Your parents were okay with that?"

"They were a little worried at first, you know, but we pitched in to help her out until she got it figured out. She's a great mom."

"You seem very proud of her."

"I am. I admire her."

Their lunch came and they ate in silence for a few minutes.

"I don't know anything about babies," Danielle blurted.

"Nobody does until they have one."

"No. I mean I know zero. I never babysat. No nieces or nephews." She drew a horizontal line with her hand. "Nothing."

"You can take a class or read online." He sipped his soda. Then jumped in with both feet. "Or I can teach you."

She was silent for a few minutes. He didn't know what to expect. "Okay."

He smiled. That meant she was willing to consider having him around after the baby was born.

He took her hand again. "I want to be there for you Danielle."

"Why? Why would want to be there for me when I'm carrying another man's baby?" She lowered her voice to a whisper and gripped his hand.

"Am I the only one feeling a connection here?"

Her lips turned up into a slow smile. "No." Her voice was soft, and her eyes conveyed more than she could know.

"Good." He pulled back and pushed his plate away. "Take a deep breath, Danielle. Everything is going to work out." Even as he said the words, he knew they were for him.

He was going down a path he'd only been down once before. A path he had sworn he would never go down again. Last time, with Jessica, he'd had it all planned out. This time, he was taking it day by day.

He'd just committed to be there for Danielle when he was going to be in Dallas.

He was going to be doing a lot of flying.

Danielle picked at her food. Her mind was going nine million miles an hour.

A baby.

Before last Friday, the whole idea of having a baby was so far off her radar, that world didn't even exist.

Now, in just the span of one week, she'd gone from a girl on a dating moratorium to a pregnant girl with a guy who wanted to connect with her. A guy whose kiss she couldn't get out of her mind. And on top of all that, said guy was a pilot. And Danielle had sworn she would never ever get involved with a pilot. Again.

Yet here he was. The man of her fantasy world sitting in front of her. Kind. Gentle. Attentive. Understanding.

A pilot.

Fate had a sense of humor.

She would never have an abortion. The idea of a life growing inside of her was the strangest and most wonderful feeling she'd ever had. Even if Joey was the sperm donor.

And that, she vowed, was how she was going to think of him from now on.

Samuel had said she needed to tell him about the baby. As far as she was concerned, he'd lost that right when he'd cheated on her.

The baby was hers. And she wasn't going to share it with anyone else.

Well… maybe Samuel.

Samuel left Danielle at her office with a promise to go to her apartment after work. It would be the first time he'd been inside, and in the evening too. Progress.

It turned out Danielle's mother wasn't the only person coming into town that week.

After he dropped Danielle off at her office, he was headed out to do some errands when he got a text from his boss.

Do you have time to meet in about an hour?

Samuel laughed. When Noah put someone on the payroll, he really expected them to be available.

He sent back a quick answer in the affirmative. A couple of quick texts, and they agreed on a place to meet not far from where Samuel was now.

He ordered a coffee and took a seat in the back of the Starbucks to wait for Noah. Noah was no doubt here to see his daughter and would see her later. A man like Noah would certainly not fly from Dallas to Houston, then drive an hour to meet with an employee who was on the payroll but not yet doing much other than check in on his daughter "now and then." Unless Danielle had told him, he wouldn't know that "now and then" was much more.

And if Samuel had his way, that much more would continue to grow. The problem was going to be all about location. Samuel was falling hard and fast for Danielle, and he wasn't about to let logistics get in his way.

Samuel recognized Noah the minute he walked into the door. Noah Worthington wore success like others wore an old t-shirt. He wore it confidently and barely seemed to notice it was there. Samuel stood up. Noah waved, ordered a coffee, then sat across from Samuel.

Noah was a busy man and didn't mince words. Apparently there were two things he was interested in. "Will you be moved and ready to go to work next Monday?"

Samuel nodded. "I plan to drive up Saturday." He was really thinking Sunday, but he didn't want to sound like he was breezing into town at the last minute for his new job.

Noah waved him off. "I'll send someone down to fly you up."

"My truck…"

"I'll take care of it."

"Alright," Samuel said. So much for his plan to slide into Dallas Sunday. One less day to spend with Danielle.

As though he read his mind, Noah asked his next question. "How's my daughter?"

She's going to have a baby. I think I love her. "She's good."

"You said you were driving her to an appointment last week."

"And I did."

Noah sat back and seemed to relax. "She needs to move New York where driving isn't required."

"Why won't she drive?"

"I don't even know if she knows. She just never had any interest in it. It's almost un-American."

"It's very unusual." Samuel agreed.

"You've been driving her around a lot?"

Samuel nodded.

"And after this week, you won't be here."

Samuel wasn't sure how to respond. Noah stated exactly what Samuel had been wondering. Also, Noah had no idea how much more she was going to need him as her pregnancy progressed. Surely, Danielle would tell him soon. It was a difficult secret to keep, especially with Noah's pointed questions.

"I'll have to think about that," Noah sipped his coffee and after his phone chimed, sent a quick text. "My wife, Savannah."

Samuel smiled. Danielle had spoken fondly of Savannah. Apparently, Savannah was the one person, other than Danielle, that Noah would walk on water for.

"Are you seeing Danielle today?" This conversation would be so much easier if Noah already knew Danielle's circumstance. "I saw her at lunch, and she didn't mention it."

Noah smiled sheepishly. "I had some time, so I thought I'd pop in and surprise her."

"Ah." Noah couldn't have picked a worse day to pop in unannounced. Unless… it was possible that they were close, and she could use the support. Maybe it would be good for her to go ahead and tell Noah.

Not my business.

"I'm gonna go ahead and line you up with some flights for next week."

"Sounds good."

"See you Monday morning. I'll email your itinerary for the week." Noah stood up. Held out his hand.

The two men shook hands, and Noah looked him in the eye. "Don't let me down."

Twenty-Eight

Danielle tinkered with the cover on her computer, but her heart wasn't in it. She changed the font color. Again.

She was going to have a baby. With Jo... with a sperm donor. Joey wasn't bad-looking, and was smart enough. He didn't read a lot, but he was quick with math. If he'd gone to college, he could have gotten a degree in engineering easily.

And she knew his parents. They were good people. No diseases as far as she knew. So decent genes on his side.

She sighed. If only she carried Samuel's child. They would have beautiful children.

She fiddled with the placement of the author's name, her mind racing with about a million things. She would prefer to tell her father first, but since she needed to do it in person, it looked like her mother was up first.

Maybe she should move back to L.A. to be near her mother. But she had a nice apartment here and a job that she liked. She was left alone to be creative in her own space. Some of the more seasoned cover artists worked from home, so maybe she could do that after the baby came.

She would have to get baby furniture. She needed to look into classes to learn about caring for an infant, much less a child.

Samuel would know. Samuel had nieces and nephews. He knew how to take care of a baby, and he'd offered to help out. But Samuel was going to be in Dallas. Her father lived in Alabama and ran a business based in Fort Worth. Somehow, he managed it, but he mostly supervised the other pilots now. He only did a few contract flights himself. Most of his flying was between Auburn and Fort Worth, and L.A. to see her, until she'd moved. He hadn't been to see her since she moved to Houston. In fact, she had been a little nervous about telling him that she had moved here, much less followed Joey here, but now there was so much more to tell him.

She missed her father terribly.

She could drive up with Samuel this weekend and fly back. She checked the calendar. She'd have to ask off for Monday.

Her head jerked up at three knocks on her door. After Joey showed up unannounced, she was wary of anyone coming to her door unannounced.

Noah stood leaning against the door jamb watching her. "Daddy!" She cried and ran to throw herself in his arms.

Hugged close and safe to her father, she started to cry.

"Hey," Noah said, rubbing her back. "What's this?"

Her breath hitched. "I just haven't seen you in so long. It seems like… so much has happened."

"Besides breaking up with Joey? Has Samuel been helping you out?"

"Samuel. Yes." She wiped at her eyes. "Wait. You knew about Joey?"

"Of course I knew about it."

Danielle sighed. "I was so worried about telling you."

He took her chin in his hand. "Danielle, don't ever be afraid to tell me anything. You know that right? After all we've been through?"

"Of course, Daddy." All those months of counseling. "It's just. It was such a big move. To come here to be with Joey, and it didn't last."

"Speaking of-- Can you leave? Can we get out of here? I'd like to see your apartment."

She snagged a Kleenex from her desk and wiped at her eyes. "Sure. Do you have a car?"

Noah laughed. "Of course I have a car."

Danielle gathered up her things and together they went downstairs, and he followed her directions to her apartment.

"This looks like a nice area." Noah commented as he pulled into her apartment complex.

"I like it." She bit her lip. She did like her apartment and had just gotten moved in and gotten it set up just the way she liked it. She was proud of her apartment and was comfortable here. No. She decided right then. She would stay here. She could raise her baby here.

Once inside, Noah walked around and stuck his head in each of her three bedrooms. Checked out her huge walk-in closet, and came back to the living area. "Nice," he said. "Now come here and tell me what's bothering you."

He sat on the sofa and patted the seat next to him. She sat next to him and took deep calming breaths. Daddy had been through intense therapy with her. She could tell him anything. Right?

"Daddy."

Noah rubbed her back. "You can tell me anything, Princess."

She looked up and stared into her father's loving eyes. Her breath hitched out. "I'm pregnant."

She watched as a range of emotions washed over his face in a matter of seconds. Then he pulled her to him and hugged her again. "It's okay, baby."

"I'm so sorry to disappoint you." She breathed against his chest.

"You could never disappoint me. Never. No matter what you ever do."

She wiped at her eyes.

"Is it… Joey's?"

She rolled her eyes. "He's now referred to as 'the sperm donor'."

"Got it. How do you feel?"

"Better today. I've had morning sickness all day long, every day."

"How did you stand it?"

"Samuel brought me crackers." She laughed. "Oddly enough, it really helped."

"Samuel's been taking care of you."

"I really like him."

"Like him, like him?"

She smiled. "Yeah. I do."

Noah rubbed his eyes with his palms. "That explains it."

"Explains what?"

He looked at her. "I saw Samuel earlier today."

"When? Why?"

"I'm paying him, remember?" Noah had a lopsided grin on his face.

"Right. And you're taking him away. To Dallas."

"Fort Worth."

"Whatever."

Noah laughed. "Working in a different city doesn't mean it can't work. It's a lot harder though."

"I don't even know what we're going to do about it." She said as her phone chimed. "I forgot." She looked up at Noah. "He's supposed to be coming over tonight."

"Okay," Noah said, but she could see the disappointment in his face.

"I'll cancel with him. He's knows you're here, so he'll understand."

"Savannah keeps telling me I need to stop showing up places unannounced."

"It's okay, Daddy. It's who you are."

He grinned. "You, on the other hand, take after your mother in all the good ways."

"You mean, I call before I show up?"

"It's a good quality to have."

"What do you think Mom's gonna think? About the baby?"

Noah shook his head. "I don't know. She's a lot different now that she's with Grayson."

"She's coming here in two days."

"That doesn't give you much time with Samuel, does it? Between the two of us."

"It's okay. I'm supposed to be in a dating moratorium anyway."

"Who said that?"

"It's self-imposed."

Noah stood up and paced to the window where she had a nice view of the pool. "Want some fatherly advice?"

"Always."

"I don't know Samuel very well, but he seems like a nice guy. His background checked out." He looked at her sheepishly. "I like him well enough to hire him. If you like him, you shouldn't let what happened with J…"

"Sperm donor."

"Right. You shouldn't let what happened with 'sperm donor' affect the possibility of a relationship with Samuel."

"That's kind of what I've been telling myself." She got up and went toward the kitchen. "Do you want anything?"

"Just some water." He glanced at his watch. "You know what? If I leave right now, I can make it home in time to have dinner with Savannah."

She handed him the water bottle. "She'd like that."

"But, if it's okay with you, I'd like to come back next week, when Samuel is working, and spend the night. We can talk about what all we need to do to prepare for the baby." A stunned look appeared on his face. "I'm going to be a *grandfather*."

Danielle laughed. "You never thought you'd see the day, did you?

"No. Now I really need to talk to Savannah. She can talk me down off the cliff."

"Daddy, it's okay. You'll be the youngest and coolest grand-father ever."

"I love you, little one."

"I love you too, Daddy. I'm so glad you came by."

After Noah left, Danielle sent a text back to Samuel. *Daddy left already. You can still come at seven.*

That gave her three hours to take a long hot bath and figure out something to cook.

Twenty~Nine

Samuel stood at the flower shop in Kroger and shifted from one foot to the other. He hadn't come to buy flowers. He stopped in to get deodorant, but the flowers had gotten his attention.

He hadn't had a date since Jessica. The only flower he ever took Jessica was actually a plant, an ivy. She didn't like girly things, and Samuel had picked up pretty quickly that she wouldn't appreciate a flower that would last no more than a few days.

Danielle, however, was the complete opposite. In fact, he thought wryly, he could almost go with the exact opposite of anything he'd done with Jessica.

Roses seemed too formal. This wasn't a formal date. It was just a couple of friends getting together. Friends who were moving toward something else, but weren't quite there yet. It would be nice to have a playbook – a place where he could look up the appropriate thing at each stage in a relationship. It would be especially helpful if there was a section on *what to do if your girlfriend is already pregnant.*

He looked at every flower in the shop. Then he went back to the one that had gotten his attention when he was just walking by. It was a little bouquet of white daisies. It looked fresh and happy. Simple and uncomplicated.

Making a decision, he took it to the woman behind the desk and asked her to wrap it up for him.

He left Kroger happily with deodorant and flowers, heading home for a quick shower before he went to Danielle's apartment.

As he was heading to what he referred to as his apartment behind the house, his mother came out the back door and stood on the deck. "Samuel."

He stopped. Busted.

"Is there something you haven't told us?" His mother asked, gesturing toward the flowers.

"They're for a... friend."

"A girl?"

He rolled his eyes. "Really Mom. I wouldn't take flowers to a guy."

"Well, that's just convenient, isn't it? Since you're leaving Sunday."

He sighed. He might as well get the bad news over with. "It got moved to Saturday."

"Then I guess I'll have to ask everyone to come over Friday instead of Saturday."

"Mom, please. Don't invite everyone, wait until the next weekend. I'll come back, and I'll have something to talk about."

"Too late."

"I wanted to just have a nice quiet evening at home."

"You have to bring her."

He was already shaking his head. "I can't do that. I actually like this girl."

"I kinda thought you did, since this is the first girl I've known you to show any interest in since… in quite a long time."

Samuel sighed. His family was still tiptoeing around talking about Jessica's death. Maybe it was time to give them someone else to talk about. "Okay, Mom. I'll make you a deal."

"What deal is that?"

"Leave off the party this weekend, and I'll bring her by to meet everyone the first weekend I'm back in town."

Minutes later, with the hot water running over his head, Samuel found his thoughts again consumed by Danielle. He replayed that kiss again in his head. He'd played it a hundred times in last two days. He wanted more.

It was time to move their relationship from the friend zone and to build upon the foundation they'd established with that kiss from heaven.

CHAPTER
Thirty

It felt a little strange having Samuel there in her apartment.

The white daisies, she'd put in a vase in the center of the dining room table; they brightened the whole room. He'd brought her the perfect flowers. She smiled as she put on an oven mitt and slipped the lasagna back into the oven. It was just one of many hot dishes her mother had taught her to throw together in a few minutes. She'd put it together and left it covered in the refrigerator until she made sure Samuel was planning to eat with her.

She looked across the counter, past the dining room table, to the living room, where she'd left Samuel with her laptop.

He'd asked to look at some of the covers she'd created, so she'd opened a file for him to look at while she checked the lasagna in the oven.

Every nerve was on edge having him here in her apartment. They hadn't called it a date, but it sure felt like one.

As she watched, he set the computer on her coffee table and walked toward her to the kitchen. She smiled and turned.

"Tomorrow, I get to cook."

"Tomorrow?"

"I have to leave Saturday." He stepped closer until he was close enough to touch her. "And I want to see you every day."

"Is that so?" She asked.

"And every night."

She backed up until she bumped against the counter. He placed his hands on each side of her, pinning her in front of him.

Her breath hitched at the intensity of his gaze. She'd seen that look in the photos they'd taken when he was about to kiss her. She hadn't seen it then because her eyes had been closed.

She had dated a lot of guys, but she couldn't remember any of them ever looking at her quite like this.

Without touching anywhere else, he placed his lips against hers, ever so lightly. Then he leaned back enough to smile into her eyes.

Her heart flip-flopped, and she smiled back.

His grin turning devilish, he reached down, put an arm beneath her knees, and picked her up. She squeaked and threw her arms around his neck. He carried her as though she was light as a feather to the sofa. He sat down with her in his lap.

Her heart was racing ninety to nothing as he put his lips against the corner of her mouth and a hand behind her head to hold her close.

He tasted minty. She recognized the faint smell of his cologne. His lips sent tingles all through her, and she wanted his lips on hers.

She turned into the kiss and sighed when he pressed his lips against hers. This. This was what she'd been craving since that kiss two days ago. Only now, without anyone watching through a camera lens, it was even better than she'd remembered.

His fingers threaded through her hair as he moved his lips against hers. She never wanted to stop. Ever.

They kissed until the timer on the stove went off. He pulled back and ran a finger along her swollen lips.

It was almost perfect. If only she dated pilots.

CHAPTER
Thirty~One

They sat on the sofa and ate with their thighs and shoulders touching. Samuel didn't want to let go of her.

Though she wasn't physically pulling away, she hadn't made eye contact since they'd stopped kissing.

"Alright. What's wrong?" He asked.

She smiled. "It's just something I have to work out."

"Maybe I can help, since I have a feeling it involves me in some way."

"You won't like it."

"Maybe I can change it."

She laughed. "Okay, but don't say I didn't warn you."

"Duly warned."

"I don't date pilots."

"Me either," he said without a hitch.

She stared at him. Then took another bite of pasta. Then she chuckled. "You're a pilot."

"This is really good," he said as he filled his fork. "Don't think of me as a pilot."

"Okay… What should I think of you as?"

"Anything. Think of me as your yard boy."

She laughed. "Why would I need a yard boy? I live in an apartment."

"I'm sure you can think of something for me to do. As your yard boy, I can run errands. I'm really good at running errands. I even do returns."

"What about when you're off flying a plane?"

"Just a taxi driver. Not a pilot." He winked at her and nudged her shoulder with his. At least she was looking at him again.

"I'm serious." She insisted.

"So am I." He set his empty plate on the coffee table.

"Just because you don't call yourself a pilot, doesn't mean you aren't one."

"And just because I'm a pilot, doesn't mean you shouldn't date me."

She shot him a look of fake exasperation.

"What do you have against pilots anyway?" He tucked a strand of hair behind her ear.

"They're always away. Remember, I have first-hand experience as the daughter of a pilot."

"A famous pilot."

"I don't know about famous, but definitely successful."

"In the pilot world." He lifted one eyebrow. "He's a famous pilot. So besides being gone a lot, what else do you have against my breed?"

She pulled her feet under her and hugged a pillow to her. "Pilots aren't... monogamous."

"What? Really? Why am I just now learning about this?" He feigned shock.

She chuckled. "It's the stewardesses. They're like candy for y'all."

"Oh, well, you're doubly safe. They don't have stewardesses anymore, only flight attendants. And I don't eat candy."

"You don't eat candy. Ever?"

"Never."

"What about a brownie?"

He shook his head. "No sweets for me, unless I'm with you." He leaned back and put an arm across the back of the sofa. "So, if I'm a taxi driver by day and your yard boy by night, does that grant me exception status?"

"I'll have to think about it."

"What if I promise to send you flowers every day?"

"Now you're just teasing me."

"How about if I drive you around, and you never have to drive or take other transportation?"

"But you're not here, remember?"

"Oh right. Then when I'm here. And don't forget, I do errands."

"I'll have to get back to you. What else do you have to offer?"

"I can do foot rubs."

"Really? I might have to see if you're any good."

"Ah. I can offer a free sample right now. If you want."

"Sure. I never turn down a foot massage."

"Here." He held out his hand. She shifted her feet toward

him. He took her shoe off and put her foot across his knees. She leaned back against the pillows. He started with her toes and worked his way to the bottom of her feet to her ankles. She had adorable red toenails.

She closed her eyes, and he moved to the other foot.

He shifted to pull her toward him, holding her close. "I also offer unlimited heavenly kisses." He whispered against her ear before claiming her mouth again.

Thirty~Two

The next morning, Danielle managed to stay focused enough to get a draft of the cover she was working on ready to send to the author.

She held her breath as she emailed it. It had a completely different couple on it from what they agreed on. Danielle wasn't sure what she was going to do if the author asked for the original couple. It was a good thing she hadn't posted her picture on Facebook or the company website. She'd prefer that no one know that she was the girl on the cover.

She was watching the door more than she was watching her computer as she scrolled through a website looking at potential images to make a premade cover.

The minute he stepped off the elevator, she saw him. Her heart rate increased to dangerous levels, and she stared at her computer screen so he wouldn't know she was watching for him.

He pulled off his sunglasses and grinned at her. Her heart

melted. He hadn't shaved today, so he had a bit of a shadow on his face. She wanted to run her hands along his cheeks to see what it felt like.

Instead of sitting across from her like he usually did, he walked up to her and kissed her right on the lips. "Hi," he pulled a white rose from behind his back and handed it to her.

"Hi." She gazed at him, unable to think. She sniffed the rose and held it next to her cheek.

"What are you working on?" Apparently, he didn't have the same problem with his thought processes.

"Oh, I um… I finished the cover."

"Can I see?"

She opened the file and pulled the cover up on her screen.

He studied it with a ridiculous grin on his face. "We look good," he said. "And the cover is nicely done, too. I'm impressed."

"Thanks. I just hope the author likes it. This one's a little more personal."

"So the author won't know it's you?"

"I hope not."

"That's probably good. Avery was right. We look like we need to get a room."

Danielle laughed. She could see it, too. Then she gasped. "Oh no."

"What is it?"

"My colleagues are going to see it." She nodded toward her door leading to the other offices.

He seemed unconcerned. "They might want to hire us as models. It could open a whole new career for you."

She patted her stomach. "I think not."

"Right. Well, you won't be pregnant forever."

"Are you sure?" It seemed like it was all she could think about.

"Do you want the usual for lunch?"

"Do you mind terribly?"

He leaned over and kissed her lightly on the lips. "Your heart's desire is my command."

Taking her hand, he led her through the lobby. It was empty, but it felt like a public announcement that they were seeing each other.

"Did I tell you my mom is coming in tomorrow?"

"You mentioned it," Samuel held the elevator for her. "Did she say how long she'll be staying?"

"Not yet."

"How long does she usually stay?"

"I don't know. She's never visited."

"Really? Never?"

"I lived at home until I moved here."

"Ah." He held the elevator door open when it stopped on the first floor.

"What about you? Where do you live?"

"Similar, I guess. My parents have what I guess you'd call a pool house behind their house. I live in it. It's a little two-room place, but I have privacy. Until now, I was rarely home anyway."

"Right. The whole taxi driver thing."

He grinned and helped her into the truck. "You're a fast learner."

He walked around the truck and got in the driver's seat. "So… do I get to meet her?"

"You want to meet my mom?"

"Why wouldn't I?"

She shrugged.

"Too soon?" He put on his blinker and made a U-turn to get into the Pappa's parking lot.

Danielle laughed. "Maybe."

"Are you going to tell her about the baby?"

"I told my dad, so, yeah, I need to get that over with, too." She bit her lip as she said the words and looked down.

"Want me to be there with you?"

"She might get confused."

"Really? I thought your mom was a successful business owner."

Danielle laughed. "She is. Okay, I might get confused. Or distracted."

He took her hand as they walked into the restaurant. The guy at the counter already knew what they were going to order.

It was crowded today, so they sat across from each other at a small booth for two.

He held out his hand, and she put hers in his.

"You haven't told me anything about your dating history." A shadow crossed his features and wiped away his smile. She immediately wished she could take back the words. "You don't have to talk about it."

"No. It's okay. I'll tell you. It's just not a good story."

"I'm not looking for a good story. I just want to know about you. After all, you kinda know about me." He definitely knew what she'd done with her previous boyfriend.

Samuel smiled again. "You don't have to tell me." His expression growing serious, he took a deep breath and lifted his chin. "Six years ago I met a girl – Jessica. We started dating and got engaged after about two years. Right after that, she was deployed to Afghanistan. She actually did one tour, came home, and had just started her second when she was killed."

Danielle gasped. "Oh no!"

"Yeah. That was two years ago. I haven't dated anyone since."

"I don't know what to say."

He shook his head. "There's nothing to say. She was my only serious girlfriend. So… I don't date. Until you."

Danielle gazed into his eyes and squeezed his hand. This man who hadn't put himself out there until her. It made it all the more special that he liked her.

"I've gone on lots of dates," she told him, lowering her voice. "But I only slept with two. Scout's honor." She raised her hand and made the Vulcan "V" with her fingers.

He laughed, as was her intent.

"I'm not worried about your past. As far as I'm concerned, we're starting with a clean slate."

"I like that."

Maybe it was time she began thinking of him as a boyfriend.

Thirty-Three

Samuel hadn't wanted to tell Danielle about Jessica. He'd wanted to start fresh without bringing that cloud along with him, but it hadn't seemed fair to keep it from her. She needed to know that he could do long-term relationships, and he didn't trifle with girls. Even when he was traveling.

She had been right about pilots, at least some of them. Samuel had heard stories and he'd seen things with his own eyes. Otherwise good men, even some married ones, going home with flight attendants for one-night-stands or even having long-term affairs.

But he didn't do that. Still, it would be a hard thing to prove. Traveling so much made trust difficult to establish and maintain.

He knew firsthand from both sides. When Jessica was in Afghanistan with the male soldiers, it had been difficult. They'd gotten through it by constantly staying in touch with daily phone calls and emails.

He had some time to kill after an appointment out toward

Katy, so he stopped back by the Memorial City Mall and walked aimlessly waiting for the time to pass until he could see Danielle again. He wanted to get her something for the baby. He wanted to be the first person to give her a gift. Had she even thought about decorating the baby's room yet?

She'd had so much to process in such a short time, it probably hadn't even occurred to her yet. A baby gift would open the door to allow him to offer to help her decorate.

He hoped she would find out ahead of time whether it was a boy or a girl. His older sister had waited to find out, and the whole nursery had been decorated in yellow and green. His younger sister had learned from that and was able to do the room in pink beforehand—a much better choice in Samuel's opinion. Practicality was totally underrated.

He wandered around a bit until he came to a Build-A-Bear shop. He had gotten one for each of his nieces and nephews. Perfect.

He spent the next hour shopping among the store full of mothers and children picking out the perfect teddy bear and outfit for it.

After choosing a dark gray bear, he looked around at outfits until he found a pilot's uniform. Grinning, he picked it up and took it with him. On the way to get the bear stuffed, he passed accessories and snagged a little stuffed camera.

"Do you want to pick a sound?" The girl, not a day over eighteen, asked.

"Sound?"

"We have sounds now. You can pick out whichever one you like." She explained how the kiosk worked and played some of the different sounds for him.

"Can I add one later?"

"Of course."

Next, he had to insert a heart into the back of the bear. Following the lead of a six-year-old, he kissed the little heart and tucked it carefully into the bear's stuffing.

Finally, it was time to create a birth certificate and name the bear. "Cute." The girl commented as she checked him out and tucked the bear into a little box. "Enjoy!"

He was left with just enough time to take a quick shower, stop by the market, and head over to Danielle's.

When she answered the door, she looked different. She was wearing a dark blue sheath dress with navy ankle boots. Besides being dressed up, she looked different.

"Whoa. What's the occasion?"

"Nothing," She tossed her very straight hair.

"Did I forget something?"

"No." She smiled. "I just stopped by the Dry Bar for a blow out."

He followed her inside and she closed the door. "A blow… what?" His mind went down a path he couldn't even follow.

"I had my hair blow-dried."

He reached out to touch a soft strand of hair that lay against her shoulder. "It looks great." He followed her into the kitchen and set down his bags. "You're dressed up."

"Yeah." She ran a hand down her dress. A dress that accented her tiny waist – she wasn't showing yet. "Pretty soon I won't be able to wear these clothes anymore. At least not for a while, so I thought I'd just wear them."

"I thought I'd missed something."

She grinned. "What did you bring?" She peaked in a bag.

"Kale vegetable salad. Since you're eating for two, I thought we'd try Tuesday healthy night."

"That's a great idea." She said.

Except that now that he'd said it out loud, he realized that it was a terrible idea, because next Tuesday he wouldn't be here. Or any Tuesday after that.

Damn. This was not working out like he wanted it to.

He would have to make the most of what he had. "I brought you something." He kept his voice light, despite his sudden despondent mood. "It's for you, but also for the baby."

He brought out the box with the bear and handed it to her.

"Oh! A baby gift. What is it?"

"Open it."

She took it over to the dining room table and examined the air holes in the box. "Is it a kitten?"

He shrugged, and mentally filed away the idea that she might like a kitten.

She opened the box and pulled out the traditional bear that he'd chosen for her. "A teddy bear." Her face exploded into a smile.

"I wanted to be the first person to give the baby a gift." He reached into the box and took out a certificate. "I made it myself and dressed it in the little pilot uniform. And look; it has a camera. And I gave it a name."

She looked at the paper. "You named it Pappa."

"Yeah. For Pappa's Burgers."

Her eyes grew moist.

"What's wrong?" He drew her close and wrapped his arms around her and the bear. "You don't like bears?"

"Nobody ever made a bear for me."

"Oh honey. It's going to be okay."

She pulled back and wiped a tear from her cheek. "It's like a combination of both of us."

He smiled. "I know."

She ran her hand along the bear's fur. "I apologize. I'm not normally this emotional."

"It's to be expected. You have a lot going on. I brought you this too." He reached inside the box and pulled out a baby name book and a yellow highlighter.

"A name. Oh. My. I forgot I had to name it. There's so much to think about."

He chuckled. "That's why I'm here." He took her hand and led her to the sofa. "You sit here. Put your feet up, and spend some time with this book while I make dinner."

Tomorrow, he would pick up a copy of *What to Expect When You're Expecting*.

The more time he spent with her, the more he knew that he needed to be here with her. Not in Dallas. Not flying people around the country.

What kind of spell had she cast over him to make him want to stay on the ground and out of the sky?

Thirty-Four

The next morning, Danielle put on some leggings and a sweater dress. Her mother was coming in sometime that afternoon, so she wanted to be presentable. She also liked the reaction she got from Samuel when she'd dressed up.

They'd had a surprisingly good kale salad with lots of different vegetables, then sat talking on the sofa for a while, looking at some of the names she'd highlighted. They'd ended up kissing until midnight. Samuel declared that he would not be responsible for her turning into a pumpkin.

"Cinderella doesn't turn into a pumpkin."

"Well, something does, and I won't be responsible."

She walked him to the door in her bare feet, then kept his lips on hers for another twenty minutes before she told him to get out so she could get some sleep.

As a result, she was a little tired today. Her mother was planning to only stay one night, so Samuel was going to be on standby, but the plan was for them to skip tonight.

That meant they only had three more evenings together. She thought several times about calling and asking her mother to wait until next week to visit, but her mother wouldn't show up without a good reason.

She took an Uber to work as always and was absorbed in her work when Samuel showed up at her door.

"Is it noon already?"

"I'm early. I wanted to give you this." He handed her a book about being pregnant.

"I never even thought about getting a book. I seriously don't know what I'm going to do without you."

He hadn't answered her, but instead had helped her into her coat. "My younger sister has a copy with highlights and color-coded tabs."

"I am not that organized."

"Creative people usually aren't." They headed toward the elevator. "The usual?"

"You know what? About that-- I was thinking maybe we could have Mexican instead."

His face lit up. "I know just the place."

Relief washed over her. She'd been reluctant to change their lunch spot since he'd gone to the trouble to get her a teddy bear and even named it Pappa. Technically, she supposed he'd gotten it for the baby. But still…

When they were seated at the restaurant, she asked something she'd been curious about. "So technically, you're working for my father right now?"

"Yeah. He's paying me for two weeks to pack and relocate."

"But are you? Relocating?"

"No. I'm keeping my house, and I've rented an Air BNB in Dallas for the next two weeks. So it'll be like staying in a hotel."

"So what do you do all day?"

"I spend a lot of time with you."

She smiled. "Other than that."

"I actually am packing and doing errands. One of my specialties, if you recall."

She nodded.

"And I've met with two people about an airplane."

"An airplane? What do you mean?"

"I'm looking into buying a small airplane."

"Wow. You haven't mentioned that."

"Yeah. I haven't decided for sure that I'm going to do it. It's a big investment. I'm not even sure that I'll have time to use it after I go to work for your father. It's my understanding that he keeps his pilots flying four to five days a week."

"Huh." There were so many implications in what he had just said that she needed to process everything."

"I wouldn't be able to buy it outright." He clarified. "I'd have to borrow most of the money, so I've met with a couple of banks, too."

"You've been busy."

"Yeah. I'm not fond of driving. I mean I don't mind driving around Houston at all. But I really try to avoid driving long distances. And with my family here, I'd like to be able to get here quickly and often. It's something I've been thinking about since I took the job with your dad. Then this week, I really started to take some steps to make it happen."

"Since it's getting closer to time for you to leave."

"Yeah. That and you."

Me. Did that mean he wanted to be able to continue to spend time with her? There was a big difference in driving from Fort Worth and flying.

Of course, after he rented a car and drove from the airport, the time would probably just about equal out.

Danielle received a message on her phone. "I think it's the author."

"She's just now responding?"

"I think she's had the flu or something." She read the message, then passed her phone over for Samuel to read it.

"She loves it." Danielle nearly bounced in her chair.

"She said she's never seen such chemistry portrayed on a cover."

"She likes it."

"We should celebrate," Samuel said. "How about a strawberry lemonade?"

Danielle laughed with a burst of happiness. She had a happy customer and a handsome boyfriend who celebrated with her by buying her lemonades at lunch.

She'd always heard that it was the little things that make people happy.

CHAPTER
Thirty~Five

Claire Beauchamp Worthington Moore arrived at Danielle's apartment in a limo. She stepped out wearing a black sheath dress with a short black jacket and black pumps with red bottoms.

Danielle watched from the window as her mother waited for the limo driver to unload her luggage. She took out her phone, and Danielle's rang.

"Hi Mom."

"Where are you?"

"I'll be right there." Danielle smiled and went out her door and hugged her mom.

Claire pushed back and, putting her hands on the sides of Danielle's face, examined her daughter. "You look good."

"Thanks. So do you. Come on in."

Claire motioned for the limo driver to bring her luggage, and they followed Danielle into her apartment.

Much as her father had done, Claire walked through the apartment and gave her nod of approval. "Nice place."

"Thanks. I like it here."

"Do you want to get dinner?"

"Sure." Danielle opened her phone. "We'll have to get a taxi." Her mother didn't use Uber.

"The limo driver is waiting. Do you know a good place?"

"There's a nice Italian place nearby."

She climbed into the limo and sat next to her mother. "How long do you have the limo?" Danielle asked.

"Just tonight. It's a long way down here from the airport."

Half an hour later, when they were seated at a table, Claire ordered a club soda instead of her usual red wine.

Following her mother's lead, Danielle ordered the same.

Claire was quiet, but she fidgeted with her napkin, her fork, and finally leaned forward. "I have to tell you something."

"I have something to tell you, too."

"Okay."

"You first," Danielle said. Her mother looked like she was about to burst.

"Okay I'll go first. Danielle, I'm pregnant."

Danielle stared at her mother, who was obviously ecstatic. "Wow."

"I know. Grayson and I are so excited. I wanted to come and tell you in person."

"How far along are you?"

"About seven weeks."

Close to where Danielle was. Surely this was not happening. "I don't know what to say."

"I know it's unexpected."

"I'm happy for you." Danielle hoped she sounded happier than she felt.

"What did you want to tell me?"

Danielle couldn't do it. She couldn't tell her. She couldn't risk taking that ecstatic grin off her mother's face by shocking her mother. Claire, after all, was happily married.

"I have a new boyfriend." She blurted.

Thirty~Six

"How did it go with your mom?" Samuel stretched out his legs across from Danielle's desk. He'd brought them coffee from Starbucks – hers a caffeine-free latte. It was early, not even nine o'clock, but he'd missed seeing her last night.

"Interesting." She put her elbows on the desk, her brow furrowed.

"Somehow, I have a feeling she didn't take it so well."

Danielle bit her lip. "I didn't tell her."

"Oh. What happened?"

Danielle looked at him for about a minute, then looked down. "She had something to tell me as well."

"It must have been something important."

She took a deep breath and looked back at him. "She's pregnant."

Samuel didn't say anything. He was too stunned.

"I had the same reaction," Danielle said.

"That's got to be… um… kinda weird."

"It's so weird, I can't begin to wrap my head around this."

Samuel laughed. He couldn't help it. "It's not funny."

But then Danielle was laughing with him. "How am I going to tell her?"

Samuel sobered. "We'll fly out and tell her."

"We?"

"Yeah. I'll have my new plane by the end of the week."

"You got it?" She jumped up and ran around to kiss him on the lips. "That is so exciting."

"Exciting and scary all at once."

"I'm so happy for you."

"Do you want to see pictures?"

"Of course." She sat down next to him, and he scrolled through pictures on his phone of the little plane he'd just bought. It had a single black stripe down the tail.

"When are you going to take me up?" She asked.

"Well, it won't be this weekend, but if everything goes as planned, how about the next weekend?"

"Sounds perfect."

He was going to ask her to meet his family that weekend, too, but he wasn't quite ready to broach the subject. They only had two more evenings together, and he didn't want to overwhelm her.

"Do you still want Mexican food?" He asked. "Or are you craving seafood again?"

"Mexican sounds great."

As they sat together on a bench waiting for a table, Samuel reached over and took her hand. He didn't want to leave. He didn't want to leave Houston anyway – his home and family – but he especially didn't want to leave Danielle.

Though it was just under two weeks instead of two years, it was like Jessica all over again. Only this time, he was the one going away. At least he wasn't going to war, and he could come back any time he wanted to.

Danielle reached up and ran a finger between his eyes. "Such deep thoughts."

He turned and looked into her green eyes. "I don't want to leave you."

"But it's exciting to be starting a new job."

He shook his head. "I don't care about the job. I mean, I'm honored to be working with your father, but I'd rather be with you."

She smiled, and he kissed her.

"Since you're not sick any more, do you want to get out and do something tonight? Maybe see a movie?"

Thirty-Seven

"I have feeling that's the last time I go out to a movie." Danielle settled on the sofa with Samuel, pulling a blanket over them as he handed her a mug of hot chocolate.

"Why would you say that?" He sipped on his own steaming hot chocolate.

"I had to get up way too many times and go to the restroom." She counted four times. "At least with a movie at home, we can pause it."

He laughed. "Alright. But after the baby comes, you should be good."

"Ha. I think I'll be staying home taking care of said baby for a very long time."

"I don't know." He looked at her sideways. "Aunts and uncles make great built-in babysitters."

"Ah. But I don't have any siblings. Yet. And my one half-sibling is going to be my baby's age, so no babysitters there."

"I, on the other hand, have three."

Danielle lifted an eyebrow. "And that helps me how?" She knew it was a leading question, but she couldn't help herself. Besides, he was the one who brought it up.

"Well, when we want to have a night out, we'll have a babysitter."

"Maybe." Danielle shrugged, but her heart was racing. He was talking many months from now. Was he talking about a long-term commitment?

"Alright." His voice sounded a bit challenging. "Come with me a week from Sunday to lunch. You'll get to meet my whole family, and you'll see that they're babysitter-worthy."

"You want me to meet your family?"

"Lunch is at Pappa's." He added with a grin.

"Well, why didn't you say so?" She picked up the teddy bear that she kept on the sofa. She would never, ever tell him that she had been taking it to bed with her.

"Did I pick out the perfect name for him or what?" Samuel asked, tipping her chin up with a finger to kiss her on the lips.

"Of course you did," she said, handing him her mug to set down. Right now, the only thing sweet she wanted was kissing.

"And speaking of being here." Samuel set their mugs on the coffee table. "I get my plane tomorrow."

"Oh wow. Exciting! Do I get to go see it?"

"You want to?"

"Of course I do."

He wrapped his arms around her and pulled her against him. He kissed her forehead, her eyelids, her cheeks, then finally her lips. By the time his tongue lightly touched the roof of her mouth, she was no longer worried about movies or meeting his family or anything else.

Thirty-Eight

Samuel should have been over the moon excited about getting his plane. It was used, of course, but it was a sleek little Mooney single-engine airplane. They didn't make them like this anymore. The previous owner had painted a black stripe along the tail. Samuel didn't mind. It made it distinctive.

He'd thought about bringing Danielle with him up to see it, but decided he would wait until he came back next week. This was their last evening together, and he wanted it to be special.

He'd made reservations at Masraff's on Post Oak Boulevard, and he'd sent a text asking if she had a formal dress. He'd laughed at her response.

Of course I do. Unfortunately, they're all in LA. Are you giving me an excuse to go shopping?

He written back. *Absolutely!*

How formal?

Black tie.

I'm intrigued.

See you at seven… after lunch.

LOL.

He'd shown her pictures of his plane at their new lunch spot – the Mexican restaurant – and she'd told him about her new client.

He was going to miss their daily lunch date.

As he drove back toward the city, he wondered what Danielle was doing. She'd said she was going to take the afternoon off and go shopping at the Galleria.

His fingers itched to text her. To see if she was safe. He would have gone with her if he hadn't needed the plane for tomorrow. Noah had taken it in stride that he'd be flying himself up.

Leaving her here, pregnant, was going to be difficult. What if something went wrong, and she needed him? What if he was in the air, and she couldn't reach him?

For the hundredth time, he wished he hadn't taken this job. But, damn, it was too good to turn down.

It occurred to him then that Noah didn't know they were in a serious relationship. Danielle had asked him to wait until he'd been working there a bit to tell him. She'd told her mother she had a new boyfriend, but hadn't said he was a pilot, much less Noah's newest employee.

It was going to be difficult. Samuel wanted to tell everyone. Besides, if Noah knew, it might afford him some leeway to visit his daughter. Samuel wasn't above using whatever avenues presented themselves to see her.

Getting the plane had taken longer than he'd expected. He had lots to do in less than three hours.

Thirty-Nine

Danielle sprayed some perfume in the air and walked through it. She'd gone with classic black. She already had black pumps to go with the dress she'd gotten. The strapless dress fell straight to the floor in a sleek, modern look. Pressing her hand against her stomach, she could feel just a little baby bump. But looking in the mirror, she couldn't see it. She shook her head. It was much too soon. It had to be her imagination.

Nonetheless, a little blip of excitement shot through her, and she couldn't wait to see if Samuel could feel it.

The dress was probably not one of the wisest purchases she'd made. She probably wouldn't wear it but once, and then all bets were off whether or not she would be able to wear it post-baby.

She'd had her hair styled at the Dry Bar. She blamed Savannah, her stepmother for getting her hooked on that luxury. Her sleek hair cascaded around her shoulders. Tonight was the last night she would see Samuel for a whole week.

He wanted it to be special, and she wanted to look her best. At a quarter to seven, she went into her living room and sorted through her mail, cleared off her coffee table, leaving just the baby name book, and paced back to the bedroom. She decided at the last minute to wear her diamond pendant. A gift from her father on her college graduation, it had five small round diamonds sprinkled along a platinum chain.

As she took one last look in the mirror, her doorbell rang. By the time she got to the door on the other end of the apartment, she was a little breathless. She opened the door, and Samuel stood there in a black tux, holding a single red rose.

She stood there a moment, her hand on the doorknob, taking in his handsome smile and letting the warm emotions flow throw her.

"Wow," he said. "You look absolutely stunning."

"You clean up pretty nice yourself." She stepped back, opening the door wide, matching his smile with her own.

He held out the rose, and she took it from him to put in a vase. Before setting it on the counter, she inhaled deeply and ran her fingers along the soft petals. She sighed.

Stay in the moment. He's still here.

She turned brightly and took his hand. "Ready?"

He brought her hand to his lips and kissed her knuckles.

It only took a few minutes to get to Masraff's. "Have you been here?" He asked.

"No." She said as they pulled into the parking lot. Samuel gave the keys to the valet, then came around, helped her out of the truck, and took her hand as they crossed the parking lot.

They were a few minutes early, so they went into the bar and sat near the fireplace. Samuel ordered sparkling water and held up his glass. "To us."

"To us," she repeated as their glasses met in a toast. *Us.* She would have to think about that later.

"It'll be Thanksgiving in a couple of weeks," Samuel said.

"I know. Then Christmas already. Savannah, Noah's wife, is graduating with her doctorate in a few weeks, so I'll be travelling to Auburn."

"And we have to fly out to see your mother."

"Are we taking your plane?"

He shook his head. "It's too small. I'll probably see if I can use one of your dad's."

Danielle studied the flames in the fireplace. Their lives were quickly becoming enmeshed. She'd gone from not dating anyone to having what looked to be a relationship in a flash.

Samuel took her hand. "Your dad will be alright with us seeing each other, right? I mean, eventually."

"Sure." Her father had always been supportive. He'd always been there for her. Besides, he'd already suggested that she not let her previous relationship disaster prevent her from moving forward with Samuel. Something held her back, though, from telling him that yet.

The hostess appeared at their side and led them to their table.

They ordered crab cakes for an appetizer, and they each ordered the sea bass for their entrée.

Soft music played in the background. Danielle was determined not to let this being their last night together for a week overshadow the moment. Nonetheless, she had to blink back tears before lifting her chin and putting a smile on her face.

"Are you excited?" She tapped a newly-manicured nail against her glass of sparkling water. "About your new job?"

"It'll be good to fly again, but it's hard to be excited when I'll be leaving you."

She sucked in her breath. "I'm not excited about it either."

"You know," he said, lacing his fingers with hers on the table. "We have a good thing here. Do you think?"

She smiled. "I think so, too."

"Danielle, do you want to be my girlfriend?"

She laughed. "You mean like your steady girlfriend?"

"I don't know what they call it now. Exclusive maybe?"

"Whatever they call it, yes."

He leaned over the table and sealed it with a light kiss on her lips. "I'm happy. Are you happy?"

"Yes, but Samuel? Are you sure?" She ran a hand down her stomach. Felt the little baby bump. Later, when he took her home, she would see if he could feel it. "I come as a package."

"I don't mind. In fact, I'm kind of excited about the baby."

She grinned. Life was finally going the right way.

Forty

Samuel wasn't thinking about anything other than spending some quality time with Danielle on her couch. If he'd been clear-headed, he would have seen Joey sitting on the steps leading up to her apartment.

Hand in hand, they were almost on him before Danielle spotted him. "Joey! How did you find me?"

"You're not hard to track," he said.

"What do you want?"

"I just wanted to talk to you." He wobbled a little when he stood up. He'd been drinking, but Danielle didn't seem to notice.

"Okay. About what?"

"Can we go inside?"

She glanced at Samuel. He nodded. He'd rather get this over with now while he was here with her. He wasn't concerned about their safety. One swing and he could take Joey down.

He waited while Danielle unlocked the door, and Joey

followed her inside. Samuel hung back behind him, so he could make sure Joey didn't touch her.

"Come in," She looked uncomfortably at Samuel. She mouthed "I'm sorry," behind Joey's back. He shook his head. "It's okay."

"Nice place you have here." Joey walked into her living room. Looked around.

"What do you want to talk about?" She stood with her hands on her hips, and Samuel moved to stand next to her.

Samuel knew the moment Joey saw the book on the coffee table.

"What's this?" He reached down and picked up the baby name book. He flipped through it, seeing the highlighted names and handwritten notes they had made.

He took a step toward Danielle. "It hasn't been that long. Are you?"

"Yes, Joey. I'm pregnant."

"Whose is it?" He glared at Samuel.

Samuel stood his ground. He had no idea how this would go. Maybe letting him come inside wasn't the best idea after all.

"Whose do you think it is?" Danielle quipped.

"How would I know?"

"You're the one who slept around."

"So, it's mine?" He was glaring at Danielle now.

"You're the father," she said.

"When were you planning on telling me?"

"I'm not sure I was."

"I have a right to know."

"You relinquished your rights the next day."

"I told you that didn't mean anything."

She scoffed. "Funny how you guys always say that."

He dropped the book on the coffee table. "Are you gonna keep it?"

She glared back at him.

He glanced down at the book. "Guess so since you're naming it."

"I thought you were a decent guy, Joey. We were together for a long time. I followed you here, to be with you. But that isn't what happened, so I don't want to see you again."

"So you're gonna have this baby by yourself?"

Samuel stepped up to stand one step in front of her. "Not by herself."

Joey smiled sarcastically. "Nice going, Danielle."

She took Samuel's arm. "It's not your business. Why did you even come here?"

He shrugged. "Good question. Like you said, we were together a long time. I just wanted to make sure you were okay."

She scoffed.

"She's great," Samuel said. "As you can see. Why don't I walk you to the door?"

Joey shook his head. "Sure. Why not?"

Samuel followed Joey to the door. It was time to settle this thing once and for all.

Forty~One

Danielle sat on the sofa and realized she was trembling. It had been a mistake letting Joey come inside. Never again. Besides, he had ruined a perfectly good evening.

She heard them talking at the door, but couldn't make out their words. Maybe it was wrong to let them talk. But she was suddenly exhausted, too drained to care. After the rush of shopping and getting ready for her date with Samuel, then the adrenalin of the date itself, followed by the confrontation with Joey, she couldn't take any more.

She kicked off her shoes and curled up on the sofa. She wrapped her arms around the teddy bear and laid her head on one of the throw pillows.

When she woke, she opened her eyes to darkness. It took a second for her figure out that she was in her bed, under the covers. She was wearing nothing but her underwear and a t-shirt.

Alarmed, she sat up.

"Hi," Samuel said. He sat next to her on the bed, still wearing his tux. "How do you feel?"

"I don't know. What happened?"

He tucked a strand of hair behind her ear. "You fell asleep."

"My clothes?"

"The dress was too pretty to sleep in. I hope you don't mind terribly. I promise I was good."

She didn't mind. Though she couldn't fathom how he'd managed to undress her while she slept. "What time is it?"

"About midnight."

"So much for our last night together."

"Danielle," he said, pulling her to him. "It's not our last night together. We're going to have lots of nights together. Just not for a while, until we get things figured out."

She nestled her head beneath his chin and put her fingers in his hair. Maybe he really would come back and spend time with her. Joey had taught her a lesson. Never follow the guy. That wasn't something she was likely to forget. "What happened with Joey?"

"He won't be coming back."

"How do you know?"

"We had a man-to-man talk." Samuel rubbed his knuckles.

Danielle gasped. "You hit him?"

"Maybe just a little. Mostly, I just told him how it was gonna go, man-to-man."

She chuckled. "And what exactly does a man-to-man talk entail?"

"Sometimes fighting." She shifted, but it was too dark to see if he had bruises.

"Fortunately, this time fighting wasn't required."

"But you hit him."

"We just punched each other on the arm for good measure."

"Oh. My." She sighed.

He laughed. "Are you worried about me or him?"

"You," she murmured against his chest. "Only you."

"Good. Because all I want is for you to be happy."

"I am happy. Samuel?"

He rubbed her back. "What is it, love?"

"Will you really be back?"

"Danielle. I don't think you understand." He shifted to gently take her chin in his hands. "I'm so in love with you, I can't see straight. This baby you're carrying… I feel like it's my baby, too."

Danielle's lips curved into a smile, and her heart swelled. She put her arms around him and held him close. "I love you, too, Samuel Johnson."

"So, will you wait for me? Will you be my girl and put up with me being gone until we figure out how to be together?"

"Yes," she whispered. How was it possible that she'd fallen so deeply in love so quickly? Her grandmother had told her once that love was like that. Sometimes people grew to love each other over time, but other times, it was a sudden, unexpected meeting of the hearts.

If you ever have that happen, don't let it go. And don't let anyone stand in your way. Not even your family.

Danielle wasn't sure what her grandmother had meant about

family. Her family was supportive, but she supposed she was one of the lucky ones.

Forty~Two

The following Wednesday morning, Danielle sat working at her desk. She hated to do it, but she sat looking through stock photo images. After the experience of working with Avery and Jacob, she didn't feel like dealing with exclusive models at the moment.

When her phone rang with Samuel's ringtone, all thoughts went out of her head.

"Hi love," he said when she answered.

"Hi." She melted when he called her that – every time. This was the first time he'd called her in the morning since he'd left. Since he was flying during the day, they spent hours talking in the evenings.

"Do you want to have lunch?"

Her breath hitched. "Of course I do, but you're just teasing me."

"Nope, I'm serious."

"Okay." She glanced down at her casual pants and t-shirt. Did she have time to change?

"There's a catch though. I need a huge favor."

She laughed. "You want me to fly to Dallas?"

He chuckled. "Any time you want to, but not this time. This time, I'm coming there."

She smiled into the phone, but kept her voice calm. "Alright."

"They need to see my birth certificate up here for something. Insurance, I think. My mom had to go to work, but she put it in an envelope and taped it to her back door. If I send you the address, can you go get it, then meet me at the airport? I was thinking it would be a good excuse to see you."

She bit her lip. "Sure." She checked the time. It was only nine o'clock, so she had plenty of time. Even time to get home, change clothes, and maybe stop by the Dry Bar to get her hair styled.

They set up the details, and she shut down her computer. She was thankful she had a job that was based on commission, leaving her free to come and go.

While the taxi driver waited, she changed into some jeans and a new green sweater to match her eyes. She threw some makeup in a bag and rushed back to the taxi. Since Samuel had been driving her around, she'd gotten in the habit of using taxis instead of Ubers. He had given her about twenty reasons why she should stick to taxis.

After she had her hair washed and blow dried, she went into their restroom and took extra care with her makeup. She was so excited about this unexpected visit from Samuel that her hands were shaking as she applied mascara.

It was such a wonderful surprise. She'd resigned herself to a boring, lonely week, and Friday couldn't get here soon enough. Maybe this long-distance thing could work. Sure, he was coming to pick something up, but still, he was coming. She didn't have to wait all week to see him again.

She called another taxi and gave him the address Samuel had texted her. Today was one day she was second-thinking her no-driving thing. Maybe she would have to look into getting a car. Especially with a baby coming. She was going to need a car seat and who knew what else. Yes, she was definitely going to start looking for a car after the new year.

She asked the driver to wait while she got out at Samuel's house. It was a new two-story modern house with a well-mani-cured lawn. She went around back and stopped to study the pool and the little house on the other side of it where Samuel lived. If the taxi driver hadn't been waiting for her, she would have peeked through one of his windows. Not in a creepy way, just to catch a glimpse of the way the man she couldn't stop thinking about lived.

She would be meeting his family in four days. Just four days. In the meantime, she could focus on being productive. It certainly wouldn't hurt her career to have her weeks free to do nothing but work. She'd take a lunch to work and stay at her desk all day. Immersed in her work, maybe she wouldn't miss him quite so much.

Forty~Three

Danielle sat in the back seat of the taxi, Samuel's birth certificate tucked safely in her handbag as they approached George Bush Intercontinental Airport. The driver took her around to the Signature Flight Support building. She was familiar with this type of private area. Unlike commercial flights, she would be allowed to wait for him in the lobby.

She'd loved airports since she was a kid, probably because her father loved airports and airplanes and anything related to flying. His exuberance had been contagious and had become a part of her as well.

Still, she had butterflies in her stomach. It had been five days since she'd seen Samuel, though they'd talked on the phone daily. He would only stay long enough for them to eat lunch, then he'd be on his way back to Fort Worth.

After arriving at her building, she paid the driver and entered the lobby. It smelled like fresh-baked cookies and popcorn. She smiled at the nostalgia associated with private lobbies over the years from flying with her dad.

She was early, so his plane wasn't there yet. She took a seat where she could watch the incoming planes.

She thought of Samuel now as her boyfriend, though it was going against her rule about not dating pilots. She supposed that since she'd made the rule, she could break it.

Her father and Savannah made it work. Surely she and Samuel could also. How many men would be willing to raise another man's baby?

She shook her head. She was getting ahead of herself. He'd offered to help her out, he certainly hadn't committed to raising the baby as his own.

She recognized the plane coming in from pictures he'd shown her before it even landed. The single black stripe down the tail distinguished it from the others. She stood up and leaned against the window to be able to see him the minute he stepped from the plane.

The sky was a beautiful clear blue dome today; a perfect day for flying. He'd promised to take her up this weekend, probably Saturday, since they were having lunch with his family on Sunday. She reached inside her handbag and pulled out the envelope with his birth certificate.

She grinned as he stepped from the plane. He was wearing black pants and a white oxford shirt, the uniform her father insisted on. It was the first time she'd seen him in uniform, and her heart skipped erratically.

After he stepped from the plane, he turned and helped an attractive woman with long wavy brunette hair, looking to be about their age, step from the plane. The woman had on shades, heels, and wore a red trench coat over a short skirt. Once the two of them were on the ground, she took his hand, and they faced each other. They were too far away, but it looked like they were talking. She couldn't see Samuel's face, but the girl looked serious, then smiled.

Then they hugged. A long hug. Danielle held her breath, but even when she had to breathe, they still hugged for a few more seconds.

And then the girl stretched up and kissed him. Danielle couldn't tell if she kissed him on the cheek or the lips. As they turned and walked toward the limo that had pulled up, she slipped her hand around his elbow, their heads bent close in conversation. She kissed him on the cheek before he relinquished her to the care of the limo driver. He watched as the car drove off.

Stunned, Danielle watched as he walked back to the plane to speak to one of the line crew before approaching the lobby. She was trembling, and her thoughts were completely incoherent.

Her ears ringing, she sat on the nearest chair. She stared at the door he would be coming through shortly.

Samuel came through the lobby door a couple minutes later and quickly spotted her. A wide smile on his face, he strode toward her.

She sat, frozen, watching him walk toward her.

He stopped in front of her, and his smile disappeared. "What's wrong?" He held out a hand to help her up.

She flinched away. "No," she breathed.

"Danielle, what is it?"

"No." She stood up, threw the envelope at his feet, and practically ran toward the exit. The tears were blinding her.

"Danielle. Wait." He followed, quickly catching up with her.

He grabbed her arm. She could barely see him through the tears. She jerked away. "Leave me alone." She turned and hurried down the hallway, ignoring the people who stopped to stare at her.

When she was outside, she stood pressed against the wall until she could catch her breath. She'd been wrong about him.

He was no different from the others. No different from Joey. No different from Richard, who'd broken her heart when she was in high school. No different from other pilots who had relationships with flight attendants and passengers. She'd been so gullible. So desperate to be loved, that she'd believed him.

She had believed that he was different.

But he was like all the rest.

CHAPTER
Forty~Four

Annabelle Lawson had a crush on Samuel since she was twelve years old. She was sixteen now, but Samuel would bet his life that she could get into any club with absolutely no problem. Her grandfather, Nathaniel Shannon, had doted on her – a hundred times over the level of doting on his daughter, so it was off the charts. Nathaniel lived in Houston, where he made millions running a company called Steri-Waste – medical waste removal and recycling. His daughter married a man who ran a big oil company in Dallas, so Nathaniel bought a couple of airplanes that he didn't know how to fly.

He'd gone to Louisiana Tech University and asked the flight director if he knew any recent graduates who could fly him around. Samuel's chief flight instructor had automatically called Samuel, who'd jumped at the opportunity. He'd logged countless hours flying both Nathaniel and Annabelle back and forth between Houston and Dallas. Nathaniel had preferred flying over driving, so he had kept Samuel busy, and he paid well.

Samuel had saved his money, and now, at age twenty-five, he'd bought his first airplane.

As Nathaniel's flight schedule slowed and Annabelle got caught up in high school cheerleading… and boys, Samuel began looking around for other options. He was in no hurry, and didn't want to leave Houston, but when a job with Noah Worthington opened up, he had no choice but to take it. In Samuel's opinion, it was even better than getting on with a major airline.

But now Nathaniel was dying. Annabelle had called him in tears asking for a flight to Houston. The timing couldn't have been better. He'd done what he could to distract her, but she was devastated. He'd given her his sunshades to cover her swollen eyes.

He'd probably never see Annabelle again until she booked with Skye Travels some day when she was grown up. Even if then, it would be a long time. She was planning to go to university in Europe.

He watched as Danielle took the first taxi away from the airport. Had she seen him hug Annabelle? Was that what this was all about? If so, it was just a misunderstanding. He needed to follow. Would she go home or to the office? Didn't matter. He'd find her.

His phone chimed.

Damn. It was Noah. He needed him back ASAP.

Forty~Five

Danielle sat in the back of the taxi and stared out the window. She watched the traffic and the buildings of downtown approaching. She wiped her cheeks and batted back the tears that threatened to spill out.

She just needed to get home to her apartment and close out the world.

She'd had nothing good happen since she'd moved here. She'd gotten pregnant with the cheating boyfriend that she'd moved here to be with. She fallen in love with a pilot who'd moved away and now had cheated on her as well.

She'd spent enough years in therapy that she should know how to handle any crisis.

The words of her therapist came back to her with absolute clarity. *If your life isn't going the way you want it to, do something different. Think back to when things were good and try to recreate some of the good things that were working for you.*

Los Angeles. When she was in L.A. living with her mother, her life was good. She made better decisions.

She didn't fall in love in a matter of days. She dated and moved on. Or took her time with a long-term boyfriend. The fact that he eventually cheated didn't factor into her equation. He cheated in Houston, not L.A.

There was nothing here for her in Houston. She had no real reason to be here.

That was the answer. She would go home.

She laid her head back against the seat and concentrated on the things she needed to do to move. She would have to get out of her lease. But she was pregnant. That shouldn't be a problem. Extenuating circumstances.

She would quit her job. Either quit or she could work from L.A. Besides one meeting a week, she never saw anyone else at the company anyway. She could work better from the study next to her bedroom. It was much more conducive to creativity than the sterile office environment where she worked now.

Why hadn't she considered that before? She'd been grieving the loss of Joey, then Samuel had come into her life and clouded her thoughts.

She would have her mother and Grayson to help with her baby.

A smile fluttered about the corner of her lips as she realized that she and her mother could raise their babies together. They would be like siblings.

Stranger things had happened.

She let herself into her apartment. She would gather up her personal items, pack a suitcase, and call a moving company to ship everything else she needed back to L.A. The apartment had come furnished, so she didn't have furniture or appliances to deal with. The apartment had been easy to move into and would be easy to move out of.

Without looking back, she turned and walked to the apartment office. Thirty minutes later, she was free. She had until the end of the month to get out.

She could be out by this time tomorrow.

She got on the phone and arranged the moving company and set up a flight out for tomorrow afternoon. It would have been so very much easier to just call her father and have him come get her.

But she wasn't ready to tell him.

She felt like her life was a total wreck, and she didn't want him to know just yet how bad things were going for her.

Tomorrow morning, she would go to work and talk to her boss about either quitting or working from L.A. All she had to do was to tell them she was pregnant. Everyone so far had reacted in such a cooperative way. Pregnancy was like a golden ticket to getting whatever she needed.

She hauled one suitcase onto the bed and began packing her clothes. After a few minutes, she rolled out her large suitcase. Just about everything she owned was going to fit in these two suitcases.

Her phone rang while she was in her closet gathering up shoes. She recognized the ring tone. It was Samuel. She didn't answer.

A few minutes later, her phone indicated that he'd left a message. He rarely left messages. He said he always managed to bungle them up.

As she pulled underwear from the dresser, she got a text. She ignored that, too.

She had nothing to say to Samuel Johnson and didn't want to hear anything he had to say.

She was done. She was going to take herself and her baby out of here.

By sundown, she had two suitcases standing by her front door and yellow sticky notes on everything she wanted to have shipped. Her Apple TV, a painting she'd brought with her, and a few other things.

She pulled out a trash bag and emptied the refrigerator. As she dragged it out to the trash bin at the curb, her phone rang again.

She went back inside and looked around. Everything was done.

She took a glass of orange juice from the refrigerator, one of the few things left, and went to sit on her sofa next to the teddy bear Samuel had made for her - Pappa. With his little flight suit and goggles, wearing a little stuffed camera around his neck.

What she wouldn't give for glass of wine right now.

She put her feet on the sofa and picked up the baby name book she and Samuel had spent so much time highlighting and laughing about. There were times she'd forgotten, and it had felt like it was their baby she was carrying.

She was exhausted. She remembered how he'd cooked for her while she rested. But Samuel wasn't there to make dinner. Or rub her feet.

Those days were over. Yet she was surrounded by reminders of him.

With the baby name book in her lap, she unlocked her phone and played back her messages.

Forty-Six

As Samuel taxied down the runway at Dallas Fort Worth Airport, he checked his phone. His only message was from Noah.

Nothing from Danielle.

He called her number, but she didn't answer.

"Danielle, it's me. I really need to talk to you. Please call me back." He paused. He hated leaving messages. Once something was said, it couldn't be taken back. "I'm confused about what happened. Noah called me back to Dallas. I didn't know what to do, so I'm back here to see what he needs. But anyway I'll call back as soon as I know. I hope you're okay."

Irritated now that he hadn't been able to follow Danielle, he went into Noah's office with a scowl on his face.

"Where have you been?" Noah asked.

"I just flew to Houston to pick up my birth certificate."

"Oh. Ok." Noah frowned at him. "And?"

"And I had plans to eat lunch with Danielle when you called

me back." He left out the part about where she had run away from him in tears for some reason he could only guess about. Yet, the more he thought about it and replayed the whole thing in his mind, the more he realized that she must have misconstrued his interactions with Annabelle. He had to fix this. He had to make this right.

Noah relaxed. "It's okay. She's used to the pilot's schedule."

Exactly. Noah missed the whole point. The pilot's schedule was the major thing she didn't like about him. That and his hug with Annabelle.

"You have something on your cheek." Noah pointed out.

Samuel rubbed his cheek and came away with red lipstick on his fingertips. He groaned. He'd forgotten that Annabelle had kissed him.

This was not good. He had to fix this.

"I think she's upset. I need to go to her. To fix this."

"Does this have anything to do with a girl named Annabelle?"

Samuel blinked and had nothing to say. "I saw the flight logs. You can have tomorrow off to fix it."

"Thank you, sir." And that was exactly why Noah had endeared himself to the pilots who worked for him. "What did you need?"

"I need you to take a client to Phoenix."

"Now?"

Noah smiled. "Welcome to my world. You'll be back late."

Forty~Seven

Danielle sat holding her phone with her face in the teddy bear's fur. She was crying so hard that she could barely breathe. The person she needed the most wasn't there.

He'd apologized, though he said he didn't know what it was he had done. She hadn't answered. Not a single text or phone call.

Though she had his phone number halfway memorized, she blocked his number from her phone and deleted his contact information.

It was the only way she could deal with it. She had to rip the Band-Aid off quickly. She'd learned a long time ago that dragging out a break up was not the way to go. It caused too much heartache. This way, she never had to see or hear from him again.

He'd sounded tired in the last message she'd gotten only a few minutes ago. He said the girl was the granddaughter of an old friend. He said he'd given her a ride to see her dying grandfather.

Maybe he was telling the truth. Maybe he'd only been comforting an old friend. But she saw what she saw. She couldn't unsee it. Now, whenever she saw him, she'd have that image in her head. That image of him embracing another girl.

But she wasn't that vulnerable girl she'd been at seventeen when she'd had no coping skills; when she'd felt that life wasn't worth living without her boyfriend.

The tears started again. She couldn't go through the whole thing all over again. What Joey had done had drained her and left her emotionally fragile. It probably didn't help that her hormones were all out of whack from the pregnancy.

A baby. She had a baby to take care of. That's all that mattered right now.

She would go home. She would go back to where she felt safe.

And her first appointment when she got back would be to her psychologist's office.

She needed to get over Samuel Johnson and get on with her life.

She set the teddy bear aside.

Forty-Eight

It wasn't until he was flying back from Phoenix, in the dark, by radar, that Samuel realized Noah must have put it together that he was seeing Danielle. Noah had asked him to look after his daughter. And he wasn't dumb. Nonetheless, Samuel had kept Danielle's wish and hadn't said anything to her father.

He had gotten back to Dallas after Midnight, then driven the short distance to his rented apartment and fallen into bed. He had tomorrow off to see Danielle, so he didn't set a clock.

Big mistake. He didn't wake up until nine o'clock.

There was no way he would be there to take Danielle to lunch. He sat on the edge of the bed in his pajama bottoms and dialed her number again. No answer.

He jumped in the shower and threw on some jeans and a sweater. The sooner he got there, the sooner he could straighten this thing out.

He usually found being in the air calming, but not today. He couldn't shake the unease. He'd hated seeing the pain on her face and it was ten times worse knowing he'd somehow caused it.

After he landed, he grabbed the car he'd requested to be waiting for him. He assumed she would be at work, so he went to her workplace first. Her computer was turned off and had a yellow post-it note on it. Danielle wasn't in her office. He walked around her office space and knew she wasn't there and she wasn't coming back. Her space felt... different.

He wandered down the halls looking for someone to ask about her. He found two open doors. Both women shrugged and shook their heads. "People come and go all the time," one of them told him.

Her boss was out, so there was one else to ask. He needed to get to her apartment.

He rode down the elevator and dashed to her place. The apartment door stood open. Never a good sign. Was she hurt? Is that why she didn't answer? His irritation turned into true gut-wrenching concern. She could be here hurt or dying and no one would know. Except maybe the two guys taking a picture off her wall.

"What are you doing?" He stood in front of the man holding Danielle's art work. It was one of the few furnishings left that didn't have a yellow sticker on it.

The worker shrugged.

"Where is Danielle?" The pit of his stomach dropped out as it occurred to him that they may have already taken her body out.

One of the two workers took pity on him. "She moved away, man. We're gonna be right behind her, except we're driving."

"Where did she go?"

His new friend looked at the other guy who shrugged. "I don't know about her, but we're going to L.A."

Samuel dropped to the sofa that obviously didn't belong to Danielle since it didn't have a sticker on it. He allowed this information to sink in. That's when he noticed the teddy bear left on the sofa. She had left Pappa! And Pappa wasn't wearing a yellow sticker. He picked it up and ran a hand along the fur on its head. The fur was damp.

It was like a stab in his heart that she left Pappa. Samuel couldn't leave him here. He was glad he'd come here and found the little teddy bear.

Gathering up Pappa, he waved to the movers and headed out the door.

Forty-Nine

Danielle sat in the back of the taxi, riding from LAX to her house - her mother's house. She hadn't called her mother. She was just going to show up. She smiled to herself.

I am my father's child.

Her father rarely called before showing up. Both her mom and stepmother had tried to break him of that habit. His new wife had come closest.

The driver stopped in front of her house and took her two suitcases from the trunk. After he set them on the curb, Danielle paid him and the driver drove off.

Danielle stood on the curb between her two suitcases, with a tote bag on her shoulder. She watched as the taxi turned the corner and drove off. She then turned and faced her mother's house.

It was Thursday afternoon, so no one was home. She was about to upset their evening. She grabbed a suitcase with each hand and dragged them to the front. She went to the door, keyed in the code, and let herself inside.

And was met by her cat, Charlie. She picked up the cat, squeezed him to her, and carried him with her into the living room. She needed to bring her suitcases inside, but decided she was too tired to drag them up the front porch steps. She grabbed a throw, and curled up on the sofa. She was exhausted from the trip. Exhausted from crying about Samuel. She buried her face in the cat's fur and was soothed by its purring.

She was sad that she'd left Pappa in her old apartment. It had been done in a brief moment of anger. She grabbed her phone off the coffee table and dialed the apartment complex phone number.

It took her ten minutes to convince the girl to send someone to her apartment to look for the stuffed bear. It took another thirty minutes for them call her back. The movers had already come and gone.

And there was no sign of Pappa.

When Danielle woke up, her mother was sitting on the coffee table watching her. She rubbed at her eyes and sat up. Someone had brought in her luggage. "Mom. I must have fallen asleep."

Claire nodded. "It's almost six o'clock."

Danielle hugged a throw pillow and avoided her mother's intense gaze. "I should have called."

"I guess you came by that honestly." Claire said softly.

Danielle blinked back the tears, but felt her chin trembling. Then her mother was sitting next to her, and Danielle buried her face against her mother's shoulder and cried until her tears were spent.

"Now Danielle Worthington." Claire put her hands on either

side of Danielle's face and forced her to look at her. "Tell me what's going on with you."

"Everything is falling apart." Danielle's chin trembled.

"Whatever it is, I'm sure we can fix it." Claire released her.

Danielle shook her head. "I don't think so, Mom."

"You're too upset for this to be about work." Claire tilted her head. "I know you broke up with that Joey, thank God, but you said you had a new boyfriend."

"It's so complicated. I don't know where to start."

"Start at the beginning."

Danielle's breath hitched. "I'm pregnant."

Claire sat up straight. That was her only reaction. *Years of etiquette classes.* "You're pregnant?"

Danielle sniffled. "But that's not the worst part."

"Worse than being pregnant?"

It all came out in a rush. "The worse part isn't being pregnant. It's because the father is Joey. And because I love Samuel. He would have been a great dad, but he found someone else."

Her mother scowled at her. "It might take a little time to sort all this out."

Danielle almost smiled. She'd made the right decision to come home.

CHAPTER

Fifty

Samuel sat between his two grandmothers at Pappa's Burgers and stared at his food. He ordered fried catfish – something he'd never ordered here before. He'd eaten a few bites and moved his food around on his plate.

It was Sunday dinner with the family. The day Danielle was supposed to meet his family. Samuel had been a ghost of man since he'd walked out of her deserted apartment.

He'd never known anyone to be so determined to break up that they'd moved across the country the next day. In all fairness, though, he understood her wanting to be with her mother.

But he just needed her to listen. To understand that he hadn't done anything wrong. He'd been so excited to see her. And then she'd run off – across the country.

"What's gotten into you, dearie?" His grandmother Veronica asked.

He shook his head and straightened in his chair. "It's nothing." He attempted to smile.

"You were supposed to bring your girl today."

Everyone knew of course, but Veronica was the first person to bring it up. "She's not talking to me right now."

"Nonsense. Why wouldn't a girl want to talk to a handsome young man like yourself?"

"It was a misunderstanding, but she's made her decision. She doesn't date pilots."

"Samuel Johnson." He turned to face his grandmother. His affable grandmother looked rather stern at the moment. "I know it hurt when Jessica was taken from you."

Samuel looked away. It had crushed him to lose Jessica, but since he'd met Danielle, she'd become a memory to him. He was ashamed to admit it.

Maybe his grandmother was the one person he could talk to about Danielle.

"Grandma. There's something about her I was wondering if I could talk to you about."

"You can talk to me about anything."

"She says she doesn't date pilots." His moment of resolve crumbled at the last minute.

"Nonsense. She'll get over that. What is it you really wanted to ask me about?"

Samuel chuckled. "When I met her, she was expecting a child with her ex-boyfriend." He kept his eyes down. Now, at least, his grandmother would stop asking about her, and he would start finding him someone *respectable* to date.

When his grandmother didn't respond, he looked up at her.

She shook her head. "Samuel. Is that why you let her go?"

"I didn't..." He looked away from his grandmother's piercing gaze. "She left me."

His grandmother patted his arm. "How do you feel about her being pregnant?"

"I wish the baby was mine." Samuel blurted.

"Why did she leave?"

"She saw me with a client. A young girl. And she must have misinterpreted. She... the girl hugged me. Maybe Danielle thought I was cheating on her."

"Were you?"

"No. Of course not. I love—" He looked at his grandmother. "her." It was first time he'd said it out loud. *I should have told her.*

His grandmother grinned. "Listen to me," Veronica said. "If you want this girl, then you have to do whatever it takes."

"I don't think there's anything I can do. She won't answer my calls, and she moved to California."

"Well, that is a bit of an obstacle." Grandma Veronica took a swallow of sweet tea. "But if a man wants the girl..."

He turned and looked into her eyes. "If you want this girl, then you've got to find a way to win her back. This is not the same as what happened to Jessica. You have a chance to turn this girl around. She may say no, but you surely have to do anything and everything to get her back."

"But—"

She held up a finger. "No buts, Samuel. It's time for you to take control of your life."

Fifty~One

Danielle was home alone when she got the flowers. And the letter.

Her eyes widened when she opened the door to the delivery guy holding the vase of three red roses.

Then she caught herself. They would be for her mother, of course, from Grayson. He was always doing little things to surprise her.

"I have a delivery for Danielle Worthington." The delivery boy said, holding the vase toward her.

"Me?" She took the flowers, but kept them at arm's reach.

"Are you Danielle?"

"Yes."

"The guy asked me to give you this letter, too."

Danielle took the envelope, too, and glanced past him, but didn't see anyone watching. "Who?"

"I don't know. Some guy who came into the flower shop. I think there's a card."

"Okay." Danielle took the flowers and closed the door, the delivery boy forgotten. Her mind whirled. Whoever had sent her flowers had bought them in person. Who would be in L.A. to personally buy flowers to send her when they could have brought them?

Her mind darted to Samuel, but surely if he was here and knew where to find her, he'd come by. *He doesn't know how I would react.*

She took the flowers to the coffee table and opened the card. Someone had scrawled *Best Wishes* on it. Not helpful at all.

She opened the sealed envelope.

Dear Danielle,

I hope you're doing well. I'm sorry I wasn't the boyfriend you were looking for. I'm just not ready to settle down. I hope you're happy with your new boyfriend. He seemed like a nice guy, even though he did give me a black eye when I told him I didn't even know if I was the father.

Danielle rubbed her forehead. Samuel had managed to leave that part out.

I know I'm the father. You're a good girl. You deserve to be happy. So I'm not going to bother you. I'm going to leave you to raise our child as you see fit. If there ever comes a time when you need me for anything, you know how to get in touch with my mother. I told her about you and the baby. She wasn't happy about my choice, but she agreed to contact me.

Joey

P.S. If you want child support, just let my mother know, and I'll take care of it.

She read the letter a second time. The only really new information was that Samuel had given him a black eye. She wasn't quite sure what to think about that. Samuel did not seem like the kind of guy who would hit someone.

The fact that he had hit someone in defense of her honor sent a flurry of emotions through her that she couldn't even begin to sort out.

And what had prompted Joey to send this letter to her? He could easily have just let the whole issue alone. A touch of conscience perhaps? They had known each other a long time after all.

Nonetheless, it was a relief that he wasn't planning to seek custody of their child – her child. And she didn't need or want his money. That wasn't even an issue.

She was on her own. Thoughts of Samuel swirled in her mind. She had thought he would be there for her. But she had chosen to block him out of her life. She wanted someone whom she could trust with all her heart.

Fifty~Two

One Month Later

Samuel stood next to Noah Worthington at the window overlooking the tarmac at Dallas Love Field Airport. They both wore black pants, white oxford shirts, and black hats with silver braiding, the uniforms of Skye Travels.

"I should probably call Savannah or Danielle to let them know we're running late." Noah said, but made no move to do so.

"Yeah," Samuel kept his gaze on the storm gathering in the west. He swallowed the lump in his throat at hearing Danielle's name.

"It's okay," Noah held his iPad toward Samuel. "We can still make it."

Samuel looked at the radar showing the storm. He closed his eyes and squeezed the bridge of his nose.

He tried to ignore the pain in his heart. There was nothing he could do about it at the moment.

"See that break in the storm – here," Noah held a finger over a clear area on the radar. "We can take off and get above the clouds."

Samuel opened his eyes and blinked. *Focus.* He pointed to the image near Birmingham. "You know they won't approve it. And even if they did, look at this area. We'll never be able to land."

Noah checked his watch. "I can't call Savannah."

"Why not?" Samuel asked, but his thoughts were already back on Danielle. Danielle was with Savannah right now. They were getting ready for Savannah's graduation from Auburn University with a Ph.D. in psychology.

"I don't want her to know I screwed up," Noah wore a miserable expression. "I can't let her down."

Well, hell. Samuel was still confused about why Noah had brought him on this flight. Noah had to remember that he and Danielle were no longer together. Samuel hadn't tried to contact Danielle after he found Pappa in her deserted apartment. The message was too loud and clear.

Even though it went against his better judgment, the least he could do was to go along with Noah. He understood Noah's need to be there for his wife.

He followed Noah out onto the tarmac and boarded Noah's Cessna with the name Skye Travels emblazoned in red across the fuselage.

He sat in the copilot's seat and watched patiently as Noah checked the radar again and called in to the Airport Traffic Advisory System and listened to the recording.

This was Samuel's first time to fly with Noah. By reputation, Noah was one of the best pilots. As far as Samuel could tell, Noah was about to make a decision based on emotion instead of good judgment. He bit his tongue as Noah radioed in to the control tower requesting permission to take off.

Samuel put on his own headset so he could listen in. "We're not going," he said after the negative confirmation came through.

Noah turned in his seat and looked pointedly at Samuel. "We will go."

Samuel shrugged and sat back in his seat to prepare for a long wait.

After about ten minutes of silence from Noah, the rain began to slow, and it looked like the storms were moving away.

Noah sent in an emergency request to take off.

Samuel closed his eyes and tried not to think about Danielle. He tried not to wonder what she was doing right now. Three months pregnant. She would be starting to show a bit now. A baby bump. Danielle was adorable. He imagined that now that the nausea had subsided, she was already getting that glow that only expectant mothers got. They would say it was too early for her to be glowing, but Samuel had seen it. He saw it in the glint of her eyes when she smiled at him.

When she hadn't thought he was watching her work on a design.

"Go ahead, Skye Flight 23. Ready for take-off Runway 31 right," the controller said in his headset, knocking Samuel out of his reverie. "No way." He straightened in his seat.

Noah grinned as he flipped switches bringing the aircraft to life. "You have to have faith," he said.

"Determination is more like it."

"Semantics." Noah guided the plane down toward the runway. "Let's go see our girls."

Samuel kept his focus on the controls and ignored Noah's words. He would think about that later. For now, it was going to be interesting to see the famous Noah Worthington at work. All he had to do was keep his mind off anything Danielle-related.

Once they were in flight, however, there wasn't a lot of distraction to keep his thoughts in check.

Noah wanted him to go to Savannah's graduation reception with him, even knowing Danielle would be there. He had a sick feeling in his stomach when he thought about seeing Danielle. It had been about four weeks. Would she be with someone else? Probably not. Since Noah had brought him along, she must not be seeing anyone else, at least not seriously.

She would probably be showing now. How was she coping with being pregnant? He thought that by now, he'd be rubbing her feet, at least on the weekends. He knew now that anything beyond weekends would have been a challenge. He was usually up at six, flying all day, then just time for a quick happy hour before falling into bed. Only to get up and do it all over again the next day.

He'd spent the weekends at home, mostly with his family. With the holidays coming up, his mother had kept him distracted with decorating the house. But despite her efforts, it made Samuel even sadder that he didn't have Danielle to do things with.

He kept a picture they had taken together the Friday before he left. They'd had a nice dinner until her ex had shown up. Samuel hoped the guy hadn't followed her to L.A.

He wasn't opposed to tracking him down if he thought Joey was harassing her.

He had lots of other pictures of them, too, from the photo shoot. Though they hadn't started seeing each other at that point, those pictures conveyed intimacy. An intimacy that had begun growing even before they knew it was there. Looking back, Samuel was enchanted from the moment he met Danielle.

She had never returned any of his phone calls or texts. If Noah knew that she'd moved, he hadn't said anything to Samuel. In fact, they rarely talked about Danielle at all.

Samuel was trying to let her go. But being around her father, working with him, even now flying with him, left the wound open. Sometimes, he'd say something or make a facial expression that reminded him of Danielle. He thought about her all the time.

He glanced over at Noah, who was checking the radar again. Noah knew. He knew Danielle had gone back to L.A., Samuel would put money on it. There was no way his daughter moved across the country without her father knowing about it. Noah was just being respectful of Samuel's feelings by not bringing it up.

It was a little odd, though, that he sometimes acted like they were still together. Like today. *Let's go see our girls.*

One day. One day he would have the chance to talk to her again. To straighten things out between them. Probably not today, though, since today was about Savannah and family.

It was time though. Time to put this misunderstanding behind them.

Danielle sat on the sofa surrounded by family at Savannah's house on Lake Martin near Auburn, Alabama. Her mother, Claire with her new husband, Grayson were there. Her stepmother, Savannah, was there of course, with her baby, Aria. Danielle's grandmother, Emily, was there, too.

It was interesting that Noah's ex-wife and current wife had become friends of sort over the years. Danielle supposed that she was the link holding them together. Mother and stepmother. They were similar in many ways. Very cultured. Neither one of them would be caught yelling or slamming a door. They probably wouldn't run away from a relationship like Danielle had, either.

The only person missing from today's gathering was Noah – Savannah's new husband.

And Samuel.

Danielle hadn't known that she could miss someone quite so fiercely as she missed Samuel.

She knew that Noah and Samuel were flying in together. What she didn't know was whether or not Samuel would be coming to the graduation party.

It didn't keep her from watching the door.

The rain was falling in torrents now. She shifted her gaze toward the windows along the back of the house and watched the storm roll in across the lake. Someone had turned on the electric fireplace. That and the lights from the Christmas tree reflected in the window. The tune *I'll be home for Christmas* played in the background.

Danielle checked the cell phone she held in her hand. Even now, after a month, she missed the frequent texts she'd become so accustomed to from Samuel.

Savannah sat on the other end of the sofa, also staring at her silent cell phone.

"No word from Noah?" Danielle asked.

"No. You?" Danielle heard the anxiety in Savannah's voice.

Danielle shook her head. *Samuel would have stayed in touch.*

"They must be in the air." Savannah was known for her optimism.

"Probably," Danielle agreed. Still, a tendril of anxiety slithered up her spine. Her father had done a one-eighty since he'd been married to Danielle's mother. He stayed in touch now. His marriage to Savannah was nothing like his marriage to Claire.

Still. Danielle maintained her conviction that once a man was away, it was far too easy to lose touch and for a relationship to fall apart. The current circumstance was a case in point. Her father had missed Savannah's graduation. Without a single word.

"Did you text Samuel?" Savannah asked.

"We broke up," Danielle responded automatically, though she knew that Savannah was well aware of this.

"Right," Savannah said.

Danielle tapped her phone. Looked back toward the window.

"Still," Savannah insisted, "he'd probably answer you. Then we'd at least know that Noah is okay."

Danielle frowned. Damn Savannah for invoking the fear and anxiety that she had learned to live with regarding her father's flying.

Noah was a good pilot. "No," Danielle said. "He's late because of the storm. He'll be here when the weather clears." She took a deep breath and reached out and touched Savannah's arm. "I'm sorry he missed your graduation. I can't imagine what a huge disappointment that must be."

"It's part of the package. I knew that going in. I trust him. I trust him with every fiber of my being."

"He'll be here." Danielle ignored Savannah's comment about trust. They weren't talking about trust. *Everyone knows.* Everyone had to know that she broke up with Samuel because she didn't trust him. Maybe Savannah thought it was unjustified.

"You're right," Savannah said. Waited a beat. "I guess it was a little strange to think about marrying someone so much like your father."

Danielle didn't want to talk about Samuel. She missed him so much it ached. The fact that he was like her father wasn't strange. One of the things she liked about Samuel was that he was like her father. It was the thing that she most liked and most feared.

She feared days like today. Days when he didn't call. Just like Noah hadn't called.

"I met him a couple of weeks ago. He seemed like a nice guy, but then… you would know him better than anyone else."

Danielle fought the urge to walk away from her stepmother. She turned away from Savannah, her chin trembling, as she considered her words.

Yes, Samuel was a nice guy. And yes, she knew him better than anyone else. She was the one who knew just how kind he was. How generous. And how much he had cared about her.

Savannah's mother, Emily, walked over, Aria on her hip. "I think we should go ahead with the cake," she said.

Savannah nodded. "Of course." And took her child from Emily.

Emily served cake and punch. Danielle ate a few bites, but barely tasted it. Savannah also barely touched her cake. Danielle's heart went out to her, despite her irritation with her stepmother's accurate observations. Savannah was in obvious pain, and it was her graduation party.

Danielle stood next to the Christmas tree, facing the front door - she couldn't help herself. Besides, it wasn't strange to be worried about her father. In fact, she was worried about both of them – her father and the man she still loved.

After Savannah tossed her plate into the trash, she picked up her daughter, who'd crawled behind her into the living room.

With the exception of the Christmas music in the background, the room was quiet. Waiting.

The doorbell rang. As far as Danielle knew, no one else had been invited to Savannah's small celebration. Noah wouldn't ring the doorbell. *It could be Samuel coming in before Noah.* Samuel would ring the doorbell.

Danielle and Savannah reached the door at the same time. Danielle realized what she was doing and stopped to stand back. It was Savannah's house.

Savannah opened the door to two men wearing black suits. That little tendril of fear was more like a full-blown fire now.

"Mrs. Worthington?" The older of the two asked.

"Yes," Savannah said, handing Aria over to Danielle. Danielle took the cooing baby and cradled her close, but her eyes were locked on the men at the door.

"We're with the FAA. You're listed as next of kin on Noah Worthington's contact record."

Savannah grabbed the edge of the door and fell to her knees. "Noah," she said, just as Danielle reached her side.

Fifty-Four

About thirty minutes out, Noah gave Samuel control of the plane. "There's a thunderstorm just north of Auburn Airport," he pointed out. "We'll go in from the south and land on runway 36."

They began their descent to Auburn Airport. "We're in the correct position," Samuel said, but even as he said the words, the plane shifted.

"We're in a microburst." Noah said.

"Descending…" Samuel gave the plane full power, but the descent continued.

Altitude warning alarms began beeping. "What the--? Give me the controls."

"Landing gear!" Samuel flipped a switch.

Noah pulled out of the drive with full power. "Something's wrong with the system," he muttered.

"We're gonna stall."

"I'm going to do a controlled descent."

"We're too high." Samuel held onto his seat, his knuckles white.

"I switched off," Noah said. "We'll recover out of it."

"Yes," Samuel agreed. "We're leveling off. Everything's fine now."

Noah exhaled. Gauges indicated the runway ahead. They were on path. Samuel blew out his breath. Everything was good.

"We made it." Noah engaged the thrust reversers to start slowing them down.

The plane was set in full reverse, but they were going too fast, and the end of the runway was getting close. Seeing the end of the runway was something he *never* wanted to do.

Noah hit the brakes, but the plane started sliding on the wet runway.

They checked the antiskid. Engaged.

System failure.

Something wasn't right. Noah checked the annunciator light to see if there was system failure, but it was on.

Samuel gripped the edges of his seat as they slid off toward the end of the runway. "We're gonna crash," he said through his teeth.

They were going too fast. Much too fast to stop now. They braced themselves as they went into a full skid off the runway.

The last thing that flashed through Samuel's mind was an image of Danielle smiling up at him and the feel of her lips on his.

Fifty~Five

They made it to East Alabama Medical Center in Opelika in record time. Grayson drove Emily's SUV with everyone else packed into the seats, Aria included. There had been no time to think. Someone, Emily and maybe Grayson, had grabbed all their handbags and ushered them out the door.

Savannah had known where to go and what to do. Everyone else just followed. Danielle was in a daze. The men from the FAA had said Noah was alive, but that they needed to get to the hospital.

They hadn't said anything about Samuel.

Noah was in surgery, so the whole family was sent to a waiting area to sit. And pace.

Her father had to be alright. Though she'd dogged Savannah's heels and listened to every conversation, no one had indicated that he was very bad off.

And no one mentioned Samuel.

Danielle paced across the waiting room floor a couple of

times. Emily had gotten Aria to sleep. Savannah was on the edge of her seat. Claire sat with Grayson, their attention on his iPad.

Without a word, Danielle went out to the nurse's station. "Can you tell me where Samuel Johnson is?"

The nurse looked at her over her glasses, typed on the computer, and shook her head. "We don't have anyone by that name."

"Maybe he came in without a name. He was with Noah Worthington. In the crash."

The nurse shook her head. "The ambulance only brought in one person."

"That can't be," Danielle said, turning on her heel and running back to the waiting room.

"Savannah, are you certain Samuel was with Dad? The nurse said he isn't here." Her words came out in a rush. *What if he hadn't survived?*

Savannah's brows furrowed. "Yeah. When I talked to Noah this morning, he said they were both coming. He said Samuel was excited to see you."

"He knows we broke up."

"Well, either way, he was bringing Samuel with him to graduation and to the party."

"The ambulance only brought in one person. Where is he?"

Savannah frowned. "That airplane is rated for two pilots. There was another pilot on that plane." She was out of her chair and on her way to the nurse's station.

"Danielle," Claire called.

Danielle stopped in her plan to follow Savannah and instead went to sit next to her mother.

"Are you okay?" Claire asked, placing a hand on Danielle's arm.

Danielle shook her head, feeling the tears gathering in her eyes. "No one knows where Samuel is. He was on the plane with Noah."

Claire glanced at Grayson. "How can that be?" Her voice trailed off with an unspoken realization.

Grayson shook his head. "Not necessarily," he muttered.

Danielle stood up, took a step, and came back to stand in front of them. "I have to find him."

Savannah rushed back. "They took him to Birmingham - UAB."

"Oh no!" Danielle said. That could only mean the worst. "How is he?" She bit her lip even as she asked.

"She didn't know," Savannah said. "But they flew him straight to UAB by Lifeflight."

Danielle felt the bottom fall out of her stomach. No. No. Not Samuel. Not sweet, kind, loving Samuel. "I have to go. I have to go to him." She turned to Claire and held out her hand. "I need the car."

"Danielle, honey, we flew. We don't have our car."

Danielle put a palm on her forehead. "Right." She couldn't think straight. She needed a car.

Emily stepped forward and held out her keys. "Take mine," she said.

"Mom! How will we get home?" Savannah asked.

Emily raised her eyebrows at her daughter as Danielle took the keys from her hand. "We'll figure it out."

Keys in hand, Danielle raced from the room toward the front

of the hospital. Did she even know which car belonged to Emily? It was an SUV. *I'll find it.*

She dashed out into the cold and looked around the parking lot for an SUV. Fortunately, there was only one in sight.

Getting into the driver's seat, she put her head on the steering wheel and took deep breaths. She had no idea which way to go.

"I'm the daughter of a pilot," she told herself. "I've lived in L.A. and Houston. Surely, I can drive to Atlanta."

If only I had an airplane. I could navigate myself there.

GPS.

With sudden inspiration, she used her phone to map her way to the hospital in Atlanta.

The SUV felt huge in her hands. She knew how to drive. She just didn't like to drive.

Within minutes, she was on Highway 280, and it looked like a straight shot from here.

She relaxed her hands on the wheel for the first time since she'd put the vehicle into drive.

Maybe she should have waited to see how her father came through his surgery. But surely, he was going to be okay, since they'd kept him there in Auburn. *Or maybe he was too critical to leave.*

No. Samuel's words came back to her. *Take a deep breath, Danielle. Everything is going to work out.*

Remembering how Samuel had held her hair while she threw up, her eyes teared up, and the road in front of her blurred. She blinked back the tears to be able to see better.

He'd been there for her every step of the way. He'd known

she was pregnant before she was, and had taken her to the doctor.

He'd even offered to be there for her and to help raise the baby.

When Joey had shown up, her ex had left with a black eye and wounded pride.

And she'd walked away from him without even a word; without giving him a chance to redeem himself.

With the perfect man standing right in front of her, declaring his love.

She'd been afraid. Afraid of being hurt. Again.

It was stupid. Being apart from him hurt like hell.

They'd been attached at the hip from the moment they met.

Now, for nearly a month, she'd been nothing but miserable. And for what reason? He was lying in a hospital – perhaps even fighting for his life. She may never even get to see him again. To talk to him. To hold his hand. To kiss him.

What she wouldn't give to have just one more day with him. One more day to have things back the way they were before.

I was wrong. It hurts more to be without him than to be with him.

There was nothing wrong with being like her father. Noah Worthington was a good man, and Samuel didn't even have her daddy's bad quality of not staying in touch.

Samuel wasn't Noah. And he certainly wasn't Joey. Or Richard. Samuel hadn't cheated on her. In her heart, she knew that he'd been telling the truth about his passenger.

As she got into the city traffic, she forced herself to focus and not to think about Samuel, a nearly impossible task.

When her phone rang, she hit speaker. It was her mother.

"Noah is out of surgery and is doing fine."

"Thank God," Danielle said. "I have to go, Mom. I'm hitting traffic."

"Are you sure you're okay to drive? You don't even know where you're going."

Danielle laughed a humorless laugh. It sounded like something between a laugh and a croak. "It's a little late to be worried now. I'm fifteen minutes out. I'll call you when I know something."

She got off the phone and sat forward in the seat.

I have to make this right. When I see Samuel, I'll tell him.

I'll tell him I love him.

Fifty~Six

When Samuel woke up, he was in a helicopter with an oxygen mask over his mouth. As he lay there with his eyes closed, slowly getting his bearings, the last thing he could remember was seeing the end of the runway ahead of them. They'd crashed then.

When he opened his eyes, the medic greeted him cheerfully and removed the mask. He quizzed Samuel on the basics – his name, the date, where he was when the accident happened.

"Where are you taking me?" he asked.

"UAB."

"Where's that? I'm from Houston."

"Birmingham. One of the best hospitals in the country."

"Noah?" His held as breath as he waited for an answer. Danielle's father had to be okay.

"They took him to the local hospital. He had a broken bone. Probably doing surgery, but he'll be okay."

Samuel blew out a breath, and the medic put the oxygen back on his mouth. Noah would be okay then.

He began replaying the last moments before the crash. System failure. That's all it could have been. Noah did everything right. They would try to blame it on the weather and pilot error, but Samuel had landed in worse. The weather had nothing to do with it. Noah had accounted for the slippery runway.

"We're ten minutes out. Is there anyone we can contact for you?"

Danielle.

Danielle was always his first thought. But she'd made it clear that they were no longer a couple. That she didn't want a future with a pilot. Not in words, but in actions.

Something had gone wrong. Terribly wrong. She had been right. He could have been killed.

The irony was that he now had an automatic four months off. A pilot couldn't fly for one hundred twenty days after a concussion. It was almost perfect timing. He would have been around all the time to help her get ready for the baby. The baby that he had been ready to claim as his own.

The helicopter landed at UAB, and Samuel was carried inside on a stretcher. He'd hesitated long enough to avoid answering the medic's question about who to contact about his accident. He felt well enough. He didn't want to alarm his family. The last thing he needed was for them to come flying out here to Alabama from Houston when he was fine. He would tell them all about it at their next Sunday dinner.

Since he was about to have four months off, he could spend some long overdue time with his family.

The next couple of hours were spent with doctors and an

MRI. And more doctors. They finally decided that they would keep him for observation for forty-eight hours.

After getting set up in a private room, a nurse came in with a plastic bag containing his clothes and his cell phone.

He grabbed his cell phone like a man dying of thirst would grasp a cup of water. He had only one text message. It was from his sister reminding him to be there for Sunday dinner. Since it was in two days, he wouldn't make it this week. He'd make an excuse later.

Finally left alone, he laid his head back and closed his eyes. Maybe after a little nap, he'd call his sister. He wasn't over the breakup with Danielle and now this crash. He could use a friendly voice in his ear.

The sense of isolation – being stuck here in a hospital somewhere in Alabama – was overwhelming. To get through it, he imagined he was flying in his Mooney single-engine high above the clouds. His thoughts soon settled enough that he was able to drift off to sleep.

In what seemed like only a few minutes, he opened his eyes to a smiling blonde standing over his bed. He blinked. She wasn't wearing a uniform, and she didn't look familiar.

"I'm sorry," the girl, who looked to be college-aged, smiled. "You didn't answer when I knocked, so I came on in to see if you needed anything."

Samuel shook his head. Why would this girl, this stranger, be here to check on him?

"I'm here with the Sigma Kappa Sorority, and we're visiting people at the hospital with Alzheimer's Disease. I know you don't have it, but since you hit your head, you were kinda the closet person I could find to talk to that would count."

Samuel groaned. The girl was talking, and he couldn't quite follow what she was saying. He closed his eyes and drifted back to sleep. When he woke, Danielle was there, leaning over him. His heart soared. He held out his hand and squeezed hers. She'd come!

"I'm so happy you're here. I've missed you more than you can ever know."

Danielle rushed into the ER and found her way to the desk.

"Samuel Johnson," she struggled to catch her breath.

"Your name," the clerk peered at her over narrow glasses.

"Danielle." She tried to smile. Anything to keep from grabbing the computer from the woman and looking herself.

The woman's hands remained in her lap. "We have a family-only policy for giving out information."

"I'm his fiancé," she blurted.

The woman tilted her head as she seemed to consider.

"Please," Danielle pleaded. "Just tell me if he's even here. I just drove in from Auburn. And we're from Houston." She didn't fight the tears that filled her eyes. Crying on demand was a talent that she'd never mastered… until becoming pregnant. Now, the pregnancy hormones had opened up a whole new world.

The clerk tapped on her computer keys. "He's in room 532," she said.

"Thank you," Danielle said and took off toward the elevators.

When she got off the elevator and approached his room, she stopped. What was she supposed to say? *Hi. I know I broke up with you. But I was so worried.*

Maybe it was best if she didn't say anything.

Her heart pounded in her chest as she put one foot in front of the other. Now that she was here, it took every ounce of strength to keep moving forward.

She heard female laughter as she approached his room. Probably a nurse trying to cheer him up. She put a hand on the doorknob and turned it. As the door opened, she wondered if she was supposed to knock first. Danielle had no experience with hospitals. She'd gone with her mother once to visit her grandmother, but that was it.

As the door swung open, Samuel smiled. With a two-second sweep, she took in the situation. Definitely not a nurse.

Samuel sat propped on pillows in the bed. His attention was on a young lady standing at his bedside. Definitely not a nurse. As she drew closer, she saw that he was holding the girl's hand. She took another step, though her brain was frozen. She stopped just inside the door and heard Samuel's words. "I'm so happy you're here. I've missed you more than you can ever know." It barely registered that his eyes were half closed.

The girl saw Danielle first and turned, concern and confusion shadowing her face. Samuel followed her gaze. His eyes widened in disbelief. "Danielle," he breathed. He looked back at the girl standing next to his bed, holding his hand.

Danielle felt a wave of heat setting her blood to boil. This. This was exactly why she would never marry a pilot.

"You're here." He murmured, looking back at the other girl. "How?" Then turned his gaze back to Danielle.

"I drove." Her voice was barely a whisper, but her heart was in her throat.

"Wait."

Danielle turned around and quietly walked back down the hall. *Never make a scene,* her mother had told her a million times.

Once she was in the parking lot and inside the vehicle, she locked the door and the tears wracked her body. She cried harder than she had ever cried before. Even harder than the time she had taken her mother's Xanax with her father's alcohol.

That had been years ago, and she had never felt that way since.

Not until now. Now she felt like her world had crashed at her feet in a thousand pieces. Even as she'd broken up with Samuel, she'd clung to the belief in her heart that he was different. That he would never hurt her.

He had no idea what it had taken for her to drive to this hospital. Not only the drive itself, but to take the risk that he might want to see her.

He hadn't needed her after all. He'd moved on. Without her. Just like she'd known he would.

It will pass. Years of therapy coalesced in that moment to give her strength. She wiped away the tears and lifted her head. It was raining now. She watched the raindrops slide down the windshield and let them wash away her pain along with it.

Maybe it was the hormones, but whatever it was, it was too much. Samuel deserved better.

I need to get myself together.

Every instinct had her going back up to his room. It was a misunderstanding. She could straighten it out in a minute.

Samuel deserves someone he can make a baby with. His own baby.

I love him too much. I have to let him go.

She put on her seatbelt and put the SUV in reverse.

She needed to get Emily's car back to her. Then she needed to get back to L.A. and back to work. Authors were waiting on their covers, and she had to design them.

And more importantly, she had to get ready to bring home a baby.

Fifty-Eight

Samuel had his feet on the ground before the nurse darted into the room and grabbed hold of his ankles. "Where do you think you're going?" she admonished.

"Danielle," he said, pulling away.

"You can't leave," she told him.

"I can." He made it as far as the elevator. As he stood waiting for the elevator, he knew. He knew he wasn't going to catch her.

She had been moving too fast, and he had lost precious time before he reacted. And that nurse had held him back, and now that same nurse was there grabbing one arm while an orderly took the other. "It's not a good idea for you to leave right now," The man's voice was gentle. Understanding. Unlike Nurse Ratched whose fingers were digging into his upper arm.

He allowed them to lead him back to his room – as if he had a choice. He had some things to think about anyway.

First, and most importantly, Danielle had driven here from

Auburn; the other side of Auburn if he remembered correctly. For a girl who never drove, that was quite an accomplishment.

The girl from Sigma Kappa was still there when he got back into his room. "I appreciate your kindness," he told her, "but I'd like some time to myself now."

The girl left as he climbed back into his bed and lay there with his eyes closed.

He had quite a few things to think about.

CHAPTER
Fifty~Nine

Two weeks later…

Danielle now remembered why she avoided commercial flying when at all possible. The hassle had gotten out of hand. Especially at this time of year, just days before Christmas. She sighed as the older woman sitting next to her pulled a tote bag of merrily-wrapped presents from under the seat in front of her. Yes, she should have taken her father up on that offer.

She walked through the gate at the airport in Fort Worth. Her pulse rate was a little too high. Maybe it was from flying commercial. Her father had offered to send someone to pick her up, but she'd said she needed some time alone. To think.

Fortunately, the expense of booking a flight over and back the same day was so ridiculously outrageous that she had booked a one-way ticket. She had made a good decision in counting on her father getting her back to California.

Or Samuel.

She had come to Fort Worth under the guise of visiting her father, but in truth, she wanted to see Samuel. Maybe it was the sentiment of the holiday season, but she wanted to make things right with him. She hadn't given him a chance to explain himself either time before running away. Something nagged at the back of her brain about the two incidents. Maybe it was his bewildered expression. And that it just didn't fit with what she knew about him. Whatever it was, she wanted to see him. To talk to him.

Her father stood waiting for her just outside the door. It was one of the perks of being a pilot that he had free reign at the airport. He greeted her with a big bear hug, as always.

"I'm so glad you're okay." It was the first time she'd seen him since he was in the hospital, and she had to blink back tears.

"So am I. It's good to see you, too. No luggage?"

"Nah. I'm just here for the day."

"Alright. Let's get lunch." Together, they walked through the airport, then outside to his car. "Are you craving anything in particular?"

"Pizza." She'd run through seafood, then Mexican, now anything with cheese.

"Pizza it is." Driving away from the airport, he took them straight to a small pizzeria.

"You knew just where to go." Danielle said.

Noah looked a little sheepish. "You know pizza is my weakness. I eat here whenever I can come up with an excuse. Just don't tell Savannah."

Danielle laughed. She loved that she and her father were close enough that they had things they did. Things that neither

her mom nor Noah's current wife, Savannah would need to know about. Like eating pizza.

After they ordered, while they waited on their pizza, Noah peered at his daughter. "I know you didn't fly all the way over here to eat pizza. Although I have to admit I've done it myself."

"Yeah." She looked away. There was nothing she couldn't tell her father. That didn't mean it was always an easy thing to do. "I was hoping I could see Samuel."

Noah's eyes widened. Danielle's heart tripped. Surely, if something had happened to him, someone would have told her.

"You didn't try calling him?"

"Dad. I deleted his phone number."

"Pumpkin, you probably shouldn't do things like that."

"I know. But is he here today?"

"He has a mandatory one hundred twenty days off after a concussion."

"So… is he coming back?"

Noah shrugged. "I don't know."

The only way Danielle had communicated with Samuel was through his cell phone. "Daddy, does he still have the company cell phone?"

"Yeah, but he doesn't answer it."

Danielle stared into space. There had to be a way.

"Danielle." Noah pulled her attention back to him. "What happened with him?"

"I saw him. In Houston. At the airport. With another woman."

"When?"

Their pizza arrived, giving Danielle time to think back to

enough details to answer her father's question. "It was the day he had me bring him his birth certificate."

Noah gaped at her. "I remember. He came back so obviously upset, but he wouldn't tell me what was wrong. He'd just taken Annabelle to Houston to see her dying grandfather."

"Annabelle?" Danielle didn't feel so good.

"Yeah." He shrugged. "A client."

"Daddy. I think I messed up."

She told him about how she'd seen Samuel at the airport and stormed off. She also told him about seeing him with the girl at the hospital. "He'd just had a concussion. I think he might have been confused." She blinked back tears. "What should I do Daddy? What would you do?"

CHAPTER

Sixty

Two months later…

Danielle sat at her desk in her home office on the second floor of her mother's house in Los Angeles. She had to give her mother credit. She'd accepted Danielle's pregnancy without a hitch, and together, they had converted a guest room into a home office for Danielle to work. Danielle had an enviable view of the back yard – a manicured lawn with evergreen trees blocking the neighbors.

She was lost in the world of shape shifters. This was her biggest author yet. And the author's release date was in just six months. And big name authors got their books out there for preorder early.

She glanced at the calendar next to her desk and noted the date.

February 14.

She'd gotten through Christmas and New Year's without a boyfriend. She could get through Valentine's Day without one.

As though to remind her that she wasn't alone, the baby in her abdomen kicked. A little feathery kick, but a kick nonetheless. She smiled.

"Just you and me kiddo. We'll get through this just fine."

She ducked back into her work. A couple of minutes later, a movement at the door caught her attention.

She looked up and blinked.

Samuel.

Holding a bouquet of red roses.

She sat back and stared at him, then blinked again to make sure she wasn't hallucinating.

"I have a delivery for Miss Danielle Worthington."

A smile played at the corner of her lips. "Did my father send you?"

He smiled then. "No. As a matter of fact, these are from…" He shifted the bouquet. "Let me just check the card." He looked at the attached envelope. "They're from a mister Samuel Johnson. Do you know him?"

"Hmm." Her lips curved into a slight smile. "I believe he's a pilot from Dallas."

"Oh no," he said. "That's not the same person. This is Samuel Johnson, flight instructor, of L.A."

She frowned at him. "There must be a mistake. The only one I know works for my father."

"Nope," he said. "This one lives right here in L.A. Um. Can I come in?"

"Of course," she said. "I wasn't thinking." She hit save on her computer and slid it aside. "Are those for me? Really?"

He looked wounded. "And who else would they be for?" He set them on the desk, the silver vase glittering in the sunlight streaming through the window. "They're yours if you'll have them."

"It's impolite to refuse a gift." She leaned forward and sniffed one of the perfect rose buds. "Even if it is Valentine's Day."

"Is it Valentine's Day? I wondered why there was such a long line to buy flowers today."

"Ha. Ha."

He shrugged. "It seems we have a tradition. Birthdays. Valentine's Day."

"You missed Christmas." She pointed out.

"You weren't in the office," he said.

"And neither were you." *Nor did you answer your phone even after I found your number on my cell phone statement.*

"I've been off the grid for a while."

She decided to let his statement go. She wanted to see how he planned to play this out. "So how are you feeling?" She asked. "After the crash and all."

"The doctors released me."

"Both you and my father were very lucky. They said it was system failure."

"Luck had nothing to do with it. It was all due to your father's skill and experience that we came out basically unscathed."

"If you call a concussion unscathed."

"Considering the circumstances, I do."

She studied the red rose buds for a moment. They were high quality flowers. Her mother had taught her how to discern quality. "So, really, what brings you here? I'm not expecting my father."

"Your father has nothing to do with my being here."

"How did you get away? He drives a hard bargain with his pilots."

"Right." She wouldn't tell him she'd asked her father about him and already knew that. "I have a mandatory one hundred twenty-day moratorium on flying."

"For the concussion?"

"Yes. And I also quit my job."

She scoffed. "You did not."

"I most certainly did. Ask him."

She glanced at her phone. "I'm not going to ask him."

"Cause then you'd have to believe me."

"Of course I believe you. You've never lied… to… me." She said the last words slowly, realizing that those were the words she should have said to him three months ago.

"And I never will."

She nodded. Trust. Something that he had earned, despite her reluctance to give it. "So, you're visiting." She wasn't quite sure what he was telling her.

"I think we need to talk," he said.

"Right," She stood up and gestured to the day bed across the room. It was perfect for naps, but now it seemed, it was good for entertaining. Next to the day bed was a crib with pink blankets.

Samuel stopped halfway across the room and stared at the crib with a silly grin on his face. "It's a girl," he said.

Danielle smiled as she ran a hand along the now unmistakable baby bump. "Yes. I had to know."

They sat on the day bed, and she wondered where to begin. He looked good. She'd stared at his photo enough to memorize every line on his face, but he was even more handsome in person. When he looked at her, his eyes twinkled with a light that couldn't be captured in a photo.

It seemed he already knew what he wanted to say. "When I saw you in Alabama, I knew I had to do something. Whatever it took to be with you."

His words were like a warm balm settling over her soul. "Samuel…"

"Even if you hadn't left Houston, I didn't want to live like that. I didn't want to live apart and only see you on weekends. You deserve more than that."

"Even that's more than most people have."

"Maybe so. But it isn't for us."

She knew exactly what he meant. They weren't just a romantic couple. They were best friends. They wouldn't be one of those couples who only saw each other in the evenings or weekends for dinner. They were part of each other's daily lives. Or had been until she'd disappeared on him. "I guess I knew you would find me."

"You knew I could."

"And hoped you would." Words she hadn't even admitted to herself. Until now. Seeing him here, it was even more clear how much she'd missed him.

"So," he continued. "I *did* quit my job with Skye Travels."

"You really quit?"

He nodded. "I really did."

"Wow. My father didn't say anything."

"I asked him not to. To let me tell you. And I didn't tell him until two days ago. I waited because I wasn't sure how long he could keep it from you."

She waited for him to say more. He took her hand and wove his fingers through hers. "Danielle, I've moved to L.A."

"But your home is in Houston. Your family. Houston is in your blood."

"I'll get a stronger plane."

She thought about her father and how she hated that he lived so far away – in Alabama, but he worked in Fort Worth and visited her often here in California. There were perks to being a pilot, but not an unemployed pilot.

"What will you do?"

"I'm an instructor."

"I know. You said. But I mean for a job?"

"It is a job. A job that will allow me to be home in the evenings in time to make dinner and take care of you."

She stared at their hands linked together. A flight instructor. Still a pilot. She sighed. "I think I might have mentioned that I don't date pilots."

"Danielle. Seriously? Surely we've gotten past that. Give me a chance."

How could she not? She nodded.

"Will you let me take you flying?"

She laughed. "Flying is all you pilots think about."

"True. But there are some people I'd like you to meet."

CHAPTER
Sixty-One

Samuel sat next to Danielle at Pappa's Burgers, squeezed in between his two grandmothers.

"I'm so glad we finally get to meet you," Veronica Johnson said to Danielle.

"It's nice to meet you all, too."

"You'll come back to the house with us after lunch, won't you? We'd like to spend time with you."

Danielle glanced at Samuel. He shrugged.

He wasn't having to say much today. Everyone was focused on Danielle. They were so excited he'd finally brought a girl to a family function, they practically had them married off.

"Have you set a wedding date?" His older sister asked from across the table.

Danielle had the deer-in-the-headlights reaction for only a fraction of a second. He was probably the only one who saw it. "No," she said, keeping the smile on her face. "We haven't talked about that."

He'd warned her that they would be invasive – in a loving and accepting way. He squeezed her hand. It was so very nice to have someone to share his family's intensity with.

His younger sister chimed in. "You'll get married before the baby comes?"

Samuel scowled at her. He hadn't told anyone that Danielle was pregnant. When she glanced at him, he shook his head.

He could see her thoughts whirling as she decided the best way to go with this. "There's plenty of time before July to figure everything out."

He heard his mother and father whispering from his left. "A baby?"

"Did you know about this?"

His mother beamed. "Another grandchild."

"Like you don't have enough."

His mother elbowed his father. Then when there was a lull in the conversation, she said loud enough for Danielle to hear. "Welcome to the family, dear."

Danielle flushed and squeezed Samuel's hand.

Then their food arrived, and as the server distributed their plates, the conversation moved to other things. Preschools. His brother's new job. With such a big family, there was lots to keep up with.

Danielle relaxed a little and smiled at him. "I tried to warn you," he whispered.

"And I wholeheartedly appreciate that."

He chuckled. "I guess you'll believe me next time."

"Believing and experiencing are a leap apart."

CHAPTER
Sixty-Two

Danielle and Samuel were swept away to his grandparent's house along with the rest of the family after lunch.

"Can I show you around?" Samuel asked.

"Sure." The rest of the family settled into the living room and spilled into the kitchen. The house was full of large windows with an open floorplan. He led her around to the parlor.

"It's a pretty house," Danielle said, looking at Samuel.

"Let's take a break from the family for a few minutes."

"Okay." *Thank goodness.* She hadn't wanted to say anything. Everyone was being so very kind. It was just such a big family. She was a little overwhelmed.

He took her hand and pulled her into a hug. "Are you happy?"

"Of course." She pulled back and his lips went to hers.

"Let's sit." He nudged her toward the sofa.

She turned to sit and stopped. Her thoughts froze. There was a teddy bear there on the sofa. A teddy bear that looked like Pappa, the one Samuel had given her.

In her fit of anger, she'd left him at her apartment here in Houston. She'd called the movers and the apartment office, but no one had seen him. She'd kicked herself a hundred times for leaving him behind in anger.

Maybe everyone in the family had one of them.

She sat next to the teddy bear and couldn't resist picking it up. "This looks like…"

The bear had a pink ribbon tied around its neck. "Pappa."

She ran her hand along the ribbon that was looped through a ring. She lifted the ring. It was a glittery diamond.

"Samuel," She turned, the bear in her hands. "Is this…?"

He was on his knees with a grin on his face. "Pappa and I have something to ask you."

She held her breath.

"Danielle." He took her hands. She inhaled raggedly.

"Is this my bear?"

"Yes. It's your bear. Your bear and I want to ask you something."

"Okay."

He squeezed the bear's paw. And the words "Will you marry me?" came from the bear.

He slipped the ribbon off the bear and held up the ring. "Will you marry me?"

"Yes," she breathed, going into his arms and into a kiss.

After a few minutes, she asked. "How did you get Pappa? I thought he was lost."

"I went to your apartment the day you moved out. The movers told me you'd left. I couldn't just leave him."

"Samuel, I called everybody looking for him."

"Then I'm glad I rescued him."

"I am too." She got off of the floor and sat on the sofa, pulling him with her. She pressed the bear's paw and giggled. Pappa had learned to talk. Then, with her expression serious again, she turned back to Samuel. "Are you sure? You're taking on some serious baggage."

"Hey. I knew about the baggage before you did. Surely that counts for something."

"True. I'm not sure what that says about me."

"I think it means we're an awesome pair."

"We do work well together."

"I was thinking more like we play well together."

She flushed. "We play well together, too."

"So," he said, "since you said yes, I don't have to help you slink out the back door. Everyone's waiting out there."

"They knew?"

"Don't even try keeping something like this from my family. All it takes is for one person to have a suspicion, and suddenly everyone is all over it. I think they have cake."

She laughed. "Then let's not keep them waiting."

And together, they went out to announce their engagement to his family.

Sixty-Three

With family living in Alabama, Texas, and California, and two pilots in the family, choosing a wedding location hadn't been easy.

It was Samuel's younger sister who first suggested a destination wedding. "Danielle's dad can fly us anywhere. Why wouldn't we take advantage of that? I, for one, wouldn't mind getting away for a few days."

Mrs. Johnson admonished her daughter for bringing it up, but the idea took on a life of its own and Savannah said almost the same exact words as Samuel's sister.

Savannah and Noah voted for the mountains in Colorado. Samuel's siblings wanted New Orleans. Samuel and Danielle were thinking a warm Florida beach.

But when Claire's doctor restricted her from flight travel, they went with the Long Beach Museum of Art with its beautiful view of the ocean at sunset.

The wedding was outside on a perfect April afternoon. It

was a family-only affair. Nonetheless, her mother hadn't been able to resist small details like a white carpet for her to walk down the aisle on and rose petals scattered everywhere.

Samuel, Noah, and Grayson all wore tuxes – Danielle's soon-to-be husband, her father, and her stepfather. Danielle smiled at the sight of the handsome men in her family.

As they waited for their cue to walk down the aisle, Noah pulled Danielle aside. "Danielle. You know you don't have to do this. Between me and Savannah and your mother and Grayson, we'll help you raise the child. You'll have plenty of help."

"I'm not worried about that, Dad."

"We can stop now. It isn't too late."

"I thought you liked Samuel."

"I do like Samuel, but I want you to be sure. Not to feel like this is a train you can't stop."

"You couldn't pull me off this train if you tried."

Her father kissed her on the cheek. "Okay then. If he ever hurts you, you tell me, and I'll take care of it."

"Dad." She laughed. "I love Samuel. I *want* to marry him."

"Is everything good?" Grayson asked as they came back to stand in their places.

"Everything's perfect." Danielle hugged her stepfather.

Samuel stood waiting as her two fathers walked her down the aisle – one on each arm.

Danielle wore white – an empire A-Line floor-length wedding gown. It was sleeveless, but the skirt had mounds of tulle with layers and beading. She didn't hide her pregnancy, but she didn't accent it either. Unless she placed a hand beneath her stomach, it wasn't evident. For *something blue,* she wore flat Superga sneakers in blue. For something old, she wore a diamond necklace that her grandmother gave her, and for something borrowed, she wore a little homemade ring that her father had made for Savannah in college, but never had the chance to give to her.

When they reached the front of the aisle to stand in front of the priest, Danielle stood next to Samuel and the rest of the world faded away.

He had become so very dear to her. The way his lips curved up at the corners when he looked at her. His eyes that focused on her and only on her. The way their hands seemed to magnetically snap together when they were close.

Then there was the way he seemed in-tune to the nuances of her mood and to know her every need before even she did.

She was only content when he was near. She could no longer imagine a day without him in it.

When he said "I do," he said the words softly, only for her, leaning forward with his lips almost touching her cheek.

Then when the priest paused and looked at her, she said "I do" before he even said the words. It didn't matter what he said, what the words were. She wanted this man for the rest of her life.

Then Samuel leaned her back, Hollywood-style, and kissed her. Though she instinctively put her arms around his neck, his arms around her back were strong, holding her secure. Seconds ticked.

It wasn't until everyone started clapping that he set her back on her feet and grinned at her.

And just like that, she was Mrs. Samuel Johnson.

Sixty-Four

Danielle woke Samuel in the middle of the night. At first, he thought he was dreaming. "Samuel?"

"Samuel." She shook him this time.

He sat up in the bed, his heart racing. "What?"

"It's time."

She was already sitting up.

"Now?"

"Now."

"I need to send your mother a text." That was the plan, he'd send a text to her mother, and she would start the chain reaction that would send everyone to meet them at the hospital.

"I sent it already."

"Oh no! You can't take my job. Your mother will hate me."

She smiled smugly. "I sent it from your phone, silly."

"We should go then."

"Probably."

How was she so calm? Her father and Savannah were

staying in a hotel not far from here and on the way to the hospital. Claire and Grayson were on standby. Samuel's family would come out later after they were settled in with the new baby.

Samuel got dressed, brushed his teeth, and helped Danielle from the bed. "Do you want me to carry you?"

"We'd both be on the floor. I can walk."

Their overnight bags were already in the car. He just had to grab their cell phones, wallet, and keys, and they were good to go.

It was all too simple.

Halfway to the car, the contractions hit her again. Danielle went to her knees in pain. Samuel, helpless to do anything other than comfort her, waited until she could walk again.

Another wave hit her in the car. Samuel drove faster.

When he got to the ER, everyone was already there. Noah met them at the car and helped Samuel get Danielle out and to the door.

Someone showed up with a wheelchair.

Samuel wheeled her inside.

Everything for the next three hours was a blur.

The only thing that Samuel remembered clearly was when the doctor put the squirming little baby in Samuel's arms. He sat on the bed next to Danielle and gingerly placed the baby in her mother's arms. Danielle smiled up at him.

It was in that moment that Samuel knew that from this moment forward, he would think of the baby as his. It didn't matter that she wasn't his biologically. He and Danielle had brought this baby into the world together. They would raise it together and love it together.

"Have you decided?" They had talked about so many

different names. They had finally decided that they would know when the baby got here.

Danielle looked down at the cooing infant. "Samantha Skye."

Samuel beamed. His first choice. Samantha after him, and Skye just because it was such an awesomely fitting name for the daughter and granddaughter of a pilot.

Samuel bent over and kissed her on the tip of the nose. "I love it. And I love you."

Sixty~Five

Danielle felt like she'd been through hell and back.

But it didn't matter. She had a beautiful baby girl to show for it, and Samuel was going to be the most awesome father.

Her heart warmed as he placed the baby carefully in her arms.

"Before I bring in the rest of the family, I'd like to ask you something."

"Okay." She took a deep breath. "But keep in mind, I may not be exactly coherent."

"That's kind of what I wanted to talk about."

She waited. Was this where he told her this was more than he could handle?

"Was it so terrible? Having a baby?" He reached and smoothed her damp hair.

"It was awful and wonderful all at the same time."

"But look what we have to show for it."

"She's beautiful." Danielle put the baby's tiny little hand in hers and counted her fingers. Again.

"So… I was thinking."

"Oh boy."

He laughed. "I was wondering how you felt about thinking – just thinking – about us making one of these little guys together."

"I've been thinking about that for quite some time, actually." She smiled into his eyes.

"So have I. But not just the process. Once you're over your pregnancy, but to have one to go with this one."

"That's something I'm willing to take into consideration."

He took her hand and kissed her fingers. "But then if you decide you never want to go through this again, I totally wouldn't blame you."

"I totally want to give little Samantha a little brother or sister."

"I never want to tell her."

Her heart stuttered a little. "You never want to tell Samantha?" She rocked the sleeping baby gently.

"I want to be her father. I never want her to doubt that I chose her. I don't want her to know about the… sperm donor."

"Deal." Danielle had been thinking similarly. "It may come up again, but I won't bring it up."

He pressed his lips against hers. Her eyes fluttered closed.

Today was her daughter's birthday.

And the man of her dreams was here next to her.

Maybe happily ever after wasn't just a myth after all.

Danielle straightened her skirt and slipped into her heels. Today was her daughter's birthday. She was one-year-old today.

And in about one hour, her house would be filled with family.

She and Samuel were waiting a bit to start on baby number two. Right now, their hands were more than full with little Samantha. She was a good baby, but with both of them doting on her, she took most of their time.

Neither one of them had been apart from her at night yet.

They were working on that.

In fact, tonight, after the baby's party, she and Samuel had reservations at an Italian restaurant down the street.

With Danielle's family there, they had agreed that it was the perfect time for Danielle and Samuel to have their first post-baby date.

She peeked out the back window where Samuel was busy

with the grill. Samantha played at her feet. She scooped the baby up and went downstairs to the kitchen.

There was nothing left to do. The cake was ready. The gifts were wrapped.

When the doorbell rang, she knew it would be her mother and Grayson before she even looked. She hugged both of them, and Grayson took Samantha.

In his other hand, Grayson carried little Beau – named after Claire's maiden name Beauchamp - in a little baby carrier.

Danielle and Claire had no more than gotten to the kitchen when the doorbell rang. It was her father and his wife Savannah.

Samuel came in through the back door and took it in stride that everyone was an hour early.

"We're a little early," Noah said.

"I couldn't keep him away." Savannah said reaching for the baby, Samantha.

"Who couldn't keep who away?" Noah said.

"It's great," Samuel grinned. "Let me just wash up, and I'll get you all something to drink."

"I'll help you." Grayson shrugged when Claire rolled her eyes.

"He gets a little nervous when there are too many babies around."

"I do not."

"Since everyone's here," Danielle said, "there's no reason why we can't go ahead and get the babies ready for the party."

"Sounds like a great idea." Savannah agreed.

Claire set down her diaper bag. "I couldn't agree more. Then the babies can take a nap while we rest and have a glass of wine. I'm exhausted."

Savannah nodded. "Danielle, you did it right. Don't wait until you're our age to have a baby. If you think you're tired now, just imagine having twenty years on you."

"At least you know what you're doing."

Both Savannah and Claire laughed. "If only."

"Sounds like our cue to head out to the barbecue pit." Noah said.

"Men." Both women said at the same time.

Danielle followed Samuel into the kitchen and put wine glasses on a tray while he washed up.

"It's kind of amazing that your divorced parents get along so well."

"It is, isn't it? My mom and dad had sort of an arranged marriage. And now both of them are back with their high school sweethearts."

"I hope you don't get any ideas like that."

Danielle handed him the bottle of wine and the corkscrew. "Not a chance. You're stuck with me."

"I'm just glad we don't have to deal with Joey."

"I know. I haven't heard from him since the letter."

"I don't think he'll bother us."

Danielle laughed. "Me either. I don't know what you said to him that night at my apartment in Houston, but he's staying away."

Samuel shrugged. "I'll never tell."

"We should probably leave the wine in here until the babies go to sleep."

He chuckled. "That's probably a good idea."

Danielle carried the birthday cake, and Samuel carried the plates and forks.

"If we're doing the cake now, I'll have to get the guys back inside," Savannah said.

"I think we should do it while the babies are still awake." Claire pointed out.

They set up the dining room table while Savannah got Noah and Grayson back inside. Then they rounded up the babies, and, after putting little Samantha in her high chair, both Savannah and Claire sat with their babies in their laps.

They sang *Happy Birthday*, passed out cake, which soon went everywhere, and Danielle helped Samantha open her presents – practical nonslip socks from Grayson, a fly and learn airplane from Noah, a little red wagon from Claire, a Manhattan treetop adventure activity center from Savannah, and a sit-to-stand walker from Mom and Dad.

An hour later, the house looked like a tornado went through it, but the babies were all three asleep.

Savannah collapsed on the sofa. "We need wine."

"And we need to get the barbeque going." Noah suggested.

"We have that taken care of." Danielle said.

Samuel poured wine for everyone, but poured sparkling water in his own glass.

"What's up?" Danielle leaned over and asked.

"Someone has to be a designated driver. With three infants in the house, you never know. Besides, I'm driving to the restaurant."

"Good point. I'll have water, too."

"Um Samuel." Danielle looked up from her phone. "I think you missed the turn to the restaurant."

"I'm taking the scenic route." He winked at her, and she went back to her phone.

"We got some really good pictures of Samantha. I'm sending some of them to your family."

"Thanks, love."

A few minutes later, Danielle looked up again. "Where are we going?"

"The airport."

She frowned at him. "Why? We're going to miss our reservation."

"I think we're going to just make it."

She answered a text on her phone. "You're acting strange."

"I know. I told your dad I wouldn't be able to pull it off."

She groaned. "Oh no. What did my dad talk you into?"

"Actually it was my idea. He just helped with the details."

"Are we flying somewhere?"

"Yes." Samuel beamed at her. "But I'm not supposed to tell you. It's supposed to be a surprise."

She almost pressured him into telling her. It wouldn't take much effort. But instead, she decided to go along and let him surprise her.

Besides, it was kind of fun wondering what he had planned. With Savannah and Claire at their house, she felt safe leaving Samantha there under their watch.

And… she could peek at the Nest cams at any time.

She leaned her head back against the seat and rested her eyes until they got to the airport.

They climbed into his little Mooney airplane, and she watched as he prepared to fly. She loved it when he went into pilot mode. Other women may find firemen attractive or even doctors, but for Danielle, it was pilots— or maybe just one pilot in particular.

An hour later, they were flying over the Magic Kingdom at Disneyland. Danielle beamed at her husband as their wheels touched down at John Wayne Airport.

After he turned off the plane and helped her down, he said. "I seem to recall that on the day we met, you told me that your perfect birthday would be to have dinner at the Magic Kingdom castle. Since we couldn't go on your birthday, I thought our daughter's birthday would be the next best thing."

She put her arms around him. "It isn't the next best thing." She kissed him on the lips. "It's perfect."

THE END

Turn the page for a preview of Just Stay…

KATHRYN KALEIGH

Just Stay

FOR THE LOVE OF THE FLIGHT

CHAPTER 1

Isobel LaFleur adjusted her sunglasses. The bright Dallas sun coming in through the windshield of the little Cessna Citation, one of Noah Worthington's newest private jets, was brutal.

She was just back from a quick turnaround flight to Denver. Dropping off a woman and her Australian shepherd for a visit to her daughter's house.

Isobel had spent some time vacuuming up the dog hair and wiping down the windows and seat. Dogs invariably drooled on windows. Every time.

As she went down her pre-flight checklist, she absently swept away a floating dog hair. There would be dog hairs in the cabin for days.

Otherwise, it was a light day for her, especially for a Friday, and she had a long weekend ahead.

She had to take a passenger - she glanced at her clipboard - Matthew Rodgers - to a small town in Louisiana, then fly him back to Dallas on Sunday.

The drive to Marigold, Louisiana wasn't more than four hours at the most by car, but to each his own. Besides, those who preferred the convenience of flying over driving paid the rent.

The biggest problem was that Isobel was from a small town just north of Houston. She'd worked hard to get out of there, vowing to herself that she'd never live in a small town again.

So the prospect of spending two nights in a town so small she'd never even heard of it was off-putting to say the least.

But taking care of clients was Noah Worthington's first and foremost policy. He'd built Skye Travels out of nothing more than a dream and now landing a job flying for him was more coveted than flying for any of the major airlines.

Isobel had been with Skye Travels for about eighteen months now. And the job so far had lived up to her expectations and then some.

She absolutely loved it. She could pretty much set her own schedule, within reason, of course. She could request short out and back day trips or she could ask for longer trips.

That particular perk of the job - reasonable freedom - came with a give and take.

When a flight like the one she was on today came up all of a sudden - as so many of them did - Noah looked for volunteers.

Isobel hadn't had anything on her schedule for the weekend. And to be honest, flying was flying, even if it did involve spending two nights in a little town in Louisiana.

And it got her out of her best friend's wedding dress try on thing. She'd already done two of them. And sitting in a wedding dress shop while her friend came out in various dresses wasn't all that exciting. The most exciting part was holding up little hand-painted signs that read things like *Love it* or *Next* or *No Way*.

But the whole process would take the better part of half a day and, though Isobel had a high tolerance for boredom, she found waiting for her friend to change from dress to dress interminable.

Isobel was excited for her friend, but her personal idea of a romantic wedding involved a flight to Vegas.

She didn't get into the whole tradition of trying on a million wedding dresses and tasting wedding cakes and... monogramed cookies, for God's sake.

And, of course, with the whole Vegas option, there was flying involved.

Matthew Rodgers was late.

With the way commercial airlines had people trained to be early, it was unusual for a passenger to actually be late for his flight.

She thought about calling him. She had his phone number right there on her clipboard.

But decided instead to use the time to help Gretta sort through some dresses.

Gretta had found a cool app that she and all her friends could log into. They'd swipe right if they liked a dress or left if they didn't.

After everyone went through the dresses, Gretta would be able to see which dresses her friends thought would be best for her. It was supposed to cut down on the trying on and modeling part of the process, but Isobel doubted that would actually happen. Gretta enjoyed trying on dresses way too much.

Isobel started swiping. Then stopped and sent Gretta a quick text. *Really... I can fly you two to Vegas.*

She got a quick message back. A cute emoji of Gretta shaking her gorgeous head of long blonde hair.

Ah well. It was worth a try. It wasn't the first time she'd offered and it wouldn't be the last. The wedding wasn't until December, so she had at least six months to change Gretta's mind.

Ten minutes later a limo pulled out on the tarmac and stopped near her plane.

Isobel tamped down her negative thoughts about the entitled rich and put a smile on her face. Just because he drove up in a limo... and was late... didn't make him a bad person.

She went to the door of the plane and waited for the driver to unload Matthew's luggage onto a cart. A baggage handler then loaded the passenger's luggage - three big suitcases and a trunk - alongside her one suitcase.

She was reminded of a trip she and Gretta had taken together. It had been the one time Isobel and Gretta had gone on a cruise. Gretta had taken practically every outfit she owned, making Isobel look like a pauper next to her.

Gretta had loved the cruise. The whole dressing up - a different outfit for every activity. Isobel had been in hell. She would have left after the first day. But of course, that wasn't an option.

After that, Isobel hadn't taken any more trips where she didn't have access to either a car or an airplane.

The driver opened the passenger's door and after a few minutes a man with a set of crutches stepped out.

That explained a lot. She'd never been on crutches herself, but it made sense that everything took longer to do.

The man who stepped out of the limo and took the crutches had to be Matthew.

He wore a cast on the bottom half of his left leg.

A blue baseball cap on his head plastered with a large T and dark sunshades hid most of his appearance. But he was tall with a lean muscular build. He was wearing a tee-shirt and gray jogging pants. Quite comfortably dressed for the short flight. Most of her passengers flew at least in their Sunday best. But then most passengers weren't wearing a cast.

Isobel went back to the cockpit and waited. She didn't want to stare as Matthew laboriously made his way to the plane.

It took a bit of maneuvering, but after handing his crutches to the driver, he climbed aboard.

Isobel adjusted the black captain's hat that was part of her uniform and came out to greet her passenger.

"Hello," she said with a bright smile. "I'm Isobel LaFleur. I'll be your pilot today."

Matthew didn't even look at her. He frowned as he adjusted his leg and removed his sunshades. His eyes, flickering in her direction for only a second, were the bluest blue Isobel had ever seen.

"Then we should get going, don't you think?"

"Of course." Isobel kept the smile on her lips, but it faded from her eyes.

She took her seat and began going down the pre-flight checklist.

He was the one who'd been late.

She'd been quite patient waiting on him.

And now he wanted to *get going*.

Isobel would get going alright. She knew how to be professional but distant.

Matthew Rodgers better hope he didn't need anything extra.

CHAPTER 2

Matthew Rodgers was in hell.

Going anywhere. Doing anything was an ordeal. Even sitting here on the little airplane.

Since he couldn't drive, his little sports car sat in storage for who knew how many weeks.

He'd torn his calf muscle completely in half. And besides the pain in the neck of using crutches, the pain that radiated through his calf was almost unendurable at times.

He took a sip of the clear seltzer water the pilot had provided. He hadn't had any special requests. But the girl on the phone at Skye Travels kept asking.

So he just made up something. He didn't even like seltzer water. Plain old tap water suited him just fine.

He would have stayed home through all this if he'd had a

choice, but when he made a commitment, he did everything he could to follow through.

And he wasn't about to subject any of his friends to a weekend with his family. Or vice versa.

And right now, the Rangers were willing to pay for whatever it took to keep him happy.

It wasn't even their fault. He'd been standing on the field during baseball practice, sure, but it could have happened anywhere.

He'd simply taken a step backwards and his calf muscle had popped, leaving it torn completely in two.

That kind of thing normally happened when an athlete was doing something athletic. Not taking a step backwards.

The doctors called it a freak accident.

Matthew could have used a little less freakiness in his life.

The pilot was pretty and she seemed sweet.

He just wasn't in the mood for pretty or sweet.

Besides, being a pilot, she'd also be smart. And Matthew hadn't been around that many smart women lately.

He wasn't sure he had the energy right now to keep up his end of a meaningful conversation.

He just wanted to get this weekend over with and get back to his apartment.

Then he could stew in his misfortune. Alone.

But he only had one little sister and she was getting engaged.

He needed to meet the guy before all this went too far along the path.

If he was honest with himself, he had to admit that it was already too far gone or they wouldn't be having this engagement party.

That's what happened when he put his career first.

Family slid into second place and little sisters got engaged.

The flight was smooth.

And he promised himself he'd be nice as the wheels touched down on the little runway in Marigold, Louisiana.

The airport was out in the middle of nowhere. A wide-open space surrounded by trees on all sides. Just one opening for a little blacktop road that led to the highway.

It would be okay. He wouldn't be here long.

A visit didn't mean he would be stuck here. He'd gotten away from the small town and a visit didn't mean anything more than a visit.

If he could just talk his sister into moving to the city...

The plane came to a stop and after a few minutes, the pilot opened the door.

The smile she'd had for him earlier was gone. In its stead was a serious professionalism. He'd caused that.

"Do you need any help getting out?" she asked.

Matthew shook his head. "Nah. I can manage." He maneuvered himself out of the plane and stood on his crutches.

The doctors had been smart. They'd arranged the cast so that he couldn't put any weight on his leg.

Still, every little movement hurt like hell.

Isobel looked around at the little runway that passed for an airport. No other planes. No cars.

Nothing.

"Um. Do we need to call anyone?" she asked.

Matthew pulled his phone out. "My brother's supposed to be here." He sent a quick text. Drake was always late.

Though Matthew had previously prided himself on being on

time, this leg injury was pulling him into the family trait of being late.

"I can unload the luggage." Isobel seemed a bit unsure of how to proceed. Matthew got the feeling that she wasn't comfortable with the little runway. He wondered if she'd ever been to an airport this small.

An airport that was only a runway. Still it had a designation. ML1.

A text came in from Drake.

> Ten minutes out.

Matthew shot back.

> Don't text and drive.

> Just answering your question.

Matthew blew out a breath. It was going to be a long weekend.

"Please don't," he said. "My brother will be here shortly.

Just minutes later an ancient green pickup truck came lumbering out of the trees toward the runway. Matthew heard the truck before he even saw it.

It was just like his brother to pick him up in the family's forty plus year-old beat up truck.

Drake loved to make fun of the fact that Matthew lived in the city in what he called a fancy apartment with regular cleaning service that took care of his house cleaning, laundry, etc.

Something only a brother could get away with.

Drake stepped out of the truck. His tall, lean body wearing faded jeans and a plaid flannel shirt.

Drake was really playing it to the hilt.

Matthew took a step forward, then stood there balancing on his crutches.

Drake took one look at Isobel and broke into a wide grin.

Isobel stood warily watching the two of them. She was slim and petite. Not more than five four or so. Her sleek brunette hair was pulled back in a ponytail beneath her captain's cap.

A few strands of hair had escaped the ponytail and fell about her face. She absently swept the hair away, keeping her attention on his brother.

Drake held out a hand. "Welcome to Marigold," he said. "My name's Drake."

Matthew had to bite his tongue.

He had, after all, seen her first.

Isobel smiled at Matthew's brother, Drake.

Drake looked like the typical small-town guy. Blue jeans and a flannel shirt.

The kind of guys she'd grown up with.

She smiled back. At least Drake was friendly. Unlike Matthew. Matthew was cranky and difficult.

And obviously very rich. Matthew didn't belong here. At least not the Matthew she'd seen so far.

But Drake did.

She shook Drake's rough and calloused hand. "Thank you, Drake." She was pleased with herself for not cutting her gaze toward Matthew. She wanted to say *See. Your brother knows how to behave properly.*

But she didn't. *She* behaved properly. Matthew was her client. Not Drake.

It was an important thing to remember.

"The prodigal son returns," Drake said.

"Only for our sister, Tara."

Drake folded his arms. "She sends her best."

"What have you done with her?" Matthew looked like he needed to sit. He was wobbling a bit on his crutches. "She was supposed to come with you."

Drake shrugged. "The boyfriend beckoned, I guess."

"Great. Just great."

"Look," Isobel said, stepping between the brothers and turning toward Drake. "Can you just grab his luggage while I call an Uber?"

Drake laughed. "An Uber."

She stepped aside. "Yeah," Isobel said over her shoulder as she opened the Uber app.

It took about half a minute for her to figure out that Marigold did not have Uber service.

She wiggled her toes in her high heeled pumps. There was no telling how far it was to town and the one hotel. The only hotel in the world that didn't take reservations. According to the scheduler at Skye Travels their policy was, *We always have rooms, honey. You don't need a reservation.*

As Drake transferred Matthew's luggage piece by piece from the plane to the old truck, Isobel gathered up her little crossbody bag and iPad and locked the plane. She'd just have to rent a car and come back for her luggage.

She tapped the iPad screen and held it out to Matthew to sign. Balanced precariously on the crutches, he scribbled his name.

"I'll see you Sunday at ten o'clock," she said as Drake walked past with the last of the suitcases. The solid black one with the pink and green luggage tag.

He had her suitcase.

"Wait," she said. "That one's mine."

Drake paused, holding the heavy piece of luggage with obvious ease and looked to Matthew.

"They said you'd be staying," Matthew said to Isobel.

Isobel looked from one brother to the other. "I am."

Matthew looked at her with a crooked grin. "Never knew a female to leave her luggage behind."

Isobel acknowledged the bristle that went up her spine. Let it go. She was, after all, a female. And she was actually kind of secretly pleased that he'd noticed.

"I'll walk to town. I'll rent a car and come back for my suitcase."

Drake set her suitcase on the ground and put one hand on a hip as though he had all the time in the world to watch how this unfolded.

Matthew just started hobbling toward the pickup, grimaces of pain shooting across his face. "Suit yourself," he said, "but it's a ten mile walk to town."

Isobel felt her jaw drop. Ten miles.

She exercised. On occasion. At least once a week she forced herself to the gym for a three-mile run on the treadmill.

The thought of walking ten miles - in high heels or barefoot - was unimaginable. She tried to calculate how long it would take to go ten miles. She could run four, maybe five miles an hour, but walk about three and a half miles an hour. Before she went too far down into the math, she remembered that she'd brought white sneakers.

She slid her suitcase away from Drake, pulled her white

sneakers from the outside pocket of her suitcase and while the two men watched, changed shoes.

"What?" she asked, as she carefully stuffed her heels into her luggage.

"There's room in the truck for you," Drake said, watching his brother.

The two of them exchanged a look and Drake lifted the suitcase into the back of the truck.

"I..." she said, eyeing the truck with trepidation.

She was seriously trying to weigh out the choice of walking ten miles or riding in the pickup.

Even growing up in a small town hadn't prepared her for riding in something that looked so unsafe. It probably didn't even have seatbelts.

Matthew leaned against the open truck door and grinned at her. All traces of cranky and difficult were gone.

Instead, he was grinning at her with such charm that it nearly took her breath away.

Ten miles was a really long way and it would be dark by the time she got to town.

She shook her head. There was stubborn and there was stupid.

She didn't consider herself to be stupid.

"Fine," she said, as she walked toward the truck.

Matthew chuckled. "You'll thank me in the morning."

She slid across the bench seat. It was surprisingly clean. The leather was soft, like it had recently been replaced.

But she'd been right. No middle seatbelt. "No seatbelt," she said under her breath.

"Don't worry," Matthew said sliding onto the seat next to her and settling his crutches beside him before he fastened his waist only seat belt. "I'll hold you."

He went to wrap his arms around her, but she ducked away. Just as Drake took his seat on her left.

"Whoa," Drake said. "There's plenty of room for all of us. And don't worry about the seat belt. I happen to know the sheriff."

"I was more worried about the lack of safety," she said, crossing her arms.

Drake turned the key and the motor flared to life. "Matthew will keep you safe."

Isobel glanced at Matthew out of the corner of her eyes.

The pain was back on his face as he adjusted his leg. Maybe she'd just imagined the charming version of the man who sat beside her.

Maybe she'd seen what she needed to see to keep her from walking the ten miles to town.

Either way, it wasn't the seatbelt that was she worried about so much at this point.

It was Matthew.

Charming Matthew had her heart racing in a way that was not a good sign.

It was going to be a long three days.

Fortunately, she would get to spend most of it alone in the little town of Marigold.

A town so small the hotel didn't take reservations.

She sighed.

Yes, it was going to be a long weekend.

Matthew clearly remembered why he only visited for a couple of days at Christmas.

It wasn't just the small town of Marigold itself that kept him at bay, Matthew mused as they traveled along the highway and turned left onto Main Street.

Ok, maybe it wasn't quite ten miles. But for a girl like Isobel, wearing not only a tight black pencil skirt and matching fitted jacket, but high heels to boot, it may as well be a hundred miles. The thought of her walking along this highway was not something he could even consider allowing to happen.

The town was quiet this morning. The morning rush would happen soon. A few would crowd into the pizza parlor and a few into a little sandwich shop. But most people brought their lunch from home. Much different from Dallas / Fort Worth where lunch was a time for escape and business meetings.

If the small-town culture of Marigold wasn't enough to keep him away, it was his family.

His brother Drake who was guaranteed to give him hell. Like picking him up from the airport in the green pickup. He had to know that he'd have a pilot with him. A pilot who would need a ride to town. Apparently Drake found humor in that.

His sister Tara. Who'd promised she'd be there to pick him up at the airport, but when it came time to be there, she'd taken the better offer. She'd smile that smile of hers that lit up her innocent face and no one would say another word.

Then there were his parents. His mother would be off doing some society thing or working at her little shop. His father would be working, of course. In his mind, the bank couldn't run without him.

And perhaps his father was right. It was a small local bank and Walter oversaw everything. The children had always been expected to make their careers there, eventually taking over.

But his sister had no interest in working at all. Fresh out of high school, where she was the homecoming queen and head cheerleader wanted nothing to do with the bank. She wanted to be a wife and mother. And she was clearly headed straight forward on that path.

Drake wanted nothing to do with corporate life on any level. Not even the small-town kind. He worked as a forester, choosing to spend his days outdoors.

And, of course, Matthew, the only one of the three who'd gone to college, had graduated with a degree in aviation. Matthew was a pilot and no doubt a secret disappointment to his parents.

If that wasn't enough to keep Matthew away from his family, he didn't know what was.

Drake slammed on the brakes as the one traffic signal turned yellow. Normally Drake never slowed for yellow lights.

Matthew instinctively put an arm across Isobel's waist to hold her in place. She grabbed hold of his arm with both hands and shot Drake a look that he ignored.

"I'm sorry about my brother's driving," Matthew said. "He spends most of his time walking about through the forest."

Drake shrugged. "Sorry." Matthew was certain he didn't mean it. "Since Tara bailed, I didn't take the time to go home and change out vehicles. So you get the pleasure of riding in my work truck. It's not so smooth as the other cars, but it'll get us there."

Since Isobel held onto his arm, he left it there as they sat through the light.

He recognized old Mr. Parker passing by in front of them as they sat there. It was funny how so few changes happened in Marigold.

Some people would see that as part of its charm.

"We'll be there in a few minutes," Drake said as he shifted the truck into gear and turned left.

They passed by the little hotel - a two-story cottage with yellow trim. "Is that my hotel?" Isobel said, pushing Matthew's arm away.

A *No Vacancy* sign hung clearly out front beneath the Marigold Inn.

"It's the only hotel," Matthew said, moving his arms away from her.

"They said I didn't need a reservation," she said, a mix of confusion and frustration and not a little desperation in her voice.

"Normally, they'd have rooms," Drake said. "But with my sister's engagement party, a lot of people are in from out-of-town."

"Why wouldn't they just tell us that?" Isobel said.

Matthew looked at her sharply. Her lower lip was quivering just a little. He did not want her to cry. *Please don't cry.*

"You'll stay with us," Matthew said quickly. "We'd planned on it anyway."

But she was shaking her head. "I can't do that. It's not proper."

"Proper?" Drake looked at her sideways.

"We have plenty of room," Matthew wondered why Drake was driving so slowly. He must be going a good five miles below the speed limit.

His family lived on the other side of town from the airport. Most inconvenient from his viewpoint.

They had at least another fifteen minutes to sit cramped up here together at this rate. Not that he was complaining about sitting next to Isobel.

But if she was going to cry, he wasn't sure he could handle it.

"I'll just call them," Isobel said. "Maybe they saved a room for me after all."

Drake opened his mouth. "They only have-"

"Drake," Matthew interrupted sharply. "Let her call."

There was a hopefulness in her voice that Matthew couldn't bear to crush.

There was no need to tell Isobel that the Marigold Inn only had six rooms. And his cousins had booked all of them this morning.

"I see. Thank you for your time." Isobel ended the call and pressed her phone against her chin.

"Any luck?" Drake asked.

If Matthew had been close enough to his brother, he would have elbowed him in the stomach.

Drake knew as well as Matthew did that the rooms were all booked. His mother had sent out a group text just that morning letting them all know.

No one really cared, but it turned out to be relevant now with the lovely Isobel sitting next to him looking crushed.

"The rooms are all booked." She looked at Matthew. "Are there any other hotels nearby?"

Keep Reading Just Stay…

Sign up for my NEWSLETTER to get all my romance releases, sales, Kickstarter announcements, and a **FREE** romance, SEALED WITH A KISS

ALPINE FALLS

DON'T MISS ANY OF THESE BESTSELLERS

www.kathrynkaleigh.com

DON'T MISS ANY OF THE SILVER PINES SECOND CHANCES SERIES:

www.kathrynkaleigh.com

**A new boss.
A fake girlfriend.
A secret identity.
What could possibly go wrong?**

**What would you do if the very system you
believed in, worked for, even lived for,
turned against you?**

DON'T MISS ANY OF THE BOOKS IN THE **VOWS OF PROTECTION** SERIES:

www.kathrynkaleigh.com

A ghostly presence...
A rip in time that never healed...
An impossible romance...

A Storm
A Spell.
A Step Back in Time.

INTO THE MIST
TIME TRAVEL SERIES

A Bride for all Eternity.

Sign up for my NEWSLETTER to get all my romance releases, sales, Kickstarter announcements, and a **FREE** romance, SEALED WITH A KISS

Vows of Inheritance Series

(Reading Order)

Vow to Protect

Vow to Redeem

All of the books in the Vows of Inheritance Series are standalone and can be read out of order. However, some books have characters from the previous stories in them.

CONTEMPORARY

(ALPINE FALLS)

Stranded in Alpine Falls

Belonging in Alpine Falls

The Spirit of Christmas in Alpine Falls

Christmas Wishes in Alpine Falls

Secrets and Second Chances

Honeymoon with a Stranger

Finding True North in Alpine Falls

A Ghost of Christmas Magic in Alpine Falls

(SILVER PINES)

The Way Back to You

Back to Where We Began

When We Were Us

(ONCE UPON FOREVER)

My Forever Guy

Our Forever Love

Forever Vows

Finding Forever

Accidentally Forever

(TRUE NORTH)

Borrowed Until Monday

Still Mine

The Moon and the Stars at Christmas

Perfectly Mismatched

On the Way to Forever

A Merry Little Christmas

On the Way Home to Christmas

It was Always You

(UNBREAK MY HEART)

Begin Again

Love Again

Falling Again

(FOR THE LOVE OF THE FLIGHT)

Just Stay

Just Chance

Just Believe

Just Us

Just Once

Just Happened

Just Maybe

Just Pretend

Just Because

(MAGNETIC NORTH)

Second Chance Kisses

Second Chance Secrets

First Time Charm

Three Broken Rules

Second Chance Destiny

Unexpected Vows

(FALLING FOR CHRISTMAS)

The Heart of Christmas

The Magic of Christmas

In a One Horse Open Sleigh

A Secret Royal Christmas

An Old Fashioned Christmas

(CITY SKYLINE BILLIONAIRES)

Billionaire's Unexpected Landing

Billionaire's Accidental Girlfriend

Billionaire's Fallen Angel

Billionaire's Secret Crush

Billionaire's Barefoot Bride

(TRULY, MADLY, DEEPLY)

The Lady in the Red Dress

On the Edge of Chance

Sealed with a Kiss

Kiss Me at Midnight

The Heart Knows

(STOLEN ECHOES)

When Cupid's Arrow Strikes

Chasing Fireflies

A Chance Encounter

(EDGE OF THE HORIZON)

The Forever Equation

Pretend Boyfriend

All our Tomorrows

Kissing for Keeps

Out of the Blue

The Princess and the Playboy

(RED LIPSTICK KISSES)

Red Lipstick Kisses and Small Town Wishes

Stolen Dances and Big City Chances

Chance Connections and Upside Down Plans

A Christmas Kiss on the Twenty-Fifth

Believe in the Magic of Christmas

ROMANTASY

(IN THE SPIRIT OF LOVE)

Spirits of the Heart

Out of Dreams and Ashes

Etched Upon the Heart

WESTERN ROMANCE

(LONE STAR HEARTS)

Wanted by a Texas Ranger

Saved by a Texas Ranger

(WHISKEY SPRINGS)

Finding Natalie

Promising Samantha

Falling for Allyson

Saving Savannah

Claiming Charlie

Rescuing Keira

Protecting Gabriella

Courting Isabella

TIME TRAVEL

(INTO THE MIST)

Written in the Wind

Scripted in the Stars

Destined in the Twilight

Promised in the Mist

Trapped in the Melody

(DRAGON'S BLOOD)

Dragon's Blood

Lavender Blue

Champagne Silver

Twilight Frost

Mountbatten Pink

(WHEN HEARTSTRINGS BECKON)

Rescued in Time

Meet me in 1879

(WHEN HEARTSTRINGS ECHO)

Messages Across Time

Falling Through to Forever

Once Upon a Winter's Spell

(BECKONED)

Before the Storm

Twist of Fate

When the Stars Align

Once Upon a Christmas

Once in a Blue Moon

A Wish Upon a Star

(BEGUILED)

When Lightning Strikes

Storm of Time

Midnight Storm

When the Moon Falls

Stormborn Angel

(SPELLED)

Time Tempest

The Heart Remembers

A Moment in Time

Moonlight Shadows

HISTORICAL

(TAPESTRY OF BLUE AND GRAY)

Shadows Beneath Magnolia Blooms

Secrets Among Southern Roses

(IT HAPPENED BY ACCIDENT)

Accidentally Alluring

Accidentally Married

(SOUTHERN BELLE CIVIL WAR)

Beyond Enemy Lines

Love Always

Hearts Under Siege

Hearts Under Fire

Away Down South in Dixie

The Reluctant Bride

Stay with Me

Jasmine Kisses

Magnolia Kisses

Gardenia Kisses

(THE QUINNS)

Wait for Me

Take Me Home

Keep Me Safe

FATED MATES

Riley's Mate

Aiden's Mate

Brayden's Mate

STANDALONE SUSPENSE

Lost and Found

All I Want for Christmas

Serenity

Courting Alley Cat

All of the books in each Series are standalone and can be read out of order. However, some books have characters from the previous stories in them.